Dear Reader,

When Pocket Books brought my novel *By Love Unveiled* back into print, I was thrilled at the chance to revise and refresh one of the eight novels I penned under the name Deborah Martin. Those early works set the stage for my career to come: first, the historical detail, passionate action, and darker tone of the Deborah Martin novels. And later on, the sensual entanglements, sexy repartee, and lighthearted spirit of my recent Regency series, the Duke's Men and the Hellions of Halstead Hall. Both romantic styles are infused with the sizzling sexual tension my readers have come to expect in my works. Every writer dreams of digging deep and finding the distinctive and authentic voices that make their stories come alive for readers. I'm profoundly grateful to be living that dream!

Now I'm delighted that *Silver Deceptions*, another Deborah Martin novel, is available to you once again in this revised edition. For this tale of a London stage actress with a hidden plan and a seductive marquess trying to unravel her secrets, I heightened the drama and the danger, enriched the story line, tightened the dialogue, and stoked one very hot passion to make it burn brighter than ever. It was an exciting and rewarding undertaking, and one that, I sincerely hope, makes *Silver Deceptions* a satisfying and unforgettable reading experience for you.

Enjoy!

Sabrina Jeffries

THE HELLIONS OF HALSTEAD HALL

THE TRUTH ABOUT LORD STONEVILLE

"Delectably witty dialogue . . . and scorching sexual chemistry."

—Booklist

A HELLION IN HER BED

"Jeffries's sense of humor and delightfully delicious sensuality spice things up!"

—RT Book Reviews (4½ stars)

HOW TO WOO A RELUCTANT LADY

"Steamy passion, dangerous intrigue, and just the right amount of tart wit."

—Booklist

TO WED A WILD LORD

"Wonderfully witty, deliciously seductive, graced with humor and charm."

—Library Journal (starred review)

A LADY NEVER SURRENDERS

"Jeffries pulls out all the stops. . . . Not to be missed."
—RT Book Reviews (4½ stars, Top Pick)

"Sizzling, emotionally satisfying. . . . Another must-read."
—Library Journal (starred review)

"Superbly shaded characters, simmering sensuality, and a splendidly wicked wit . . . *A Lady Never Surrenders* wraps up the series nothing short of brilliantly."

—Booklist

Also by Sabrina Jeffries

THE DUKE'S MEN SERIES

How the Scoundrel Seduces

When the Rogue Returns

What the Duke Desires

THE HELLIONS OF HALSTEAD HALL SERIES

A Lady Never Surrenders

To Wed a Wild Lord

How to Woo a Reluctant Lady

A Hellion in Her Bed

The Truth About Lord Stoneville

THE SCHOOL FOR HEIRESSES SERIES

Wed Him Before You Bed Him

Don't Bargain with the Devil

Snowy Night with a Stranger
(with Jane Feather and Julia London)

Let Sleeping Rogues Lie

Beware a Scot's Revenge

The School for Heiresses
(with Julia London, Liz Carlyle, and Renee Bernard)

Only a Duke Will Do

Never Seduce a Scoundrel

THE ROYAL BROTHERHOOD SERIES

One Night with a Prince

To Pleasure a Prince

In the Prince's Bed

BY SABRINA JEFFRIES WRITING AS DEBORAH MARTIN

By Love Unveiled

SABRINA JEFFRIES

WRITING AS
DEBORAH MARTIN

Silver Deceptions

POCKET BOOKS

New York   London   Toronto   Sydney   New Delhi

Pocket Books
A Division of Simon & Schuster, Inc.
1230 Avenue of the Americas
New York, NY 10020

This book is a work of fiction. Any references to historical events, real people, or real places are used fictitiously. Other names, characters, places, and events are products of the author's imagination, and any resemblance to actual events or places or persons, living or dead, is entirely coincidental.

Copyright © 1994, 2015 by Deborah Gonzales

Originally published in 1994 by the Penguin Group

All rights reserved, including the right to reproduce this book or portions thereof in any form whatsoever. For information, address Pocket Books Subsidiary Rights Department, 1230 Avenue of the Americas, New York, NY 10020.

First Pocket Books paperback edition January 2015

POCKET and colophon are registered trademarks of Simon & Schuster, Inc.

For information about special discounts for bulk purchases, please contact Simon & Schuster Special Sales at 1-866-506-1949 or business@simonandschuster.com.

The Simon & Schuster Speakers Bureau can bring authors to your live event. For more information or to book an event, contact the Simon & Schuster Speakers Bureau at 1-866-248-3049 or visit our website at www.simonspeakers.com.

Cover design by Min Choi
Cover illustration by Jon Paul Ferrara

Manufactured in the United States of America

10   9   8   7   6   5   4   3   2   1

ISBN 978-1-4767-6105-3
ISBN 978-1-4516-6553-6 (ebook)

To my agent, Pamela Gray Ahearn of the Ahearn Agency,
thank you for twenty-five wonderful years together.
Here's hoping we have twenty-five more!

Prologue

NORWOOD, ENGLAND
MAY 1667

"Death, in itself, is nothing; but we fear,
To be we know not what, we know not where."
—John Dryden, *Aureng-Zebe*, Act 4, Sc. 1

Dark clouds, their bellies full of cold spring rain, hovered over Norwood's square waiting to dump their burden, and dirty piles of winter slush lined the bleak patch of ground. It was a perfect day for a hanging.

Twenty-one-year-old Annabelle Taylor drew the hood of her woolen cloak forward to cover her hair and pushed through the crowd. No one must notice her.

But she needn't have worried. As she gained a spot near the gallows, the crowd that watched for the cart with sickening jubilation paid her little heed.

No one would expect her to watch her mother's hanging. That was why her plan just might work. The sheriff and his men would be taken so off guard when she claimed the body herself that it might not occur to them to prevent her and her servant Charity Woodfield from carrying Mother's body away in the wagon Charity's father was bringing.

"I have terrible news," a voice whispered at Annabelle's elbow.

With a sudden foreboding, she glanced at the buxom, fair-haired widow who'd come to stand at her side. Only five years her senior, Charity was more like an older sister than a servant to her. "What is it? What's happened?"

"The surgeon can't take yer mother."

"What do you mean? I gave him all the gold I had. He swore he'd do what he could to revive her!"

She'd read tales of men revived after a hanging. If the neck remained unbroken, a person could still live through it, fainting before actually dying. Only last year, friends of a man in the next shire had secretly carried his hanged body off to a surgeon, who'd warmed and bled it until the man had revived. He now lived healthy as a horse in London, or so she'd heard.

"It isn't the surgeon's fault." Charity looked grim. "Some runagate told the sheriff about yer plans, and now there's soldiers at the surgeon's house waiting to seize you and the body if you come near the place. They'll only let you take the body to the graveyard."

Despair clogged her throat. "It was my only chance to save her."

The pitiful hope that Mother might beat death

in the end was what had seen her through Mother's short imprisonment, trial, and sentence of death by hanging for murdering Annabelle's father.

No, he was her stepfather, a fact she had only recently learned.

She choked back a sob. No one cared that Ogden Taylor had been beating her or that his poor wife could no longer endure such cruelties to her daughter. In the world's eyes, Squire Ogden Taylor had merely been administering a proper punishment to his daughter when his wife had lost her wits and plunged a kitchen blade through his brawny chest.

Tears slipped from between her lashes. "She can't die, Charity. I can't let her. If it weren't for me—"

"Don't start blamin' yerself. He pushed her to it, he did. At least yer mother had the satisfaction of seein' him suffer in the end."

Annabelle couldn't pretend to have loved the man, nor even to wish Mother hadn't killed him. She only wished Mother had done it less publicly.

The moment those wicked thoughts appeared, a superstitious fear made the sweat bead up on her forehead. *Please, God, I didn't mean it. Only let her live. If you save her, I'll . . . I'll . . .*

How could *she* tempt God into overlooking Mother's crime? Her stepfather had called her the "spawn of the devil" because she suffered his punishments in silence. He'd said it was unnatural.

Perhaps he was right. Then again, he didn't

know how she became someone else inside her mind to endure his beatings, how she pretended she was suffering in battle as the warrior queen Boadicea or the goddess Athena or even Joan of Arc—anything to escape the pain.

"What do I do now?" Annabelle whispered raggedly to Charity.

Charity placed a soft hand on her arm. "It's out of your hands, dear heart. There's naught left but to flee this wicked place, turn yer eyes from the evil here, and set yer feet toward London."

"Not until the end." With a shudder, Annabelle stared at the gallows crosspiece, the rough wood worn smooth in the middle where the rope was tied. "A miracle could happen. God may yet spare her."

"Yer mother's put herself beyond helping," Charity said without rancor. "Come on with you. We'll travel to London and join my actress cousin. She says the theater's full of women like us. With yer genteel manners, you could get a position easy."

"I'll go soon enough." Annabelle strained to see if anyone yet came down the road. "I have no choice—no one wants me here. But you don't have to leave your family. You've got a chance for a good place as a cook."

"Fie on that! I want to seek my fortune on the stage. My cousin says the nobles fight over the actresses, and any bonny woman can find a duke willing to set her up—"

"Don't even think such a thing!" Annabelle

hissed. "That sort of behavior is what landed Mother here. If she hadn't taken up with a dissolute nobleman, she wouldn't have been abandoned with me in her belly. Then her parents wouldn't have forced her to marry the squire and live the hellish life that drove her to—" She broke off with a sob.

"My poor dear." Charity stroked her mistress's back soothingly. "Come away. You shouldn't be here."

The noise of the crowd suddenly increased, and Annabelle's gaze shifted to where the cart track split from the road.

First strutted the sheriff in his sable robes, appearing very dignified and aloof for a man who'd already purchased the Taylor lands from the Crown, since her stepfather had no heirs. Meanwhile, he'd made *her* an offer of a different kind that she had refused. No doubt that was why he sought to prevent her from any attempt to have Mother revived.

She gritted her teeth. He completed the wheel of torment fashioned by Ogden Taylor and the unfeeling nobleman who was Annabelle's real father. A plague on them all! How she hated them!

Suddenly, the cart carrying Mother rumbled into view. Chains held her, with thick iron shackles that dwarfed her delicate wrists and ankles. Her beautiful, silver-streaked jet hair had been shorn, highlighting her expression of helpless confusion. As she knelt on the wobbling cart in her white gown, she clasped her hands before her, lips moving in prayer.

"Mother!" Annabelle cried out and started forward.

Charity held her back. "No, no, dear heart. They'll be waiting for you to make a fuss, so they can throw you into gaol, too. Don't give the bastards the chance."

This last was said with such venom it gave Annabelle courage. Annabelle let that venom seep into her soul. She'd need the strength of her hatred to avenge Mother.

Not against the townspeople. Some were wretches, but most had been relatively kind to her and her mother. No, she must find her real father, the lord whom Mother had called Maynard, whose gifts—a signet ring and a poem with the signature *The Silver Swan*—Mother had sent her to retrieve from their hiding place in the harpsichord. Mother had told her of him only two days ago, urging Annabelle to seek him out and ask his protection.

She'd sooner cut out her tongue. Instead, she would make sure he paid for abandoning Mother when she'd needed him most.

A drunk voice in the crowd called out, "What a collar day! Perfect day for a murderess to be twisted!"

Though someone hushed him, the word *twisted* made Annabelle's fingers curl into fists. And when a hawker nearby cried, as if this were some merry-making fair, "Mutton pies for sale, good and hot!" she would have lunged for him if Charity hadn't slid an arm about her waist to restrain her.

"Don't torment yerself by staying here," Charity muttered. "Yer mother is as good as dead now. You promised her you'd not witness the hanging. Keep that promise."

"I can't leave her!" Annabelle hissed.

Charity shook her head but remained at Annabelle's side.

The rough-hewn cart stopped a few yards in front of them, beneath the gallows with its dreadful rope hanging down like a hideous outstretched claw. Annabelle ached to run to Mother's side, but she resisted the urge. If Mother saw her, it would make her last minutes intolerable.

A man whose somber clothing and executioner's mask marked him as the hangman jerked Mother to her feet, and the hot hatred filling Annabelle was so intense she thought she'd burst into flames.

As the wind whipped Mother's white gown around her, the hangman slipped the noose over her bowed head. He tightened it around her neck, and Annabelle's own throat went numb.

Please, God, save her. You must save her!

The hangman stepped off the cart. The sheriff of Norwood repeated the sentence in a booming voice, then asked if the condemned had any final words.

Her mother's soft "Nay" incensed the crowd, who would rather have heard a long confession of her past sins.

The hangman led the horse forward, while Phoebe Taylor's feet dragged the bottom of the cart until they no longer found purchase.

Annabelle shut her eyes. The silence of the crowd

maddened her, because it allowed her to hear the gallows creak with her mother's weight. But Annabelle didn't scream or even cry. Instead, she prayed more fervently than she'd ever prayed in her life.

Let the rope break, God. They'll not hang her again if the rope breaks. They'll take it as a sign. Let her live, and I'll be pure and holy all my days, I swear it. Save her and I'll be your servant forever. Please, God, I swear it!

She didn't realize she was babbling the words aloud, her voice rising above the hush of the crowd, until Charity began dragging her backward.

"Come, dear heart, we're leaving now," Charity whispered. "God has taken her into his bosom, where she belongs. He ain't going to release her. Come on!"

A clap of thunder sounded nearby, and Annabelle's eyes shot open. It was an answer, wasn't it? God would spare Mother?

Then she saw the gallows, and she screamed. She wrenched her gaze from the horrifying sight before her, one last supplication tumbling from her lips.

The rope held.

In that moment, Annabelle shoved her soul and her childhood dreams into a cupboard in her heart, then closed it against the pain threatening to overwhelm her reason. And as she hardened her heart against men and all their cruelties, she vowed that one man at least would pay for taking her mother from her.

Her father.

Chapter One

"Robes loosely flowing, hair as free:
Such sweet neglect more taketh me,
Than all the adulteries of art;
They strike mine eyes, but not my heart."
—Ben Jonson, *Epicœne*, Act 1, Sc. 1

A mischief upon all Fools!"
Act 3 of Dryden's *Sir Martin Mar-All* was well in progress when those words temporarily lessened the din in Lisle's Tennis Court, which had served as the playhouse for the Duke of York's acting company since the theaters reopened. All eyes were on the actress who'd spoken the line with contemptuous pride.

Colin Jeffreys, Marquess of Hampden, who'd just arrived, surveyed her from a first-tier box with particular interest, then glanced at the playbill to make certain she was the woman whom the Earl of

Walcester wanted him to spy upon. It read, *Rose, played by Mrs. Maynard.*

That certainly fit. Although the earl had mentioned she was unmarried, all the actresses were called Mrs., married or no, and Colin doubted there was more than one going by the surname of Maynard.

His gaze followed the tall woman as she crossed the proscenium stage. She played the witty servant Rose very well, which intrigued him. Few of the actresses had much interest in their profession; most were on the stage to find a protector.

Not that this one couldn't if she wished. Although the requisite short curls framed her face in front, the rest of her hair tumbled to the middle of her back, a shimmering robe of ebony in the light of the theater's candles. She was well proportioned and fine-limbed, and she moved with the bearing of a queen.

Yet she still projected an elusive quality of innocence. That took some fine acting indeed. And perhaps a bit of cosmetic manipulation—while Moll Davis wore a heavy shade of rouge on the cheeks of her white-powdered face, Annabelle Maynard wore little and thus looked fresh and unspoiled as wild rosemary.

In short, she was the perfect antidote to the jaded sensibilities of an oversophisticated court . . . and not at all what he'd expected. Perhaps he indeed had the wrong woman. He hadn't been to a play at the Duke's Theater since he'd returned from spending three years in Antwerp in the king's service, so he wasn't familiar with all the players.

"Sir John!" he called to his friend over the loud hum of voices. How on earth did anyone listen to a play in this din?

"Not now." Sir John Riverton drew closer the giggling vizard-mask who sat between them, plying her whore's trade. "Can't you see this poor girl's lonely?"

The "poor girl" was sliding her bejeweled hand up Colin's thigh even while her other hand worked at tantalizing Sir John.

"*Lonely* isn't the word I would choose," Colin said dryly as he brushed her hand away. "She can wait. Tell me about the actress in white."

Sir John turned his attention to the stage. "The Silver Swan, you mean?"

Ah, yes, Colin had forgotten that bit. He noted the beauty's slender neck and graceful gestures as well as the silver ribbons she wore not only in her hair but threaded through her lace cuffs and in bows on the tips of her white satin slippers. On her bodice, a silver brooch winked in the lights. A swan, no doubt.

She was certainly going to a great deal of trouble to foster that nickname. Perhaps Walcester was right to be alarmed, though she did seem rather young to be engaged in the sort of intrigues that the earl had once been part of. Colin would judge her to be no more than twenty-three. "Yes, the one with the dark hair."

Sir John shrugged. "She's only been with the duke's players for . . . oh, six or seven months. She plays mostly smaller parts, but there's talk that she'll soon be moved to larger ones."

"Moll Davis had better look out, then." Because Mrs. Maynard was clearly the better actress. "How well do you know the Silver Swan?"

Sir John's chuckle carried to him over the chatter in the surrounding boxes. "Well enough." When Colin fixed Sir John with a speculative glance, the man added, "But not in that way, you understand, although there are some who have known her more . . . shall we say . . . intimately."

An inexplicable twinge of disappointment made Colin frown. "Typical actress, is she?"

"That's what I've heard. Serene and aloof onstage, but a fiery wench in bed." He laughed. "I imagine pearls and baubles will open the thighs of any pretty actress. And she's no exception. So they say."

Colin flicked his gaze over the woman, searching for some sign of this wanton side. "Who exactly are 'they'?"

"Somerset, for one. Claims he's practically put himself into debt buying her jewels, and you know the man can't afford it. He says she repaid him . . . as only a woman could. He's undoubtedly waiting in the wings for her this very moment."

Colin frowned. "That stunning beauty with a fop like Somerset? I can hardly credit it."

"He's the sort of man she seems to find attractive. Or at least the only sort I've seen her with."

Hard to believe. She looked intelligent, and she obviously knew her trade. She even had the old matrons in the upper gallery eating out of her hand. So why dally with prancing coxcombs? It made no sense.

Not that anything in this fool's errand for Walcester made sense. "I want to meet her."

Sir John shifted in his seat, adjusting his bad leg. "When?"

"As soon as possible."

"All you need do is slip into the tiring-room and wait for her."

"With the other gallants? No. I want to meet with her alone, where we can speak."

"Speak?" Sir John laughed. "'Is that what you're calling it these days? I suppose her maid can set up an assignation, assuming her mistress is willing." He stood, ignoring his pouting companion. "Wait here, and I'll arrange it."

Colin returned his attention to the stage. Mrs. Maynard exited, prompting cries of "Swan, Swan!" from the raucous gallants in the pit. Clearly the woman had a score of men, both young and old, seeking her favors.

Then he would do so as well. How better to learn what Walcester needed to know? Colin owed the earl much for having saved his life while they were both in exile in France. The earl had been instrumental in gaining Colin his position in the king's service, which had led directly to His Majesty's bestowing on Colin the title of Marquess of Hampden. Colin would be forever in Walcester's debt. So dallying with a pretty actress to find out her secrets for the earl was the least Colin could do to repay the man.

Not that it would be any great sacrifice. It had been a long time since he'd found a woman who stirred his interest, and this one intrigued him. He'd grown too jaded in his years at court and as a spy. Perhaps it was time to explore something different. *Someone* different from his usual fare.

The play went on, tedious now that Mrs. Maynard had left the stage. Just as the act ended, however, Sir John returned with a full-figured, youngish blond female at his side.

With his usual merry smile, Sir John said, "Lord Hampden, meet Charity Woodfield."

The chit bobbed a curtsy, and Colin noted that Sir John cupped her elbow to urge her to rise before resting his hand in the small of her back with obvious familiarity. No wonder the man knew so much about Mrs. Maynard. He had a clear interest in the woman's servant. And judging from how she didn't shy away from him, either, the interest was mutual. That could only help Colin's case.

"I wish to meet your mistress," he said without preamble.

"So do a great many men, milord, if you don't mind my saying so. She's a fine actress, and the gallants all find her fetching."

He smiled at her shameless and entirely unnecessary attempt to raise his interest. "As do I. So what must I do to ensure I get a fair chance with her?"

"Oh, but yer lordship wants a bit more than a fair chance," she said tartly, "or y'd be down there right now, trying to get her attention."

"You're a saucy wench," Colin said. "Is your mistress as bold with her tongue as you?"

The maid lifted a brow at his double entendre. "Bold enough to cut you to ribbons with it, and leave your pride hanging by a thread."

"Now that's a feat I'd like to see."

"Then you'll have to enter the fray behind the stage with the others."

"No reason for that." He opened his hand to reveal several gold sovereigns. "I'm willing to buy my way into your mistress's good graces. I'll wager that's more than those other fools would do."

A coldness spread over Charity's face, and she curtsied stiffly. "I'm afraid you've mistaken my mistress for a whore, milord. I don't think the two of you would suit."

Without another word, she pivoted on her heel, brushing off Sir John's hand when he tried to halt her exit.

"Wait!" Colin called out. At least now he knew that the Silver Swan wasn't just looking for money.

That argued against her being a spy for pay. When Charity kept on going, he added, "I didn't mean to offend. I've heard tales, and sometimes rumors don't distinguish between women who take lovers and women who are whores. But I do know the difference, so please accept my apologies."

The maid halted to cast Sir John an accusing glance, obviously having guessed who'd been at fault for the rumors. He shrugged, unrepentant as usual.

Charity stared Colin down. "Very well, milord, I accept your apology." But her tone was still cold. "What exactly is it you wish me to do?"

"To arrange a meeting between your mistress and me. One where we'll have complete privacy."

"Of course," she said, her voice positively icy.

"I simply want to talk to her."

"Of course," she repeated, but when he refused to take the bait and offer more assurances, she added, "So it won't bother you if the meeting takes place in the tiring-room, here at the theater?"

"As long as I can speak with her alone, I don't care if it takes place in the middle of London Bridge."

That seemed to bring her up short. And soften her a fraction. "Come to the tiring-room tomorrow an hour before the play begins. I'll make sure you've got her to yerself." She fixed him with a dark glance. "But I'll be right outside in the hall. That's as close to having her alone as you'll get."

It was a start, anyway. "That's good enough,

thank you." He smiled broadly. "I see that your name is fitting. You're the very soul of charity, and I won't forget it."

For the first time since she'd entered the box, she returned his smile. "Oh, don't you worry, milord. I don't intend to *let* you forget it."

Then she whisked out of the box to the sound of his chuckle.

ANNABELLE EXITED THE stage at the end of act 3 and looked around for Charity. How odd. The maid was usually right here when she left the stage. Thinking to find her in the tiring-room, Annabelle entered it but found an orange vendor instead, resting her weary feet on a chair.

"Something to whet your whistle for the next act?" asked the girl hopefully.

"That bad today, is it?" Hitching up her skirt, Annabelle drew a few pence from the pocket in her smock and handed it over to the orange girl, who couldn't have been a day over thirteen.

"Thankee kindly," the vendor said as she handed Annabelle her fourth orange that day. "Even with the crowds, no one is clamoring for fruit. And Maggie'll 'ave my 'ead if I don't give 'er somethin' to show for my efforts."

As the girl left, Annabelle hefted the fruit. The other three oranges would go to the urchins outside the theater as always, but today she was in the mood to actually eat one.

Charity walked in just as she was peeling it.

"Where have *you* been?" Annabelle asked.

"Are you throwing your pence away on the orange girls again?" the maid countered as she began searching Annabelle's costume for signs of disrepair. "'Tis no wonder you can't afford that new gown you want. How many is it today? Two? Three?"

"Four, if you must know," Annabelle said testily.

"You're such a soft touch. That's why they follow you about. You shouldn't encourage them."

"I can't help it." Annabelle sighed. "They remind me of myself at that age. I know Maggie beats them when they come up short. And what's a new gown compared to that?"

Charity sniffed.

"Besides," Annabelle continued, biting into one juicy section, "I like oranges. You can't be a true member of the theater and *not* eat them."

Softening, Charity smiled enigmatically and knelt to study Annabelle's loose hem. "The theater does suit you, dear heart." She drew out the needle and thread she always held ready and began to sew.

"I do believe it does." Annabelle liked the smell of hot wax from the hundreds of candles, the intensity of the audience in the pit when a scene went well, the sound of lutes wafting down from the musicians' box. She even liked flirting with the gallants, though most of them were foolish pups. Yes, the theater had been good to her.

What's more, she actually excelled at acting. She should probably thank Ogden Taylor for that. If not for his beatings, she would never have learned to lose herself in imaginary characters.

The thought of her stepfather's cruelties sobered her, reminding her of the one dark thread through her bright tapestry. Seven months in London and she still hadn't found her real father.

She'd set the trap for him well enough. She'd taken his name as a surname. And since he'd signed *The Silver Swan* to that poem he'd left behind with Mother, she and Charity had worked hard to get the entire theatergoing court to call her by that.

Nonetheless, no one by the name of Maynard had approached her, and certainly no one pretending to be the Silver Swan had shown up.

Charity finished the hem and rose to plump Annabelle's drooping coiffure. "All that heat and damp air is taking the curl out of yer hair and ribbons."

Annabelle tore herself from her obsessive thoughts and ate another section of orange. "Never mind that. Act four will start any moment, and I've forgotten the line I enter on."

"Well, don't expect *me* to remember it. If I could memorize lines, we'd *both* be on the stage." Charity frowned. "Nobody warned me I'd have to learn such long speeches. I'd rather sell pork pies in the market, I would, than spend my time wracking my brain for some poor bit of verse."

"Fortunately, I don't have to wrack my brain.

Just look in that copy of the play over there and tell me what it is, will you?"

As Annabelle finished off the orange and licked her fingers, Charity read aloud, "Mr. Young says, 'Good luck, and five hundred pound attend thee,' and then you and Moll come in."

"Oh, right. It follows that absurd scene where Warner and Lord Dartmouth plot to find a husband for his pregnant mistress." Annabelle scowled. "Mr. Dryden has obviously never known what it's like to be a bastard or he wouldn't write so blithely about illegitimacy and men who don't do their duty by the women they seduce."

"Don't start thinking on such dark things in the middle of the play. It'll mar your performance." Putting aside the script, Charity came back to work on one of Annabelle's silver ribbons, curling it around her finger in a useless attempt to revive it. "And make you brood on the past."

"I don't mind brooding on the past," Annabelle said. "It strengthens my resolve to set things right, so Mother can rest easy in her grave."

"She's gone where you can't help her anymore. You have to think of yourself now."

"I *do* think of myself."

Annabelle caught Charity's hand and moved it to trace the crescent-shaped scar on her temple where her stepfather had once lost his temper and cuffed her so hard that his ring had gashed her. She'd been six years old.

"I think of how it felt to have my own blood dripping down my face," Annabelle went on fiercely. "I think of the mother I'll never see again. Ogden Taylor may have wielded the lash that led to her death, but it wouldn't have happened if my real father hadn't abandoned Mother. 'Tis only fair that I punish the man who started it all."

Charity caressed the spot. "I understand how you feel, but don't let your thirst for revenge sour yer heart."

"Too late for that." Pushing away Charity's hand, Annabelle turned to pace the room. "I only wish that 'Maynard,' whoever he is, would simply take the bait. I thought certain when he saw me using the names Maynard and Silver Swan together, he'd have some reaction. I paid a pretty penny to have this brooch specially fashioned, and it has brought me naught so far."

Charity shrugged. "Perhaps he don't live in London no more. Who knows? The man might be dead."

"He'd best not be. I want my vengeance!"

Mother had said her father was a wounded Roundhead captain named Maynard, whom her family had taken in until he could rejoin his regiment. Since even the officers in Cromwell's army had been of good birth—and the man had left a signet ring behind—she knew her father had to be someone of consequence. So the last thing he would want, especially if he was as sober-living as most of the Roundheads, was to have his wild behavior unveiled.

Which was why she planned to confront him with her bastardy, then rub her stage experience and scandalous adventuring in his face. Her unveiling would be public, a supper perhaps, to which she would invite all the gallants and nobles. There she'd announce her real parentage.

Then he would become the laughingstock of London for the bastard daughter he couldn't control, who mocked his good name before everyone. To tread the boards was a shame no family could bear. And she would make sure that the association was an embarrassment beyond endurance. She would send her creditors to him, she would joke of him to her friends, and she would take a string of supposed lovers. His name would ever be on her lips. London would know that he was her father, and he would cringe that they knew.

"I will make sure that the barbarous arse squirms for what he did, abandoning my mother to the squire," she hissed.

"Madam!" Charity cried. "I swear yer letting those gallants turn all yer proper words into obscenity. How will you ever find a decent husband like that?"

"I don't want a husband, and certainly not a 'decent' one, who will tether my tongue. I like being able to mock the world and be praised as witty for it. That only happens in the theater." And as long as she couched her words in dry humor, no one could guess at the pain beneath them.

Least of all the gallants who courted her. "Besides,

if these so-called wits who surround me are any indication of the sort of man I would have to choose from, I'm better off alone. They're a lot of conceited popinjays."

"And they're not that witty either," Charity pointed out. "Lord Somerset is so enamored of his own face, he don't have time to sharpen his brain."

Annabelle smiled. "Nor the inclination. The viscount seems entirely concentrated on preening and bragging about his supposed bedding of me to his lackwit friends."

"Ah, but he was a sight the morning after." Charity giggled. "Waking up groggy after swigging my tea, and not even knowing he'd merely been sleeping beside you the whole night. You should have seen his face when I entered to announce you were wanted straightaway at the theater. The simpering fool didn't know whether to admit he didn't remember his evening with you or boast about his success."

Annabelle snorted. "Of course he chose to boast."

"'Tis a good thing for you that he did. If y'd had a real man in that bed, he wouldn't have let you go till he'd taken another tumble, no matter what I told him about where you was to be."

"That's why I chose Somerset. He'll believe whatever I say about his prowess and leave when I tell him to." Her smile faded. "It wouldn't do for me to find myself in Mother's position . . . my belly full and no man near to claim the babe."

Letting the world think her a whore might be necessary to her vengeance, but she refused to do more than play the role. If her stepfather hadn't cowed her, she certainly wouldn't let some foppish gallant do it.

Besides, one day she hoped to have a real life somewhere in the country where she could just be herself. Where she could find a man to marry who would love her as she loved him. And when that day came, she meant to be chaste. She of all people knew how men could be if they discovered that their loves were not.

"Still," Charity said, "if y'd gone one more month without letting them think *someone* had bedded you, one of those so-called wits would have had his way with you, willing or no."

And Annabelle was *never* going to let that happen. So far, every man she'd met in London was either a fop or a brute, and she had no use for either.

A knock at the door and a warning that her entrance was coming up made her start. When Charity gave Annabelle's gown a quick once-over and bent to straighten a ribbon on her slipper, a lump filled Annabelle's throat. The youthful widow could have left her long ago for one of the many gallants attracted to her lush figure and sharp wit. Yet she stayed at Annabelle's side.

"Have I thanked you for keeping me sane these past few months?" Annabelle asked softly.

Charity glanced up in surprise. "You thank me, dear heart, every time you smile."

Tears stung Annabelle's eyes. "Then clearly I shall have to smile more often."

The call came again from outside the tiring-room. When Annabelle started to leave, Charity said, "Mr. Harris came by and mentioned that he wants to rehearse next week's play with you in the morning an hour before this one starts."

"What? Why?"

Looking suddenly nervous, Charity rose to go fold some costumes. "He's worried about his part, that's all. Wants to go over some lines. You know how nervous he gets about performing a new play."

That was true enough. And since he was a favorite with the theater owner, she was in no position to refuse his request.

"Fine," she said as she headed out the door. "Just make sure the tiring-room is cleared when he arrives. You know how he is."

"I do indeed," Charity said cheerily.

Briefly it occurred to Annabelle that Charity was being a bit *too* cheery about having to come early for an extra rehearsal.

But then she stepped onto the stage and the errant thought left her mind entirely. Once again she lost herself in Rose, and the real world faded around her.

Chapter Two

"Queen and huntress, chaste and fair,
Now the sun is laid to sleep,
Seated in thy silver chair,
State in wonted manner keep . . ."
—Ben Jonson, *Cynthia's Revels*, Act 5, Sc. 3

The next morning as Annabelle entered the tiring-room, she swore to find it empty. Where the devil was Henry Harris? He wasn't in the theater, and he wasn't back here.

Annabelle would have asked Charity, but the maid had mysteriously disappeared yet again. Shivering, Annabelle headed to the hearth to lay a fire, and as she knelt, a sharp pain made her suck in her breath. Devil take her tight laces! She always suffered pain on days when the winter damp seeped into a person's bones. But it had only been a year since the squire had thrown her down, then kicked her hard enough to break three ribs. Perhaps in more time they would heal.

A grim smile crossed her face. At least she no

longer had to fear being tormented by her wretch of a stepfather.

She fought for control over the ache, and in moments had a comfortable blaze going in the fireplace. As she gazed into the flames, she touched her hand to her brooch. The poem "Captain Maynard" had left behind was engraved on her memory after all the hours she'd studied it, looking for some clue to his identity:

> The bard cannot reveal himself,
> Except in song, one last refrain,
> To beg sweet Portia tread with Beatrice
> Far away from the martyr's plain.
>
> Her heart she must keep close and mute,
> Her tongue must whisper not a cry
> Else she be forced by crown-less hands
> To sing the hangman's lullaby.
>
> With fond hopes,
> The Silver Swan

Obviously the poem had been intended as a message to someone. Was "the bard" meant to be Shakespeare, and the message to Portia to "tread with Beatrice" intended to be the establishment of an assignation?

If so, how had Mother been part of it? Mother

had said that even after she'd secretly become intimate with Captain Maynard, she'd known little
about his past. Then one day, he'd asked her to
carry a sealed poem to his friend at a tavern in Norwood. To ensure that Phoebe could verify that the
message came from him, Maynard had given her his
signet ring.

Mother had met Maynard's friend as planned.
He'd read the poem and, when some people had
entered the room, thrust the letter back at her and
told her to leave. Not certain what to do, she'd
returned home only to find that Captain Maynard
had fled.

Her mother never knew why the poem was
signed *The Silver Swan* or what became of her
lover. Why had "Captain Maynard"—the only
name Mother had known for him—left her to bear
an illegitimate child alone?

Annabelle recited the poem's lines aloud, searching yet again for any hidden meaning, but it didn't
seem to make any sense.

"Rather morbid verses for such a beautiful and
accomplished actress," said a man's voice behind
her.

She whirled, then tensed at the sight of a tall,
broad-shouldered stranger just outside the open
door. Alone in the tiring-room, she would prove
easy prey for any scoundrel.

Though he stood in the shadows, she could just
make out his rich clothing and rakish plumed hat.

That eased her alarm. This was no footpad looking to rob or assault her, but another forward gallant. She could easily handle one of *those*.

"It appears that you have lost your way, sir," she said smoothly. "The pit is behind you to the left."

"So you would banish me to the pit for daring to admire you?"

The deep, faintly mocking voice put her on her guard. "Better the pit than to be turned to stone, like those who gazed on Medusa."

His low chuckle contained enough charm to seduce a stone. "You are hardly a Medusa, madam. I've heard it said that Aphrodite is *your* muse."

She sucked in a breath. Aphrodite's bird was the swan.

But that meant nothing. Everyone knew her nickname.

"Then I will pierce you with Aphrodite's arrows," she said, determined to have the last word with this unsettling stranger.

"I'll risk it."

He stepped into the room, and she caught her breath when eyes green as a forest in spring raked her with insolent amusement. She tried not to notice his solid build, nor the cleft in his square chin, nor even the golden hair that streamed over his shoulders from beneath his wide-brimmed hat to glint in the firelight.

She tried not to notice . . . and failed. How strange that she had never seen him at the theater before. She certainly would have remembered *him*. Like Adonis, the only man who'd ever been spared Aphrodite's shafts, he was almost too handsome to be believed.

Not that it mattered. She wasn't in the market for a lover of his sort, no matter *how* handsome.

So it annoyed her when he made himself right at home, resting his hip against a scarred oak table a scarce two feet from her.

"I'm waiting for someone," she told him coldly. "You can't stay."

"You're waiting for me. Just ask your maid."

She blinked, then groaned. "Devil take that woman! 'Tis so like her to do something like this."

"I take it you weren't informed of our appointment?"

"Of course not. If she'd told me, I wouldn't be here."

"Then I must thank Charity for her discretion."

She leveled a scathing gaze on him. "No, you mustn't, for her discretion will get neither of you anywhere. My maid does not decide whom I will see, so I'm afraid you must leave."

"Ah, but we haven't even been introduced." With the smooth, frightening grace of a tiger, he whisked his plumed hat from his head and bowed. "Colin Jeffreys, Marquess of Hampden, at your service."

A marquess, no less! No wonder Charity had agreed to arrange a meeting. Still, Annabelle wouldn't let something like a title tempt her. Men with titles could be as treacherous as men without them, if not more so. Her experiences in the theater had taught her that.

"A pleasure to meet you, my lord. Now, would you please go?"

"You can't throw me out yet. We're just beginning to get acquainted."

When he tossed his hat onto the table behind him, she stifled a groan. "There's plenty of time for that later." She flashed him a simpering smile, wishing she had a fan to flutter coyly. "Why don't you return after the performance? Many others do."

"Precisely, which is why I'm here now."

Stubborn ox. Time for another tack. She headed for the door. "You are becoming incredibly tiresome, Lord Hampden. If you don't leave, I shall seek out Sir William to remind you of the rules."

His low chuckle gave her pause. "Go ahead. Sir William and I are good friends. We'll share a fine laugh over the 'rules,' and when we're done, I'll still be here."

A tingle of alarm ran down her spine. It had to be alarm. What else could it be? "What do you want from me, my lord? What must I do to have peace?"

He crossed his arms over his chest. "Surely you could guess that." Pointedly he allowed his gaze to travel the length of her.

Color suffused her face, though she fought to maintain her aloof, bantering persona. "Ah, but that would take the enjoyment out of hearing you make the proposition."

He pushed away from the table to approach her with slow, deliberate steps. She stared him down, no longer able to pretend amusement.

When he halted very near her, he reached out to smooth one curl from her face, much as Charity might have done. Only his gesture wasn't soothing or helpful. His was calculated to seduce. His fingers brushed the skin of her cheek, the merest tickle, but enough to make her heart's pace quicken.

It was nicely done. No doubt he'd perfected the technique by practicing it on other actresses.

Then his eyes locked with hers, their glittering depths offering interesting promises that she knew he'd never keep. Still, the intelligence in that look gave her pause. She didn't realize she'd stopped breathing entirely until he dropped his hand and a long, drawn-out sigh escaped her.

He swept his gaze down to her brooch. "Such a lovely piece of work. Where did you find it?"

That put her instantly on her guard. It wouldn't do to admit she'd bought such an expensive piece of jewelry on an actress's pittance. "Oh, I scarcely even remember. Some admirer or other gave it to me, I suppose."

"Have you so many admirers that you forget their gifts that easily?"

He was mocking her, the devil. "I have more admirers than you can possibly imagine."

"And not a one that you favor with your affection."

The surprising insight startled her, then worried her. He'd been digging into her affairs. She'd better take care. "Of course I've favored some with my affection." She fluttered her lashes. "What poor actress could resist the sweet blandishments of London's gallants?"

"Then why are you resisting mine?"

Uh-oh. This was beginning to feel distinctly like a trap. "At any other time, with your being a handsome marquess and all, I'd be tempted." She found it increasingly difficult to play the part of jaded, vapid actress with this fellow. Something about him gave her pause. "Unfortunately, I have quite a tendre for Lord Somerset. We spend every waking moment together."

He arched an eyebrow. "When you're not in the theater, you mean."

"Exactly."

"Such a pity. The Silver Swan deserves someone better than a fop. Particularly when she bears the name Maynard."

Her pulse jumped into triple time. First he'd commented on her brooch, then her name. Was this about more than just a gallant looking for pleasure?

No, how could it be? A lord of his consequence never did anything useful. And he was too young— and of the wrong name—to be related to her quarry.

But that didn't mean she couldn't get information

from him. "What does my surname have to do with anything?" With studied nonchalance, she moved to put a chair between them.

Lord Hampden's gaze turned calculating. "It's an important name in London, attached to a great family. Certainly greater than Somerset's, no matter how glib his tongue and how fashionable his clothing. The man is all sparkle and no spark, all flash and no explosion. Rely on him for your maintenance, and you'll find yourself eating cabbage when you ought to have caviar."

"And I suppose *you* would give me caviar, spark, and explosions." She cut a coy look up at him. "Sounds dangerous."

His eyes gleamed at her, momentarily driving out all rational thought. No man should be allowed to walk around with eyes that arresting. He must make ladies trip over their feet wherever he went. "Ah, but you seem the sort of woman for whom danger has a certain appeal."

Hardly. And she needed to bring the subject back to the Maynard family. "I'm not sure which Maynards *you've* been associating with, but this particular one prefers diamonds to danger. And reliable gentlemen to rakish ones."

"You consider *Somerset* reliable?" He snorted. "You're more naive than I thought. If it's diamonds you're looking for, you're better off with me. Ask any of your rich relations. They can all vouch for my character."

"So you know these . . . rich relations I supposedly have?"

"I know everyone of any consequence." He cast her a dark smile. "Which is why you'd be better off spending your time with me than with Somerset."

Ah, so that was why he was making much of the "Maynards" . . . as a way to gain her favor. Little did he know, in her eyes the fact that he might know her "rich relations" didn't say much about his character.

"So, my sweet swan," he went on, "I pray you will allow me to call on you in your lodgings on the morning after tomorrow. Two days should give you time to ask around about me and find out if I'm worth your trouble."

His request threw her into a quandary. He knew some wealthy Maynards and might even know her father, but he also clearly wanted to bed her. And letting him wouldn't be wise.

Still, she'd fooled Lord Somerset easily enough; surely she could do the same with Lord Hampden. It was worth the risk for the chance of finding out who her father was. "You may call on me in *three* days, my lord."

"Two is plenty enough to determine my suitability."

His businesslike treatment of their impending assignation began to annoy her. "Perhaps I should ask for letters of reference," she said tightly.

With a glint in his eyes, Lord Hampden rounded

the chair. "I take it that you think me cold-blooded. I see I'll have to explain myself better . . . so you'll understand exactly what sort of association I propose." His suddenly hungry gaze dropped to her lips, and his arm snaked about her waist to draw her close.

"Truly, my lord, I don't think that's necess—"

His lips on hers cut her off, causing a surprising tingling in her belly that took her utterly off guard. He dragged her tighter against him, then thrust his tongue inside her mouth, slowly . . . deeply . . .

Boldly. And she was swept up in a kiss of such fathomless intensity, it made her body ache. The plunge of his tongue in her mouth, mimicking the act he meant for them to share, made her pulse quicken and her eyelids slide shut. With a groan, he clasped her head in both hands so he could steal the breath from her with his ravening kisses.

Her knees grew weak and her blood ran hot. So this was seduction—this unexpected hunger that made her want to arch into him, to pull him into herself. Good Lord in heaven, what was he doing to her?

When at last he drew back, she stared at him through heavy-lidded eyes, her body awash with need. She couldn't have spoken if she tried. As his heated gaze played over her face, he stroked her lower lip with his thumb.

"Two days," he murmured. "How will I wait two days to have you?"

The words sent a ripple of desire through her, then alarm. None of the fumbling gallants who'd kissed her in dark corners behind the theater flats had affected her so profoundly.

"This is madness," she whispered.

"Aye." He drew her against him until they were plastered to each other from thigh to chest. "A very pleasant sort of madness, I think."

He lowered his mouth again. Knowing that she'd never survive another searing kiss, she strained away from him, and in that moment Charity burst through the door.

Then halted to cast them a speculative glance. "Beg pardon," she said dryly. "Didn't mean to disturb you. I'll just go—"

"No!" Annabelle pushed free of the marquess. "His lordship was just leaving."

What had she been thinking, to let this powerful lord tempt her from her purpose, no matter how much he might tell her? She'd never be able to control him. Never.

She forced a smile. "Lord Hampden, I've changed my mind. You needn't bother me again, though I thank you for your visit today. It's been most . . . enlightening."

He chuckled. "For me, too." He reached for his plumed hat and settled it on his wild mane of curls. Then he added in a distinct tone of command, "Two days, Mrs. Maynard. Use them well."

"You don't understand—" she began, but before

she could finish, he'd stalked from the room, leaving her alone with Charity.

Annabelle whirled on her maid in a fury. "How dare you set up an assignation for me with that man without telling me!"

Charity shrugged. "Looks to me like you two got on pretty good. Looks to me like you weren't complaining about him the *whole* time he was here."

A blush heated Annabelle's face as she tried desperately to regain her composure. "You still should have told me of it."

"Would you have met with him if I had?" At Annabelle's scowl, the maid added, "That's what I thought. And I could tell just from talking to the man that the two of you would suit. I was right, wasn't I? If I hadn't come in—"

"Nothing would have happened."

Charity snorted. "*Nothing?*"

Annabelle avoided Charity's eyes. "All right, I'll admit I allowed him certain . . . ah . . . liberties. What else was I to do?" She shot Charity a faintly accusatory glance. "He had me trapped here. I had to rid myself of him somehow, and the only way to appease these gallants is with a kiss. So I let him kiss me . . . out of pity, of course, but—"

"That man got more than a pity kiss from you, I'll warrant. Don't try to tell me otherwise because I won't believe a word."

And with that, Charity began to lay out the items of Annabelle's costume. As silence descended in the room, broken only by the rustle of rich fabric, Annabelle pondered the disquieting Lord Hampden.

What he wanted was clear. But was there something she might get from *him*? "Charity, when you set up this assignation with Lord Hampden, did he mention he knew a rich family named Maynard?"

"His lordship knows yer father?" Charity asked, clearly startled.

"I'm not sure. But he claimed to be friendly with some Maynards."

"That's good, ain't it? Perhaps his lordship will help you find yer father." Charity cast her a sly glance. "And you must admit he's a fine figure of a man."

"Aye, but he's not stupid. I can't afford to have him guessing my game. His eye is too sharp and his tongue too quick to serve my purpose."

"I take it you got a taste of that tongue firsthand."

"You're having a pleasant time with this, aren't you?" Annabelle snapped.

Charity hid her face, but not before Annabelle glimpsed her smile.

Annabelle sighed. "I can't decide what to do. He means to come to my lodgings two days hence, and you know what he wants."

"So give it to him."

"Charity!"

"Nay, I mean it." Charity moved behind Annabelle to undo her laces. "Let him sniff about your honeypot, and then ask him yer questions while he's in the throes of passion. When a man's breeches is open, he'll say anything to keep you in his bed."

"And you complain about *my* language! My 'honeypot' indeed."

"'Twasn't original with me. Sir John says the rakes are always buzzing about the actresses' honeypots."

"You shouldn't listen to Sir John," Annabelle grumbled as she stepped out of her gown. "That man will lead you astray faster than you can *say* 'honeypot.'"

"Aye. Well I know it."

Annabelle glanced over in time to catch Charity's dreamy smile. "Surely you're not interested in a thorough scoundrel like Sir John."

"He's not a scoundrel." Charity sniffed. "He may not be a marquess like yer Lord Hampden, but he's still a nice man."

"The marquess is not *my* Lord Hampden," Annabelle bit out.

"Oh, but he will be, you wait and see."

"He will never marry me," Annabelle warned, "if that's what you're hoping for."

Charity planted her hands on her hips. "No, but he'll give you some enjoyment, which you sorely need."

"And then what? After I leave here and want to have a real life again—"

"You'll pretend to be a widow, that's all." She shook her head. "Hoping to keep your virtue while making yourself out to be a whore to shame your father is trying to have your cake and eat it, too."

"Doesn't everybody want that?" Annabelle quipped.

"Aye, but it never works. Mark my words," Charity said with conviction, "this game you're playing will land you in some man's bed. So why not let it be that of a fine man like his lordship?"

Before Annabelle could retort, Mrs. Norris and Moll Davis entered, discussing their latest conquests. Charity grinned, then vanished out the door.

Faith, but the woman was cocky.

As for Lord Hampden . . . Though he could prove useful if he really did know some Maynards, he'd said nothing specific, and it might all be just for show.

Meanwhile, allowing the man too close could prove dangerous. He would never be put off as easily as Lord Somerset, and she refused to follow Charity's mad advice and go willy-nilly into the man's bed.

So if she was serious about her vengeance, she must halt his pursuit of her before it went any further.

Chapter Three

"For secrets are edged tools,
And must be kept from children and from fools."
—John Dryden, *Sir Martin Mar-All*, Act 2, Sc. 2

Two days after he'd tangled with Annabelle Maynard, Colin stood in the doorway of the coffeehouse The Grecian in Threadneedle Street and grimaced. In the three years since he'd last been here, things had certainly changed. No longer was it just a gathering place for wits and men of science; now there were also fops showing off their latest petticoat breeches and brocaded vests. London had become a city of fawning peacocks like Somerset.

That reminder of Mrs. Maynard's "companion" made him scowl, then curse under his breath. Why did he care if the woman had lovers?

But he did. And it annoyed him. He wasn't used to being put out of sorts for anyone, even a pretty female.

By God, she *was* pretty . . . and lush and sweet and intoxicating to kiss. Her mouth held more mysteries than a sultan's harem, and her skin was silky soft, as fragile and delicate as the fine filigree of her swan brooch.

Yes, that damned swan brooch. She had grown decidedly nervous when Colin asked about it, which made him wonder if Walcester was right to be worried about her. Could it be coincidence that she and the earl not only bore the same surname, but that the gallants called her by the same nickname that had served as Walcester's code name during the war?

It didn't seem likely, but "The Silver Swan" *was* a popular madrigal. Perhaps Mrs. Maynard simply liked music. Then there was her quoting of that morbid poem. What did that mean?

Most telling, however, was her reaction to his remarks about her "rich relations." Colin had to admit—that alone made her behavior a little suspect. At least it warranted further examination.

Unfortunately, it wasn't her behavior that he ached to examine. 'Sdeath, it had been a long time since a woman had heated his blood so fiercely. In Antwerp he'd been too busy doing the king's business to spend much time wenching, and since his return, he'd grown disenchanted with the court's single-minded pursuit of pleasure at the cost of the country.

Yet here he was, unable to stop thinking about Mrs. Maynard—the scent of oranges that clung to her, the way her lush body curved into his arms. If he didn't watch himself, he'd be sucked into the merry-go-round of the court's sexual abandonment. Then he'd be nipping at her heels like the other bucks, without a thought for his future.

He frowned. That was absurd. He could handle his desire for a woman, if anyone could. Surely it was just part of the general restlessness he'd felt ever since his return. And it wasn't because of a lack of anything to do—the king wanted to send him somewhere else to gather intelligence, yet he'd been balking. He couldn't even explain why.

"Hampden!" called a voice from a table at the back of the dimly lit room.

It was Sir John, whom he'd come to find. And with him was Garett Lockwood, the Earl of Falkham.

Colin broke into a smile of genuine pleasure as he headed for their table.

"Decided to brave city life for a while, have you?" Colin asked Falkham as he took a seat on the bench opposite his closest friend in the world.

Falkham gave a rueful sigh. "It seems that even Mina has the urge to acquire a new gown once in a while." He shook his head in the way affectionate husbands always do when speaking of their wives. "Besides, she's been eager to attend the theater. She's got her eye on some play called *The School of Compliments*."

Colin's smile slipped. A certain actress was said to have a role in that upcoming play.

"Now, that's the face of a man who's been rejected

by a beautiful woman," Sir John told Falkham with a laugh.

He gritted his teeth. No doubt Sir John had heard from Charity about Colin's useless attempts to capture Mrs. Maynard, the roving target. Those two were thick as thieves these days.

"How can that be?" Falkham said. "I thought Hampden had perfected the art of seduction. In fact, my poor wife despairs of his ever finding a wife, since he has enough women to warm his bed *without* benefit of clergy."

"Your wife ought to know by now that I will die a bachelor."

"I daresay you will, since beautiful women have finally begun rejecting your advances." Falkham dug his left elbow into Sir John's side, and the two men laughed like witless fools.

Hell and furies. Now he wished that Falkham hadn't decided to visit. The man had been waiting years for a chance to pay Colin back for flirting with Mina when Falkham had her in his sights. Sir John's gibes were bad enough without Falkham gleefully joining in.

Falkham smirked at him. "So tell me, what female is wise enough to spurn *you*?"

"She's not spurning me," he ground out. "She's merely avoiding me, a small circumstance I mean to remedy shortly."

According to Charity, Mrs. Maynard had disappeared from her lodgings at morning's first light. He had watched the place half the morning after that, but Mrs. Maynard hadn't returned.

Sir John snorted. "Why don't you admit that the woman isn't interested in you? She prefers a man she can twist around her little finger. The Silver Swan can't abide being told what to do, and we both know you can't abide keeping your opinions to yourself." He winked at Falkham.

"The Silver Swan?" Falkham asked.

"She's one of the duke's players," Sir John explained. "You'll have a chance to see her if you attend *The School of Compliments*. Rumor has it she'll be playing the lead role instead of Moll Davis."

Falkham shot Colin an assessing glance. "An actress isn't your usual preference."

"No," Colin clipped out.

And his friend knew why. Colin's mother had been a vain, pretentious French actress and sometime courtesan. Over the six-year-old Colin's frightened protests, she'd eagerly relinquished her son to Marlowe Jeffreys, Colin's father, when the wealthy merchant had come to France in search of his bastard son.

Colin thrust those dark memories from his mind. How he felt about actresses had nothing to do with this. He was pursuing Mrs. Maynard only on Walcester's behalf.

Right. And clouds were made of cotton.

"So what do you plan to do about Mrs. Maynard?" Sir John pressed when Colin wasn't forth-coming.

"Don't worry. Just because she's been avoiding me all day doesn't mean she'll escape me forever. She can't bow out of the play, can she?"

"Will you abduct her from the stage, then?" Sir John asked.

"There are better ways to deal with Annabelle Maynard, I assure you." Like how he'd dealt with her in the tiring-room. His blood heated at the mere memory of the way she'd responded to his kisses.

"Just be certain Charity doesn't object to your methods," Sir John pointed out, "or you'll have not one but two angry women on your back."

"That's why I need your help." Colin caught a passing serving boy and ordered more dishes of coffee all round. "This afternoon I want you to keep Charity busy while I . . . deal with Mrs. May-nard."

Sir John laughed. "Now, that's a mission I am more than happy to be charged with. I didn't real-ize until you started dealing with her mistress that Charity was such a fiery little thing. But now that I know, I am happy to help in any way I can."

"Which means he intends to seduce her," Falkham put in dryly.

"Why not?" Sir John said. "That's what Hamp-den intends for her mistress."

Colin merely smiled. He wasn't entirely sure *what* he intended for Mrs. Maynard. Walcester had said nothing about seducing her, and Colin could find out her secrets well enough without that.

No, what he wanted was to understand her. Why was she coy one moment and wary the next? What did she fear? *Whom* did she fear? And why the devil was she perfectly happy to give herself to a fool like Somerset but skittish about giving herself to a marquess of twice his consequence?

One way or the other, he meant to figure that out. If it took seduction to do that, then so be it.

AS THE FIRST act of the play ended and Annabelle exited, the tenor who was to provide the musical interlude between acts brushed past her as if she were invisible. Too bad she couldn't *be* invisible. Because Lord Hampden was out there in the audience. She'd felt his gaze on her even when she couldn't see him, and it still made her pulse race and her palms go damp.

In the two days he'd given her, she'd asked about him . . . to her infinite regret. She'd discovered that the Marquess of Hampden was a powerful man with powerful friends. Rumor had it that he'd been a Royalist spy during the war. The king held him in highest esteem, as did several influential nobles.

But was her father one of them? Could she find out who he was at last just by cozying up to Lord Hampden?

No, that method was far too risky. Best to avoid the overbearing and too-fascinating marquess entirely.

Thus it was with great alarm that she found the cause of her distress leaning against the wall as she approached the tiring-room. She forced nonchalance to her face. "My lord, what are you doing here?"

He pushed away from the wall with a dark glance. "Reminding you that we had an appointment for this morning. One you missed."

"I believe I made it clear that I changed my mind about our appointment."

"So you're a coward after all," he murmured. "Tell me, why would a woman with a reputation for enjoying the finer pleasures of life turn tail and run after one paltry kiss?"

He had her there, devil take him. She couldn't let him think she was anything except a wanton actress. Unfortunately, if she accepted the challenge, it would be like trying to cage a tiger. But if she refused, it would be like trying to outrun one. Either choice was bad.

Suddenly the door to the tiring-room burst open and Moll Davis sailed out. Through the open door, Annabelle could see Lord Somerset, tapping his foot with impatience as he attempted to fluff out the flounces of his petticoat breeches.

To her relief, he glanced up and spotted her. He sauntered out to join her, followed by Sir Charles Sedley, a pretty-faced rake known for his outrageous exploits, most recently for disporting himself naked on a balcony.

"Hello, angel," Lord Somerset cooed. "You are captivating tonight as always."

He stank of some strong perfume that nearly made her choke. Still, when he bent to kiss her cheek, she turned so that his wet mouth met hers. He drew back, his surprise at her response showing in the lift of his plucked eyebrows.

Fighting the urge to wipe her lips, she ignored Lord Hampden's scowl and took Lord Somerset's arm. Today the man wore three patches on his rouged cheeks. Together with his new periwig of flowing yellow ringlets, they made him look like a truculent child awaiting Mother's treats.

"I've missed you," she leaned up to whisper.

Now his surprise became full-blown. "Can't have that, can we?" He tossed his horrible corkscrew curls, then lowered his mouth to hers again.

Lord Hampden cleared his throat loudly, prompting Lord Somerset to peer into the shadows. "Ah, Hampden. Decided to have a look at all our lovely actresses, have you?"

"Only one in particular, although the woman has apparently forgotten our assignation." Lord Hampden's gaze steadied on her. "Such a damnable shame, too, since I very much looked forward to stroking the dear creature's feathers, if you know what I mean."

"Indeed." Lord Somerset slipped his arm around Annabelle's waist to draw her closer. "Even this wild creature is prone to the occasional shy moment."

She wasn't sure she liked being called a "wild creature," but at least the viscount hadn't realized whom Lord Hampden was hinting at.

"Oh yes," Sir Charles put in. "We all know the Swan hides behind her feathers whenever possible."

A pox on Sir Charles! Fortunately, Lord Somerset was obviously too intent on peeking down her low-cut gown to realize he was being mocked. "Yes, yes," was all he said as he smoothed his hand down her derriere.

"I can scarcely believe Mrs. Maynard hides from anyone," Lord Hampden snapped.

"I know," Lord Somerset said. "She can be a bold little thing at times. Quick-tongued, you know."

Sir Charles grinned. "Well, not all of us have had the privilege of receiving the end of Mrs. Maynard's tongue."

Annabelle shot Sir Charles a murderous glance.

"She saves her tongue for me," Lord Somerset said, preening a bit.

"Because she enjoys slicing you to ribbons with it?" Lord Hampden said, with thinly disguised irritation.

"As long as she allows me a thrust or two of my own occasionally," Lord Somerset joked, "I don't mind her barbs."

Normally, Annabelle could tolerate all the double entendres, but not today in front of the marquess, especially with Sir Charles laughing at her expense.

Though Sir Charles's laugh was cut short by Lord Hampden's glare. And when Lord Somerset, pleased with his wit, pressed a kiss to her hair, the marquess stiffened. "You know, Somerset," he drawled, "I'm glad to see you enjoying yourself. After the terrible news you received this morning, I thought—"

The viscount's head snapped around. "What terrible news?"

Lord Hampden feigned surprise. "You didn't know? Hell and furies, I've spoken out of turn. Of course, perhaps I misunderstood His Majesty . . . Yes, I'm sure that's it. Never mind."

Sir Charles, always one to make trouble where he could, took up the theme with glee. "I believe I heard the same thing."

Lord Somerset released her. "Out with it, man! His Majesty spoke of me? What did he say?"

The marquess shrugged. "I don't know if I should tell you. Perhaps I'm wrong."

"It's my petition, isn't it? His Majesty has refused it." Lord Somerset whirled on Sir Charles. "You heard it too?"

"It's possible that I misunderstood as well, but . . ." Sir Charles trailed off meaningfully.

"God-a-mercy!" The viscount turned to Annabelle. "Listen, angel, you won't mind if I go to Whitehall for a bit, will you? I must find out about my petition. Terribly important."

Silently cursing Lord Hampden, she forced a

smile for her inamorata. "As his lordship says, they may have misunderstood. Must you leave before the play's over? If you stay, then perhaps after the play we could go back to my lodgings and . . . well . . ." She trailed off with a seductive smile.

He blinked and looked as if he might change his mind. Then he shook his head. "Later, angel. I won't be gone that long. You understand, don't you?"

"Of course she understands," Lord Hampden said in a steely voice. "Don't worry, Sir Charles and I will watch over her to make sure the other gallants leave her be. Since my own companion hasn't yet arrived, I might as well make myself useful." His smile of victory made her itch to slap him.

"Thank you!" the viscount gushed. "I'd be most grateful for that kindness, sir." Grabbing her hand, he pressed a kiss to it and then was gone.

She whirled on the marquess. "You, my lord, ought to be ashamed of yourself for telling such monstrous lies!"

"I never lie," Lord Hampden said dryly. "The king does have some terrible news for Somerset. As I recall, it concerned the situation in the colonies or . . . some affairs of state or . . . What was it, Sir Charles, that His Majesty said?"

"I believe His Majesty threatened to exile Lord Somerset to the colonies if the man didn't stop boring him with endless tales about his tailor."

"You see?" Lord Hampden drawled. "I wasn't lying a bit."

She wanted to snatch his sword from him and break it over his head. "You are the most annoying, insolent—"

"Devil?" Amusement glittered in his eyes. "Be glad for it. I just saved you from enduring that popinjay's slobbering ministrations all evening."

Annabelle sniffed. "Better a popinjay than an arrogant brute who presses his attentions where they're not wanted."

His expression darkened. "They weren't so unwanted two days ago in the tiring-room."

At Sir Charles's laugh, she whirled away, but the marquess caught her by the arm and drew her behind a scene flat to shield them from Sir Charles and the other players.

"The choice is yours." His breath burned hot against her cheek as he pressed her against the painted image of an idyllic garden. "Either explain why my kiss so upset you, or meet me after the play as agreed. I'll take nothing else."

Why in heaven's name was he so persistent? She fumbled for an excuse that wouldn't give away her secrets. "Your kiss demonstrated you were too rough a man for me. I don't like being mauled. It might behoove you to remember that."

"You don't know what 'rough' is, you little fool," he leaned in to murmur. "You keep toying with these fops and gallants, and one day you'll find yourself in serious trouble. They're not all as easy to manipulate as Somerset."

You certainly aren't. "I can take care of myself," she said stoutly.

"Then why are you so afraid to meet me?"

Dear heaven, he kept coming back to that. And the truth was, if he found her refusal odd enough, he could ruin all her carefully laid plans by speculating with the other gallants about her supposedly wanton character. The house of cards would come tumbling down if the men started comparing notes and figuring out that she wasn't nearly the wanton she was painting herself to be.

Besides, if she trod carefully, she might get the marquess to help her determine which Maynard had abandoned her mother. She really should just give in and handle this cocky lord as she'd handled the rest, by playing on his vanity and pretending to capitulate.

"Very well," she said haughtily, "I'll meet you after the play, though I don't know why you've fixed on me for your advances. Any number of actresses would be only too glad to oblige your raging passions."

"I know," he said baldly. "They earn little enough without spurning the honest attentions of a wealthy man. So why are *you* so reluctant, eh, Aphrodite? It tempts a man to wonder what you're hiding."

As she hesitated, unsure how to answer, he took her hand. She swallowed hard as he pressed a kiss to it that bore no resemblance to Lord Somerset's sloppy one. Then, with his eyes gleaming up at her, he turned her hand over to kiss her palm so provocatively it made her shiver.

"I'll be waiting for you by the tiring-room after the play," he said, running his finger over her wrist, where her madly beating pulse gave away her reaction to him. "If you're not there, I'll find you. We made an agreement, and I intend to see you hold up your part of the bargain."

Then he released her, and with a bow he left. Meanwhile, she remained standing behind the flat, her heart pounding madly in her chest.

So the insufferable beast intended to bed her after the play, did he? Well, he'd find himself in bed, all right. And if she planned it right, he'd awaken tomorrow with such a horrendous headache, he'd never approach her again.

Chapter Four

"Words may be false and full of art,
Sighs are the natural language of the heart."
—Thomas Shadwell, *Psyche*, Act 3

Colin waited with Mrs. Maynard in the doorway to the Duke's Theater as sheets of rain pelted the road, transforming the already muddy thoroughfare into an unnavigable mire.

He scowled. Of all the wretched luck. He'd walked to the theater, knowing that her lodgings were close by. But, with the rain, all the hackney coaches were gone.

Not that it mattered. The road now resembled a marsh, with enough mud to stall even the largest hackney. No, the only thing for it would be to keep close to the buildings, where the ground was firmer, and to take their chances with the bitterly cold rain.

He glanced over at his companion, who'd wrapped herself so tightly in her drab cloak that she resembled a sparrow more than a swan. But he knew something of what lay beneath the brown wool. The knowledge burned deep within his belly . . . and lower . . . a fire that wouldn't be quenched.

Hell and furies, but the woman threw him off balance. Instead of gaining the information he'd promised Walcester, he was letting himself be drawn in by her obvious attractions, her clever mind . . . and the mystery of her inexplicable reluctance. He wasn't used to women refusing him, especially not for the likes of Somerset. Nor was he used to the irrational anger that surged up whenever he thought of Somerset's leer and Sir Charles's sly talk about tongues.

He was a spy, for God's sake, known for his cool detachment and careful perceptions, not for letting a female get under his skin. He must keep his wits about him.

But what man could, with a sweet wench like her at his side?

"I suppose we'd best stay here for a while," she said. "Of course, you don't have to wait, if the rain doesn't bother you."

He bit back a laugh. Did she think it would be as easy as that to rid herself of him? "It'll slacken soon, and then we can take it at a run."

"Perhaps *you* can afford to ruin your attire in mud and rain and grit, but I can't afford even to ruin my hose. Clothing is dear for us humbler folk, my lord."

"Don't worry, I'll buy you more hose . . . and a new gown and cloak and whatever else you desire."

She blanched. "Must you be so blatant about all this? You have a way of making a woman feel like a trollop."

"You're the only actress I know who'd regard a simple offer of clothing as a vile insult," he muttered as he scanned the dark street.

She did have the oddest scruples. Why treat him like an uncaring brute for offering what Somerset had no doubt already given her? Damned if he could figure out how the woman's mind worked.

Suddenly two urchins, a boy of about twelve and a girl of ten, came out of the rain to approach Annabelle. "Have ye any oranges for us today, miss?"

With a ready smile, she dug into her cloak's deep pockets. "I do believe there's a couple here." She put two oranges into the outstretched hands.

The children's eyes lit up. "Thankee, miss," they cried as they tore greedily into the fruit.

Annabelle smiled as she hunted in her pockets once more. "I think I may also have a cross bun in here, too, that I didn't have the chance to eat."

When she handed it over, the girl's eyes filled with tears. "Y're an angel, miss." The girl broke the bun in half and handed the other portion to her companion. Within seconds, it was gone.

The two started to leave, but the boy paused to glance back at Colin. "Best ye be nice to the orange lady, milord," he said boldly before his friend worriedly yanked his arm. They scampered back into the rain.

Colin stared after them. "Do you do that often? Give food to the street urchins?"

With a shrug, she mumbled, "Once in a while."

Oranges weren't cheap. She'd complained about the cost of new hose, but had no compunction about feeding street urchins off her modest salary? He didn't know what to make of her.

They stood there in silence until the rain slowed to a drizzle. Then he murmured, "Time to spread your wings," and pulled her into the street.

She kept surprisingly good pace with him, despite the mud sucking at their feet. They'd rounded the corner into the alley where her lodgings lay when the skies opened again. "Hell and furies!" he growled as a wave of wind and water whisked his hat from his head and soaked his coat. The same sheet of water whipped her cloak from around her and threw back her hood, exposing all of her to the merciless elements.

He snatched her up in his arms and ran for the lit door at the end of the alley. Fortunately, it wasn't latched, and in moments he'd maneuvered his way inside.

But he didn't set her down right away, enjoying the soft weight of her and the clean rain scent that rose from her soaked clothing. She stared up at him guilelessly. Candlelight played over the slope of her pale brow, the fine curves of her cheeks, the slender nose with its pert tip.

And it glinted off the naked sorrow in her eyes.

She watched him from behind lashes dusted with tiny drops, like honeysuckle nectar, like rain tears. He bent his head, wanting to kiss them away, and perhaps with them that dark hint of sadness. Then she blinked and the moment passed.

With what sounded like a sigh, she murmured, "You can let me down now, my lord."

"Only if you call me Colin. Considering what we are to be to each other, I should think Christian names are more appropriate . . . Annabelle."

"Very well. You may put me down, Colin." Her husky voice speaking his name sent shivers of anticipation through him. He obliged her but only because he feared if he kissed her here, they'd never reach her rooms.

Water dripped from them both, forming ever-widening puddles on the wooden floor. She attempted to wring it out of her wool skirts, but that was futile.

Removing her cloak, he gestured up the stairs. "We have to get out of these wet clothes."

Fear flashed in her eyes, catching him off guard. Then, as if she drew her soul into herself, she changed into another creature entirely. Gone was the vulnerable, hurting maiden and the gentle woman who fed oranges to urchins. Even the coy coquette had disappeared. The reserved actress had returned, as prickly and unapproachable as her swan namesake.

"My rooms are upstairs," she said regally. Then

she took a brace of candles from beside the door and motioned for him to follow.

They'd gone only a few steps, however, when a door beneath them flew open and a wizened old man appeared.

"Mrs. Maynard, what . . . who . . ." the old man stammered.

Annabelle halted to cast the man a brittle smile. "Good evening, Master Watkins. I'm sorry for the water on your floor. We got caught in the rain."

"You wouldn't be bringing the gentleman up to yer rooms, now, would you?"

Her smile wavered. "Surely you won't mind if my brother visits with me a short while."

Colin bit back a smile. He'd used that ploy once or twice himself, but he'd never thought to have a woman use it for him.

"Yer brother?" Master Watkins assessed Colin with a look of pure skepticism.

"Colin Maynard, at your service," Colin said easily, all too accustomed to pretending to be something he wasn't.

But Master Watkins only regarded him with even greater suspicion. He scowled at Annabelle. "You know that me wife don't like you bringing men to your rooms, Mrs. Maynard. After that last gentleman, she said if you brought more, she'd toss you in the street. We run a respectable house. Can't be having talk going 'round about us."

After that last gentleman. It had to be Somerset.

Annabelle planted her hands on her hips. "I don't understand why in heaven's name I can't bring my own brother—"

"Yes, yes. Yer brother," Master Watkins said with a sigh. "Go on with you, then. But don't let me missus see you."

"Thank you, Master Watkins," she said like a queen, then continued up the stairs, her back stiff and proud.

Colin nodded to the landlord and followed her up, trying not to dwell on the fact that other men had walked these steps before him. He didn't care. He'd never cared before; why should he care now?

Yet the idea of it irritated him sorely, which only showed how important it was that he bed the woman—so he could end this foolish obsession and get on with his real purpose.

Once she'd unlocked her room and beckoned him in, she shut the door and whirled on him. "Now see what you've done? Thanks to you, I may find myself in the street tomorrow, if not sooner!"

"Don't blame it all on me. If I understood your Master Watkins correctly, I wasn't the first man to enter these hallowed rooms." 'Sdeath, was that jealousy in his voice? It couldn't be. He'd never been jealous in his life.

"I told you before that Lord Somerset and I were—"

"Lovers?" he said snidely. "No, you never said so, but I'm no fool." Oh yes, that was jealousy all right.

A blush stained her cheeks.

"Not that I care," he lied. "Somerset isn't here now. I am."

"So you are." She glanced about. "But where the devil is Charity? She should be here, since she wasn't at the theater."

He gave her a bland smile. Sir John had done his job well. "Perhaps she has found a swain of her own."

"Women like Charity and me don't have swains."

"You have bedfellows."

The blunt word made her pale. "Exactly." Then she swept about the room, lighting candles. "And since you mean to be one of them, you should take a look at my lodgings and decide if they meet with your approval."

The woman had a way of spreading such contempt on her words that any man would think twice before willingly letting her near.

Of course, Colin wasn't just any man. He scanned the room, noting the cold hearth with two armchairs placed before it, a lace-covered table surrounded by four sturdy chairs, an oak cupboard, and a looking glass with gilt edges that represented the most expensive piece of furniture.

Despite the cheap materials and rough workmanship of her furnishings, she'd created a pleasant, homey atmosphere. That made sense for the woman who gave oranges to urchins, but not for the woman who supposedly lived her life for pleasure and naught else.

Once again, she'd managed to perplex him.

"Will it do, my lord?" she asked. "Or are you already planning to hire workmen to remake it to your preference? Do let me know your plans, so I won't be a nuisance." Despite her acid words, a faint tremor in her voice betrayed her anxiety.

"At the moment, my only plans are to remove these wet clothes." He lifted her cloak. "Is there somewhere I can hang this?"

"I'll take it." She approached him. "And your coat and vest."

He peeled off his sodden outer garments and handed them to her. Her eyes went wide, scanning his wet lawn shirt and snuff-colored breeches, which clung to him like a second skin. Was that a blush on her cheeks? It hardly seemed likely. She had to have seen men in less clothing than this.

At his questioning glance, she seemed to recollect herself, and she crossed the room to drop their garments onto an armchair.

But when she knelt to build a fire in the grate, he said, "Let me do that." He came up to take the bundle of kindling from her, and her icy fingers brushed his.

Jerking away, she jumped to her feet. "I'll see about your coat." She draped her cloak over one armchair and arranged his clothing over the other.

Once the fire caught, he rose to watch her work. God, she was skittish for a woman rumored to take lovers where she pleased. She stood stiffly beside the chair that held her cloak, plucking at its folds and rearranging it to better catch the heat from the fire.

She was stalling. He knew it, and so did she. He just couldn't figure out why. "Annabelle—" he began in a low voice.

"Tea! We must have tea." She headed for the cupboard. "You need something to warm you."

"I can think of something better than tea to warm me," he rasped.

"It'll take but a moment." After setting a kettle on the hob to heat, she started toward him, then caught sight of herself in the mirror and stopped short. "Faith, but I look a fright!"

"On the contrary," he drawled, "I've never seen a more fetching sight than you in a wet gown."

She eyed him askance. "Oh, but my hair is a wreck. Meanwhile, your curls are still crisp and tight. You must give your secret to Charity. No matter how hard she works at my unruly waves with the irons, she can't train my hair to form perfect ringlets."

"It helps when the ringlets are natural," he said dryly.

"I should have known," she said, shaking her head ruefully. "Every other rake has to work at being fashionable, but you, of course, were born that way."

Sensing her babbling was meant to stave off her nervousness, he sought to put her at ease. "Ah, but I wasn't born with Somerset's knack for choosing patches."

A sudden sparkle lit her eyes. "A dire handicap indeed."

"And I could never match his biting wit."

"Which only bites *him*," she quipped. Then, seeming to realize she was being disloyal, she mumbled, "Though, really, he can be witty when he wishes."

"I don't want to talk about Somerset," he growled. "And you should get out of that gown before you catch your death of cold." God, how he ached to see her without her gown.

She arched an eyebrow. "Are you concerned for my well-being? Or just eager to see me in dishabille?"

"Both. And why are you so nervous around me, Annabelle?" He searched her face. "Answer that question to my satisfaction, and I'll leave right now. I have no desire to bed a woman who is frightened of me."

"I'm not frightened of you," she said, forcing a smile. "Don't be ridiculous." Then she hurried to the fire to take the kettle off.

He watched her warily. He still wasn't sure what he intended to accomplish with this assignation. Did he really mean to bed her just to find out what Walcester wanted to know?

No. The bedding was because he desired her, and he could swear that she desired him . . . when she wasn't flitting about acting like a maiden on her wedding night. She intrigued him, with her armor of words and her changeable moods and her strange reluctance. Beneath it all lay a real woman whom he itched to unmask. Because she plainly wasn't who she appeared to be.

Could she really be the spy that Walcester feared she was? For the Dutch or the French perhaps? If Walcester was right and she was trying to draw him out, she could be working for almost anyone.

Then again, perhaps her secrets were more mundane.

Whatever they were, he meant to ferret them out before the night was over. He dropped into an armchair and began to pull off one of his muddy half-boots.

She was at the cupboard with her back to him, fooling with the kettle and some items she'd taken from a drawer. "Time for tea," she said cheerily as she turned to face him with a tray in her hand.

Then she froze, her gaze dropping to where he was now removing his other boot.

"I hope you don't mind," he said. "I decided to make myself comfortable."

"Of course," she murmured as she went to set the tray down on the table. But her hands were shaking.

"I'm curious," he remarked in his best casual tone. "Where are you from originally? You don't have a London accent."

With a quick nervous gesture, she brushed a damp lock of hair back behind one ear. "Well . . . ah . . . the country, of course. I was born and bred in the country."

He dropped his boot, noting how she flinched at the sound. "That doesn't exactly narrow it down. At least give me the county. Yorkshire? Lancashire?" He paused. "Or perhaps not England at all. Perhaps Ireland?"

She shot him an irritated glance. "Don't be absurd. I'm as English as you are."

He merely kept staring at her. As a young spy in France, he'd learned that remaining quiet and fixing the subject of his questioning with an expectant look got better results than dozens of questions. People disliked uncomfortable silences.

Annabelle was no exception. "Northamptonshire," she remarked after a moment. "I grew up in a small village you've probably never heard of."

"Oh, I doubt that. I roam our fair country a great deal. I'm sure I've been in your neck of the woods at some time or another."

"Why does it matter where I'm from?"

Ah, he thought, the skittish swan had reappeared.

"It doesn't." He leaned back in his chair to watch her pour tea into a chipped bowl. "Believe me, I understand your reluctance. You can't risk people carrying tales to your family. No doubt your parents would haul you back home and marry you off instantly if they knew you were in London on the stage."

She blanched. "My parents are dead."

The glint of sudden tears in her eyes made him gentle his voice. "I'm sorry. I didn't know."

She squared her shoulders. "'Tis no matter. At least I can care for myself, which is more than some orphans can do."

Ah. That was why she fed the street urchins.

"But I did hope, when I came to London," she went on, "that I might find other members of my family. So tell me about these relatives of mine you seem to know."

Back to the Maynards, eh? This got more suspicious every time she opened her mouth. He had to play this carefully, for Walcester's sake.

He wracked his brains for information about the earl's family and distant relations. "Let me see. There's Joseph Maynard, of course, a lawyer and a knight."

"Oh?" She spooned some sugar into the bowl and stirred. "A knight?"

So that was important, was it? "Aye, although he only received that honor recently when he was made the King's Serjeant."

She looked disappointed.

"There's Leticia, his sister, a bitter witch with a penchant for tearing apart other women's reputations."

Annabelle just stared at him. Clearly Leticia didn't interest her.

"Oh, and Louis, the poet. Let's not forget him. Not that anyone could, since he persists in circulating his ridiculous verses at court to anyone who will give him the time of day."

"He's older?" she prodded.

"Actually he's about my age."

Her interest seemed to vanish. Age must be important to her, too.

"I almost forgot," he said casually. "There's Edward, the Earl of Walcester, a widower of about fifty. Now, that's a relative you should cultivate. His fortune isn't vast, but it's certainly enough to keep a woman like you in gowns and slippers for some time, especially since he has no heirs."

He knew he'd hit the target when she froze.

Damn. He'd begun to hope Walcester was wrong about her. Because what reason could she have for trying to "draw the earl out," especially after all these years? Did she intend to blackmail the man for something related to his tenure as the Silver Swan? If so, how could she know anything about it? She hadn't even been born when Walcester was a spy. This still made no sense.

Which was why seducing her might be wise. Women told confidences to men who bedded them.

He ignored the part of his conscience that said his debt to Walcester had nothing to do with why he wanted to bed her.

A shaky laugh left her lips. "A nobleman? I hardly think I'm related to nobility." Nonetheless, she carried his tea to him with trembling hands.

He took the bowl and set it on the floor. "Oh, I can well believe you have connections to nobility." When she started to move away, he clasped her hand. "A woman of your beauty and obvious

refinement can't help but move in high circles." He
pulled her to stand between his thighs. "And now,
my dear, it's time we engaged in a more intimate
discussion."

She pushed away from him none too gently and
went to sit at the table. "Let's have our tea first. It
will do us both some good."

Again with the damnable tea. He started to tell
her he wanted *her*, not the tea. Then, noting how
she watched him, he lifted his bowl and sniffed
unobtrusively.

Valerian root and tarragon. He couldn't mistake the fragrance meant to mask the most important ingredient in a sleeping decoction—laudanum.
Mina had taught him and his companions at the
Royal Society how to brew the special tea.

Hell and furies, the wench was trying to drug
him. He became certain of it when he set the bowl
on the floor untouched and alarm crossed her face.

He struggled to hide his temper. What did she
hope to accomplish? Robbery? Blackmail? Did she
detest him that much?

Then the truth hit him like a well-placed blow.
The maidenly behavior, the way she'd retreated
after he'd kissed her, her strange refusal to let him
pursue her . . . She feared seduction.

No, how could that be? She'd lain with Somerset.

He sucked in a sharp breath. Perhaps. Or perhaps she'd drugged that fool, too, to make him

think he'd bedded her. Until he spoke with the man to determine what he remembered, Colin couldn't be certain, but that made sense. The question was, why?

He was getting ahead of himself. First he had to be sure of his theory.

With a grim smile, he rose from the chair. Her eyes widened. Then she set down her bowl so quickly, some of the liquid splashed out.

"Aren't you going to—"

"Drink my tea?" Sarcasm dripped from his words. "Not right now. I'm going to kiss you instead."

She rose as if to flee, but in two strides he was before her and catching her in his arms.

He saw her defenses go up seconds before his mouth seized hers, but he didn't care. He held her without remorse, knowing she'd never intended this to happen. His lips plundered hers as he entangled his fingers in her long, damp hair, holding her head still.

She remained stiff as a sword and just as cold within his embrace, clinging to her precious shield of detachment. But he knew that the Annabelle who reveled in his kisses was in there, no matter how much the Silver Swan tried to keep her hidden. And he meant to unveil the woman beneath the mask if it took him half the night to do so.

Chapter Five

"There's beggary in the love that can be reckoned."
—William Shakespeare, *Antony and Cleopatra*, Act 1, Sc. 1

Annabelle didn't know what had set Colin off, but from the moment he'd set down his tea and come for her, she'd known all was lost. The man's gaze stripped her bare as a maple tree in winter, seeing into places she hadn't wanted him to see.

He was angry, too—she could tell. It made her all the more determined to fight him. Unfortunately, she was already losing that fight, and she knew it.

To keep herself remote, she silently chanted a litany of memories about her mother's torments, of her distrust of men. Yet it changed to gibberish as his mouth invaded hers.

When at last he drew back, she sighed with relief, knowing she wouldn't have lasted much longer. But then he began to kiss her brow, her closed eyelids, the tip of her nose. His anger seemed to have abated and the fierceness to have drained from his kisses. Now they were soft and so tender that they made longing well up in her throat.

Then his mouth closed over hers again, and devil take her if she didn't respond this time. She hated herself for the weakness, for the cracks appearing in her wall of resistance.

But how could she help it? Faith, the man kissed like a god. Adonis. Adonis had her in his thrall, and there wasn't a blessed thing she could do about it, not with her body melting like a snow woman under the spring sun. He made her feel alive for the first time in years, made her want and need and yearn.

His hands slid over her shoulders and down, taking the top of her bodice with them. When the air chilled her shoulders, she barely registered it. Until his fingers brushed the upper swell of her breast. Rising from her sensual fog, she tore her mouth from his. But the way he stared, so raw, so hungry, sent her emotions skittering in a thousand directions.

"I want to see you without your feathers," he rasped.

She closed her eyes in a wordless acceptance. He slid one finger beneath the edge of her gown and her smock, running it all along the top, right over the nipples of her barely covered breasts.

The tips tautened into hard pebbles, and her eyes fluttered open. The raw desire shining in his gaze sent a shudder of longing through her.

He kept his gaze on her as he loosened her gown's front with expert ease. Of course. He *was* a rake, after all. No doubt he'd undressed many women.

Futilely she tried to restore her armor of resistance. Why was she standing here letting him strip her of her dignity, her freedom?

Because his gaze riveted her with its knowledge. He seemed to know her as no other gallant had. She couldn't say why, but the realization paralyzed her. No one else saw beneath her role to the real Annabelle.

No one but Lord Hampden.

Only when her gown loosened did she find the power to speak. "Please . . . let go of me . . . my lord."

"My name is Colin, dearling." He pushed her gown down to her waist. Nothing but her thin holland smock covered her breasts. With a tact she hadn't expected, he refrained from looking at them, but his hand . . . faith, his hand covered one cloth-draped breast.

A sharp pang pierced her, making it hard for her to breathe. Her breast filled his hand as if made to fit. Then he slanted his mouth across hers once more.

His mouth also fit.

Only this time she didn't soften. She refused to acquiesce, refused to succumb. She'd fight him with the weapon she'd learned would wound him most. Indifference.

She fell back on the trick she'd used during the squire's beatings, playing a role. He kissed her thoroughly, enticing her, seducing her. So she became the goddess Diana, wild and free, mocking all men as she hunted alone in the forest.

Diana, I am Diana, she chanted silently, and it helped her to withstand the astonishing temptations Colin offered.

Barely. Only with great concentration could she maintain the role. Colin's thumb circled her nipple through the cloth of her smock, eliciting a sweet ache with each passing, and a moan bubbled up in her throat. She closed it off just in time.

I can do this. I can fight him if I try.

He drew back, his expression taut with unbridled desire. "I won't hurt you, dearling. You need not fear that. 'Tis not my wish to take your pride or bend your will to mine. I want only to give you pleasure."

Where his seductions failed to break through her defenses, his gentle words succeeded. Her lips began to tremble, her chin to quiver. He saw it and caught her fear with his kiss. She tried again to summon up her image of Diana, but she couldn't think of anything but his reassuring words, his infinitely gentle tone.

Scarcely knowing she did so, she opened to him, her heart slamming in her chest. Such sweet strokes his tongue gave. Such intimate, gentle nibbles his teeth took of her mouth.

He undid the ties of her smock, then slid her smock off her shoulders until it dropped to form a kind of apron over her half-fallen gown. A moan sounded deep in his throat as he filled both hands with the soft weight of her bare breasts, shaping them, caressing them until she thought she'd faint away right there with the pleasure of it. Unconsciously she pressed against his hands, her own hands finally stealing around his lean waist.

Where had all her pride gone? His fingers worked their magic and his mouth plundered hers with honeyed kisses. How could she have forgotten the lessons Mother had taught her?

A tear of regret slipped between her lowered lashes. Apparently, he felt the damp trail against his own cheek, for he pulled back and his hands stilled on her breasts.

Eyes green as a night forest bored into her. "I want to coax your body to sing, my beautiful swan," he murmured, brushing soft kisses along the path her tear had taken. "Is that so terrible?"

"You want a swan song. If I give you that, I die."

He stiffened, then lifted his hand to smooth one damp lock of hair from her cheek. "Even swans mate. And they don't die afterward."

She must tell him something, must give him some excuse for her hesitation. How could she do so without explaining that her maidenly fears came from being a maiden? She must play this role exactly right if she were to escape his trap.

There was one thing she could request without being thought odd. It wasn't a part of her role she relished, but if it would protect her. . . .

She forced a knowing smile to her lips. "I'm sorry, my lord. This swan requires more wooing before she mates."

Suspicion glinted in his eyes. "Wooing?"

"Sweet words, public attentions . . . gifts."

"Ah." Though the warm light in his eyes faded to a cold cynicism, he didn't release her. Instead he kissed her fiercely, almost angrily, as she fought to remain unmoved.

He drew back to mutter, "I promise to bring you all the gifts you want tomorrow, my greedy miss. But tonight, we shall find another pleasure."

"Nay." She pushed his hands from her breasts and donned an expression of disinterest, though she had begun to loathe that part of her role. "I'll find no pleasure with you until I see some material proof of your affections."

His eyes glittered with a sudden anger and the remnants of desire. But he stepped back and drew her smock in place, tying the ties with quick, jerky movements.

"I should have known." He pressed his body to hers, letting her feel his arousal. "You'll have your . . . ah . . . gifts, my coldhearted swan, as soon as I find ones to suit your beauty. In the meantime, you'd best accustom yourself to my presence, for I don't intend to relinquish the pursuit."

His words thrilled her, although she hated herself for it. Without another word, he released her and went to don his clothes. She stood there numbly watching, only half thanking the heavens for her reprieve.

Colin headed for the door, but paused there to fix her with an angry gaze. His eyes raked her so slowly, they set her afire again.

"Oh, and Annabelle," he said in a warning tone. "I don't know who mixes your tea, but I recommend she use prickly lettuce in her sleeping decoction instead of valerian. It's quick and effective, and best of all, the scent is easier to mask."

He actually smiled then, although the smile stopped short of his eyes. His gaze locked with hers, a challenge in its depths. Then he left.

She dropped into a nearby chair to gaze at the full bowl of tea he'd left on the floor. *Oh, sweet Mary, I am undone. He knows. Devil take the man, he knows.*

AFTER COLIN LEFT, Annabelle tossed and turned half the night, tormented by fitful dreams. She awoke to find her hand caressing her breast.

She shot upright. Lord help her, what had the man done to her? He was turning her into a wanton!

And sadly, she didn't mind nearly as much as she should. Hugging her knees to her chest, she surveyed her bedchamber. The gray morning light seeped into the windows like a mist off the Thames, hiding as much as it revealed.

'Twas like her evening with Colin. Every time

she'd thought to determine his true intentions, he'd shifted tactics, throwing her off guard.

His last tactic had been particularly effective. She raised her hand to her throat, then let it drift down to her smock, following the path of Colin's kisses. Fie, but she'd come close to sharing her bed with him. With his words and caresses he'd woven a magical veil around her so impenetrable she could no longer see the world as before.

She dropped back against the pillow with a dreamy sigh. Despite his talk of buying her gowns, he'd not treated her like some doxy to be tumbled at his whim. And he was witty and intelligent and attractive . . .

The man has bewitched me.

She touched her fingertips to her lips, which felt far too heated for a somber winter dawn. He had a sorcerer's touch, that was certain.

A sorcerer's all-seeing eye as well. Unfortunately, he used the very intelligence and sensitivity she admired to see beneath her roles and discern all her deceptions. She shivered as she remembered his final words. What would he make of her drugged tea? Could he guess at her plans just from that?

Suddenly, she heard the door from the hallway open, jolting her from her ruminations. Then Charity appeared in the doorway to the bedchamber, obviously distracted.

As the woman passed the bed in a dreamy daze

on her way to her own bed, Annabelle said, "Where have *you* been?"

Charity jumped. "Faith, but you frightened the life out of me! What are you doing up so early when you don't have to be at rehearsal today?"

Annabelle noted Charity's mussed hair, slightly askew clothing, and reddened lips. "What are *you* doing out so late?"

A bright red blush spread over Charity's cheeks. "I . . . I . . ." She got a stubborn look on her face. "I was with John."

"Sir John Riverton?" Annabelle clutched her pillow in her arms. "Oh, Charity, surely you didn't let him—"

"I did." Her expression shifted, becoming soft and dreaming. "And I don't regret it for a moment."

Annabelle sighed. Charity had always said she'd tasted respectability with her husband and now she sought to taste wickedness with a lover. They'd argued over it, with Annabelle trying to convince Charity that taking a lover, wealthy or not, would represent a disastrous fall into degradation. But Charity had continued to insist that once Annabelle experienced the joy of bedding a man, she'd not be so keen to leave it behind either.

She doubted that. Charity's description of how it was done made her wonder if it would be like so many other things in life—more fun for the man than for the woman. How could anyone find enjoyment in having something resembling a hefty sausage stuck up inside you? Yet Charity insisted it was pleasurable.

Oh yes, Annabelle had known all along what Charity wanted. Still, the widow's defection left Annabelle feeling bereft. "Is Sir John going to . . . to keep you now?"

Charity dropped onto the bed with a sigh. "'Tis too soon for that. In truth, I was rather surprised that it happened at all." She plucked at the folds of the counterpane. "He's always flirted, but I never thought he was much taken with me until yesterday, after the play, when we started talking in one of the boxes. It got late, and he apologized for keeping me so long without my supper. Then he . . . he asked me to sup at his lodgings. So I went."

Annabelle groaned. Men were such sly creatures when it came to finding their pleasure. And Charity was so warm and open, she'd fallen right into the hands of a rake like Sir John.

She could see why Charity found him attractive, with his masses of chestnut hair barely silvered by threads of gray. Though everyone knew he'd been in trade before he'd been knighted for service to the king, Charity would never care about that. Nor would she care about his limp, the result of a battlefield injury. She saw only his smiling brown eyes and ready wit. But he was an incurable rake.

"I knew what I was about," Charity said, laying her hand on Annabelle's. "I promise I wasn't forced."

"No, you were seduced." *As I nearly was myself last night.* "He didn't even have the decency to offer to keep you."

"Oh, but he did," Charity protested, then clapped a hand over her mouth.

"I thought you said . . ." When Charity stared down at their joined hands, Annabelle realized the truth. "You refused because of me."

"Now, now, dear heart, don't be angry. It's not the time for me to be setting up housekeeping elsewhere, and well you know it." Charity flashed a sly smile. "Besides, I believe in letting a man stew. They say that a fellow loses interest once he breaches a woman's defenses, but that's not true. It's feeling sure of her before he knows his own mind that makes him run. Sometimes a woman's got to help him know his own mind before she lets him see her own."

Annabelle thought of Colin's fierce assurance that he'd pursue her to the end. "I only wish Colin didn't know his own mind quite so well," she grumbled.

"*Colin?* Faith, but I'd completely forgotten that Sir John said you were off with his lordship! What happened? I don't see the man lying about. Did you put him to sleep?"

Annabelle grimaced. "I tried to get him to drink the tea, but he sniffed out the sleeping potion and wouldn't touch it."

Charity grew thoughtful. "Did he, now?"

"Before he left, he even had the temerity to suggest that next time I use prickly lettuce."

"Did he, now?"

"For heaven's sake, stop repeating that! He did, he did! He insinuated himself in here, sniffed out my ruse in one evening, and nearly bedded me before I could stop him."

Charity's eyes twinkled. "Oh, did he, now?"

"Devil take you, Charity Woodfield! I don't find this the least amusing!"

Charity sobered. "*Nearly* bedded you?"

"Aye," Annabelle said, coloring slightly. "But not for want of trying."

"Hmph, if his lordship had wanted to force himself on you, you would have been bedded, and no doubt more than once."

Charity had a point. He'd stopped when she'd asked, even knowing that she'd tried to drug him. What man would do that? Certainly not Sir Charles or Lord Somerset or any of their ilk. Most rakes would have taken her against her will after such a deception.

But he hadn't. What's more, she'd trusted him not to. It had only fleetingly occurred to her that he might harm her in his anger.

She hugged her pillow to her chest. That was the worst of it—he'd already begun making her trust him, the sweet-tongued devil. Dear heaven, but the man truly did have a sorcerer's powers!

"So did he kiss you?" Charity asked.

Heat rose in Annabelle at the memory of the many touches and kisses he'd given her mouth . . . her neck . . . her breasts. Her face flamed.

A mischievous smile crossed Charity's face. "I figured his lordship knew how to woo a woman."

"How to seduce a woman, you mean," Annabelle said tartly.

"Seducing's part of wooing, if you ask me."

"No one asked you."

Charity laughed. "I see that 'Colin' is a mighty sore subject." She caught her mistress's scowl, and her smile faded. "So what d'ye intend to do?"

Annabelle shook her head. "I don't know. If he's discovered the sleeping-potion ploy, he may eventually determine that I use it on other men as well. Once he knows that—"

"'Tis of no consequence. Even if he guesses that, all it means is y're afraid to bed men. It wouldn't reveal yer deeper purpose."

The Maynards. She'd forgotten all he'd said about them. And how odd that he'd been able to tell her so much about so many of them.

"Speaking of that, Colin told me something of the Maynards in London. One in particular would be the right age to be my father. But he's an earl. That doesn't make sense."

"Why not? If yer father was a captain during the war, he could have been a second son who inherited later."

"But he was a captain for the Roundheads, not the Royalists."

"There were noblemen who sided with Cromwell."

"I suppose." She rested her chin on the pillow.

"And if he's a Puritan nobleman, he'll be even more angry about his daughter strutting the stage. And you'll have your vengeance, which is all you want."

"Yes." Something occurred to her that hadn't before. "Colin seems to knows an awful lot about the family, and in both of our encounters he made a point of mentioning them." She felt a sudden sinking in the pit of her stomach. "What if he and my father are friends? What if my father put Colin up to finding out about me?"

The very thought that Colin might be manipulating her in such a manner nauseated her. She'd allowed him much closer than any other man.

Charity pursed her lips. "Can't see Lord Hampden being put up to anything by anybody, can you?"

Annabelle tried to shake off her queasy feeling. "No, I suppose not."

"Even if his lordship does somehow determine who you are and tell yer father, it won't change anything."

"It might. My father could go running off to the country or France to avoid being made a fool of."

Charity snorted. "If yer father is as lofty as you

think, he ain't going to care about some chit of an actress until you *make* him care. That sort is arrogant. And that's how you'll get him. Besides, I doubt that Lord Hampden will guess that you're the man's daughter unless you tell him."

"Still, it worries me."

"Actually," Charity said, her eyes narrowing, "if he knows yer father, it gives you even more reason to let him pursue you. You might even tell him who y're searching for. Just don't tell him why until he leads you to the man."

Annabelle considered that possibility. "That might work *if* I can get Colin to sympathize with my quest." She added, dryly, "And if he doesn't ravish me before I find out what I need to know."

"*Ravish* you? Now you sound like the ladies you play on the stage. I doubt it would be so dramatic and awful as all that."

Perhaps not. But she wouldn't risk losing her virtue or bearing a bastard for it. Besides, much as she wanted to believe she could keep Colin at arm's distance while finding out what she needed to know, the sad truth was she couldn't even keep the man at a finger's distance. He had this uncanny ability to slip beneath her defenses.

"All the same," Annabelle said, "I think it best I avoid the man entirely. I should content myself with exploring the one name he's given me and not attempt the harder task of trying to manage Colin's passions."

A knock sounded at the door to the hall, making them both jump.

"Are you expecting anyone?" Charity asked.

"Do you think his lordship would return so soon?"

With a shrug, Charity slid off the bed. "John says the man is taken with you. Who knows what a man captivated by a woman will do?"

As Annabelle smiled at the absurd idea that Colin was captivated by her, Charity moved into the other room and opened the door. A low-voiced conversation followed. Then Charity returned with a boy prettily dressed in a rich burgundy and gold livery.

"We have a visitor from the marquess," Charity said with a grin.

The boy showed no trace of surprise when he saw Annabelle in her smock. Given his master's rakish reputation, he was probably used to women going about in their smocks. In truth, many actresses received guests in dishabille. Annabelle had become so accustomed to changing gowns before an audience in the tiring-room that she wasn't the least bit modest anymore.

Except with Colin.

At Charity's prodding, the footboy came to stand beside the bed. "My master sent this for you, madam." He held out a package wrapped in gold cloth and tied with a burgundy velvet ribbon.

A gift from Colin? Dear heaven, he'd taken her at her word last night when she'd said he must woo her with gifts. Shame washed over her.

Then alarm. He would take her acceptance of the gift as a tacit approval of his pursuit. She might as well announce, "Come learn all my secrets."

With a sigh, she waved the boy's hand away. "Return it to your master, and tell him I don't want his gifts."

"But, mistress, you can't mean that!" Charity exclaimed. "Why, you haven't even seen what it is!"

"I don't care what it is. I do not wish to encourage Lord Hampden's advances, and you know quite well why. Show the boy out, and give him a shilling for his efforts."

With a mutinous glance, Charity snatched the package and opened it.

"Charity!" Annabelle protested, but the woman was already removing the contents.

"God in Heaven! 'Tis a gold ring with diamonds and rubies!" Charity held it up to the light. "You can't be wanting to return a gift like *that*!"

The cut stones sparkled in the sun, sending a thrill of pleasure through Annabelle.

"There's a note here, too." Charity opened it and read, "'For the fire and ice of my lovely swan. May my paltry gift melt her heart.'" She clutched it to her chest with a dreamy sigh.

Devil take Colin for knowing just how to soften her. No one had ever given her jewels before, and that alone was a temptation. But it was the sweetness of his note that tempted her to accept.

She sighed. She couldn't, not when she knew

what it would mean. "Charity, give it back to the boy and let him return it," she said before she could change her mind.

"But, Annabelle—"

"Give it to him and show him out!" she cried.

A moment's silence ensued. Then Charity complied, though with an ill grace. When Charity returned, she was scowling. "Faith, have you lost all good sense? Don't you think this foolish stunt will draw his attentions more than taking it would have? His lordship loves a challenge, John tells me. 'Tis like beating a hornet's nest to spurn his gift."

Annabelle rubbed her temples wearily. This game was sorely trying her wits. "Perhaps, but I dare not let him any closer." She attempted a hopeful smile. "With any luck, my refusal will convince him I'm not worth the trouble."

Charity rolled her eyes. "Clearly you know naught about men."

"If Colin refuses to heed my clear message, I shall simply have Lord Somerset impress upon him that I'm not available." She blinked. "That's it! Charity, go tell Lord Somerset of Colin's overtures. That will solve all my problems. Lord Somerset is a jealous man. He'll warn Colin off."

"Are you mad?" Charity shook her head as she began to tidy the room. "That painted coxcomb will never defend you to his lordship."

Annabelle tipped up her chin. "Thank you for

your opinion. I'll keep it in mind while you're at Lord Somerset's."

Unperturbed, Charity picked up some discarded clothing. "I suppose it *would* be amusing to watch the popinjay crumble into cowardice."

"Don't provoke him. I need him, even if he is a puppet of a man."

Charity eyed her askance. "I think y're putting yer money on the wrong cock, but I'll do what you say."

She was probably right. But Annabelle had to do *something*. She couldn't just sit here and let Colin dig into her secrets. "Oh, and, Charity? Learn what you can about Edward Maynard, Earl of Walcester. Determine if he has a family, and find out where he was around the time of my conception."

Charity planted her hands on her hips. "How the devil am I to do that?"

"Just speak with the man's servants. Or perhaps ask Sir John."

"If I ask Sir John, he'll tell Lord Hampden."

With a groan, Annabelle clutched her pillow to her chest. "True. Devil take the marquess, he's been a nuisance from the moment I met him."

"And will no doubt be more of one before this business is finished," Charity said dryly as she left.

Annabelle sank back and prayed that Charity proved to be wrong.

Chapter Six

"It holds for good polity ever, to have that outwardly in
vilest estimation, that inwardly is most dear to us."
—Ben Jonson, *Every Man in His Humour*, Act 2, Sc. 3

Did you hear about Lovelace being appointed
governor of the Province of New York, poor
man?" Sir Charles asked Colin as they stood in Sir
John's drawing room drinking wine.

Colin glanced at the door, irritated that Somerset
hadn't yet arrived. He and Sir Charles had skipped
the play and come early to Sir John's supper. Colin
had hoped Sir John could convince Somerset to
show up before the actresses.

And Annabelle.

"Why do you call him 'poor man'?" Colin asked,
keeping an eye on the door. "To be honest, I envy
him."

"Egad, why?"

Colin sighed. How could he explain the change
in him since his return? He was tired of the games
played among the nobility. Lasciviousness had
become a currency. The actresses offered their bod-

ies in exchange for a comfortable living, and the rakes seduced their friends' wives to sate boredom. It all seemed so empty. Of late he found more satisfaction out of his experiments with the Royal Society.

He could return to spying, but that began to prey on his conscience. Which was odd, because it never had before. Was it because of a certain interesting actress that he felt that way?

No, the idea was absurd.

"The colonies are filled with new flora and fauna to examine," Colin explained, "new peoples and new cultures to study. I myself might find it interesting to add something to human knowledge by exploring that abundance of newness."

The moment he said the words, he was surprised to find that he meant them. The colonies weren't something he'd much thought about, but he had to admit that retiring to Kent to run the estate his father had left him didn't appeal to him. It had already been so competently run for years by his estate manager that he felt like a guest in his own home when he was there.

Sir Charles shrugged. "I have enough trouble dealing with the new women who appear on the stage weekly to even think of traveling to a distant land. I should think you would, too, with your merry pursuit of the Silver Swan."

As Sir Charles spotted a friend and walked away, Colin scowled at the reminder of the annoying vixen who would soon arrive at Sir John's.

He might be tiring of London's glittering society, but he couldn't eliminate his interest in the ever-changeable Annabelle.

The woman was driving him mad. In all his days of spying, he'd never met a female he couldn't twist around his finger. Now here was this actress, paying him back fourfold for all his previous deceits.

She'd had the gall to turn down a very costly gift after she'd just demanded one from him! Though probably she'd demanded the gift to divert his attention from the fact that she'd tried to drug him.

Rage still seared him every time he thought of it. How determined she'd been to stay out of his bed, the little temptress!

Ah, but not entirely determined. Once or twice she'd melted under his caresses like an icicle under sunlight. Only when he'd nearly undressed her had she iced over again, acting skittish as a virgin on her wedding night.

Was he right? Was it seduction that she feared? Her reaction to him had been most maidenly. Although if she were indeed a maiden, then why did so many men seem to have known her intimately?

No, only one man—Somerset. And if anyone would have fallen for such a ruse, it was that fop.

Still, could an actress truly be chaste after months treading the boards in London?

Either way, he didn't care. He wanted her, and he would have her, despite her tricks. After all, there was his promise to Walcester to find out her secrets. And what better way to learn a woman's secrets than to take her to bed?

He groaned. That was the spy in him talking. But the thought of using Annabelle in such a manner sat ill with him now that he thought she might be a maiden. The few times he'd glimpsed the vulnerable woman who masked a deep pain behind her many faces made him loath to hurt her more.

Somerset entered the drawing room, followed by Sir John, and Colin smiled. At last. It was time to learn what part Somerset had played in her deception, assuming that Sir John had prepared the man sufficiently.

Given how nervous Somerset appeared in his presence, he had. Colin approached the man. Sir John suddenly found something to do elsewhere and took the other occupants of the room with him as planned, leaving Somerset alone with Colin.

"Good day, Somerset," Colin said coldly.

"Ahem, nice to see you, Hampden. Now, if you'll excuse me—"

"I wish a word with you."

Somerset sighed. "It's about Mrs. Maynard, isn't it?"

That startled Colin. "How did you know?"

"Her maid . . . er . . . warned me yesterday that you'd been bothering her mistress. Paying her attentions and such." He met Colin's gaze warily. "The woman doesn't want them. Her maid said I should defend her from you."

Colin couldn't help but laugh. The very thought of this fop defending anyone was ludicrous.

Somerset looked more pained than insulted. "Look here now, Hampden. Mrs. Maynard asked me to defend her, and I shall." He drew himself up like a stuffed goose. "Desist in your attentions at once. Mrs. Maynard wishes that you leave her alone."

Colin eyed the man askance. "The woman's name is Annabelle, or haven't you gotten far enough with her to know that?"

A flush darkened Somerset's powdered cheeks. "I call her Mrs. Maynard out of respect. She prefers refined gentlemen, who treat her with consideration." He swept Colin with a contemptuous gaze. "Not beasts like you with base appetites."

"Which means you haven't bedded her," Colin said dryly.

"Sir, you go too far!" Somerset tugged at his flowing cravat, then glanced around, clearly torn between bragging of his exploit and holding to his position that Annabelle Maynard deserved respect. Colin's amused expression apparently decided him. "I *have* bedded her, as you so crudely put it. Not that it's any of your affair."

Colin took a stab in the dark. "Did you bed her in your sleep? Because you and I both know you slept through your night with her."

Rage rose in the fop's cold eyes. "Did the little trollop tell you that?"

So much for respect and consideration. Hell and furies, what had the woman seen in this pompous ass? "Charity told me," he lied.

"Well, she's mistaken," Somerset said stiffly. "Ask Mrs. Maynard . . . er . . . Annabelle herself. I've given her gifts, and she's given me kisses . . . and much, much more."

His knowing glance sent Colin over the edge. "I care not what you claim she has given you," Colin snapped. "I want her, so find another actress willing to toy with your affections."

"You would take my leavings?"

Colin could barely restrain his temper. "If I thought for one moment that you'd truly possessed any part of her, you'd be welcome to her. But she's too much of a woman to have any real interest in you. That's the only thing saving you from having your face smashed in."

Alarm leapt in Somerset's gaze, no doubt fueled by the false tales Sir John had fed him regarding Colin's unpredictable temper and tendency toward violence.

"She makes a fool of you with others," Colin persisted. "Whatever her game in sending her maid to you, she is as enamored of me as I of her and has given me kisses to prove it."

He hated revealing any part of his intimacy with Annabelle, but it was the only way to keep Somerset from pawing her. She deserved better, damn it.

"God-a-mercy, I hate to give her up," Somerset

murmured, surprisingly stubborn. "She's a pretty wench."

Colin clenched his hands into fists. "And you, sir, are a pretty man. If you want to stay that way, relinquish your interest in her. Unless, of course, you want to 'defend' her on the field of honor."

"A duel?" Somerset squeaked. "Over some actress? Good heavens, no! I'm a man of peace, sir."

Man of peace, hah! Somerset couldn't win a duel with a tortoise, much less a swordsman of Colin's caliber, and he knew it. "Well, then. I see we have an understanding. You'll cease your pursuit of Annabelle Maynard, and I'll overlook your previous association with the woman."

Regret tinged Somerset's face before he waved his hand in an affected gesture of nonchalance. "You're welcome to her, sir. In truth, the woman has cost me a pretty penny. I don't envy you the expense of buying her affections."

The expense didn't bother Colin nearly as much as the difficulty he was having in making the transaction. "Good day, then, Somerset."

The man fled the room with unseemly haste, no doubt going in search of less forbidding company. There'd been a time when Colin would have enjoyed routing such a coxcomb. Now it merely saddened him to see a man so little concerned for his pride that he would rather sully the reputation of a woman he supposedly cared for than chance being forced into a fight.

How shallow the courtiers in London had grown under Charles II, how caught up in their clothes and wigs. These days he couldn't tell the actors from the real people. Everyone seemed to be in costume.

Including Annabelle. She was playing a double role—he felt sure of it now. The Silver Swan, widely acclaimed to be a wanton, had drugged at least one man to keep him from bedding her.

Why create such an elaborate scheme? To protect her virtue? Such an odd concern for an actress. And if she wanted to protect her virtue, why go with gallants in the first place? Somerset claimed she'd bled him for expensive gifts, but if this were only about money, why had she spurned Colin's ring, which had to be worth more than anything Somerset could afford?

Her resistance pricked his pride and heightened his suspicions. Hell and furies, but he couldn't figure her out. He would, however. Because if his lovely swan maiden thought spurning his gifts and provoking Somerset to defend her would send Colin running in terror, she had a surprise in store.

WITH HALF A dozen other chattering women, many of them actresses, Annabelle and Charity swept into Sir John's surprisingly fine town house. Charity had said Sir John had a good income, but Annabelle hadn't guessed it would be *this* good. His spacious hall was decked with Italian paintings of the first quality, and servants rushed to attend them. No doubt his "informal supper" would be a seven-course affair with music and dancing.

Good. After her long afternoon, she could use a fine meal and something to keep her mind off that cursed marquess. Sir John had said Colin was out of town, thank heaven, or she would never have come.

They entered the drawing room to find Lord Somerset lounging in a corner and their host watching for them. As Sir John approached them with a broad smile, Annabelle tamped down her dismay. What a shame he'd been the one to capture Charity's heart. A man of his obvious wealth no doubt had a string of mistresses as long as the Roman road.

Yet there was no mistaking his pleasure at seeing Charity. Though he conversed with them both, it was Charity who received his most fervent attention, Charity whom he undressed with his eyes.

Annabelle could take a hint. Murmuring some excuse, she left them to their cooing. She looked about for Lord Somerset, wanting to thank him for his agreement to keep Colin away from her, but he seemed to have disappeared. How odd. He usually rushed to her side whenever she entered a room.

It took her a while to find him in a parlor that adjoined the dining room, speaking with Sir Charles. She walked up to slip her hand in the crook of Lord Somerset's arm.

"Good evening, my dear," she murmured as she kissed his heavily powdered cheek.

He jerked back in what looked like alarm. "Mrs. Maynard! What are you doing here?"

"I was invited, of course." This grew more curious by the moment. "I wish a private word with you. Perhaps we could step into the next room?"

"Oh no. No no no. I was . . . er . . . just this moment leaving. Yes, exactly." He cast an anxious glance at the parlor door. "Another engagement, you see."

The man seemed oddly agitated, even for him. "What other engagement?"

"Dining with a friend. A good friend. I have to go. So good to see you." He hurried for the door without so much as a kiss of farewell.

"Wait!" she called out, but he'd already gone. How very peculiar.

"It seems you've lost your fop this evening," Sir Charles said.

"Yes," she said absently. "I wonder what that was all about."

"Perhaps he doesn't wish to fight the other men vying for your affections."

"Fight them? Why should he have to fight them?"

"Because one of them is Hampden."

Her heart plummeted. "Prithee, what do you mean? Did Lord Hampden challenge him, for heaven's sake?"

"If I had," said a voice behind her, "who would you champion? Him? Or me?"

Annabelle whirled to find the scoundrel approaching. "What are you doing here? You're not supposed to be here!"

"I don't see why not. Sir John *is* my friend."

Oh, of course. And his friend had obviously lied to get her here, curse him.

"But answer my question," Colin said solemnly. "Who would you champion? Somerset or me?"

"Neither," she choked out. "Fighting is foolish. I abhor violence." She'd seen far too much of it in her day.

She had to get away from him before she did something just as foolish—like noticing how well he looked this evening. "Now, if you'll excuse me, my lords—" she began as she turned to leave.

"Somerset and I had a very intriguing conversation," he called out behind her. "We compared notes about your tea."

That brought her to a halt. Sweet Mary, she'd been afraid of this.

Colin hurried to block her path to the door. "I believe Somerset actually had the chance to drink his, but he couldn't tell me much about it."

She snapped open her fan, fluttering it in front of her face to cover her confusion. Bad enough that Colin had realized she'd tried to drug him, but now he'd figured out that she'd also drugged Lord Somerset. What would he make of it?

"No barbed denials?" Colin said, at her continued silence. "No protestations of innocence?"

All too aware of Sir Charles listening behind them, she met Colin's gaze and forced a bored smile to her lips. "What is there to deny? I offered you both . . . er . . . tea when you came to my chambers. Or perhaps you're complaining about the tepid condition of yours." Turning to flash Sir Charles a knowing smile, she added, "The warmth of my 'tea' depends on how well I like my visitor. I assure you that Lord Somerset's 'tea' was steaming."

Sir Charles chuckled.

Colin did not. His eyes narrowed. "Perhaps that explains why he isn't returning for another serving. He must have scalded himself. I'm not so foolish. I know how to deal with hot tea." His gaze raked her, reminding her that he'd tasted more of that 'tea' than she cared to admit.

She snapped her fan shut. "Yes, but it would have to be offered to you, wouldn't it? And there's little chance of that. All I can offer you is tepid tea, Lord Hampden, and I doubt that would satisfy you."

Before he could answer, voices sounded from behind them. "There you are," Charity said breathlessly as she hurried to Annabelle's side with a worried look. "I didn't know Lord Hampden was going to be here." She flashed Sir John a daggered glance.

"Neither did I," Annabelle said as she, too, glared at Sir John, who looked utterly unrepentant. "Apparently, our host meant to surprise us."

Thankfully, Charity and Sir John were accompanied by others of the party, which gave her a reprieve from Colin's questions.

And Charity jumped in to rescue her as usual. "Lord Hampden, we were talking about the rumors of a treaty with the Dutch against the French, and Sir John here said you know the most about it, since you came from Antwerp a few weeks past. What did you find out?"

Flashing Charity a grateful smile, Annabelle chimed in even as she moved discreetly away from Colin. "Yes, do tell us about the Dutch. It sounds very interesting."

She wasn't to be let off so easily. With a smooth, leisurely grace, Colin followed her until he once more stood at her side. "I would be more than happy to entertain you with news, madam, but I heard nothing of any consequence."

"Surely you heard *something*," Charity pressed. "Are we really to be allied with the Dutch?"

"You're wasting your time badgering Hampden," Sir Charles put in. "He doesn't care about affairs of state anymore. He's too busy talking about how enjoyable it would be to sail off to the colonies."

Annabelle's startled gaze shot to Colin's. "Why would you go *there*?"

He laid his hand in the small of her back and, when she tried to shift away, hooked two fingers in the laces of her gown. Short of engaging in a tug of war, she couldn't move.

His gaze locked with hers. "Perhaps I'd like to experience living in a country of unlimited potential, where a man can create a new world from the earth's bounty. Where people are exactly who they appear to be."

She swallowed hard.

"*Is* there such a place?" drawled Sir John.

"Apparently the colonies are, if Hampden is to be believed," Sir Charles retorted. "Damned fool doesn't seem to understand that in the colonies you can only be a farmer."

"Not quite a farmer, Sedley," Colin said dryly. "But a landowner, yes. Exactly as I am here, with my estate. The land in Virginia is rumored to be quite fertile."

Annabelle could only gape at him. He would leave court, travel so far away, just to explore a new continent? That didn't seem like him. But oddly enough, it made him even more appealing, if that were possible. Curse the man.

Sir Charles snorted. "I can hardly imagine you beating your sword into a plowshare, Hampden." He glanced down at Colin's breeches. "'Twould be a waste of a good sword."

Sir John slid his arm around Charity's waist. "Aye. A sword is more amusing to a lady than a plowshare, wouldn't you say, Charity?"

The normally unflappable Charity blushed, provoking laughter from the others.

But Colin seemed more interested in working his

fingers further inside Annabelle's bodice in back. She pulled away. He jerked her back. She cast him a scathing glance. He merely grinned.

With a sniff, she said, "Perhaps Lord Hampden prefers the plowshare because his sword lies useless in its scabbard."

Her attack on his virility got a laugh from everyone else but didn't seem to bother *him.* "Plowing a fertile field does provide its own amusement," he said boldly.

The men all laughed again. These gallants would always find the double entendre in any comment. Meanwhile, Colin twisted the laces of her gown to draw her close enough that her backside pressed against his hard thigh.

A delicious shiver swept down her spine, annoying her. "Be careful, my lord." She arched an eyebrow at him. "Some of those fields are full of thorns sure to prick you."

His eyes gleamed at her. "That's why plows are made of iron, my dear. To cut through any defense."

"Now who's pricking whom?" Sir Charles called out gleefully, garnering more laughter.

She leveled him with a dark look. "Certainly not you, Sir Charles. Given the reports of your naked dancing on that balcony last week, your plow is the *size* of a thorn. It wouldn't even make a dent in my field."

While the man flushed, everyone else laughed, but before he could respond, the steward announced that supper was served. The rest of the company paired off, chattering as they headed into the dining room. But Colin kept Annabelle trapped with his fingers in her laces.

He leaned close to whisper, "My plow is more than sufficient for your field, dearling."

The endearment made her despair. He would never leave her be. And the more he pursued her, the more she wanted to be caught. If it weren't for his facility in uncovering secrets . . . "Ah, but you have to get near enough to my field to plow it, sir, and that will never happen."

They were alone in the room now. She reached back to pry his fingers from her laces, but he caught her hand and lifted it to his lips for a kiss as arousing as it was tender.

"Why not?" he rasped. "I met your terms. You said you wanted gifts, and I provided the first of many to come. Yet you returned my ring. Now, why is that?"

She tried to pull free of him, but he wouldn't let her. "I don't like small gems," she tossed out, desperate now to escape him and his tempting advances. "You'll have to do better than that if you want to win my favors."

He surprised her by chuckling. "I suspect you'd have rejected my gift even if it had been a diamond the size of a pear."

Faith, but the man was perceptive. "But you won't know that for certain until you try, will you?"

"Why try when I know what the outcome will be, when the only thing of real value you wish from me is information?"

Her stomach clenched. "Wh-what do you mean?"

"You want to know about your relatives, the Maynards."

Alarm gripped her. How much had he guessed of her true purpose in coming to London? Had he found some other source of information about her? Like from her real father, perhaps?

"What makes you say that?" she asked, fighting to still the frantic fluttering of her heart.

"Come now, don't be evasive." His smile didn't quite reach his eyes. "You're not good at it. I don't know why you're so interested in the Maynards of London, but I promise to tell you all you wish to know."

Charity hadn't been successful in questioning the Earl of Walcester's servants, who'd been suspicious of an actress's maid. All she could find out was that he was a man with high connections and very well respected by the king. That told her little she could use. Yet here was Colin offering to tell her everything. Did that mean Walcester was indeed her father? Did Colin know her father better than he said? And why was he so certain that knowledge of the Maynards would interest her?

The more she thought about it, the more panicked she grew. After all, Colin had once been a spy for the Crown. Who knew what other people he might spy for?

He couldn't be trusted, that was certain. No matter what his intentions, she doubted they were limited to making her his mistress. He might offer her information, but he would no doubt try to guess her secrets before he'd tell her anything of substance. If he did figure out what she was up to, he'd warn her father off. Then she'd never find out who the man was, never have the chance to wreak her vengeance.

And Mother's death would have been a hollow cry in the wind.

That decided her. He'd gotten far too close, and she'd let him toy with her far too long. "Sir John!" she cried.

The conversation in the next room stopped, and Colin froze, his face marked by surprise.

Sir John appeared in the doorway. "What's going on? Why aren't you two coming in to supper?"

There was only one way to rid oneself of a too-persistent gallant. It wasn't a way she relished, but she saw no other choice. "This rude coxcomb is bothering me. He's making indecent proposals and refusing to unhand me."

Colin dropped her hand as if he'd been burned and cast her a look of such contempt that she wished she could take back her words. But she dared not. It was the only way to stop his pursuit.

The unspoken rule among actresses and rakes

was that the rakes pursued and the actresses played coy. Never did they take it seriously or make their sparring publicly uncomfortable.

Sir John's embarrassment demonstrated that. Of course, Sir John didn't give a farthing for her reputation or her feelings. After all, actresses were considered little more than whores. If a gentleman insulted one, who would care?

Still, she was making a scene, and neither Colin nor Sir John would deal well with that. *Good,* she thought. The sooner she became unpopular with their circle, the better.

"Will you throw this insolent brute out, Sir John?" she persisted, determined to play the role of injured lady.

Sir John muttered a low curse. Those in the dining room had come to stand in the doorway and watch. With a glance at them, he said placatingly, "Now, Annabelle, I'm sure Hampden didn't mean to—"

"So you will allow me to be insulted by an unmannerly bastard in your home?" The word *bastard* made both men stiffen, but she went on relentlessly, "If you won't throw him out, I shall leave."

Sir John flushed. He'd never throw Hampden out. That was what made the situation galling . . . and effective. It perpetuated the humiliation. Of course, Sir John might just call her a strumpet and tell her to leave if she couldn't handle the rakes. But with Charity there, she didn't think he would.

In the end, he didn't have to. "No need to evict me," Colin ground out. "I find I have no stomach for supper all of a sudden. Good evening."

He stalked from the room without another word or glance her way.

Her heart plummeted. She'd finally succeeded in driving him away. So why did she feel so wretched?

"You're a heartless wench," Sir John muttered as the front door slammed. "Hampden doesn't deserve your sharp words. He'd show you more care than any man I know. You had no cause to spurn him before his friends."

His other guests, deprived of a spectacle, drifted back into the dining room, leaving them alone.

"He'll recover," she managed to say through the lump of guilt in her throat.

"No doubt he will. He's used to treachery from actresses." He said the word *actresses* with such contempt that she cringed. "His mother was one, and the cruel creature gave him up to his father without so much as a protest."

She blinked. "But Lord Hampden . . . I mean . . . I thought he was—"

"A nobleman? He is now. He's a bastard, but Charles saw fit to give him a title for his service to the Crown. He's become powerful enough that most ignore his true origins. Unless someone reminds them of it, that is."

Guilt ripped through her, cold as a knife blade. "I didn't know . . . I never heard . . ." Oh, how she wished she could take the words back. She, of all people, was well aware what it was like to be mistreated for one's bastardy.

"You'll never snare a man as fine as that again." Sir John's condemning gaze sliced through her. "Though perhaps you truly prefer strutting cocks like Somerset. If so, Hampden's better off without you. And you're a woman to be pitied."

In more ways than one.

She'd stopped Hampden before he could unveil her secrets—but she hadn't thought it would hurt so much to do it.

Chapter Seven

"Whilst we strive
To live most free, we're caught in our own toils."
—John Ford, *The Lover's Melancholy*, Act 1, Sc. 3

Three days had passed since she'd called Colin a bastard, and Annabelle still felt wretched. Sir John refused to talk to her, and though Charity, as always, stood by her mistress, Annabelle could detect a coolness in her.

Still, it wasn't their behavior that disturbed her; it was the thought of what she'd said. Couldn't she have found a better way to be rid of him, one that wouldn't have left her feeling like a shrew?

Now she stood in the tiring-room alone, cursing as she struggled to remove her gown. Where in heaven was Charity? Act 3 was to begin at any moment, and Annabelle had to change her costume.

This week, Sir William Davenant had given Annabelle her first major role, the one of Selina in *The School of Compliments*. She still hadn't gotten over her nervousness, even though it was her third night of playing the part. She glanced ruefully at the shepherd's disguise she was to wear for the remainder of the play. At this rate, she'd never get it on.

"Somebody help me!" she shouted as she strained to reach her laces.

"I've got it!" Charity called and rushed in. As she pulled Annabelle's laces loose, she said, "You'll never guess who's in the audience tonight!"

"Colin?"

"That's not who I meant, but aye, he's here, though I'm surprised to see him. He told Sir John that you'd driven him to the King's Theater, where he could watch a more congenial woman flaunt her charms."

They both knew whom he meant—Nell Gwyn, who captivated all the gallants these days. "Yet he came back."

"Not for you, I'll wager." Charity yanked the gown over Annabelle's head. "He's sitting with a lady of quality."

"Good," she lied, swallowing her jealousy with some difficulty.

"Anyway, 'tis not Lord Hampden I came to tell you of," Charity said. "'Tis His Majesty, Old Rowley himself."

Annabelle pulled on the breeches of her shepherd's costume. "What? The king is here? Tonight? But the royal box was empty."

Charity gave her a secretive smile. "Aye, it was. He's what Moll Davis calls 'incognito.' She says he does that sometimes—puts on common clothing and goes about town. She's seen him before, when he's come to watch her on the stage. Tonight she spotted him sitting with the Duke of York."

"Is she sure it's His Majesty?"

"As many times as she's graced his bed, she ought to be familiar with his countenance." With certain malicious glee, Charity added, "So she's none too happy y're to dance tonight, especially in those tight breeches. Mrs. 'Put-on-Airs' tried to cozy up to Sir William to convince him she would do better in the part, but of course, he's used to Moll's petty jealousies and he ignored her."

Annabelle groaned. "I wish you hadn't told me." She stood still while Charity put the shepherd's smock on her and buttoned it. "Now I shall be nervous and make a laughingstock of myself before the king himself." And Colin, too, curse it.

"Stop talking such nonsense. You'll dance and kick up yer pretty heels, and they'll all be mightily impressed."

Colin wouldn't be. And she hated to admit it, but he was the only one whose opinion she cared about.

Not that it mattered. She couldn't take back the words she'd spoken at Sir John's, and shouldn't take them back in any case. It was better to leave matters as they were.

Yet even after she took the stage, she found herself speaking every line differently, conscious of his presence. Performing for the king was nothing compared to performing for Colin. He would appreciate the nuances of her role more than anyone else, and she couldn't help but want it to be perfect.

When it came time for her dance in the fifth act, she pirouetted and swirled for Colin, the man she could never have, whom she both feared and desired.

She scarcely noticed that the gallants were cheering when the dance ended. Nor did she do more than drift through the end of the play. All she could think of was what Colin would say about it . . . if he were speaking to her, that is.

As she left the stage at the end of the last act, Charity came up to point out where the king sat, but she didn't care. Nor was she swayed by everyone's compliments over her performance. And when they returned to the stage to take their bows and the king himself smiled at her before slipping out the doors with the duke, she did little more than nod in return. She was too busy scanning the theater for Colin.

She only spotted him as they filed offstage. He sat in a box with a beautiful blond woman at his side. He wasn't even looking at the stage, but was instead whispering something in the woman's ear, to which she responded with a laugh.

Annabelle fought down the ache in her belly. This was what she'd wanted. This was how it had to be. But her steps dragged as she approached the tiring-room.

A young man waited there, an envelope in his

hand. She recognized him at once—John Wilmot, Earl of Rochester, one of the most notorious blades in London, even at the age of twenty-one. She'd seen the handsome rake often backstage, lounging among the actresses.

She started to pass him, assuming he was waiting to see Moll Davis, whom he'd reputedly bedded. But then he thrust the envelope at her with his typically mocking smile.

Curious about who could have written her a note to be carried by so important a personage as Rochester, she opened the envelope and drew out the paper. The seal at the top stopped her cold.

With her throat tightening, she read: *I enjoyed your dance tremendously. Would you give me the honor of supping with me at Whitehall this evening? I'll send Rochester for you at nine. I do hope you'll come.* It was signed *Charles.*

She'd forgotten about Rochester observing her with his heavy-lidded gaze until he asked, with faint sarcasm, "What is your reply, madam?"

Charity had come out of the tiring-room. Stunned, Annabelle handed her the note. Charity read it, then exclaimed under her breath.

"I suppose I should give you time to compose yourself," Rochester said snidely, "but I must return a reply, although I'm sure I know what it will be."

"She'll be ready at nine," Charity answered as Annabelle stood frozen. "You tell His Majesty she'll be waiting."

Rochester made a sketchy bow, then vanished into the theater.

"Odsfish, His Majesty!" Charity exclaimed. "You know what this means, don't you? When His Majesty asks a woman to sup—"

"He wants to bed her," Annabelle finished. "I can't go! You know I can't!"

"Whyever not? Here's your chance to be His Majesty's latest mistress. Barbara Palmer isn't much in favor with him these days, and we both know you'd be more apt to keep his attention than that snooty Moll Davis."

Annabelle yanked Charity into an alcove. "I didn't come to London to become the king's whore!"

Charity squeezed her hands. "There, there, I know the thought of lying with the king might frighten you a bit. Rumor has it that Old Rowley is . . . well . . . rather large in his privates. But for pity's sake, do you know how many women wish to lie with him?"

"And how many have already," Annabelle said in a tense whisper. "I can't do it, I tell you." She could hardly explain that after being touched intimately by Colin she could never let another man touch her so. "Besides, the king is as fertile as a rabbit. It's all well and good for a married lady like Barbara Palmer to bear his children, but any child I bore would be a bastard. I won't do it!"

"You have a point." Charity glanced worriedly

about them and lowered her voice. "But it isn't politic to refuse His Majesty. Sir William would turn you out if you incurred *his* displeasure. And 'tis not as if you can drug the king with yer tea."

"That didn't always work anyway." Annabelle sighed. "Colin saw right through that ploy. A pity I'm not as wily as Colin. If he were here, he'd come up with some great stratagem to fool the king."

Her mind began to race, remembering how expertly he'd rid himself of Lord Somerset whenever he wished. Colin excelled at such maneuverings. If anyone could help her out of this mess, he could.

Of course, asking him for help would be galling . . . if he didn't ignore her pleas outright. But if she didn't ask, she'd be deflowered by the king before morning. Or else turned off from the theater entirely.

"Do you think Colin has left yet?" Annabelle asked.

Charity frowned. "I know what you're considering, madam, but it's madness. Y've spurned his gifts and spurned the man himself publicly. Not likely he'll do yer bidding now."

"I have to try, don't you see? I—I can't lie with the king. 'Twould make me a wanton in more than just name."

The maid's expression softened. "Aye, dear heart, I know. But if you go running after his lordship, he'll take one look at you and run t'other way.

Let me talk to him. I'll see if I can't convince him to help you."

As relief flooded Annabelle, she hugged Charity tightly. "Thank you, thank you! Please, Charity, do catch him and bring him back here."

"Go wait in the tiring-room for me. If I'm not back in a few minutes, go on home and I'll meet you there, for I may have to track him down."

"We've got a few hours yet." With the play over, it was only about five o'clock. "But please hurry." She paused, then added in a quavering voice, "Tell his lordship I'll do anything . . . not to 'sup' with the king."

Charity raised an eyebrow. "I'll not be making promises you don't intend to keep. But I'll get his lordship back here, come what may."

Then she was gone, leaving Annabelle alone to realize she would indeed do anything to keep from supping with the king. Because, in truth, the only man she wanted to "sup" with was Colin.

"'SDEATH, MINA, WHERE is that damnable coach?" Colin scanned the road but saw nothing but a sea of other carriages. "Falkham ought to boot your coachman out the door the first chance he gets."

"Why? Because he doesn't drive fast enough to suit you and doesn't appear in the twinkling of an eye when you want him?"

He forced a smile. "Because he keeps you waiting in the bad weather."

She slapped at his arm with her closed fan. "You've spent all night frowning and complaining and now you mean to redeem yourself with one chivalrous statement? You should be ashamed of yourself. I'll tell Falkham you've lost all your wit."

Falkham would laugh to hear that, for he was generally the one accused of that. But in truth, Colin had been a bear all evening, and all because of Annabelle, damn the woman. He'd vowed to avoid the Duke's Theater, no matter what Walcester asked of him. Then he'd foolishly allowed Mina to talk him into accompanying her to the play. Now he regretted it.

He could still remember the Silver Swan dancing gracefully in that alluring shepherd's costume, the tight breeches accentuating her fine hips and thighs. It had made him ache all over to watch it. It did no good to remind himself of what a sharp-tongued witch she was. The soulful expression was of the other Annabelle, the wary one with skin of silk, who gave oranges to urchins. *That* Annabelle tugged at his sympathies with each lowered glance and sad smile.

Hell and furies, but he'd sunk far. He'd always said he'd never let a woman under his skin, and here he was brooding over the heartless Annabelle Maynard.

"She was very beautiful," Mina said beside him.

Colin eyed Mina with suspicion. "Who?"

"That actress. The one who danced."

He groaned. "I suppose Falkham's been telling you of my exploits again."

"Of course. He tells me everything. So when one of the gallants pointed out the Silver Swan, I had to take notice." She grinned. "After all, 'tisn't often I see you so enamored of a woman."

"I'm not enamored of her," he ground out, then realized he sounded churlish. "Trust me, the chit is even more tart-tongued than you, and hates me besides."

"Oh, I don't think so. As the players left the stage, she cast you a look of such longing, I almost pitied her. I swear, if she'd seen the hungry way you'd watched her throughout the play, she'd have raced through the theater to be at your side."

"I doubt that," he said irritably. Then he spotted the Falkham coach and changed the subject. "Do you think Falkham will keep up his pretense of being sick once we return to your town house?"

She laughed low, not at all fooled by his refusal to speak of Annabelle. But she humored him. "He'd rather die than admit his mistake. I believe he truly thought that if he claimed to be deathly ill, I'd not go to the play. This is the third time he's tried to put me off. I was getting very tired of it."

"I'll admit Falkham isn't much interested in theater."

Her brow creased in a frown. "Yes, but he doesn't want me to go unaccompanied either. He thought to get around me, but I've demonstrated that he can't. I'm so glad you agreed to take me. He couldn't very well refuse to let me go when you'd so generously offered to accompany me while he was . . . ill."

Colin smiled. "I'm sure he's cursing himself now."

"I do hope so. He might not be jealous of you, but he's surely pacing the floors, thinking that half the gallants in the theater are flirting with me."

He wisely kept his mouth shut. Falkham wasn't above being jealous even of Colin and was probably more than a bit mortified at the thought of his wife being out with a rake, even one he could trust.

Of course, it served the man right for not taking Mina to the theater for one damnable night, while at the same time insisting she shouldn't go alone. Then again, perhaps Falkham was wiser than Colin gave him credit for. The theater had become a gathering place for all the false creatures in London society, particularly the court, with its base gossip and petty intrigues. No man with a life of purpose would waste his time at the theater.

He shouldn't even be here. He'd thought he was fulfilling his own purpose, repaying a debt to an old friend while keeping abreast of any intrigues that might be of use to him later. Now he wasn't so sure. His experience with Annabelle had heightened his desire to find something better in life than spying, than intrigue and gossip. Court machinations disgusted him increasingly every day.

The coach rumbled up then, putting an end to his ruminations, but before the coachman had even leapt from his perch, Colin heard his name called. He turned to find Charity Woodfield rushing toward him, her pretty cheeks flushed.

"Lord Hampden," she gasped as she tried to catch her breath. She cast Mina a wary glance. "I . . . I must speak with you."

Just what he needed—Annabelle Maynard trying to sink her claws into him again. "I'm afraid that's impossible. I'm leaving."

"Please, milord, I wasn't the one to insult you. Give me a moment of yer time. I beg of you."

He gritted his teeth. He felt Mina's eyes on him, shining with curiosity, but didn't enlighten her. "Yes, all right. What is it?"

Charity glanced at Mina.

"Lady Falkham is the wife of my dearest friend," he explained. "You can speak in front of her."

With a quick curtsy, Charity murmured, "Begging your pardon, milord, but it's about . . . about my mistress."

"Of course. What does she want—a second chance to flay me with her tongue? Perhaps this time she'd like to put a dagger through me."

Charity colored. "She needs yer lordship's help with a private matter."

"Tell her to call Somerset. I'm sure he'd do her bidding."

He started to turn away, but Charity grabbed his

arm. "Oh, please, milord, I know you have good cause to be angry with her. But she thought she had no choice. In any case, she's full of shame for it. And she needs yer help. Come back to the tiring-room with me for one moment and hear her out."

"If she's so desperate for my help, why didn't she come herself?" he bit out, hesitating despite himself.

"Because I told her not to. I feared you'd run away before she could speak."

He stiffened. "Your mistress may be a coward, but I'm not."

"Then will you lower yerself to speak to her . . . if only for a moment?"

Charity's pleas affected him despite his attempts to remain unaffected. No matter what Annabelle had said at Sir John's, she wasn't the kind of woman to toy with him. If she needed his aid so badly that she'd swallow her pride and send her maid to ask for it, then she must be desperate indeed. But damn the woman, what right had she to ask at all?

"Go on, Hampden," Mina said in a low voice beside him. "What can it hurt to speak to the poor woman?"

"Believe me, Mina, the Silver Swan is not a poor woman," he ground out. "She's quite capable of taking care of herself."

"Appearances can be deceiving, as we both well know. Go on. I'll wait here in the carriage. I'll be perfectly safe until you return."

Colin sighed. What a fool he was for these sweet-faced women. Hell and furies, he might as well go. If he didn't, he'd spend his nights worrying about what trouble she was in instead of damning her to hell as he should. That could be far more dangerous to his peace of mind.

"All right, then," he growled. "But this had better be worth it."

Chapter Eight

"Errors, like straws, upon the surface flow;
He who would search for pearls must dive below."
—John Dryden, *All for Love*, Prologue

Time passed far too slowly for Annabelle as she waited in the tiring-room. Everyone had left the theater to pursue the evening's amusements.

Being here alone reminded her of the first time Colin had kissed her so temptingly. She touched her fingers to her lips. Would he ever kiss her again? Dared she let him? And what if he insisted on more?

Then she would give it to him. Between him and the king, Colin seemed a less dangerous choice. Perhaps he'd even help her out of the kindness of his heart.

A mirthless laugh escaped her. After how she'd treated him, she'd be lucky if he helped her for a price.

A knock sounded at the door and Charity peeked around the corner. "Oh good, no one's here. I brought his lordship."

"Thank heaven," Annabelle breathed, then caught her breath again when Colin entered.

Never had he looked so handsome. His hair gilded his shoulders like a mantle of gold chain mail, and his tight hose outlined every muscle of his calves. How could she have forgotten what an attractive figure he cut?

If only his eyes weren't so terribly cold. "Leave us," he commanded Charity.

The maid fled.

"So, madam, what do you want?" he asked in a cutting tone. "A new recipe for tea? Or perhaps you're short of funds and you'd like my ring back."

She forced down her hurt. "I deserve that. I had no right to call you a bastard there before God and everyone, but I didn't know you actually were— That is—"

"Spare me your tender pity. I've long accustomed myself to being a bastard. That's not what angered me. That was merely the final straw in a long line of offenses, beginning with the tea you tried to force on me. But that's neither here nor there. Tell me what you want, so I can leave."

Wishing he looked less fierce, she handed him the envelope Rochester had given her. With a suspicious glance, he opened it and read the contents. For a moment, he went rigid.

Then his gaze swung back to hers, even colder than before. "What do you need me for? To help you decide what to wear?"

The words knifed through her. She forced herself to endure his scorn. "I don't want to go, Colin. Please, you have to get me out of it."

He looked startled, then intrigued. "Half the actresses in London would give their eyeteeth to warm the king's bed, and you want to get out of it?"

She lowered her gaze to her hands. "I know it sounds . . . odd, but yes."

"Why?"

The simple word struck terror in her. How could she explain without sounding like a frightened virgin before her wedding night, which, in a sense, she was? "I don't want to be involved in these court intrigues. I don't understand all the machinations, and I—"

"Don't be absurd, Annabelle. He wants a quick tumble, not a female spy. He doesn't give a fig for your behavior in court. Unless he makes you his mistress, which isn't likely at the moment, he'll have his way with you, send you off with a piece of jewelry or some gold, and not trouble you for anything else."

She flinched at the description of what sounded suspiciously like a transaction between a whore and her customer. Still, she couldn't give him her real reasons, for then he would want to know it all. "I don't think I could please His Majesty."

His jaw tightened. "Well, then, I can't help you with that. I draw the line at giving lessons on that sort of thing when another man plans to benefit from them."

Nettled by his apparent calm, she cried, "Devil take you, Colin, do you *want* me to lie with His Majesty?"

With a curse, he crumpled the note from the king. "No. In truth, I don't want you anywhere near him. It's probably just my stung pride. I'm afraid to discover that he might succeed in melting your heart where I failed, but I don't want you to go."

Relief seized her. He did still feel something for her. "Then help me. I know you can find a way out of this. I have but three hours to come up with a plan that will work. You've got to help me!"

He fixed her with a hard stare. "Why don't you just admit the real reason you don't want to 'sup' with His Majesty?"

She blanched. "I don't know what you mean."

He advanced on her. "It's not that you're afraid you won't please him or know how to handle the court's political intrigues. It's because you're a virgin. And that's an explanation even I can understand."

"I'm not a virgin any more than you are," she protested weakly.

"Don't think you can play your 'wanton' role with me. It won't work." He scoured her with a long glance. "You smile like a virgin, you walk like a virgin . . . in every way, your innocence shows. It's a beacon to all the debauched rakes in London." His tone grew harsh. "'Tis why they flock to you, wanting to wipe their grimy paws all over your sweet body. Our king apparently is no exception."

She fought to keep her composure. "You obviously pay no attention to the gossip, or you'd know I'm rumored to be quite free with my favors."

For the first time since he'd entered, a smile crossed his lips. "Haven't you yet learned that I'm not like the other witless fools at court? I'm a master of rumor and innuendo. I honed my skills very well during the war, and I can detect a false tale hidden beneath beds of roses. That one is certainly a false tale."

"Why would anyone tell such a tale about me?" she whispered, trying to hold on to her role.

"Obviously, someone started it for a good reason." He crossed his arms. "Someone like you, perhaps." Her startled expression elicited another smile from him. "Of course you started it. Why else would you be drugging gallants to maintain it? Or associating with fops like Somerset? As for why . . . well, that I don't know. But I mean to find out."

Of course he did. "Believe what you wish about my virtue. I still don't wish to meet with His Majesty. Will you help me or no?"

She could see the indecision on his face, the terrible struggle between his pride and his sense of compassion. Then he growled, "I'll help you, damn my soul. I can't very well send a virgin off to be sacrificed to our regent god, can I?"

Her breath escaped in a whoosh. "Thank you, Colin!" She wanted to kiss him but knew it was likely to annoy him.

"Don't be so hasty in your thanks. My help comes at a price."

She sucked in her breath, an unwarranted thrill coursing through her even as she cursed him for being such a rogue. "Anything you ask," she choked out.

His eyes narrowed as he guessed what she was thinking. He allowed his insolent gaze to linger on her body. "I admit that the offer is tempting. But it isn't your damnable virtue I wish to exact from you."

"Then . . . then what do you want?"

"The truth. If I'm to keep you out of the king's lecherous clutches, then I expect you to tell me everything—why you pretend to be a wanton . . . why you came to London . . . and why my advances so frighten you."

She said in a small voice, "I'd rather you take my virtue, my lord."

He gave a dark chuckle. "No doubt you would. And perhaps I will have that, too." Before she could react to his presumption, he added, "But I'll not take it as a payment for my service to you. 'Tis only of value if freely given."

The burning awareness in his eyes seared her, challenged her . . . and frightened her sorely. "You think I will give it to you?"

"We'll see, won't we?" With a rakish grin, he leaned back against the wall. "So, dear Annabelle, do we have a bargain? My help for your secrets?"

She stepped to the window and stared out at the streets below as she considered his proposal. She daren't tell him all, but perhaps she could tell him enough to assuage his curiosity. "Aye, we have a bargain."

"Good. Then I have a plan. But we must work quickly. My friend Lady Falkham awaits me in her carriage. I think I can persuade her to take us to your lodgings and help us."

Annabelle spotted the lone carriage waiting at the end of the alley. "Is Lady Falkham the new woman in your life?" She cursed herself for sounding less than nonchalant.

Especially when Colin laughed. "Don't tell me that my coldhearted swan is jealous."

She refused to face him, afraid he would read the jealousy in her face. "I merely thought it interesting that you waited so little time after relinquishing your pursuit of me before engaging in the pursuit of another."

With a curse, he crossed the room and swung her around to face him. "Listen to me well, my sharp-tongued beauty. Lady Falkham is the wife of my dearest friend, the Earl of Falkham, and I have never so much as touched her hand without her husband's express permission. She's a gracious lady who will most likely help you this evening, so I suggest you be civil to her. I won't have you scoring her with your cutting words."

The truth of what he spoke shone clear in his

face, filling her with a quick shame. She glanced away, hurt by the obvious respect he felt for this lady and the comparative contempt he held her in. "I'm sorry," she whispered. "I'll be more than courteous, I assure you."

He glared at her for a long moment. Then his expression shifted to one of desire, of yearning. It was the first time he'd touched her since she'd insulted him before his friends. Both of them were intensely aware of it.

He cupped her cheek, his fingers cold as iron against her flushed skin. But his eyes burned hotter than any smelting furnace. "You twist my heart when you stare at me that way. Did you know that? I only wish I knew what terrible storm lies beneath those sad eyes."

She swallowed. "Sometimes 'tis better not to know these things."

He searched her face, as if he could gain her secrets that way. Then, with a sigh, he released her and turned for the door. "Perhaps," he muttered.

But somehow she knew he didn't believe it.

TO ANNABELLE'S VAST relief, Lady Falkham proved to be a woman of wit, with a soft heart and no apparent scruples about associating with an actress. During their short ride, Colin told her of the problem facing them. Once they reached Annabelle's lodgings, Colin laid out his plan, which involved making her appear to be ill.

"I got the idea from Falkham," he told her ladyship. "It may not have worked well for him, but it might work for Annabelle, if you can make it convincing."

Apparently Lady Falkham was a healer, or had been before her marriage.

"I agree." The noblewoman paced the floors of Annabelle's front room. "I'll use a balm of oxeye daisy to make her skin flush. Rubbed all over her body, it will simulate a fever nicely. If it's made properly, it won't hurt her."

Colin's eyes narrowed. "If it's made properly, Mina?"

Lady Falkham went on as if she hadn't heard him. "It will warm her skin for a bit, but it won't last. And we can achieve a dramatic effect if we use an emetic to make her vomit—"

"No," Colin interrupted, with a glance at Annabelle, "I don't think we should do anything that will be uncomfortable for her."

"Won't be nearly as uncomfortable as bedding the king," Charity put in.

Colin scowled.

"The discomfort doesn't bother me," Annabelle broke in, tired of hearing them discuss her as if she weren't there. "I'm willing to have a real ague if it saves me."

"No need for a real one, but we can certainly have a pretend one." Lady Falkham put one finger to her chin. "We can manufacture the fever and the vomiting. The coughing and other effects will simply be good acting." She smiled at Annabelle. "From what I saw at the theater, you'll have no problems with that."

Annabelle blushed at the compliment.

"No problem at all," Charity put in proudly. "My mistress can play a role to perfection when she wishes."

Colin's gaze locked with Annabelle's, and she knew he was thinking of the last time he'd been in her lodgings. "I can attest to that," he said dryly. "Annabelle is one of the most accomplished actresses I know."

"Then it's settled. Annabelle will have an ague." Lady Falkham added, with a glance at Colin, "And 'tis best to use the emetic. After all, His Majesty is sending Rochester to carry her to Whitehall. So it must be convincing."

"That's why I wanted your help," Colin put in. "Since His Majesty knows you're a healer, he's more likely to believe her truly ill if he hears you're attending her. If the king even hears a hint of this deception, he might be insulted enough to have her discharged from the duke's company. I don't think she'd want that."

"Nay," Annabelle put in, "I could ill afford it."

"Yes, where else but in our wild theater could you find ready entertainment and a host of fops slobbering at your heels?" Colin snapped.

When Annabelle glared at him, Lady Falkham

said, "Pay Colin no mind, dear. He's become tedious these days, I'm afraid. He probably thinks men should be allowed to dance and sing and sow their seed freely while women sit prettily at home waiting for their poor drunken lords to show them some attention."

"That's a lie, and you know it," he protested. "Besides, when did you become so freethinking, Mina? I don't see you allowing every gallant in London to follow you about."

"Ah, but that's because I don't have a poor drunken fool for a husband. Though if I ever found him sowing his seed anywhere but in my field, first I'd crush his plow, then not waste one moment in finding myself a string of gallants."

"A ruthless woman," Colin said with a laugh. "Well, if the time ever comes for you to seek interests farther afield, pigeon, do remember me."

Lady Falkham rolled her eyes. "Oh, of course. I could join the other fifty women who've tried to capture your heart."

With a scowl, he glanced at Annabelle. "It hasn't been so many," he muttered and rose to go stand by the window.

"Gossip has it to be a hundred," Lady Falkham teased. "Be glad I've allowed for some exaggeration."

Though Charity smothered a laugh, Annabelle found it impossible to smile.

"Well, that's neither here nor there," Colin

growled. "We should be discussing our plans to save Annabelle from a rogue who truly has had a hundred women. Or more."

Lady Falkham flashed her a knowing smile. Annabelle liked Colin's friend more than she'd expected. Anyone who could parry Colin's witty comments word for word drew her admiration.

But she did envy Lady Falkham her easy friendship with him. Not to mention the respect he showed the woman. Annabelle would give anything to have him consider her in such high esteem. Alas, Lady Falkham was nobility—a countess, no less—and . . . and . . .

I'm nobility, too.

Mother had been a knight's daughter. Yet Annabelle no longer felt like a noblewoman or even a gentlewoman. The theater had made her wonder who she was. Squire's stepdaughter? Earl's daughter? Actress? Wanton? They seemed like so many roles disguising Annabelle of Norwood.

Oh, if only she could simply be Annabelle of Norwood again.

"Well?" Colin asked impatiently. "What are you waiting for? Let's get to it. We don't have all night."

With a laugh, Lady Falkham sprang into action. She sent Charity to the apothecary's for oxeye daisy and black alder while Colin went in search of a boy to send a message to the Earl of Falkham about his wife's whereabouts.

He returned just as Lady Falkham finished mixing up the balm. Annabelle couldn't help noticing that he seemed tenser now.

"I supposed Garett will be furious with me when I arrive home," Lady Falkham commented when Colin entered.

"No doubt. But I'm sure you can sweeten his temper with a kiss, pigeon." Colin sat down at the table, his eyes on Annabelle, who was spooning soot out of the fire grate to use to blacken under her eyes. "Where's Charity?"

"She's gone down to tell my landlady how ill I'm feeling. It wouldn't do to have the woman give the lie to our tale."

"Well, it's done," Lady Falkham announced, wiping her fingers on a rag. "Are you ready to have this ghastly mess rubbed in?"

Annabelle sighed. "I suppose we'll have to put it all over."

"Certainly anywhere that might be exposed when you leap out of bed to vomit. Your back, neck, legs, arms, upper chest . . ."

That got Colin's attention. "Can I watch?"

"No!" both women cried in unison. Then they went into her bedroom. Annabelle stripped down to her smock and slipped into bed.

Lady Falkham appeared embarrassed. "If I could let you rub it on yourself, I would, but in truth, I worry about the amount. Too much and it might blister your skin. Too little and there will be no effect. Better if I do it myself."

"It's all right." Annabelle forced a smile. "In the theater, I've grown used to being seen half-dressed."

To Lady Falkham's credit, she managed not to expose much of Annabelle's skin at a time. Her matter-of-fact chatter as she worked put Annabelle at ease, too. Until she had Annabelle turn onto her stomach.

Just as Annabelle realized that she shouldn't let Lady Falkham see her back, the noblewoman drew down her smock and gasped.

Colin rushed in at the sound, and Annabelle turned swiftly onto her back. She should have thought to prepare Lady Falkham for the scars from her stepfather's whippings. The woman looked white as chalk.

"What is it?" Colin demanded. "'Sdeath, Mina, you haven't hurt her with that concoction, have you?"

With her eyes, Annabelle begged her ladyship not to speak. If Colin knew, he'd ask a million infernal questions.

Lady Falkham gave her the barest of nods. "I merely knocked my knee against the bedstead, Hampden. Now, get out, so I can finish."

Colin stared at them a moment longer, then left.

"Thank you," Annabelle whispered.

Annabelle could see the questions in the woman's gaze but could never answer them, not when Lady Falkham was such a good friend of Colin's.

After that, they finished quickly. Colin went off to Lady Falkham's carriage across the street, where he could watch for Rochester. Charity bustled about trying to make the bedroom appear more like a sickroom. And Lady Falkham held the emetic ready to give Annabelle as soon as Rochester arrived.

Then they settled down to wait.

Chapter Nine

"Age cannot wither her, nor custom stale
Her infinite variety; other women cloy
The appetites they feed, but she makes hungry
Where most she satisfies . . ."
—William Shakespeare, *Antony and Cleopatra*, Act 2, Sc. 2

As Colin waited in Mina's carriage, all he could think about was Annabelle and their ruse. What if it didn't work? What if she either made a fool of herself and Mina or found herself bound for Whitehall despite it all?

If she made a fool of Mina before Rochester, Falkham would never forgive him. Mina had enough problems with her reputation as it was, since people regarded her abilities as a healer and her half-Gypsy blood with suspicion. Colin didn't even want to think how Falkham might react to hear that his wife had been involved in some scandalous actress's scheme.

Then again, Mina was glad to do it, and what other choice had they had?

You could have refused to help her.

Yes. Then he'd have sentenced himself to the torment of imagining her in the king's arms. Hell and furies, but this one woman roused in him a peculiarly possessive instinct. No doubt about it, the Silver Swan had bewitched him.

Still, whenever he thought of her fear and the silent sadness in her eyes, he knew he would do it all over again if he had the chance. What gentleman could have resisted an appeal as desperate as hers?

The sound of a carriage approaching interrupted his thoughts. He pushed aside the velvet curtain just in time to see Rochester's coach pull up across the street. His heart hammered as the earl climbed out and sauntered inside.

Damn the man! Colin hated to think of Rochester going within two miles of Annabelle in her smock.

So Colin waited with his pulse quickening by the moment. He could see only Annabelle's window and the light on in her rooms. After an ungodly amount of time, Rochester came out of the lodging house looking quite green.

Alone.

The relief that flooded Colin was so intense he marveled at it. He hadn't realized until now how fearful he'd been that they wouldn't pull it off. It was all he could do to wait until Rochester's coach turned the corner, leaping from Mina's carriage and hurrying back into Annabelle's lodging house.

He'd made it halfway up the stairs when he heard peals of laughter coming from Annabelle's room.

Damnable women! Didn't they have enough sense to keep up the pretense until they were certain Rochester was gone for good?

Determined to teach them a lesson, he took the remaining steps two at a time, then rapped on the door with imperious insistence. Everything went silent.

Charity's voice asked, "Who is it?"

In his best approximation of Rochester's bored tones, he said, "Lord Rochester."

"One moment, milord," Charity called out.

He could hear them scurrying about inside. Then the door swung open to reveal a white-faced Charity and Mina standing behind her.

As Charity slumped in relief, Mina cried, "For shame, Hampden, scaring us like that! You're no gentleman to play such a trick on us."

He entered and shut the door behind him. "I could hear you hens cackling all the way down the stairs," he grumbled. "Rochester could easily have come back for . . . for—"

"For what?" Annabelle asked as she came out of her bedchamber. She still wore only her smock, and although her face was flushed, he thought her the loveliest woman he'd ever seen. Only Annabelle could fake an illness and still look ravishing.

"For another look at you in your smock," he growled.

Annabelle and Mina glanced at each other, then burst into laughter.

"Me in my smock?" Annabelle said between gasps. "I don't think he noticed. He was too busy recoiling from my vomiting!"

"I assure you, Hampden, he hadn't a thought in his head about Annabelle's attire," Mina put in. "You should have seen this pair. Annabelle moaned like a woman on the verge of death. Then when she emptied her stomach in the chamber pot, Charity set up a pretend wailing for her poor mistress that would have awakened the dead."

"'Tweren't all pretend, milady," Charity said with wide eyes. "I tell you, I never saw anybody cast up her accounts so violently in all my life."

Annabelle grinned. "That emetic worked quite well. Lord Rochester couldn't wait to escape the smell."

"Everything turned out splendidly, didn't it?" Mina exclaimed. "It was delightful fun, for me at any rate. I only wish you could have seen it, Hampden. I had to force Lord Rochester to put his hand on Annabelle's head to feel her 'fever.' He wanted to bolt the moment she swung her head over the side of the bed."

Her eyes twinkled. "But we kept him a bit longer just to torment him, and the whole while he was edging toward the door. I swear, it'll be a long time before Lord Rochester agrees to play messenger for His Majesty again."

At Mina's mention of the king, Annabelle's smile faded. "Aye, I doubt Lord Rochester will return."

She shot Colin a worried glance. "But the king can always send someone else. I don't think we could manage this ruse twice."

Colin's temper rose at the very thought. "We won't have to. I'll make sure of that."

"How?" Annabelle asked.

"We'll discuss that later," he said evasively.

The seriousness in his voice dampened their good spirits, and a heavy silence descended on the room.

Colin's eyes met Annabelle's. She knew it was time for her reckoning, and he forced himself to ignore the sudden alarm in her face. He'd done as he'd promised to gain her secrets, and now he damn well deserved to have them.

"I'm off, then," Charity announced. "If none of you have further need of me. I have a supper engagement."

"Oh yes," Annabelle said dryly. "Do enjoy yourself."

"Tell Sir John I said you deserve a reward for your service to your mistress this day," Colin put in.

Charity halted to glare at him. "For all you know, milord, I'm meeting someone else."

When he arched an eyebrow, she colored, then hurried from the room.

Mina was busy tidying up, although he noticed she kept watching him and Annabelle. Well, he'd put a stop to that. This was one discussion he intended to have without an audience. "It's time you went home, Mina. Falkham will be beside himself with worry by now, despite my note. I'll walk you to the carriage; it's waiting at the end of the alley."

Mina stopped wiping the table to stare at him. "You're not coming with me?"

His eyes locked with Annabelle's. "Annabelle and I have some unfinished business."

She met his gaze steadily, acknowledging that he'd earned his payment.

Mina glanced from him to Annabelle, then hesitated, as if about to say something. But she seemed to think better of it. "Let's go, then."

As she walked to the door, Colin told Annabelle, "I'll be back shortly."

She nodded.

He and Mina descended the stairs in silence, but as soon as they'd walked out into the night air, Mina rounded on him. "Listen to me, Hampden. I don't care what Annabelle has done or said to you. She's not the kind of woman you think she is."

Her fiercely protective air irritated him. "How do you know what kind of woman I think she is?"

"You think she deserves your censure. You treat her like a woman who can't be trusted." She tipped her chin up. "Perhaps she can't. I don't know."

"No, you don't."

She ignored his acid comment. "But no matter what she's done, she deserves some consideration from you. That woman has suffered. I don't think you should make her suffer further."

Mina had obviously become attached to Annabelle, so it would do him little good to try convincing her of Annabelle's coldhearted side. Still, it annoyed him that Mina should presume so much about his relationship to the woman.

"When did you become so concerned about the private affairs of an actress?" he snapped.

"When I discovered that the actress was intelligent, witty, and interesting. Not at all like the barely educated women they pull out of the slums and throw into the theaters these days."

"You're right about that. Annabelle is anything but ordinary."

"Then I hope you admit she should be treated with care."

Stung by her lack of faith in him, he glowered at her. "Have I ever treated a woman otherwise?"

"Nay. But neither have I ever seen you react this strongly to one. I suspect she's capable of rousing your anger more than any."

'Sdeath, but the woman could read minds. "What lies between me and Annabelle is none of your affair," he bit out.

"It became my affair when you brought me here to help her."

"Annabelle would find that amusing, I'm sure." He tried for a flippant tone, but managed only to sound bitter. "She considers herself quite capable of fending off any unwanted attentions."

"She hasn't fended them all off successfully, I assure you."

That raised a cold chill within him. "What do you mean?"

A sudden flush suffused her face. "I shouldn't say. She wouldn't wish it."

"Has she told you something about her past?" he prodded.

"I saw something," she mumbled.

"What?" He remembered Mina's gasp while she was spreading the balm on Annabelle's back. "Damn it, Mina, tell me what you saw."

"She . . . she has scars on her back from where someone whipped her rather mercilessly. Some of the marks were recent, but some were faint, probably done when she was a good deal younger." She grabbed his arm. "Someone has mistreated that poor woman from the time she was merely a girl. Remember that when you . . . take care of your 'unfinished business.' "

Bile rose in his throat at the thought of Annabelle being whipped. "Hell and furies, what black devil would do such a thing?"

"I don't know." Mina shuddered. "We didn't discuss it. But I think she wishes you not to know, so don't tell her I told you."

He thought of Annabelle's defensiveness, of how she shied from him sometimes. It was a wonder she allowed anyone close to her at all. To think that she'd held such a terrible secret inside her all this time, never daring to trust another with her pain. It made him want to murder whoever had abused her.

"One more thing," Mina said, jerking him from his dark thoughts. "She may react later to the balm or the other herbs. If she does, she'll have trouble sleeping."

He scowled. "I thought your balm was harmless?"

"It is, it is. But if . . . it should happen to cause her problems later . . ." She pressed a pouch into his hand. "Here's a powder to help her sleep. Tell her to use it if she feels uncomfortable. All right?"

Still frowning, he tucked the pouch under the sash about his waist. How ironic that Mina should offer Annabelle, of all people, a sleeping potion.

Mina's hand still lay on his arm. "You'll be gentle with her, won't you, Hampden?"

Her sympathy for a woman she'd just met touched him. Obviously, Mina had made some assumptions about what he planned to do to Annabelle. Coming from any other noblewoman, her bluntness would have shocked him, but he'd long ago come to admire Mina for her straightforwardness.

"Don't worry." He laid his hand over hers. "'Tis not my intent to hurt or force her. I merely wish some questions answered."

She searched his face, then smiled, apparently

satisfied. "I've always thought you a good man. Now I know it."

As they walked on to the carriage, he held her words close in his heart, hoping she wasn't mistaken. After all, good men didn't spy on young women with tragic pasts unless they were prepared to take responsibility for dealing with what they learned.

He was beginning to think that in Annabelle's case, that might be a large responsibility indeed.

Chapter Ten

"For one heat, all know, doth drive out another,
One passion doth expel another still."
—George Chapman, *Monsieur D'Olive*, Act 5, Sc. 1

Annabelle waited for Colin with clammy hands and a pounding heart. She tried to take her mind off the coming ordeal by removing the remaining traces of balm on her skin. Then she donned her only mantua, a silk wrap that well covered her smock once she tied it with a sash.

Feeling better prepared, she tidied the room, opening the windows wide to dispel the foul odor. Yet when she heard Colin's footsteps on the stairs, she found herself far more tense than while awaiting Rochester.

Colin walked in without knocking, as if he belonged there, and shut the door behind him.

She tried to make light conversation. "It'll be some time before my poor rooms are back to normal. And my body, too, I suspect. I thought I'd never get the bad taste out of my mouth. Fortunately, I still had an orange in my pocket."

"How do you feel? Is your stomach still roiling?"

His concern touched her. She faced him with a wan smile, which faded when she noticed he'd removed his coat and sash and slung them over a chair. She tried not to notice how handsome he looked in his sleeveless vest and white shirt. Or how dangerous.

"No," she said, "my skin is still a bit flushed, but I've removed the balm, so it should return to normal soon. My stomach has finally settled as well." Then she couldn't resist adding, with a burst of defiance, "I'm quite capable of withstanding your inquisition now, my lord, if that's what you're asking."

Not even a raised eyebrow betrayed his thoughts. He simply continued to regard her with an oddly pitying look. "'Tis not meant to be an inquisition. But I don't think it unreasonable to want to know why we've just gone through an elaborate scenario that risked the reputation of my best friend's wife and caused you no little discomfort."

She dropped her gaze from his, reminded of how much Lady Falkham had chanced by involving herself with the affairs of an actress. "No, that's not unreasonable."

"Then let's begin with the most obvious question. Do you want me to continue to protect you from the king's advances?"

"As long as you can find a way to protect me that I can accept."

"All right." Settling his hips against the table, he

crossed his arms over his chest. "If I'm to help you, I must know the reason for your reticence. Why do you fear lying with the king? The truth, Annabelle."

She tipped up her chin. "I thought you'd already answered that. I'm a virgin, remember?"

"But even a virgin would lie with the king. 'Tis every actress's aim to bed His Majesty, in hopes that she may gain his affections and perhaps even bear him a child."

She turned her back to him, rubbing her hands over her now chilly arms. "'Tis not *my* aim," she said softly.

She heard him leave the table and move closer. "Why not?"

How could she tell him the truth without also revealing that she sought revenge against her father, who might be his friend?

As she hesitated, he spoke in a sharper tone. "If you're worried about the pain, don't be. Once you've made His Majesty aware of your innocence, he will be more than gentle with you."

She whirled on him. "Aye, and then I'll be bearing his bastard nine months hence, like all the other women he's bedded!" she blurted out. Then she realized how he would take what she'd said. In horror, she clapped her hand over her mouth, wishing she could take it back.

He went very still, his eyes hard. "I see I misunderstood your reasons entirely."

"Yes . . . no . . . oh, devil take it . . . Colin, I'm

a bastard myself. I don't know who my real father was, and I suffered . . . for being what I am. I won't do that to a child of mine. I won't!" She wheeled away from him to hide her tears.

As she stood there fighting the sobs that showed her weakness, he came up to draw her into his arms. With infinite tenderness, he stroked the hair back from her face. "Hush, don't cry. Hush, now, hush."

He was so kind, so caring. Why was the one man she could consider losing her virtue to also the one man she feared she couldn't trust?

Yet she badly wanted to trust him. Hardly thinking of what she did, she curved her damp cheek into his palm. "I'm sorry for . . . for being so blunt. 'Tis something I only learned recently. It still pains me to speak of it."

"If anyone understands that, 'tis I." He nuzzled her hair, sending a thrill through her that she tried fruitlessly to squelch.

"Then you must see why I fear lying with the king . . . or any man. You're right. I'm a virgin. And though I worry about the pain and humiliation, I mostly worry about finding myself with child. You do understand, don't you?"

"I do." He traced the line of her tears with his finger. "You know," he said, now stroking her lips, "there are other ways to make sure one bears no child."

She tensed. "Yes. I've heard of herbs that will kill

the unborn child. I know other actresses use them, but I . . . I just couldn't."

"That's not what I meant. There's a way to prevent a child from being created inside the womb."

She drew back to gape at him. "What do you mean?"

"'Tis a device made of sheep's gut. Some use it to protect themselves from disease, but I use it to keep from siring children. Like you, I have an aversion to bringing a bastard into this world."

Searching his face for signs of duplicity, she found only sincerity. "But . . . but how can sheep's gut keep a man from having a child?"

"It's a sheath that the man puts over his member to contain his seed."

She blushed, but her curiosity wouldn't let her change the subject. "Does it work?"

He shrugged. "For the most part."

Still skeptical, she asked, "Why haven't I heard of it before?"

He glanced away. "Many men don't know about it. I learned of it while I was . . . er . . . gathering information for the king in France." He paused, then added, "The men who do know don't like to use it. It limits their enjoyment."

Anger made her nod bitterly. "I should have known. Isn't that the way it is with everything? If something limits men's enjoyment, then they certainly don't tell women about it."

She left his arms to pace the room. "Never mind that women suffer through hard births every day, that they often die in childbirth." She whirled to face him. "If something limits the enjoyment of men, then by all means, keep it a secret, and let the women suffer."

A muscle worked in his jaw. "Yes, there are men like that, selfish, inconsiderate men. But not all of us are engaged in a conspiracy to make women miserable. After all, I told you about it, didn't I?"

His defensive words brought her up short. "Aye, you did tell me." She thought of all the ways he'd given her the benefit of the doubt in the past few days. "You're not like other men, Colin. I'll give you that."

With a curt nod, he acknowledged her thinly veiled apology. "I hope you're not going to use your newfound knowledge about sheaths to cut a wide swath through London's gallants."

She couldn't miss the jealousy in his tone and teased, "Even if I were interested, I can't see any of London's gallants 'limiting their enjoyment' by donning such protection for my sake."

That brought a grudging smile to his lips. "True. No man in his right mind would wish to limit his enjoyment of you."

Her mouth went dry at the blatant desire that suddenly flared in his face. She took an involuntary step back, but he refused to let her put distance between them. "Why do you play the wanton with half the rakes in London when you shy from me like a newborn colt? You said you'd tell me if I helped you. I held up my end of the bargain. Now I want the truth."

Devil take the man! She forced herself to meet his gaze, searching for a half-truth to pacify him. "What else does a virgin do if she wishes to protect herself? You know what it's like for an actress on the stage. Only last week, Rebecca Marshall was violently assaulted because she dared to resist a nobleman's advances. And she received no help from any quarter."

"Rebecca doesn't play the wanton. She *is* a wanton."

"That's true, but it's not the point. She became a wanton because she had few other choices. The rakes make whores of the actresses, one way or the other, and delight in deflowering innocents most of all. The only way I could see to escape their advances was to pretend to be thoroughly scandalous with certain companions, whom I chose for their vanity and pliable natures. My ruse at least kept most of the gallants under my control."

"Not the king . . . or me."

"Indeed." Her gaze dropped to her hands. "I didn't count on His Majesty's attention. Nor yours. Both of you seem quite intent on stripping me of my innocence."

He came very near. "If you're so determined to save your virtue, then why are you an actress at all?"

She sucked in her breath, cursing him for being so astute. His questions circled nearer and nearer to the truth. "My parents died recently, leaving me penniless. Charity had a friend on the stage and suggested that we could earn a living there. So we came. After a time, I . . . found that I enjoyed the work and was good at it, so I continued in it. The theater was a haven for me."

"Until now," he remarked dryly.

She nodded. "Until now."

He clasped her waist to pull her against him. "Why are you so afraid of me?" he whispered, his breath ruffling the curls at her temple. "Is it because you fear I'll give you a bastard?"

No, it's because you may know my father and tell him of my purpose.

"I don't want you to reveal my ruse to the other gallants," she said instead. "If they know what you know, I'll be hounded endlessly."

He cupped her cheek. "You'll not be hounded again, I promise you. Not after I make our liaison known. And I *will* make it known, as soon as I can. Because the only person who'll hound you in the future is me."

His voice was husky, cocksure . . . and incredibly tempting. Like a mating call, it drew her to look at him. What a mistake that was. He smiled as a tiger before it pounces. Then he lowered his lips to hers.

She didn't want the excitement building in her as his mouth covered hers. She didn't want her heart pounding in anticipation or her body straining against him when before it had strained away.

But somehow what she thought she wanted and what she actually did were two different things. She let him kiss her.

And oh, what a kiss. Firm, warm lips molded hers. Firm, warm hands pulled her closer until her body met his, soft thigh to hard thigh, soft belly to hard belly.

It began as a gentle coaxing, his mouth caressing hers, but it rapidly flared into something hotter, fiercer . . . harder. Try as she might to keep some part of herself separate and protected, she could not resist his heady ravishment.

He unknotted the sash of her wrap, then slid his hands inside to clasp her waist, with only the thin muslin of the smock separating their skin. As his tongue invaded her mouth with long, sensuous strokes, one of his hands covered her muslin-draped breast and began to entice it with sweet caresses.

It was too much pleasure all at once. With a low moan, she entwined her arms about his neck, kissing him back with all the fire that had long lain banked within her. A wondrous desire roused her blood, making her skin tingle.

And he obliged her in her half-named desires. He rubbed her breast with the heel of his palm until it burned and ached for more. All the while his lips feathered kisses along her jaw to her throat, where he ran his tongue over the spot where her pulse beat.

Dear heaven, she shouldn't let him do this, suck at her neck and thumb her nipple into a hard, aching knot and turn her into a mass of need. She should take on some role to protect herself from the desire flooding her.

Yet no role fit her anymore—injured virgin . . . wanton actress. Truth was, she only wanted to be Annabelle. And Colin seemed to be the only man who'd let her be Annabelle.

Tired of thinking about it anymore, she gave herself up to the delights he offered with hands and lips and tongue. She just wanted to touch and be touched, to taste and be tasted.

She slid her hands down the front of him, now eager to caress his bare skin as he was caressing hers. A pity that men wore so many unwieldy garments. She was having a devil of a time unfastening the long row of buttons on his vest.

He brushed her hands away and worked the buttons loose himself. Then she yanked at his vest, and he let her remove it, reciprocating by sliding her wrap from her shoulders until she stood only in her smock. Her fingers were already unbuttoning his shirt. When at last she slid her hands over his bare chest, marveling at the expanse of skin over iron-strong muscle and sinew, he groaned.

"Hell and furies, dearling, you'll kill me yet," he muttered as he swept her into his arms and strode for her bedchamber.

She caught at his neck to keep from falling.

"What are you doing?" she whispered, although she knew.

"Taking you to bed." His eyes gleamed at her. "You've haunted my nights once too often. Time to put an end to both our miseries."

"But, Colin—"

He stopped her mouth with a fierce kiss, and when it ended, they were in her bedchamber. Laying her on the bed, he sat down to remove his boots.

Alarm skittered through her as she rose to kneel on the bed, dragging the crumpled counterpane up to her neck. "Colin, you mustn't do this," she said in a whisper, though she watched with fascination when he dropped the second boot, then stood to unbutton his breeches.

His gaze locked with hers, wickedly taunting. "Why not?"

With quick movements, he slid off his breeches and then his drawers. Her protests died in her throat as she heeded the demands of her curiosity and gazed at his chest, then followed the line of whorled hair that began there before passing down his lean waist to end at . . . at . . .

Annabelle couldn't help it—she stared. It had been one thing to joke with the rakes about "staffs" and "swords" and "plows." It was another thing entirely to see one in the flesh. She ought to be shrieking and covering her eyes, but she couldn't stop gazing at it.

"You gaze like a virgin amazed," he said with a

rumbling chuckle. "I take it that you've never even seen a man naked before."

She knew a man's member grew with his desire, but somehow she hadn't imagined this . . . this . . . "I've seen statues, that's all," she admitted in a whisper. "But on a statue, a man's . . . I mean, yours is so . . . so . . . big."

"You've roused it from its sleep." His low, husky tone sent tremors of desire through her. He knelt on the bed in front of her. "Would you like to touch it?"

She jerked her gaze away. "Dear heaven, no!" Yet the very thought stirred a strange hunger.

What in heaven's name was she doing, kneeling on a bed with a naked man? And gawking at his private parts like a . . . like a true wanton.

Still, it was very fascinating.

"Are you sure you don't want to touch me?" he teased. "I can see curiosity in your face."

When she shook her head quickly, then attempted to slip from the bed, he caught her at the waist. He stroked the tumbled locks of her hair as she flamed with embarrassment.

"'Tis naught to be ashamed of, dearling. I'm equally curious to see what lies beneath your gown." He kissed a path from her cheek to her throat. "To touch your slender belly." He undid the ties of her smock, then pushed one sleeve off her shoulder. "To taste the honey between your legs."

She gaped at him. How did he know about *that*?

But of course he knew. She might be inexperienced, but he was not.

"Aye, that, too, my shy swan maiden," he said. "There are sensual delights awaiting us that you've never even considered. And we have all night to relish them."

His words took her breath away. She watched, both curious and alarmed, as he slid her smock completely off her shoulders. The thin material dropped to her waist, baring her breasts to his gaze. As her eyes remained riveted on his face, he put his finger in his mouth, then circled her nipple with the dampened tip.

She stayed very still, afraid that if she moved, the delicious feeling would leave her. When he replaced his finger with his mouth, she sighed and buried her fingers in his hair, giving herself up to the piercing pleasure.

He teased her breast with teeth and tongue until she thought she would melt from the excitement heating her body. She'd never dreamed something so embarrassing could be so . . . so enticing. Oh . . . sweet Mary . . .

Once he had her aching and needy, he sucked the tip of one of *her* fingers, then carried it down to smooth along his shaft. "Here is your chance to sate your curiosity, dearling," he murmured.

He released her finger, but she didn't jerk it away. Fascinated, she slid it along his hard flesh, marveling at the tight, silky skin. Half in a wondering daze, she wet her finger again and rubbed it over the tip, taking a perverse delight in seeing his knowing expression slip.

Then some instinct made her close her fingers around the firm length and pull. An explosive curse escaped him as he jerked her hand away, then pushed her back onto the pillow and covered her with his body.

She blinked up at him. "I'm sorry. Did I hurt you?"

"Not exactly." He breathed heavily a moment, his gaze glimmering at her, hard and hungry. "But I do hurt with wanting you. You do things to me that no woman ever has."

She took a very feminine pleasure in hearing that. "Does that mean you like me to touch you?" She worked her hand between their bodies to stroke his muscled thigh, inching her hand closer to his shaft once more.

He halted her hand. "Yes, but if you do that right now, this will be over before it's even begun." He stared down at her with eyes that glittered like emeralds. "It *has* begun, hasn't it?"

She swallowed. "Do you . . . have one of those sheaths with you?"

Her question seemed to startle him. Then he dropped his head onto her shoulder with a groan. "I should have known my honesty would come back to haunt me."

"Well?"

"Of course not. I'm not such a libertine that I carry them about with me."

"I see." She liked his heavy weight on top of her, and she couldn't deny that he'd made her want more of his wanton, extravagant caresses. But she wouldn't risk bearing a bastard. "Colin, I . . . I just can't—"

"It's all right, Annabelle." He tongued the pulse that beat in her neck, then murmured, "But men and women can pleasure each other in ways that won't result in conception, you know."

She eyed him with suspicion. "Oh?"

He lifted his head to grin at her as he trailed his hand down past her breasts and over her belly. Slipping her smock over her hips, he tossed it to the floor. "Do you wish me to show you?"

Her breath caught in her throat as his eyes greedily drank in her nakedness. "I—I don't know."

His hand roamed lower, until it slid between her legs to cover her mound. He rubbed there with his palm, and she gasped from the intense ache he created and soothed in the same motion.

"You like that, do you?" he whispered with a cunning smile.

His finger probed her silky folds, then darted into the slick, hot passage. A quick throb of delight shot through her.

"And that?" he said as he began to stroke, gently at first, then harder and faster.

"Oh yes." She clutched his brawny shoulders. "Oh, sweet Mary, yes!"

When he slid a second finger inside her, the sensation of tight invasion was surprisingly enjoyable. Indeed, it was near to being perfect.

She threw her head back and closed her eyes, scarcely conscious that he'd moved his head from her shoulder, until his mouth closed over her breast.

Ah, such warmth, such . . . strange, fierce sensations flooded her, barely quenching the feverish thirst he was raising in her. She drank in each delectable pleasure, marveling that he could make her feel this . . . this extraordinary bliss with only his lips and his fingers.

But he didn't stop there long. Instead he began kissing his way down her belly to . . . to . . .

Her eyes flew open as his tongue darted out to replace his fingers in their forays inside her. "Colin," she whispered as he flicked his tongue over the soft petal that ached for him. She gripped his head and arched up against his mouth. "Oh, Colin!"

"That's it, my swan beauty," he murmured. "Let it take you where it will take you."

The rhythmic plunge of his tongue drove her mad, and she writhed against him, wanting to escape the wild sensations he was rousing, yet not wanting to escape them either.

As he continued to caress her intimately with his mouth, her body strained toward some mysterious treasure that lay shimmering just beyond her reach.

As if he knew what she felt, he quickened the pace of his strokes until she thrashed mindlessly, wanting ... reaching ...

Then everything exploded into brilliant shards of diamonds, glittering with delights and pleasures she'd never known. She cried out, scarcely aware that she did so. She bucked against him, her body wracked by wave after wave of glorious enjoyment.

Slowly, she sank into the down mattress. Slowly, she became aware that Colin had stopped his sensuous torment and was resting his head on her belly.

She looked down at him. His taut expression spoke of passion suppressed, and his eyes stared off, remote, as if he fought a battle within himself. She felt suddenly bereft. He seemed so pained, so apart from her. Though he'd given her bliss with his mouth and hands, she had given him ...

Nothing. And suddenly, she wanted desperately to pleasure him, too. She wanted to make him feel the way she was feeling.

No, more than that ... she wanted him to take her. The thought struck her with painful force. She didn't care about her fears; she didn't care what might come tomorrow. The man who'd seen beneath her defenses to the real her was the only man she'd ever want bedding her. And if she let this chance pass her by, she might never get the chance again.

"Colin?" She laid her hand on his head. "I want you."

He lifted his head to stare at her with a raised eyebrow.

"I want you to . . . to lie with me."

"I already am, dearling," he said softly.

She shook her head. She hadn't counted on how embarrassing it would be to make this admission. "I mean, I don't care about the sheath. I want you to . . . to . . ." She faltered, unable to say more.

He looked startled. Then a dark, seductive gleam shone in his eyes. "To show you the full range of sensual delights?" He kissed his way up her body. "Is that it, Annabelle? Haven't I satisfied you enough tonight?"

When he tugged on her nipple with his teeth, she moaned deep in her throat. "Oh, dear heaven, yes . . . I mean . . . no . . . I . . . I . . ." Now he was rubbing his thick flesh over her thatch of hair, arousing her blood again.

"I like it when you're speechless. You know, if I take you now . . . unprotected . . . there's always the possibility—"

"Oh, hush," she whispered, arching up against him. He was already making her hot and bothered again. "Please . . . Colin . . . please . . ."

"You need not ask twice," he said with a blazing smile before he eased into her.

She gasped at the sudden tightness, the uncomfortable thickness within her. He'd surely cleave her in twain if he continued.

"You're so very sweet and tight," he murmured.

"'Twill be uncomfortable at first, dearling. You must relax."

"How can I relax?" she hissed as he inched farther, pressing against some part of her inside. "'Tis very u-unpleasant."

He stopped his movement, his features drawn as he encountered the barrier of her innocence. Not even a flicker of surprise crossed his face. "Aye. But not for long."

Slipping his hand between their bodies, he found her secret place again and began to stroke the aching bud once more. She responded immediately to the liquid fire his manipulations sent pouring through her.

"Better?" he managed.

"Yes . . . oh yes . . . oh, Colin . . ."

"Now I must hurt you, but 'tis best to get it over with." Then he plunged through her virginal barrier.

Pain gripped her. She tried to buck him off, but his weight was too great, as was the strength with which he pulled her thrashing arms to her sides. He lay motionless atop her, allowing her to adjust. A tear escaped her eye, which he kissed away.

"The bad part is over, I swear," he whispered as he nuzzled her cheek, her temple, her hair. "Now there is only delight."

At first she didn't believe him, for his movements as he stirred again inside her left her feeling invaded and sore. Then gradually the soreness gave way to a kind of heat, and the heat gave way to licking flames, and the flames to a raging fire that threatened to consume her.

"Hell and furies," he muttered as he thrust into her with increasing rhythm, rocking her body in a dance more sensual than any court minuet. "Hell and furies . . . Annabelle . . . ah . . . *Annabelle* . . ."

Then he lowered his head to sear her with a kiss, plunging his tongue into her mouth in ever-quickening strokes that mirrored the cadence of his hips. Despite the slight discomfort, she writhed beneath him, once again straining to reach those mystical delights he dangled before her.

As he pounded into her, his mouth devouring hers as his hardness invaded and plundered, any lingering pain faded into sweet, sweet oblivion, and there was nothing left but him and his thunderbolt strokes within her.

He caught her up like a hawk carrying its prey into rich blue skies, and she soared with him, wheeling into ever more lofty heights. As she dug her fingers into his muscled shoulders and reveled in his glorious strength, he transported her farther, faster, higher . . . carrying her into the brilliance of sunlit sky, into that private space where there was only him and his gift of pleasure hurtling her upward.

"Colin!" she cried out as she reached the golden peak. "Oh, Colin!"

With a roar of his own, he gave a mighty thrust and spent himself inside her.

It was some moments before either of them could move or speak. Their bodies shook together, their hearts raced equally fast, and their breathing was quick. When at last he rolled off to lie on his side next to her, she felt a little bereft. Propping himself up on one hand, he lazily stroked her skin, then spread her hair down until it fanned over her breasts, tickling them.

She sighed in contentment, and he leaned over to kiss her shoulder. "When I first saw you at the Duke's Theater, I was told you were haughty and cold onstage, but fire itself in bed. Now I see that even unfounded rumors can have truth in them."

She turned her flaming face into the pillow.

"Annabelle," he said, "you're mine. You have no need to keep up this silly pretense of wantonness now that you're under my protection."

No, she truly didn't. So what was to become of her vengeance? Was she to become Colin's mistress and abandon all her plans?

"There will be no other gallants now. Agreed?" he said more firmly.

The possessive tone in his voice both worried and thrilled her. He was sure of her already, wasn't he? Wanting to prick that assurance, she said, "Well, now that you've shown me how wonderful it is to lie with a man, I may wish to—"

"Hell and furies," he muttered as he turned her to face him. But his expression softened when he saw the uncertainty in her eyes. "I'll throttle any man who tries to bed you, Annabelle," he vowed.

"Even the king?" she asked with a raised eyebrow.

"Even the king, damn his soul to hell." He lowered his mouth to hers, then stopped an inch away, his breath hot against her trembling lips, already parting to receive his kiss. "Promise me there will be no others."

It was hard to think when his hands had begun stroking her again.

"Promise me," he repeated, then ran the tip of his tongue along her lower lip, enticing her. His fingers were filling her below once more, stroking her until she scarcely knew where she was.

"I promise," she whispered, a renewed ache for him making her willing to promise almost anything.

Then, with a growl of triumph, he made sure he wiped all thoughts of other gallants quite out of her mind.

Chapter Eleven

"No mask like open truth to cover lies,
As to go naked is the best disguise."
—William Congreve, *Love for Love*, Act 5, Sc. 4

Colin and Annabelle lay spoon fashion beneath the heavy counterpane after their second tempestuous bout of lovemaking. Feeling languid and oddly content, Colin ran his hand over the smooth curves of her waist, down her hips to her thighs, then back.

Never had he found such absolute enjoyment with any other woman. Sir John would have said it was because Annabelle was an innocent, but Colin knew better. If anything, a virgin should have given him less pleasure than a more experienced female.

Nor was there any doubt that Annabelle had been a virgin. Her blood stained the sheets that lay crumpled beneath them. It pleased him absurdly to know he'd been right about her innocence. Only he had entered the fortress of her disguises to find a woman who was neither aloof nor indiscriminate with her favors, but open, giving, and thoroughly enchanting.

He couldn't stop touching her. And anyway, why should he? She was his now. She'd promised to be his, and he would make her keep that promise.

Though he doubted it would be so very difficult. He pressed a kiss to her bare shoulder, relishing how her body leapt to life. Ah yes, he had her now. He'd caught the elusive swan.

"Mmm," she purred as he continued to drop warm kisses along her collarbone.

He drew the counterpane down and pushed her heavy mass of hair aside, intending to kiss her neck. That was when he saw the long lines of white criss-crossing her upper back. His stomach roiled. Mina had been right. They were the marks of a whip or perhaps a crop.

He tried not to think of what they'd looked like when they were fresh, but he couldn't help it. Rage against whoever had hurt her sparked in him like a brush fire. Grimly he traced one of the scars.

Annabelle stiffened, then tried to pull the counterpane up over her back.

He stayed her hand. "Who did this to you? For the love of God, who beat you so cruelly?"

She remained quiet a long moment. He peered over her shoulder at her face, noting that she looked sad as she stared off across the room.

"I want to know who, dearling," he murmured, drawing her against him. "Tell me who so I can find and murder the wretch."

"You can't," she said bitterly. "He's dead."

"'He'?" His mind raced. "It couldn't be a husband, for I know as well as anyone you were chaste. An employer? The master of a house where you were servant?"

"Neither." She sighed. "I told you I recently learned I was a bastard. Well, my stepfather always knew. Apparently Mother married him when she found herself with child by another man."

"And he punished you for it," Colin bit out.

"He punished my mother, until I grew old enough to punish, too. I suppose he couldn't stand the thought of having a child not his own. He was a . . . a very proud man."

"No," Colin ground out, "he was a cruel man to use you thus."

Twisting to face him, she gave him an odd, searching glance. "Some men would say he had every right to beat me." Pain gave an edge to her tone. "He raised me as his daughter. It was his duty to discipline me."

He trailed his finger over her cheek. "Discipline doesn't require cruelty or violence. He had a right, a duty, to discipline you as a father would. But his cruelty served no purpose but to make you distrust men."

Her eyes filled with tears, and she turned to hide her face against the pillow. With a shudder, she drew the counterpane over her scars. He let her.

"It doesn't matter now," she choked out. "He's dead. The past is past."

No, he thought. The past wasn't at all past for her, for she still didn't quite trust him. But how to make her trust him when she'd suffered so at the hands of men? No wonder she'd been so vehement about her bastardy, about the hard ways that men used women. He slid his arms around her, feeling helpless to make her see that all men weren't alike, that she didn't have to face everything alone.

She must have spent years facing the world alone. Hell and furies, what kind of mother let her daughter suffer so at the hands of a brute?

Ah, but that was easy to answer. Utterly unaffected by his humiliating sobs, his own mother had let him be wrenched away from her by the wild-eyed lord who was his father. He'd already been a nuisance to her, she'd told him. They'd both be much better off if he went peaceably to England with his father.

Now that Colin looked back on it, though, he realized his mother had probably been right to let him go. His father, a dashing, hotheaded man prone to fighting duels and provoking Cromwell's men whenever possible, had nonetheless taught Colin a great deal about honor and family. He'd left some property to Colin and done his best to provide his son with a decent education.

Years later, after Colin fled into exile with Charles II, his father having been killed in the civil war, Colin had searched for his mother. Any illusions he'd harbored about her character had been finally destroyed when, at the age of sixteen, he'd found her in a respectable old chalet in the country, the kept mistress of an ancient *duc*. Her prettiness still intact, though become more brittle, she'd accused him of wanting money and had tossed him into the street.

He shoved that painful memory to the back of his mind. "What of your real father? Did he know about this?"

She hesitated. "I don't think so. But I never knew my real father."

The faint wariness in her voice gave him pause. He began to sort through things she'd told him before. Her surname was Maynard. Her stepfather's name? If so, then why express so much interest in the Maynards of London? Had she thought her dead stepfather might have relatives in London to whom she could turn? Or was it another relative entirely she sought?

And why did she go by "The Silver Swan"? It couldn't be coincidence that it was the same as Walcester's code name. Colin had learned long ago to regard suspiciously anything that masqueraded as chance.

Gently he pressed her down until she lay beneath him. Her eyes widened as she stared up into his face.

"Was your stepfather's name Maynard?" he asked.

A hint of fear leapt into her eyes. "Why would you think so?"

"You've been very interested in my friends the Maynards from the day we met. Are you searching for someone? A relative, perhaps?"

She tried to move from beneath him, but he held her pinned. "Tell me. Where did you get the name Maynard—from your stepfather?"

"Of course," she said, too quickly, and glanced away. There was genuine alarm in her face now.

"Please don't lie to me, dearling." He gentled his tone. "After what you and I just did together, you ought to be able to trust me a little, don't you think?"

Paling, she whispered, "Hush, Colin. You ask too many questions."

A faint smile touched his lips. "Aye. I like to know about the women I care for. 'Tis an odd habit I have."

Her gaze shot to him. "Do you care for me?"

He brushed his mouth against hers. "More than I should, dearling." Between bestowing kisses on her lips, her cheeks, her bare neck, he murmured, "Is Maynard the surname of your stepfather, Annabelle?"

Her breath was quickening. "Has anyone . . . ever told you you're a rogue?"

He chuckled. "Many times. How do you think I know so much about giving a woman pleasure in bed?" He fondled her breast so deftly that she gasped. "And I fully intend to show you how it's done once more."

When he moved to caressing her below, she let out a moan.

"So tell me," he whispered, "is Maynard your stepfather's surname or not?"

"Not," she breathed, then arched up against his hand. "Colin . . . I want . . . I want . . ."

"I know what you want," he rasped. It was what he wanted, too. As soon as he got her answer. "If it's not *his* name, then whose is it?"

"Please . . . Colin . . ."

He waited until he had her panting, then murmured, "Just tell me, dearling, and I'll give you whatever you want."

"It's . . . my father's name. Or so my mother said."

He froze, her confession stunning him. This wasn't what he'd expected. Nor Walcester, apparently, either.

"Colin?" she asked, her voice trembling. He could see from her face that she hadn't meant to tell him.

He wanted to know much more. How her mother had died, why Annabelle had endured her stepfather's cruelties for so long . . . Yet he must be very careful with her if he wanted all the truth. He slid his hand up to caress her cheek, but she shoved his hand aside with a look of pure betrayal.

It struck him like a sword in the belly. "Forgive me, dearling, I didn't mean . . . I shouldn't have pressed you."

For a moment, she looked uncertain whether to trust him. Then she let out a long, harsh breath. "It's all right. You might as well know the truth."

"You came to London in search of your real father."

She nodded tersely. "I was all alone in the world. I thought . . . I'd at least look for him. Mother told me he was a gentleman from London with the surname of Maynard. That was all. Then Charity and I got here. We didn't know where to begin. So I took his name and we found work in the theater, as I told you before."

He cursed himself for pressing her so sorely. Her story made perfect sense, and he could hardly blame her for wanting to seek out her real father. He'd have done the same in her place. Slowly, he slid off to lie beside her. She curled her body into a ball, her breath coming in quick gasps.

"Why didn't you tell me before?"

She shot him a defensive look. "So you could think that I just wanted to blackmail him or something equally mercenary?"

He stared hard at her. That *was* something to consider. Although she would hardly have brought it up if that was what she intended. Would she? "Have you had any luck finding him?"

She stared up at the ceiling. "You mentioned an earl a few days ago. That's the only lead I've had."

Could Edward Maynard really be her father? She

didn't appear to resemble him much, except for her blue eyes, but then, that proved little. "I see."

She faced him, her eyes watchful. "Now that you know the truth, perhaps you could aid me in my search."

He searched her face. "Perhaps."

The tension seemed to leave her body. "If you did, it would mean so much to me."

He suddenly wondered who was manipulating whom. "Do you have anything concrete I can use to find this father of yours or at least prove that the Earl of Walcester is your father?"

She averted her gaze, her fingers working nervously at the sheet. At last she nodded. "I do have one thing." Wrapping the sheet around her, she slid from the bed. She went to her bureau and took out a box of inlaid ivory. Then she blocked his view with her body, but he could hear the sound of her setting the box down and then a faint click as she apparently unlocked it. He heard the faint click again as she locked the box.

When she returned, she held an object, which she handed solemnly to him. It was a man's signet ring of solid gold, rather ornate and bearing a coat of arms.

"Do you recognize the insignia?" she asked as she sat down.

Oh yes. It was Walcester's.

He fingered the ring a moment longer in silence. What was he to do? Tell her who her father was?

He couldn't do that without first speaking to the earl, but the yearning in her face made his gut twist. 'Sdeath, but she'd had a hard life. She deserved to know her father.

Then again, there was still one thing her story hadn't explained. "What has the Silver Swan got to do with all this?"

She looked startled. "What do you mean?"

"Why does everyone call you the Silver Swan?"

"'Tis a nickname, that's all."

No, it wasn't all, and he knew it by the flicker of alarm in her eyes. Why was she lying about that one bit of information?

He wanted to rail against her, to make her tell him the truth. It wounded him to realize she could still keep something from him after the honest way she'd given him her body.

Aren't you keeping something from her as well? his conscience whispered.

A groan escaped him. He couldn't blame her for distrusting him, when he distrusted her. Besides, he might be hasty in attributing suspicious motives to her when she might simply be anxious over discussing her absent father.

"Do you know whose ring it is, Colin?" she asked, interrupting his dark thoughts. "I do wish to find my father."

His gaze locked with hers. "Why?"

"That . . . should be obvious. Everyone wants to know who their real parents are."

"Do you wish him to acknowledge you, to give you a portion since your stepfather and mother left you penniless?"

"No!" The sharpness of her answer took him aback. "No, I don't care about money."

Yet she cared about something, he could tell. She cared very much.

That decided him. There was another who depended on Colin's discretion, a friend he'd made a promise to. He dared not tell her more until he knew more.

He continued to finger the ring. "I'm not sure about the crest, but I might be able to identify it if I ask the right people."

A relieved smile crossed her face. "I knew you could help me!"

Then why not ask for my help before?

The words were on the tip of his tongue, but he shouldn't put her on her guard by asking too many questions. He'd have to get his answers another way.

He glanced at the box on her bureau and wondered what secrets she kept so carefully locked away. Could he get a look inside without arousing her suspicions? Perhaps once she slept . . .

Suddenly he remembered Mina's sleeping powder.

Setting the ring on a nearby table, he gathered her in his arms. "Let's not talk any longer about matters that make you sad."

She easily accepted his embrace. "No, let's not."

He drew her down on the bed, and she curved her body against his, resting her head on his chest. Hell and furies, but despite her suspicious behavior, she still made him want her more fiercely than any woman he'd ever known. It took all his will to fight the stirring in his loins. Nor did it help when she started planting soft kisses over his chest.

"I don't think that's such a wise idea," he ground out.

"Why not?" A coy smile gilded her rose-red lips, tempting him to taste of them once more. "Have you exhausted your strength?"

"Nay, but your body has had plenty of excitement for one day. You'll be sore enough as it is in the morning." Nonchalantly, he added, "Tell me, do you feel quite normal now after enduring Mina's physic?"

"Not exactly normal." She licked his nipple. "But it has nothing to do with the physic."

His cock instantly responded to her teasing. Oh yes, he'd transformed her into a temptress. He tried to think of anything other than what lay beneath the sheet still wrapped around her seductive little body.

"I ask," he said in a strained voice, "because I almost forgot to give you the physic Mina left for you. She said you might feel aftereffects, and this would counter them."

Her attention effectively diverted, Annabelle propped her chin on his chest. "Really? Aftereffects?"

"Yes. In fact, I think you should take it now. I wouldn't want you to wake up ill in the morning simply because I forgot to give it to you. Mina would chasten me sorely for my omission. Shall I get it?"

She sighed. "All right, but I certainly tire of filling my body with medicines."

Quickly he left the bed before her beautiful body could tempt him into changing his mind. He found the pouch of powder and mixed it with some water, then brought the cup to her.

He watched as she sipped it, guilt stabbing him unexpectedly. In all his years as a spy, he'd never felt quite as much the varlet as he did right now. "Annabelle, is there anything else you think I should know before I go off on this quest for your father?"

He had to give her the chance to tell him the whole truth.

For a moment, he thought she might. She concentrated on the contents of the cup. At last she muttered, "Not that I know of," and drank the whole of it.

But she avoided his eyes, and he knew she was lying. It cut him down deep, in the part of his heart he'd protected all these years. This was why he had to stop all his intriguing. Because it had begun to hurt.

Especially when the intriguing involved someone he cared about.

Wiping her mouth with the back of her hand, she said, "That's nasty stuff Lady Falkham is giving out."

He nodded, his heart heavy. "Aye, but she says it works."

A few moments later, when Annabelle's head dropped onto the pillow and her eyes drifted shut, he grimly acknowledged that Mina hadn't lied. The powder worked like a charm. He waited until he was sure Annabelle was asleep before leaving the bed.

Pulling on his shirt and breeches, he headed for the bureau. Like most people, Annabelle wasn't terribly imaginative when it came to hiding places, and he found the hidden key to her box easily, tucked inside the binding of a book of poems on her bureau.

Glancing back to make certain she slept soundly, he opened the box. Inside he found a woman's usual trinkets—a pressed flower, a thin silver neck chain, a few small rings, the swan brooch. And a piece of rolled paper with a broken seal and a faded ribbon tied around it.

Carefully, he removed the ribbon and unrolled the paper. A spidery script filled the page, and he realized after reading it that it was a poem. He thought it an odd poem until he read the inscription at the bottom. *The Silver Swan.*

Quickly he scanned the lines again. This was no ordinary verse, but a coded one of the kind spies often used to pass messages. Walcester had undoubtedly written it. Judging from the yellowing of the paper, it had been penned some time ago, possibly during the earl's days spying for the Royalists.

Colin squeezed his eyes shut as a terrible hurt tore at his heart. Annabelle had lied about the Silver Swan, and Walcester hadn't been wrong to suspect her. Clearly, she knew far more about Walcester and his political activities than she'd let on, and obviously had no intention of revealing any of it to him.

He'd been duped by her sadness and tale of woe. "Damned lying actress!" he hissed. He glared at her sleeping form. A seeming innocence lit her face, her eyelashes feathering her cheeks and her hair lying in a tangle over her shoulders, making his emotions clamor riotously within him. Hell and furies, how could she affect him so fiercely?

Had her story of her fiendish stepfather and her quest for her real father even been true? She did have Walcester's signet ring in her possession, which was admittedly a sign of something, and she was the right age to be his daughter.

And there was no doubt she'd been beaten by someone.

His throat tightened. If he couldn't get answers from her, he would get them elsewhere. Quickly he memorized the poem, then locked it back up and replaced the key in its hiding place. Picking up the signet ring from where it lay on the bedside table, he slid it on his finger and donned the rest of his clothes.

If he hurried, he could visit the earl and be back before she awakened. The hour was late, but Colin didn't care. He wanted the truth, and only Walcester could give it to him.

With a parting glance at the woman lying in such glorious splendor on the bed, he strode from the room, his jaw clenched. Yes, Annabelle, sweet lying Annabelle, had made him want answers. And he'd get them if he had to shake them out of the earl.

COLIN TURNED AS the earl entered the drawing room of the Walcester town house. It had taken some talking to convince the man's steward to disturb his master, but at least Walcester hadn't kept him waiting once he was roused. Judging from his unbuttoned vest and half-tucked shirt, the earl had dressed in a hurry.

"I hope you have a good reason for wrenching me from a warm bed in the middle of the night," Walcester grumbled.

"I have something to show you." Colin handed the signet ring to the earl.

Walcester gave a start as he saw what it was. "Where did you get this?"

"Is it yours?"

"Of course it's mine. You can see my coat of arms on it. Now tell me where you got it!"

Colin watched the earl carefully. "From the actress. Annabelle Maynard."

He hadn't been sure what to expect, but it wasn't the shock that spread over the older man's face. The earl dropped into a nearby chair, his eyes riveted on the ring. "Where did *she* get it? Do you know?"

"From her mother. She claims it belonged to her father."

The blood drained from the earl's face. He stared past Colin, his eyes bleak. "What town is . . . the actress from?"

"I only know that it's in Northamptonshire."

"Norwood," Walcester said. "I can't believe it. 'Tis impossible."

"What's impossible?" Colin demanded. "That she's your daughter?"

"Yes. No." Walcester fingered the ring in an almost wild distraction. "A pox on it, Hampden, I don't know if she is or not."

No. Half the time the men didn't know they'd sired children, did they? No wonder Annabelle had been so insistent about his using a sheath. Guilt ate at him. "Is there any chance of it?"

"There's always a chance. My God, Hampden, you should know that a man on the run takes his pleasure where he finds it."

"You were on the run in Norwood? When was this?"

A shuttered look came down over the earl's face. "When I was a spy for Charles I in Cromwell's army."

Colin's eyes narrowed. "Norwood is close to Naseby."

The Battle of Naseby had ended disastrously. Not only had the Royalists lost, but some of the king's papers had been found by Cromwell's men, revealing that Charles I was plotting with the Irish, Danes, French, and God knew who else to help him regain power in his kingdom. That had given the parliamentary forces popular support as nothing else had. From there, matters had steadily worsened until the king was finally executed.

Could Walcester have been part of all *that*? It didn't seem likely, but . . . "Were you in Norwood then?"

Walcester closed up. "What does that have to do with this Annabelle Maynard woman?"

"I'm just trying to figure out her connection to you, which is what you asked me to do. So she may or may not be your daughter, born of your union with . . . whom? A milkmaid? A cook? A tavern wife you tumbled as you passed through Norwood? All of these?"

Walcester groaned. "Nay. If she's of Norwood and bears my ring, then only one woman could be her mother." The soft glow of candlelight lit Walcester's tortured face. "Phoebe Harlow, the daughter of Sir Lionel Harlow."

Colin gaped at him. *Sir* Lionel Harlow? So Annabelle's mother wasn't some chambermaid or doxy. No wonder Annabelle could play a gentle-woman to perfection. She *was* a gentlewoman.

The ramifications of that fired his temper. "You lay with an unmarried gentlewoman and left her with child? Had you no care at all for what you were doing?"

Walcester bristled at the condemnation in Colin's voice. "I never knew of the child. After I left, I heard that her family arranged a profitable marriage between her and a powerful squire named Taylor. Even if I could have returned for her during the height of the war, I couldn't have had her. She'd already married."

"Aye. Because you left a babe in her belly."

Rising stiffly, Walcester glared at Hampden. "You have no right to speak to me like that. You've no doubt left a trail of bastards. I sired only one."

Only with extreme difficulty did Colin rein in his temper. "I've taken great pains not to sire any. But even if I had, I would have made certain they were well provided for."

Walcester didn't even flinch. "My daughter—*if* she is my daughter—was raised in a wealthy squire's home. Is that not 'well provided for'?"

Colin glowered at him. "That wealthy squire beat her—quite often, apparently. I saw the marks of his crop on her back." He added, when Walcester paled, "He also beat her mother. No, I don't think either of them was 'well provided for.'"

Turning on his heel, the earl went to stand at

the window and gaze out into the cold, dark night. "You're a damned insolent pup, Hampden."

"Aye. You knew that when you asked this favor of me."

The older man cursed under his breath. "What of her mother now?"

"Both she and the squire are dead, or so Annabelle says."

He whirled around. "But the woman would only be about forty."

"Annabelle said no more than that, but I believe her when she says they're dead. She says she came to be in the theater because they left her penniless."

Walcester's expression hardened. "Ah, yes, the theater. You've done your work well. You've unearthed my dark past only to present me with a whoring daughter. Thank you for that fine favor."

Struck dumb by the vehemence in those words, Colin balled his hands into fists. "Haven't you been listening? Your daughter grew up being beaten by the man to whom you abandoned her. Knowing that, all you can say is that I've presented you with 'a whoring daughter'?"

"No doubt the wench deserved beating if she acted as she has these past months in London. From what I hear, she's taken more lovers than anyone can count." He glared at Colin. "And I should rejoice to have such a daughter?"

Colin wanted to throttle the arse, then set him straight about Annabelle's many supposed lovers.

But that would mean admitting to taking Annabelle's innocence, and he doubted that Walcester would approve.

Besides, as far as the earl was concerned, his daughter had shamed him publicly by getting herself talked about as a wanton. Walcester wouldn't care whether she really was one.

"I suppose it wouldn't do to have your aspirations damaged by having an actress for a daughter," Colin said acidly.

"You may not have an interest in politics," the earl snapped, "but some of us care what happens to England."

Colin stifled a snort. Walcester's aspirations had nothing to do with any love for his country. Like many men who had lived through the uncertainty of the war and Cromwell's machinations, the earl had seized his chance in a time of tumult to better his own prospects. The king had so admired Walcester's work with the Royal Society that he'd appointed the earl to high office. And with Edward Hyde, the Earl of Clarendon, fled in disgrace, the man had a chance to be quite powerful.

But even Colin knew how easily the earl's applecart could be upset. For one thing, the younger nobles like Rochester and Sir Charles disliked him for his sober mien and harsh rebukes. For another, the Duke of Buckingham, once Walcester's close ally, had noted his rise and become his worst enemy. The duke would delight in drumming him out of the court as he had Clarendon.

"So what does the chit want from me?" Walcester bit out. "Money?"

"She doesn't know who you are, doesn't even know that you *have* money. She came to London to search for you because she wants to know who her father is."

Walcester's cold laugh chilled Colin. "Of course. That's why she's using my code name from the war. It has nothing to do with blackmail at all."

The comment brought Colin up short. The earl had a point. And why had Annabelle kept that coded message hidden? If her mother had passed it down to her, then the woman must have been part of the earl's spying. But Walcester hadn't yet mentioned such a thing.

Which only heightened Colin's suspicions that there was something more to the earl's concerns than he was saying. "How could Annabelle blackmail you if you were spying for the king?"

Walcester stiffened so imperceptibly that anyone but Colin would have missed it. "I am just pointing out that she has no reason for using it otherwise."

Which wasn't an answer. "Perhaps her mother told it to her. She came here to seek you. How better to draw you out than with your code name?"

"Her mother didn't know it," Walcester said, a shade too quickly.

Something was wrong here. Obviously Annabelle's mother *had* known it, unless the woman had stumbled upon the coded message by accident after Walcester left Norwood. But what spy left such clues lying about?

'Sdeath, between Annabelle and the earl, Colin had to sort a veritable tangle of lies from the truth. At the moment, he hesitated to mention the coded message to either Walcester or Annabelle. If the earl was lying about the code name, what else might the man be hiding?

"What do you wish me to do now?" Colin asked, although he was already hatching his own plans.

"I'll have to think on it. But if you have any loyalty to me, you'll keep my secret until I decide."

"You mean, keep it from Annabelle." Colin bit back an oath. He owed Walcester his life, but at the moment that indebtedness hung about Colin's neck like a lead weight. "What will you do in the meantime?"

"Perhaps I'll take a look at the actress myself."

"That might be a good idea, although if you plan to speak with her, I would advise against railing at her for being a 'whoring daughter.'"

Walcester drew himself up stiffly. "I don't mean to speak to her."

"That's wise." As much as he resented Annabelle's deceiving him, he hated to think of her being exposed to her father's vitriolic temper. "She's asked me to seek you out for her. What shall I tell her to put her off?"

A startled expression crossed Walcester's face. "You've gotten quite close to her, then."

"That's what you wanted," he pointed out.

"True." The earl rubbed his chin. "Did she mention anything about the Silver Swan? Had she no reason for wearing a swan brooch?"

The man was downright obsessed with Annabelle's knowledge of his code name, even now that he seemed to believe she was his daughter. "No. She claimed 'The Silver Swan' was nothing more than her nickname."

"She's lying. You must find out what else she knows."

Colin agreed, but he was beginning to think he must also find out what the earl was hiding. "I'll do what I can."

But he'd do it outside of London. Oh yes. He'd dealt with his duplicitous mistress and equally duplicitous friend long enough. He was tired of hunting between their words for the fragments of truth they chose to feed him.

It was time to change tack entirely. It was time to travel to Norwood.

Chapter Twelve

"Is this her fault or mine?
The Tempter or the Tempted, who sins most?"
—William Shakespeare, *Measure for Measure*, Act 2, Sc. 2

Light streamed in through the window when Annabelle opened her eyes. She shut them with a groan. Her head pounded like a pestle in a mortar and her lips felt cracked and dry. Then she shifted onto her side, and the stickiness between her legs made her eyes fly open again.

Dear heaven, Colin had lain with her. She hadn't dreamed it.

Soft caresses, masterful kisses . . . he'd been magnificent. Every time his deft hands had kneaded her breasts or his mouth had teased her private places, she'd thought he was driving her mad. And at the end, with his body around and over and inside her, all thunder and storm and wild male heat . . .

She sighed. Charity was right. Being bedded was wonderful, especially when the man doing it had the looks of Adonis, the grace of a tiger, and the touch of a sorcerer.

And speaking of Colin, where was he? She sat up to look about her. Her clothes lay scattered on the floor, but his were gone. Then she spotted something on top of her bureau that glittered in the sunlight. She slid from the bed, donned her smock, then wandered over to find the ring Colin had tried to give her lying there, its diamonds and rubies winking like a dozen small lights.

Pinned beneath it was a note. *Gone to fetch us breakfast. I'll return soon.*

With a catch in her throat, she picked up the heavily jeweled band. There was no going back now, was there? Colin had bedded her. He would expect things to change between them.

Perhaps that was good. An alliance with Colin could give her much, and not just money, either. She'd no longer have to fight off the gallants. She'd have an ally in her search for her father.

She'd have to give up her plan for vengeance.

A groan escaped her. Her plan required that she make a spectacle of herself by confronting her father publicly, and that would surely cause Colin pain. How could she do that to him? He'd already been generous and kind to her even when she'd been cruel to him. If it hadn't been for his help yesterday . . .

She shuddered. Still, he wanted something in exchange—her heart, her trust, her very soul. And her loyalty. He wanted her to be his mistress. But if she did, she'd be no better than the other actresses who sold their favors to a protector. Worse yet, she'd give up her independence and any prospects for the future.

Only in London. She could still go to the country, still do as Charity said and play a widow. Find a husband. Begin a new life.

She sighed. And once more she'd be playing a role. She was so very tired of playing roles.

Yet she couldn't say she regretted last night. And the idea of being Colin's mistress intoxicated her. He at least seemed to see through to the real her. She could easily imagine being a different sort of companion to him than her mother had been to her stepfather—a woman who shared her lover's life totally, who feared him not.

She bit back a sob. Nay, she didn't simply want to be Colin's lover. She wanted to be his wife, the one to whom he confided his dreams, his hopes, his cares. And what chance was there of that? Even a gentleman born on the wrong side of the blanket didn't offer marriage to an actress of dubious origins when he had a title. She mustn't harbor dreams of more.

Besides, she reminded herself sternly, could she truly want to be his wife when he still held so many secrets from her? Or was this simply the silly dreaming of a woman who'd been bedded for the first time?

After all, nothing had changed since last night except her virginal state. Colin was no more to be trusted than before, even if he had agreed to help her find her father. That thought made her glance at her bedside table in alarm, but the signet ring still sat there from the night before. Thank heaven.

Still, she didn't know how closely entangled Colin might be with the Maynards, nor why he kept mentioning the surname to her, like a hunter laying bait, nor why he seemed so inquisitive about her past. Why did he keep pressing her about the Silver Swan? Why would he care unless he knew something about it? She didn't want to believe he'd been pretending to desire her only to get information from her, but she couldn't ignore the possibility.

Suddenly she heard the door in the other room open, and before she could prepare herself, Colin sauntered in. He stopped short when he saw her sitting beside the bureau. Did she imagine it, or was his gaze less warm than before?

He flashed her a thin smile. "I see you've awakened at last."

"Yes." A sudden shyness overwhelmed her. So much had passed between them last night, yet she felt as if he were still a stranger to her.

It didn't help that he was fully dressed and looking splendid in his noble finery. Self-consciously, she glanced down at the rumpled muslin of her smock, wishing she'd had time to dress before his return.

"I've brought some bread and cheese. Are you hungry?"

"Yes." But she didn't move from the chair by her bureau, continuing instead to toy with the ring in her hand.

He stepped closer. "I see you've found my gift. Are you contemplating returning it once more?"

At the harshness of his words, she glanced up. He stood in an attitude of defiance, legs splayed and thumbs tucked into his sash, daring her to toss his gift back to him and prove once more that she had no heart.

It tore at her. "What does it mean?"

A dry laugh escaped him. "Whatever you want it to mean."

He sounded flippant, but she could see the vulnerability in his eyes. "I'm not trying to insult you, Colin. 'Tis quite lovely. Any woman would be happy to wear it on her finger."

"But not to take the strings attached to it. Is that it?"

She winced. "I—I never intended to be any man's mistress."

With a muttered curse, he took the ring from her and placed it on the ring finger of her right hand. Then, closing his hand around hers, he placed a cool kiss on her forehead. "'Tis a gift, Annabelle, that's all. A sign of my . . . my affection, if you will. Perhaps it will remind you of me while I'm gone."

Her head shot up. "Gone?"

He glanced away. "Aye. I've been called to my estate in Kent. It seems there's some trouble with the steward that needs my management. I leave today."

She noticed that he didn't mention having her accompany him. Then again, why should he? She had her work at the theater, and it wasn't as if he'd made any promises to her.

That thought sent her emotions churning once more. "When . . . will you return?" she choked out.

His expression softening, he cupped her cheek. "I can't say, but I won't be gone long, I suspect."

Though her pulse quickened at his feathery caress, she forced herself to remain detached, unconcerned, as if he'd just told her he'd be going out for a midnight jaunt. "It shall be dull here without you."

"It will be more dull for me in Kent, I assure you." His voice sounded strained as he stroked his thumb over her cheekbone.

Abruptly, he dropped his hand. "I've taken steps to see that you're protected while I'm gone."

She blinked. "From whom?"

"His Majesty, of course. I've arranged for you to stay with an old friend. The king will stay clear of you as long as you are at her lodgings."

"'Her'?"

"Aphra Behn. She's a widow who did some spying for the king in Antwerp." A wry smile twisted his lips. "Unfortunately, the king had no monies to pay her, so she had to borrow some to return to England. Since then she's been petitioning the king for what he owes her, but Charles, of course, can't spare her a pound."

He laughed bitterly. "It has made for a very uncomfortable situation between them. The king won't go near you as long as you appear to be Mrs. Behn's intimate friend and houseguest. He'll fear that if he beds you, you'll pressure him to pay Mrs. Behn. So you'll be quite safe with her."

She wanted to ask him so many more questions, but any of them would make her sound jealous, and her pride wouldn't allow him to see that. "I'd rather stay here. Isn't there another way to make His Majesty lose interest in me?"

His dark gaze unnerved her. "Not unless you leave the theater entirely and go into hiding. I didn't think you'd want to do that. Of course, if you'd rather, I could send you to my town house—"

"No," she put in quickly, though she was confused. Why would he send her to his town house, but not take her with him to Kent?

Well, he was right to go without her. She couldn't go with him and leave the theater. She mustn't lose her place in the duke's company, not with her vengeance still unaccomplished and her future uncertain.

His tone softened. "You'll like the young and carefree Mrs. Behn, I assure you. She's a witty, outspoken woman who will take your mind off your troubles."

Young and witty, exactly the sort of woman Colin was attracted to. Was Annabelle to spend the next few days or weeks with a former mistress of Colin's, one he'd now relegated to the status of "friend"?

Don't do this to yourself. You're behaving like a jealous wife. You don't know anything about this woman.

Besides, no matter what this Mrs. Behn had once been to Colin, Annabelle had willingly entered his world of rakes and free living. Now she must accustom herself to its rules, distasteful though they might be.

"I suppose this means I must delay my search for my father."

"For a short time," he said blandly. "Don't worry, we'll find your father. I promise you that."

He sounded so sure. She stared at him a long moment, wondering what devious plans he was concocting in his head.

Then she sighed and dropped her gaze. "When do I meet Mrs. Behn?"

She hadn't realized he was so tense until her words made him visibly relax. He held out his hand to her. "After you've eaten and you're dressed and ready. Charity should be here any moment, for I sent word to Sir John's. I must go make arrangements for my trip, but I'll return to accompany you to Mrs. Behn's."

Taking his hand, she stood. She winced as her headache attacked once more, forcing her to sway unsteadily.

"Are you all right?" he asked, placing a hand under her elbow to steady her.

No, I'm not all right, she wanted to scream. *You've turned all my plans topsy-turvy and I don't know how to right them.*

But she merely nodded. "I have a headache, but it will pass, I'm sure. That medicine you gave me last night has apparently had its own effects."

Guilt shone briefly in his face. "Are you well enough to go to Mrs. Behn's today? I suppose I could delay my trip."

"I'm fine," she said firmly. She needed him to leave, to give her the chance to think. When he was around, she couldn't make a single logical decision without being influenced by him.

"You don't look fine." His voice had an edge to it. "Sometimes I think you're not being completely honest with me."

Her gaze locked with his. How was it that he always peeled back the layers of her many roles to penetrate beneath the costumes and the pretense into her very soul? For a second, she wanted to spill out the entire sordid tale, to tell him of her mother's hanging and of her quest for revenge.

Then she reminded herself that he hadn't told her everything either. There were secrets he kept from her still—she felt certain of it. What's more, at the moment, he had the upper hand. He knew the Maynards of London. She did not. If she told him everything, then she might as well give up her vengeance. And she simply wasn't ready to do that.

"I'm as honest with you as you are with me."

His eyes widened. Then a cynical smile curved his lips. "That you are, Annabelle."

He dropped his hand from her elbow with an abruptness that sent worry stealing up around her heart like vines choking a tree. She should never have hinted that she'd been less than honest with him. Then again, she hadn't expected him to be so remote and brusque after last night's kisses and caresses. It made her want to rouse *some* emotion in him, even if it was anger.

"I'll leave you to pack your belongings." His spare, indifferent words continued to dash her expectations. "Try not to take more than you need. Mrs. Behn's lodgings aren't large." With that, he strode toward the door.

"Colin?" she called out, wanting something more from him, some soft word or act that would show her how he felt after last night.

He faced her. "Yes?"

There was no softness in the chiseled planes of his face. He didn't even seem like the same man who'd made love to her with a sweet tenderness and passionate hunger bordering on obsession, the same man who'd made her promise there'd be no other gallants in her life.

"Nothing," she said tightly. "I'll be ready when you return."

He hesitated, his eyes searching her face. Then he nodded curtly and walked out, leaving her wondering how she'd ever soothe her bruised heart.

ANNABELLE KEPT SILENT and tried to hide her increasing nervousness as Colin's carriage inched along crowded, stinking Grub Street. Colin sat across from her, staring out at the jostling crowds, and she watched him with a growing despair in her heart. She wished Charity were there to break the tension, but they'd agreed that Charity should remain at Annabelle's lodgings while Annabelle was temporarily ensconced at Aphra Behn's house.

The carriage jerked to a stop before a ramshackle lodging house. Annabelle glanced out but couldn't believe her eyes. His friend actually lived in Grub Street? She'd assumed the woman was some nobleman's widow who spent her time hopping from one wit's bed to another now that her husband's money had made her independent. But no nobleman would leave his wife to live in such a disreputable place.

Annabelle cast a quizzical glance at Colin, but he was already climbing out of the carriage and shouting commands to the coachman. Then he handed her out of the carriage and brought her inside and up the stairs.

When Mrs. Behn herself greeted them at the door, she met Annabelle's expectations in one respect. She was in her late twenties and quite pretty. Though she was olive-skinned and had a rather longish face, masses of dark reddish curls fell over her shoulders and she had a pouting, heart-shaped mouth that would tempt most men. Nonetheless, the effect was somewhat ruined by the dust smeared across one cheek, over her pert nose, and along her wide forehead.

"Come in, come in," she said, swiping her hair back with one dirty hand and putting a fresh smear across the other cheek. Then she sneezed. "I'm sorry, Hampden. There's dust everywhere. I've been putting the place to rights since you came by this morning, but I'm not much of a housekeeper."

She flashed Annabelle an apologetic glance. "Can't afford a servant, you see, so I do it all myself, and I truly detest cleaning."

Still uncertain if she even wanted to be here, Annabelle didn't know how to respond. Yet breeding and a natural tendency toward courtesy made her say, "You shouldn't have gone to any trouble."

"Nonsense." Mrs. Behn ushered them into what was apparently her drawing room and motioned to the coachman to start bringing in Annabelle's luggage. "If you're letting a room from me, it ought to be clean, don't you think?"

Annabelle's startled gaze flew to Colin, but he was already reaching into his vest and withdrawing a small purse. "This should cover Annabelle's expenses while I'm gone," he murmured, pressing the purse into Mrs. Behn's hand. "You know where to reach me should you need more."

"Colin," Annabelle began, "I'm perfectly capable of paying for—"

"No," he said quickly. "'Twas my idea to move you from your own lodgings, and the cost is a trifle. Don't worry yourself over it."

Looking amused, Mrs. Behn tucked the purse into a pocket of her apron, then winked at Annabelle. "It might be a trifle to you, Hampden, but for women of the world like your friend and me it's bread and wine for some time to come."

Annabelle wasn't certain what Mrs. Behn meant by "women of the world like your friend and me." Surely Colin hadn't brought her to the house of a . . . a vizard-mask, had he?

Quickly, she surveyed her surroundings. What she saw reassured her. Not that she knew what the drawing room of that sort of woman would look like. Yet surely it would be more flamboyant and extravagant than this woefully cramped room filled with worn furniture and fraying rugs. Surely a vizard-mask wouldn't have piles of paper and pots of ink scattered about.

Noting Annabelle's curious stare, Colin said, "In addition to being a spy and an adventuress, Mrs. Behn fancies herself a writer. She means to write for the stage."

"Yes," Mrs. Behn put in bitterly, "if I can ever give off writing petitions to His Majesty and letters to all of my friends from here to the Continent requesting help in getting my due from him. I swear,

I've one foot in the debtors' prison, thanks to the king and his tight purse, and no one gives a damn."

Colin raised an eyebrow.

Mrs. Behn laughed. "Except for you, of course, Hampden. You're a dear for thinking of me when searching for a place for your friend. I know this is your roundabout way of giving me charity, since I wouldn't take your money outright."

"Not at all," he insisted. "You'll provide the perfect haven for Annabelle."

"I do hope so. I can use an actress's advice." She smiled at Annabelle.

At least the mystery of why the widow had such poor quarters was solved. Still, Annabelle burned to know the woman's relationship with Colin.

Colin's gaze rested on Mrs. Behn with friendly warmth, which didn't reassure Annabelle much. "As long as you keep His Majesty from her, I'm sure she'll be happy to help you." He turned to Annabelle. "Aye, dearling?"

It was the first time since last night that he'd used the endearment, and Annabelle noted that Mrs. Behn seemed intrigued rather than perturbed by it. That cheered her. "Aye," she said softly. "I'll be glad to tell you whatever I can, such as it is."

"Good, good," Mrs. Behn stated, "but don't worry. I'll not make you work for your keep. Besides, you'll be safe as a clam in a shell here. His Majesty avoids me these days." Her confident expression faltered. "Unfortunately."

"Well, then," Colin said brightly. "It sounds as if Annabelle will be safe here, so I'd best be on my way."

Mrs. Behn glanced from him to Annabelle, eyes narrowing. "I'll go tidy up the kitchen while you say your goodbyes." In a flurry of skirts, she bustled out. They could hear her sneezing as she entered the next room.

Colin laughed. "I somehow knew Mrs. Behn would be terrible at a mundane task like cleaning. She's much too absorbed with lofty ideas and schemes to bother. I hope you don't mind."

"No, it's fine."

At the quiet evenness of her tone, he turned to stare at her. "I know you don't like being thrust on a stranger like this, but I couldn't think of anything else. Believe me, I would have preferred that the king had never noticed you." His jaw tightened. "Unfortunately, no man with eyes in his head could have managed that, and certainly not Old Rowley."

The resentment behind his words, when coupled with his strangely remote behavior, made something snap within her. "Yes, and we know how I led him on by treading the boards before God and everyone. I ought to have realized that a woman has no right to put herself forward in public, even if she is simply trying to earn a living. How foolish of me to expect to be treated with the same dignity accorded male performers instead of like . . . like . . . any common whore."

With a curse, he clasped her elbow. "Surely you knew when you chose to be so conspicuously scandalous what would be expected of you. Yes, the world is unfair to women and always has been. Did you think the rules would change simply because you wanted them to? What did you expect?"

"I didn't expect you to treat me like a whore, too." She instantly wished she could unsay the words that showed how much his behavior bothered her.

"For the love of God, Annabelle, what are you talking about?"

She tried to pull away, but he snaked a hand around her waist to hold her tightly against him.

"I was told to expect this of men," she said shakily, ashamed at herself for being so emotional in front of him when he was already itching to leave. "Once they bed you, they want nothing more to do with you. They toss you aside and trot off to attend to their business affairs. I've seen it happen with countless actresses, but I thought—"

"Forget the other actresses," he ground out. "Forget every damnable lie you've ever been told about men. This is me, Annabelle, and I'm not tossing you aside. If you think that one night of bliss could purge you from my blood, then you're a bigger fool than I gave you credit for."

She kept staring at the buttons of his coat, her heart hammering in her chest.

"Hell and furies, look at me," he commanded,

and when she did he added, "You want the truth?" His face was all harsh angles and mysterious shadows. "The thought of leaving you here with so little protection terrifies me. I feel I hold you by the most tenuous thread, which will snap the second I leave."

"Do you trust me so little?"

His dark gaze lingered over her face. "Promise me one thing."

"What?"

"To wear my ring until I return. As a sign of your . . . affection for me. The other gallants won't bother you if they know you wear my ring. Promise me."

How could she deny him, when he stared at her with such uncertainty, such pain in his eyes? "I promise."

He released a great breath. "'Sdeath, I wish I didn't have to go, but I must. It's more important than you could possibly imagine."

How odd that he spoke with such earnestness of attending to his estate. She'd barely even heard him mention it before. Perhaps more was amiss than he was letting on.

"I'm only sorry you feel abandoned," he continued.

"I'm merely being silly. Don't mind me," she said in a whisper, fearing that her emotional outburst would drive him away even more.

"How can I not? Even when you're not near, the pain behind your eyes haunts my dreams until

I can't think without thinking of you. The orange scent of you fills my nostrils until I can't breathe without breathing you."

Her pulse beat madly from his thrilling words. He pressed a kiss to her forehead. Then his lips trailed soft kisses along her temple to her ear, and he drew her against him so closely she could feel his arousal.

"Since last night," he said huskily, "when I discovered how soft you are, how wild and sweet under my caresses, I'm even more obsessed." He spoke the words as if they were forced from him. "So how can I not care what you feel? It's all I think about. The trouble is, you won't tell me what you're feeling. I know you keep secrets from me, but I don't know why."

His lips against her hair were firing her blood as they had the night before. "I—I keep no secrets from you," she forced herself to say, although baring her soul to him sounded tempting at the moment.

He went still. He held her against him, not moving, not speaking, his breath coming in sharp gasps.

Then he released her with a tight-lipped expression. "Come now, I know you too well for that. I can tell by the way you shy from me still that you hold a great many dark secrets behind your bright smiles."

She couldn't deny it again. So she said nothing, though her heart slammed in her chest.

He stood there, his eyes boring into her, probing for the truths he seemed to know she hid. Then he muttered a low curse. "My mysterious swan, always hiding. I pray that your secrets are worth lying for. Because I may not be able to control my temper if I discover they are not."

With that dire pronouncement, he whirled on his heels and left.

Chapter Thirteen

"O heaven, were man
But constant, he would be perfect."
—William Shakespeare, *The Two Gentlemen of Verona*,
Act 5, Sc. 4

Five days after Annabelle moved into Aphra Behn's lodgings, Charity came over to help her prepare her lines. That evening the duke's players were to perform at Whitehall for the king, and Annabelle was very nervous about it. This would be her first chance to see how well her alliance with Aphra kept His Majesty at bay.

Charity gestured broadly as she read a line, and in the process knocked over a stack of heavy tomes. "Odsfish, don't this woman have a cartload of books!"

"Aphra does enjoy reading," Annabelle said as she studied her part. Aphra had gone out an hour ago to deliver another petition to the palace and was to return any moment.

"So what's she like?"

"Very clever," Annabelle said without glancing

up. "She's probably read more books than I've ever dreamed of. She's bold, adventurous, and willing to unravel any conundrum. I like her."

"John says she's wild, likes to swagger and talk of love like a rake."

With a smile, Annabelle thought of Aphra poring over her journal in the evening. "She hasn't swaggered around me. She does talk rather freely about love, although I wouldn't call her wild."

Annabelle glanced up at Charity. "Actually, she's a lot like you. She's been married and widowed, and as a result is rather cynical about courtship. She says she'd rather take a lover of her own choice than marry some old bastard simply because he has money."

"She sounds wild to *me*," Charity said with a sniff.

Grinning at Charity's apparent resentment of Aphra, Annabelle pointed out, "You took a lover of your own choice rather than marry."

"Aye, and I begin to see the folly of that," Charity muttered.

Annabelle put down her script. "Why? Is Sir John mistreating you?"

"He's been talking about setting me up in a cottage in the country." Her voice hardened. "You know, where others won't know about me. When I threaten to leave him if he closets me out away from my friends, he talks about wanting me to have his children."

"It sounds as if he's becoming quite serious about you."

"Not exactly," she grumbled. At Annabelle's questioning glance, she sighed. "John has a fiancée. So he can't be too serious, can he, when he's preparing to marry a viscount's daughter come autumn? Her family wants his money, and he wants their connections. 'Tis the same old story."

Although Charity pretended to be a worldly woman who understood such things, Annabelle could see she was hurting. "I'm sorry, Charity. I didn't know."

Charity scowled. "Nor did I at first, and when I found out, I couldn't very well get angry with him after telling him I didn't want an attachment. I tell you, Mrs. Behn may talk about taking lovers, but 'tisn't all that grand. Being free means you leave *him* free, too. And with a man, a little freedom goes a long way."

Annabelle touched Colin's ring. Might he also have a fiancée hidden away? He'd already made it clear she wasn't to be part of his life at his estate. In how many other respects was she to be kept apart, so she wouldn't embarrass him? Or would he be one of those rakes who enjoyed flaunting their mistresses and public opinion be damned?

Neither possibility appealed to her. Dear heaven, how she wished Colin were here to kiss away her doubts. If she could feel more sure of him, it wouldn't pain her so much to think of a future as his mistress.

Though she'd had time to realize there would be advantages to being his mistress. She'd have him to talk to over supper after a play . . . then to share a bed with in the evenings. A blush stained her cheeks. Ah yes, she could grow to enjoy waking up every day in the arms of the man she loved.

She groaned. The man she loved. Oh no, she could *not* love Colin. She mustn't! He didn't love her, so she had to protect her heart.

But how could she when he'd already slipped beneath her defenses with his kindness and fervent words? It was too late. She already loved him. She'd loved him almost since the day he caught her alone in the tiring-room.

Determinedly, she thrust that memory from her mind. She mustn't let him change her into a pining, heartsick woman like those wives of philanderers she saw at the theater, trying to make their husbands jealous and carrying out petty vengeances on their husbands' mistresses.

Then the sound of footsteps on the stairs made both her and Charity look up. Aphra was home.

"Good day," Aphra said as she entered, though she avoided Annabelle's gaze to focus on Charity. "'Tis good that you're here with Annabelle. She can use the company."

Annabelle wondered at that peculiar statement. "How are things at Whitehall? Did you deliver your petition without any trouble?"

Picking up the books Charity had knocked over,

Aphra began to restack them. "Oh yes. It went well, though I hate dealing with that scurrilous Master of Requests. He assured me His Majesty would attend to the petition soon. Which means, of course, that I'll be fortunate if the king even reads it in the next month."

From what the widow had said, this was no different than before. So why was Aphra so perturbed? When the woman began flitting about, straightening rugs, kicking crumbs under the table, and clearing away dishes, Annabelle frowned. "Did you hear any interesting gossip at Whitehall?"

Aphra got very nervous. "Er, no, not a word."

In the past five days, Annabelle had come to know the woman well. They agreed on many issues, particularly the need for women to have better chances for education and independence. In her limited experience, Aphra was always outspoken. *Never* evasive.

"What is it?" Annabelle prodded. "Did you hear something about me at Whitehall? Has His Majesty found out about the ruse Colin and I used to trick him? You and I can deal with that. We'll send word to Colin at Kent and—"

"He's not *in* Kent," Aphra blurted out. Then she grimaced. "Oh, pish, I shouldn't have told you. But you'd have been damned angry at me if you'd learned the truth and I hadn't said a word."

Annabelle's heart sank. "What do you mean? He said—"

"He lied." Aphra's pitying look gave credence to her words.

"Why?" Annabelle whispered.

"I don't know." Aphra sighed. "I found out by accident when I overheard Rochester and Sir Charles discussing him. Sir Charles headed out of town on the same day Hampden left, and they ran into each other at an inn, so they shared lunch. When they parted, Hampden went north. Not south to Kent."

Annabelle's throat felt raw. "Perhaps he meant to . . . to . . ." To what?

"Sir Charles told Rochester that Hampden wouldn't reveal where he was heading." The lines of pity on Aphra's face deepened. "But Sir Charles did say that Hampden asked him not to mention their meeting to you."

Annabelle choked back hot tears. Sweet Mary, and she'd been thinking how madly she loved him! This was what she got for falling into such a trap.

Devil take the deceitful man! How could he have lied to her? How could he have gone off to pursue some secret business after having just bedded her? "I should have known he wasn't telling the truth. He was so closemouthed about it."

Charity jumped up. "You stop this now, dear heart! Lord Hampden's a good man. I know he wouldn't lie to you." Her eyes filling with malice, she turned on Aphra. "Why are you telling her such nonsense? Are you smitten with Lord Hampden? My mistress has his affections, so you think to destroy her trust in him with your lies?"

Aphra's startled gaze swung to Annabelle. "Is this what you believe? Because I assure you Hampden and I have never been more than friends. I had no idea that you might assume—"

"I don't." Annabelle cast her maid a quelling glance. "Charity, I'm afraid, sees Colin as the solution to all my problems, and she fears my losing him." Annabelle's voice sharpened. "She's also been swayed by his money, I suspect."

Not to mention that the maid resented the way Aphra had become her mistress's confidante. Clearly Charity didn't like Annabelle taking another woman's advice.

Charity dropped into a chair with a sniff. "I see my opinions aren't wanted by such fine ladies as yerselves. My ideas are too coarse, I suppose."

Exchanging a glance with Aphra, Annabelle said soothingly, "Come now, Charity, you know I value your opinions. But I also know Aphra speaks the truth. Colin lied to me about where he was going, which means something is amiss." She added meaningfully, "You know what I'm talking about."

Charity's gaze jerked up to hers, and Annabelle shot her a cautioning glance. Annabelle had *not* told Aphra her purpose in coming to London. Only Charity understood what Colin's deception could mean.

Especially if he was headed north. Norwood was to the north.

Alarm coursed through her. Could Colin be going to Norwood to find out her secrets? Sweet Mary, if he was . . .

No, he couldn't be. She'd never told him she was from there; she'd merely told him her county, and he couldn't exactly travel the whole shire searching for someone who knew her. He didn't even know her real surname.

So why had he lied? Was he like Sir John, harboring a fiancée in the country? Or perhaps even a wife? The very thought sickened her. "Colin's not married, is he?"

"Pish, of course not," Aphra said. Then realizing how that sounded, she added, "I mean . . . well, not that he wouldn't, but he's always said—"

"It's all right," Annabelle bit out. "Rakes generally avoid marriage."

"Not all of them," Charity said bitterly. "Sir John's only too happy to leap into the marriage bed. With someone else, that is."

"Sir John?" Aphra asked.

"Charity's lover," Annabelle explained. "She found out that he's got a fiancée."

"Of course that don't mean he don't want me," Charity said defensively. "He wants to keep me."

"Aye," Annabelle snapped, "he wants to keep you in the country, so you and his fiancée won't bother each other."

Aphra shook her head. "I'm in love with a man who's courting a younger woman while claiming to love me to distraction. These treacherous, strutting cocks haven't an inkling of the precious fragility of love. They bid us be wantons with them alone, yet see no reason to stay faithful themselves."

A bitter sigh escaped Annabelle. Colin had made her promise to be faithful to him, but he hadn't offered her the same promise.

"I say it's time we declare war on our two-faced gallants." Climbing atop a stool, Aphra posed like an orator in Parliament. "I ask you, ladies, why should we sit at home while our men take freedoms they won't allow *us*? We of the soft, unhappy sex must fight this unequal division of love, this dishonest inconstancy!"

Charity cast Annabelle a quizzical glance. Annabelle merely shook her head. Aphra was prone to grand pronouncements, undoubtedly because of her aspirations to be a playwright.

"How do you propose we fight this battle?" Annabelle asked. "We have no rights, no money, no weapons. All of the advantages are on their side."

"Not all." With a toss of her hair, Aphra struck a seductive pose. "We have our beauty and wit. If we flaunt those before their friends while denying our favors to our lovers, it will remind them that we do have choices. These men are possessive creatures; they won't long endure being put in second place."

"You're saying to make them jealous, aye?" Charity snapped. "We do that, and they'll find other women who won't be so demanding."

"Perhaps." Aphra looked fierce. "But if our lovers treasure us only for our bodies and docile natures, then we should find other, better lovers. We must make them appreciate our wit, our kindness, our loyalty. We must remind them that we, too, can find our pleasures elsewhere. They count on our sense of modesty and honor to keep us from being as wild as they, so we must set aside those shackles!"

"And pretend to wildness to keep our men?" Annabelle snapped. "Must we feign promiscuous desires to keep them company in theirs? Nay, I will not!"

She began to pace the room. She hadn't enjoyed pretending promiscuity to gain her vengeance. Why should she do it again to taunt Colin?

Because he'd lied to her. Because he'd made her no promises.

"Our men feign constancy," Aphra said softly. "Perhaps if we feign inconstancy, we can show them how wounding it can be."

Tears stung Annabelle's eyes. Aphra thought men could be taught to care about women's wants and needs, but Annabelle knew better. Men like Ogden Taylor and Annabelle's father would always believe that women were chattel.

Still, she'd thought Colin was different, better somehow than the other rakes. For heaven's sake, she'd even thought she could marry him!

"You know," Aphra said, "if Hampden came

back to find you merrily flirting with the gallants
and behaving as if you hadn't noticed he'd even
gone, he'd not be so quick to deceive you next time.
His pride would be pricked."

True, and she sorely wanted to prick his pride
after the way he'd left her so easily. Still, what if
he had some innocuous reason for lying to her?
Or what if Aphra had misunderstood Sir Charles's
comments?

"I for one think it's a sound notion," Charity
surprised her by saying. "Sir John thinks he can
hold me by the strength of his passions—and his
money—without engaging his heart. I say, fie on
that! If I'd wanted a married lover, I'd have taken
one." She steadied her shoulders. "From now on,
I'll run that fickle rake a merry chase. If he wants
me, then he must relinquish his fiancée. Or I swear
I'll find another man to keep me warm."

The two women turned to Annabelle. "You
have pride, don't you?" Aphra chided. "I'll admit
I'd never thought Hampden would use a woman so
ill, but since he has, will you let him return to find
you pining away while he blithely attends to some
secret purpose?"

Annabelle thought of Sir Charles and the smug
smile he and Rochester would wear when she came
to the theater. *They* probably already assumed Colin
went to meet another lover. They'd smile like minis-
ters carrying the king's secrets, mocking her for her
faithfulness to him.

That decided her. She wouldn't let Colin make a fool of her. She'd hide her pain and tear out the love he'd planted in her breast.

Her vengeance already required that she play the role of wanton, so she'd play it to the hilt. Let him wonder that she still flirted with all the gallants. Let him wonder about her broken promises. When he made the same promises to her, then she'd honor her own, and not before.

Removing Colin's ring, she tucked it into her apron pocket. She'd not wear it again until he proved that it stood for more than the fee paid to a strumpet.

"All right, then, ladies, let's be merry," she said with a forced smile. "Let's show our fickle lovers what brilliant women they've tossed aside."

MORE THAN A week had passed when Annabelle was waylaid outside the tiring-room after the play one evening by a towering oaf. When he requested that she meet his master and she refused, he simply strong-armed her from the stage and dragged her, protesting loudly, down the passageway and up some stairs.

"Listen, you cur," she growled, "if you don't unhand me or tell me what this is all about, I will have you thrown out of—"

She was rudely shoved into a box at the back of the theater. She stood there a moment, disoriented, then searched about her for her captor. Whoever it was sat in the shadows, barely discernible by the light of candles from the passageway. That in itself sent a chill down her spine.

"Who's there?" she demanded. "I swear, you men think you can manhandle any woman you please without a whit of concern for her dignity."

The man gave a short, cruel laugh. "Yes, so dignified you are there onstage as you contort your body into lewd positions to tease those fools in the pit."

Her breath froze in her throat. She peered into the darkness. "Who are you to care what I do on the stage?"

"Let's just say I'm a friend, concerned about your behavior."

She doubted that very much. "If you're a friend, then why hide in the dark? What do you fear from me?"

"I fear nothing from you!" he barked, half rising from his chair. When she flinched, he seemed to note it and sat back down with the help of the cane she now saw. "But you should fear me."

Her blood ran cold. "Oh?" she asked, trying not to show that she already feared him. After all, few had servants willing to manhandle women at their command. "Because you're rude and distasteful?"

"Because you meddle in matters you don't understand. 'The Silver Swan' isn't a name to use lightly."

Dear heaven. Her father? Could this gravel-voiced stranger be her *father*? Who else would be interested in her use of the appellation? "I can't help what the gallants call me."

"Nor can you help wearing that silver swan brooch or showing a preference for silver, can you?"

He lifted his cane to tap her brooch, and she shrunk from him instinctively. Her stepfather had beaten her once or twice with a cane.

The stranger reacted oddly, muttering a coarse oath and dropping the cane at her feet. It was as unnerving as his use of it in the first place.

She forced herself to continue her questioning of him. "What do you care if I am called the Silver Swan?"

"That's none of your concern, girl. Just stop doing it."

"Was it *your* nickname, then?" she prodded.

"Because I come when I hear it? Nay, not mine. But it's too dangerous a name to be used by wanton girls without a thought in their heads."

If it wasn't *his* name, then why was he here? Was he a friend of her father's?

"You seem to know so much about my character," she said with heavy sarcasm. "Have you been spying on me, sir?"

The word *spying* made him sit up straight. "Why do you have them call you the Silver Swan? Tell me that, and I'll spy on you no more."

She stiffened. "That's for me to discuss with the

bearer of the name. If you are not he, then I have nothing further to say." She started to leave.

"And if I were to tell you that he sent me on his behalf?"

She halted, then faced him. "I would say he should come himself if he wants the truth."

"Damn you, girl! What game are you playing?"

"No game. I told you, it's a nickname, nothing more."

That seemed to provoke him beyond endurance, for he rose to loom in the darkness like a waking nightmare. "You're a brazen, selfish bitch with not a virtue to commend you, do you know that?"

Though every word seared her, she stood her ground. "And you, sir, are a rude arse. Now that we've both called each other nasty names, may I go?"

"Aye," he said sharply. "But I'll be watching you, girl, remember that. If you decide to explain yourself, leave a message for the Silver Swan at the Green Goat Tavern. I'll see that he gets it." He lowered his voice to a menacing whisper. "But if you continue this foolish charade, you'll learn that I can be a treacherous enemy. So I'd watch my step if I were you."

He had the audacity to *threaten* her? She glared at him. "And you, sir, can go straight to hell!"

With that, she left. But as soon as she could find an empty box where she could be alone, she slid inside and dropped into a chair. She was going to be sick. She fought her heaving stomach, grateful that she'd been able to find a place where no one would see her.

That . . . that wretched bastard! Could that horrible man actually be her father? Sweet Mary, she hoped not. She hoped he was as he said, a friend to her father.

But more and more she'd begun to realize how foolhardy she'd been to embark on this insane quest for revenge. She'd thought to cause her absent father pain while remaining immune, to shame and humiliate him while he stood quietly by, enduring his punishment until he admitted that he'd wronged Mother.

She hadn't counted on the possibility that he might fight back. That he might even try to harm her.

"What a naive little fool you are," she hissed. She'd held some sentimental notion that he would regret his actions. But if he was the man she'd met tonight, he wasn't a man to regret anything. He was an unfeeling beast.

And if the man in the box was *not* her father? Could he indeed have found someone to spy on her? She supposed it was possible.

At least that probably meant that Colin wasn't spying on her, for why would her father need *two* spies? Despite her anger at Colin's deception, it gave her hope to think that Colin might not be in league with her father.

So what was she to do about the man who *was*? Obviously her nickname had upset him. But why? The stranger had implied that it had a deeper, more sinister significance. That had never occurred to her.

What could it be? She thought once more of the peculiar poem that made little sense on the surface. What message had been hidden in those odd words? And why hadn't her father signed it with his own name?

Unless . . . unless he'd not wanted anyone to know what he was about. If the Earl of Walcester really was her father, then it made no sense for him to have been a Roundhead captain during the war, not according to the little Charity had learned about him. So perhaps he was living a lie. Perhaps he didn't want people to know he'd fought for the other side. Perhaps he'd been a spy!

It would explain the peculiar nickname. And though the man in the shadows had commented snidely about her wantonness, he had seemed far more worried about her use of "The Silver Swan."

Perhaps she could use *his fear* for her vengeance. He'd clearly been up to no good all those years ago or he wouldn't be trying to hide it now. And he'd dragged her mother into it, which was even worse.

But if you continue this foolish charade, you'll learn that I can be a treacherous enemy.

A shiver ran down her spine. Still, what could the man do to her? Her reputation was already in tatters because of her plans for revenge, and Colin had wounded her more thoroughly than her father or his accomplice ever could. What, then, was left for him to do to her?

He could kill her.

She caught her breath. Sweet Mary, surely even her father couldn't be such a miserable worm. Then again, he didn't know she was his daughter. And she knew nothing of his character; she had yet to be certain of his full name.

Besides, if anybody killed her, then none of them would learn why she was prancing about onstage with the name 'The Silver Swan.' And that would protect her.

For a while, anyway. But it was more important now than ever that she discover her father's identity. Unfortunately, she clearly would not be able to depend on Colin in the search. The scoundrel hadn't so much as sent word of his whereabouts in the two weeks since she'd last seen him.

Suddenly an alarmed voice calling her name outside the boxes intruded into her thoughts. It was Charity.

"I'm back here!" Annabelle called out. What was she to tell Charity about her frightening encounter?

The maid stuck her head inside the box seconds later. "Odsfish, you had me worried, you did! One of the orange girls said some brute had taken you off! She didn't know what to do, and she couldn't find anyone to help. What happened?"

Annabelle stood and tried to regain her composure. "A man wanted to speak with me. He claimed to come from my father, or rather, from the man calling himself the Silver Swan, so I assume it was my father."

Stepping into the box, Charity surveyed her from head to toe. "He didn't hurt you, did he?"

"Nay. He wanted to know why I used the nickname, and when I wouldn't tell him, he left."

Charity let out a coarse oath. "Do you still plan on going with the others to the supper?"

Annabelle groaned. She'd forgotten all about Aphra's supper at the Blue Bell, the ordinary where the players normally supped. Aphra had planned a ribald diversion, funding it out of the money Colin had given her for Annabelle's keeping. Annabelle could think of no better purpose for it than to spend it on a wild supper, since she'd already decided to pay Aphra out of her own meager funds.

And the supper was to be wild indeed. Aphra had persuaded all the actresses to come in male attire. The gallants who were invited were not to know about it until they arrived, but Aphra was well aware of how much the men enjoyed seeing women in breeches. She wanted her supper to be a scandalous affair, a sufficient taunt to the men in their lives. It was to have fiddlers and dancers and drinking till dawn.

Despite Annabelle's growing disenchantment with the games that represented life in the theater, she'd been looking forward to the supper. Until now.

"Well?" Charity demanded. "The others have already left and Aphra will be waiting for us."

Now that the two had joined forces against their men, Charity had lost her resentment of Aphra. If anything, they'd become closer. Meanwhile Annabelle couldn't seem to share their wicked delight in flirting with all the wits.

But tonight Annabelle wanted to lose herself in revelry. She wanted to forget that Colin had taken her virtue, then abandoned her, that her father was a cruel man capable of wishing harm to her. Most of all, she wanted to blot out of her heart the love growing like a weed, choking out her very lifeblood.

"Yes, I'm coming," she said.

By the time she stopped outside to empty her pockets for the urchins, and she and Charity had found a coach, nearly an hour had passed. So the ordinary was already filled with guests when they arrived. Aphra bustled about, giving orders to the serving girls and urging the musicians to play. The din was nearly as loud as in the theater before a performance, but no one seemed to mind.

The second Annabelle walked in, she was surrounded by gallants complimenting her on her performance. Forcing a smile to her face, she parried the verbal sallies of one and tapped another with her fan. When the third snatched her hand up to kiss it, his damp lips leaving a trail along her knuckles, it took all her control not to yank her hand away and slap him with it.

Colin had been right about one thing. As long as she'd worn his ring, she'd been safe from men's groping hands. They'd treated her with respect, and she'd liked it. For the first time, she'd been able to perform her roles without having her concentration broken by rude remarks. Offstage, she'd been left blessedly alone, and she'd reveled in the chance to put all her energy into performing, instead of being forced to deal with unwelcome advances.

But once she'd removed Colin's ring, the men flocked around her again, sniffing at her heels like staghounds in heat. Worse yet, her biting humor and ability to play a role no longer fended them off. They weren't pricked by her barbs or fooled by her role of haughty lady.

She soon figured out why. Sir Charles's tale of Colin's secretive journey had spread among them. Rumors buzzed about why she couldn't keep a man faithful to her, since she'd given her affections to two noblemen in rapid succession and both had apparently discarded her.

Now the gallants all treated her with contempt. She found herself being trapped more and more of late by men wanting a lusty kiss and more. So far she'd held them at bay, but she didn't know how long that would last.

The theater world that had once been her haven had become a treacherous bog where only by deft maneuvering and clever acting could she protect herself.

How she wished she hadn't come to the supper. She'd been mad to think these fools could give her any relief. The rakes only reminded her of how different Colin had seemed, and how very like them he'd turned out to be.

She had a headache, and she wanted only to go home. But she'd promised Aphra to perform her dance again for the gallants as part of the festivities, and she did owe the woman a great deal for coming to her aid.

So here she stood, playing yet another role and longing for the day when all the roles would end. And the day when her heart would stop aching over Colin.

Chapter Fourteen

"Why, I hold fate
Clasped in my fist, and could command the course
Of time's eternal motion, hadst thou been
One thought more steady than an ebbing sea."
—John Ford, *'Tis Pity She's a Whore*, Act 5, Sc. 4

Colin had been traveling hard by post horse since noon the previous day, determined to reach London in all due speed. Night had fallen, so it was well past time for the play at the Duke's House to be over. It would do him no good to search for Annabelle there.

Finding Annabelle was his first aim. He spared only a few minutes to send a boy ahead to his house and let his servants know he'd arrived. Then he continued at his same frenzied pace, for if he didn't see her soon and confront her with all he'd learned, he'd surely go mad.

Little had he dreamed how much she'd kept hidden. He'd still not entirely recovered from the shock of it. But at least now he knew why pain glimmered constantly in her eyes.

At least now he knew where she'd learned to be so fierce. "The girl is strong-willed," Charity's father had told Colin. "She had to be so to endure that wretched squire's mistreatment."

Grimly Colin turned his horse into Grub Street. *Strong-willed* wasn't the word for it. She was a proud, defiant tigress with a capacity for deception he'd never imagined. According to Mr. Woodfield, she'd come to London in search of vengeance against her father, yet Colin had never even guessed it.

Had she known of his relationship to Walcester from the beginning?

He doubted that. She clearly hadn't been sure who her father was. But Walcester had been right that she was trying to draw him out. The only question was how she meant to wreak her vengeance on the man once she found him. And Colin very much feared that he knew the answer.

Because he had also discovered in Norwood exactly what Walcester feared. Not that Colin knew the entire story, but he knew enough. Unable to speak with Phoebe Taylor's parents, who were dead, he'd tracked down her parents' old housekeeper. Thanks to her, Colin had unraveled a tale that had sent him racing back to London.

Walcester had been hiding a great deal, too, and if it was what Colin suspected, then the earl and his daughter were headed for a deadly confrontation. Colin refused to let it come to that.

Still, he must find out exactly how much she

knew before he could proceed. She had to know more about her father's past activities than she was saying. She had that coded poem in her possession, after all.

He wanted to hate her for not trusting him with the truth, but how could he, when he'd seen the marks on her back and heard what she'd suffered? Only the coldest man alive would condemn her for wanting her vengeance.

And where she was concerned, he was anything but cold.

With a grunt of anger, he spurred the horse on. Two weeks away had only made his thirst for her more acute, his hunger more piercing. It so fevered his brain that he was torn between desire and wanting to throttle her for deceiving him.

Why did she have this effect on him? Why did it make him feel drawn and quartered whenever he thought of how much she'd kept from him? Women had held secrets from him before, and he'd never experienced this mind-numbing pain.

Nay, only Annabelle had the power to draw blood. His pulse raced as he approached Aphra's lodgings. He couldn't believe it—his body already anticipated seeing her again. What kind of spell had she cast over him?

He tethered his horse, then leapt from the saddle, but he'd scarcely made it inside when he met Sir John on the stairs. The man surveyed his mud-spattered clothing and his knotted hair and growled, "Annabelle isn't here. Aphra's neighbor tells me she and Aphra have gone to the Blue Bell to supper."

That brought him up short. "Why are *you* looking for her?"

"I'm not. I'm looking for Charity," Sir John bit out. "I returned from the country a week ago to discover that Charity would no longer see or even speak to me. Mind you, I was in the country in the first place to find a cottage for her. To return and find her cold and distant . . . well, I'm afraid I was too angry to do more than refuse to speak to her in turn."

Colin fell into step beside him as they headed for the door.

"I guess that was childish," Sir John murmured. "It didn't achieve the desired effect either. Instead of making her regret her coolness, it apparently made her consider herself well rid of me. For the last week, she's been blithely flirting with every man who pays her attentions."

"I can hardly believe it. I'd have sworn the woman was in love with you."

Sir John stiffened. "I think she was, until she learned of my betrothal to a viscount's daughter. Despite Charity's apparent free-thinking ideas, at heart she's a country girl." His voice softened. "I suppose she expected me to—oh, damn, I don't know what she expected."

"Ah," Colin remarked.

"In any case, I've decided to convince her that this can work. By God, I miss the wench more sorely than I'd ever thought possible. She's a sweet-tempered lass. I can't just stand by and let her go."

Oddly enough, it wasn't Sir John that Colin sympathized with, but Charity. Being a bastard had made him much more sensitive to the ramifications of a man's having both a mistress and a wife. Men like Sir John couldn't possibly imagine what it was like to have a succession of "uncles," to have their mothers' married lovers treat them like bothersome gnats.

Nor could they know what it was like for the women, who had to share the men's affections. Colin knew. He'd watched his mother's way of life turn her into a cruel, brittle woman.

Colin had later been exposed to it from the other end, having been forced to face the disapproval of his father's dead wife's relatives once he'd come to England. They'd regarded him as an affront to the memory of his father's wife. He couldn't exactly blame them.

That was why Colin had been careful with his mistresses. He'd done his best not to sire children on them, nor to promise what he couldn't offer. He had sworn not to wed until he could find a suitable wife for a marquess as well as someone to whom he could remain faithful. He'd never found that woman. Until now.

Hell and furies, where had that come from? He couldn't be thinking about Annabelle, whose capacity for deception would surely destroy any man's hope of a peaceful life. Yet it was Annabelle he imagined as his hostess, sharing his days, warming his bed at night, bearing his children. . . .

'Sdeath, you truly are bewitched. He and Sir John mounted their horses and rode toward the Blue Bell. *The woman has unhinged you.*

They reached the ordinary quickly. Music and laughter spilled out into the silent evening. The moment they entered it was apparent that a party was going on, filling the room with loud conversation, wild music, and gay colors.

At first, he was disoriented, for the front room appeared to be crowded with men, though he kept hearing feminine voices. Then he realized why. Although everyone in the room wore male clothing, nearly half of them were women.

He glanced around. Except for the scandalous male attire, the supper was no different than a hundred he'd attended. In one corner he saw a rake deep in conversation with a pretty blond woman whose hand rested on his thigh with familiarity. Another buxom lady was flanked by two gallants making a game of trying to remove her mask as she tittered and slapped their hands away.

Oh yes, a typical gathering among the wits and beauties and actresses. Yet it left him with a sour taste in his mouth to think that somewhere in the rooms Annabelle was playing these teasing, erotic games.

Hearing music floating in from an adjoining room, he followed the sound. As he passed the table, Sir John at his side, he spotted Charity sitting beside Henry Harris, who was known for his wild, romantic exploits. Harris had his arm about her shoulders and she was laughing as she fed him a sweetmeat. Apparently, Sir John saw her at the same moment as Colin, for he muttered a low curse and left Colin's side.

Colin hurried into the next room alone. He didn't at first see Annabelle. He did see Aphra with her back to him, dressed like the rest of the women, her hand propped on one hip as she argued with Sir William Davenant.

Then he noticed a cluster of people at one end of the room. He pushed forward through the crowd, but stopped short when he caught sight of his quarry in the middle of the knot of revelers.

Annabelle was dancing, and not with the measured steps so common to English dances. She was whirling . . . and kicking her heels high . . . and tossing her hair with lively grace.

He could scarcely believe his eyes. What he saw was so completely at odds with the foolish vision of his arrival that he'd nursed through his entire journey. Fool that he was, he'd thought to find her meekly awaiting him at Aphra's chambers, desperately miserable at his absence and ready to tell him anything simply to have him promise to stay with her.

Yet here she was, performing for a crowd of gallants who cheered her every step. For a moment, he could only watch, astonished into silence.

Her face was flushed, lending her skin a rosy, seductive glow, and she laughed with every quick turn. What was more, she wore the costume she'd worn when he saw her dance in the play—snug-fitting breeches and very sheer hose. She'd abandoned her coat, if she'd ever worn one, and she'd unbuttoned the shepherd's smock beneath that, so all she wore over her breasts was a man's thin holland shirt, which clung to her like a second skin.

A terrible anger ate at him as he glanced to her hand to see if she wore his ring. She did not.

He stood there stunned, feeling gutted.

Then the music ended, and before Colin could react, Rochester, who appeared to be quite drunk, pulled a protesting Annabelle into the adjoining room. Sick with jealous fury, Colin followed them, ignoring the murmurs around him as the crowd realized who he was and parted to let him pass.

He didn't even acknowledge Aphra's presence when she pushed through the crowd toward him, words of greeting on her lips that died when she saw his expression. He had only one aim: to get to Annabelle and remind her of all her promises, her damnable broken promises.

He passed into the next room in time to see Rochester thrust Annabelle against a wall and force his knee between her legs as he covered her mouth with his. She struggled beneath him, but his mouth muffled her protest.

Colin grasped the hilt of his sword, so blinded by rage that he could scarcely think, but as he stepped forward, Rochester let out a hoarse cry and jumped back from Annabelle.

"You bith my tongue!" Rochester cried, wiping away the blood trickling from his mouth. "Damn wenth! You bith me!"

"Aye, and drunk or no, I'll bite your fingers off if you ever touch me like that again!"

Rochester lunged for her. That's when Colin drew his sword. The clang of metal made the earl whirl around. His bleary eyes showed his astonishment.

"You lay a hand on her," Colin growled, "and I'll do more than bite you, Rochester. I'll spit you like a joint of mutton and roast you over yon fire."

He heard Annabelle suck in her breath, but he dared not take his eyes off the wiry young man. When Rochester was drunk, he was wild and dangerous. The earl's hand went to his own sword, and Colin tensed.

Then Rochester seemed to catch himself. Slowly, he dropped his hand, although he didn't move away. The flow of blood from his mouth had slowed. He licked his lips with his tongue as if to test whether it still worked.

Although he swayed a bit, he had enough presence of mind to sneer, "So the marquess has returned from his secret trip at last." Apparently his tongue was functioning normally again.

Before Colin could even wonder how Rochester knew about his trip, the young man continued, "Come to claim your woman, have you?"

Colin's gaze flicked to Annabelle. She stared at him wide-eyed, her hand at her throat.

"You could say that," Colin ground out. "Now step aside."

"She doesn't want you anymore, you know," Rochester said, slurring his words. "She's got other men to keep her company while you're out running about."

Colin didn't even bother to answer that. "Annabelle, come here."

He couldn't tell from her expression whether she was pleased or not to see him, and for a second he even wondered if she'd actually wanted Rochester's attentions. Then she slid from behind Rochester and came to his side. Only then did Colin lower his sword.

Rochester slumped against the wall. "She's a damn fine dancer, you know." He gave an insolent grin as he spread his legs wide and thrust with his hips in a provocative movement that couldn't be misinterpreted. "I'll wager she's even better in bed."

In a flash, Colin had thrust forward between Rochester's spread thighs to catch the man's full breeches and pin them to the wall.

Rochester went white as he stared down at the

sword. "Gadsbud, you nearly unmanned me! Are you mad?"

"Nay," Colin hissed. "If I'd been mad, there'd have been no 'almost.' And if I ever see you with your hands on Annabelle again, you lecherous sot, I won't miss. Is that understood?"

Rochester straightened against the wall and his eyes grew amazingly alert. But then, nothing sobers a man faster than the possibility of having his privates skewered. "I understand," Rochester muttered.

"Good." Colin sheathed his sword. "Because I won't mind repeating the lesson if you ever forget it."

As Rochester began checking himself to make sure Colin hadn't done any damage, Colin clasped Annabelle's arm and urged her toward the door. "Time to fly, my pretty bird. You and I have a great deal to talk about."

Chapter Fifteen

"Use every man after his desert, and who should
'scape whipping?"
—William Shakespeare, *Hamlet*, Act 2, Sc. 2

Annabelle tried to match Colin's furious pace as he strode through the back room of the Blue Bell. Although his fingers laced through hers gave the appearance that they were in easy accord, there was steel in his grip.

Neither of them spoke, too aware of the audience eager for something to feed the gossip. Murmurs followed in their wake as people parted to let them pass, but she was still reeling from Rochester's disgusting advances and Colin's surprising rescue of her. Grateful as she was for the latter, she wondered if she hadn't leapt from the frying pan into the fire.

She stole a glance at Colin. His eyes held a feral gleam, and the hard edge to his mouth alarmed her. She couldn't believe how jealous he'd been of Rochester. It just went to prove that men were two-faced rogues. After disappearing for two weeks, he'd stormed in and claimed her as if she were a horse he'd left at a stable?

Sweet Mary, she was the one who ought to be furious, not him! It wasn't *her* fault that Rochester had made an arse of himself.

As they approached the entrance doors, she halted. "Where are we going?"

His eyes glittered down at her. "To my house, where I can be sure there will be no interruptions while we talk."

His house. Dear heaven. "I don't want to go anywhere with you when you're this angry."

Dropping his hand to the small of her back, he pushed her through the door. "Would you rather return to Rochester and his roving hands?"

"Nay, but I could go back to Aphra's."

"Not a chance." They'd reached a huge, mud-spattered bay tethered near the entrance, and, without warning, he lifted her into the saddle, then untethered the horse before swinging up behind her.

She might have fought him if his arm hadn't gripped her waist, holding her in the saddle. And in truth, a part of her wanted to hear what he had to say for himself, the wretch.

"You know," he growled as his mount trotted down the thoroughfare, "none of that mess with Rochester would have happened if you'd kept your promise to wear my ring."

The audacity of the man! "I might have kept my

promise if I hadn't learned what a deceitful, unfeeling rogue you are."

"What in God's name are you talking about?"

"I'm well aware you didn't go to Kent. I also know you asked Sir Charles to keep that a secret from me."

He muttered an oath under his breath. "I see Sir Charles has trouble keeping his mouth shut," he said unrepentantly.

Any hope she'd harbored that Sir Charles had misunderstood vanished. "You wretched, lying—"

"Bastard?"

"Aye! Bastard! Your dear friend Sir Charles didn't say a word to me, but he told every other wit at court, and that's all it took for it to get back to me. Of course everyone realized at once that you . . . that you . . ."

"That I what?"

"Hid your destination because you were going to meet another woman."

He tensed behind her. "The devil I did! You thought I was with another *woman*?"

His incredulous tone seemed awfully convincing, but she wasn't fool enough to believe him again. "Of course! You made me promise not to be unfaithful, but you gave no similar promise. Nor have you given me a reason to think you're any different than the other gallants."

"Haven't I?" Pressing his mouth to her ear, he

lowered his voice to a taut murmur. "Even when I protected you from the king and told you of matters no other man would have discussed with a woman? Our night together should have revealed something of how I feel about you."

She couldn't keep the hurt from her voice. "Not nearly as much as your abrupt departure the next morn and your attempt to cover up where you'd gone."

He muttered something under his breath.

Attempting to sound sophisticated, she added, "That's when I learned that men and women look at such things differently. Like Sir John, who expects Charity to share him with his fiancée. I would have thought him different, too, but I was wrong. Men care only about having their pleasures sated."

"Not all men," Colin ground out. "I am not like Sir John."

"No? Then why did you lie to me?"

His arm tightened on her waist. "Why did you break your promise? You took off my ring and went on teasing every fop and whey-faced wit who caught your fancy until you had them following you around like insolent pups . . ."

"Oh, it didn't take any effort on my part," she said bitterly. "When they learned you'd abandoned me, they were all too eager to leap into the breach."

He let out a low hiss. "I wanted to kill Rochester for touching you. You have no idea."

"I have some idea," she said, choking back tears. "Where were you these past two weeks?"

"Not with another woman, for God's sake," he growled. "I can't even handle the one I have."

Realizing she had begun to sound like a jealous shrew, she forced some nonchalance into her voice. "It doesn't matter. None of it matters in the least."

"Oh, it matters very much, dearling, as you'll realize after we talk," he murmured. "But not here in the street. We need privacy for this discussion."

She couldn't imagine why. Unless he meant to seduce her out of her temper.

Oh, Lord, she hoped that wasn't his plan. She was having enough trouble as it was ignoring his arm about her waist, his breath against her hair, and the intimate way they sat atop the horse. Her thighs rested on his corded ones, and she could feel every sinew through the thin breeches she wore.

Their last night together sprang into her mind, heating her blood and sending anticipation prickling over her skin. Sweet Mary, how could she have forgotten what it was like to be held by Colin?

Even as her anger smoldered, a lovely, erotic longing threatened to sweep away all her determination to resist his smooth words this time. It didn't help that the horse's pace slowed or that Colin began stroking her thigh.

She would just have to stay strong, have to keep reminding herself of the fact that he'd deceived her and seemed utterly unrepentant over it.

It took them only a short while to reach his house in the Strand, one of the most fashionable districts in London. When they drew up before the imposing marble columns of a three-story brick edifice with a dazzling array of mullioned windows, she felt sick at heart.

No wonder he'd lied to her. Men who lived in mansions didn't deign to worry about what a lowly actress might think of them. What a fool she'd been even to dream of being Colin's wife. Colin would never marry a woman like her.

Colin dismounted, then helped her down as a footman came running out to take the horse. The moment they entered, a whole slew of servants greeted him, clamoring for his attention after two weeks away and gaping at her.

Oh no, she was still dressed in her male garb. No doubt they were appalled. This awe-inspiring house, with its marble floor and walls covered with expensive paintings, was not the place for a scandalously dressed actress.

No matter how much she reminded herself that Colin was a bastard like her, it did no good. She knew she didn't belong here.

And why did this evidence of Colin's wealth sway her anyway? She'd known he was rich, that he had power and a title given to him by the king himself. So why was she standing here, gawking in amazement like the street urchins to whom she fed oranges?

Because he'd never behaved like the other wealthy men who'd frequented the theater. He'd never emphasized the difference between their stations. She'd known so many pompous men who wore their wealth and power on their sleeves and spoke with contempt to the actresses that she'd half expected Colin's lodgings to be modest to match the casual disregard he seemed to have for his rank.

But of course Colin lived in a mansion. *That* was why he'd brought her here, to remind her that his power and standing surpassed hers as sunlight surpasses moonlight.

Her heart sank. If that was his intent, he'd succeeded. She'd been a fool to believe that he truly cared for her. Who could hold the affections of a man who could buy anyone's affections whenever he wanted?

Then the steward said, "I do hope you had no trouble finding Norwood, my lord. It has been some time since I traveled that way, and I'm not sure my directions were adequate."

And her whole world tilted on its axis. Sweet Mary in heaven, Colin really hadn't gone to see a woman. He had gone to Norwood.

Her gaze shot to him in alarm only to find him regarding her with eyes as inscrutable as the ocean. "I had no trouble at all, Johnson, thank you."

Panic gripped her. How had he known where she was from? She'd only revealed the name of the county. Could Charity have said something? If she had, she would have told Annabelle about it once she'd heard that Colin had left town and lied about where he was going.

And why had he lied? Why had he gone in search of her past?

Oh, Lord, he knew it all now, didn't he? There was no way on God's green earth that Colin could have gone to Norwood and not discovered every dirty secret from her past. The only thing he didn't know was her purpose for coming to London, but she had no doubt he'd try to get that out of her, too.

"If you'd like a bit of supper, my lord—" the steward began.

"No, I've already eaten. Just bring some wine into my study."

"And for . . . for the young lady?"

Annabelle could tell the steward was choking on the phrase, but she no longer cared about any of Colin's numerous servants.

"Annabelle? Would you like something?" Colin asked calmly, as if he hadn't just jerked her off her feet.

"No," she whispered, "nothing." What she wanted was to disappear, and she doubted the steward could manage that.

"Very good," the steward murmured and left.

"As I told you," Colin said in a tone of pure steel, "I have not been with a woman for the past two weeks. And you and I do have a great deal to talk about."

His words and his tone of voice hardened her resolve as he led her up the stairs to the first floor. She didn't know why he'd gone to Norwood or why he was so obviously angry over what he'd learned, but she meant to find out.

As soon as they'd entered a large room lined with bookshelves, Colin faced her, his expression dangerously dark. "Why didn't you tell me your mother had been hanged for killing your stepfather?"

"It's not the sort of thing a person wants widely known," she attempted to say offhandedly.

That only seemed to infuriate him. "Some in Norwood claim you had a part in the murder."

Shock gripped her. "I did *not*! Surely you can't believe that I would—"

"Nay." His expression softened. "I didn't believe it. Fortunately, I found someone who'd seen everything and confirmed me in that. Of course, it would have all been clearer if you'd told me yourself."

A knock sounded at the door, and Colin barked a curt command. A footman entered bearing a tray with a flagon of wine. Colin moved away to stand by the newly laid fire roaring in the grate.

With her emotions in turmoil, Annabelle waited impatiently for the servant to leave. As the footman headed for the door, Colin said, "See to it that we aren't disturbed."

"Aye, my lord."

As Annabelle watched the door shut behind

the footman, she drew together the fractured bits of her courage. "How did you know to go to Norwood?"

He didn't answer at first. Still staring into the fire, he rested his hand on the mantelpiece. The flames limned his golden hair with fiery lights that made him look like a tigerish devil, ready to tear into her with his claws. The fire stripped away the patina of civilization he normally wore and reminded her Colin could be almost savage when his temper was roused.

"*Why* did you go to Norwood?" she persisted.

A shuttered expression crossed his face. "Because I wanted to find out all your secrets, even the ones you wouldn't tell me."

"But I never told you where I was from."

"I was a spy for the king, remember? We have ways of finding out such things. And in any case, how I found out is neither here nor there." He went to the flagon and filled a pewter goblet with wine, then downed it quickly before leveling a wild-eyed gaze on her. "The fact is, I did find out, and now I want answers."

She didn't flinch from his gaze, though the dark determination in it alarmed her. "You have no right to them. Except for protecting me from the king, for which I paid you amply," she said with biting irony, "you haven't given me many answers yourself."

He raked one hand through his hair. "What answers do *you* want?"

"I want to know what prompted you to go to Norwood, and I want to know who my father is."

"Why do you assume that I know?"

"You're the one who pointed out your abilities as a spy. If you're so accomplished at it and so knowledgeable about affairs in London, why didn't you recognize that coat of arms? Why did you rush off to Norwood to root out all my secrets when you knew how much I wanted to know his identity?"

He seemed to consider her words, then said evenly, "Your father is Edward Maynard, the Earl of Walcester. It's his coat of arms on your signet ring."

Stunned to have him state it so bluntly, she searched his face for signs that he was lying. "When . . . how long . . ."

He tossed the goblet down onto the tray. "I recognized his coat of arms the very night you showed me the ring."

She dropped into a nearby armchair. So she knew the truth at last. She'd thought she'd feel more relief or anger or *something*, but the words held little meaning. It was simply the name of another noble with a title. A man she still didn't know. Unless, of course, that had been him at the theater tonight. "Why didn't you tell me his identity as soon as you knew it?"

Colin's eyes narrowed as he approached her. "Because I wasn't sure what you intended to do with the information. In truth, I'm still not sure."

She certainly wasn't going to tell him. He would construe it in the worst way.

He leaned down and braced his hands on the arms of her chair, trapping her. "Now," he growled, his face scant inches from hers, "it's your turn. And don't think you can lie to me. I've told you what you wanted. I want my own questions answered."

"You already seem to know all the important answers." Her hands grew clammy, and she wiped them on her shepherd's smock.

"Yes, I know about the murder. Your mother killed your stepfather to protect you from him and was hanged for it. That needs no explanation."

The almost manic intensity in his gaze struck her with terror. "S-so what is it you wish to know?"

"They told me in Norwood that you were a proper girl, even religious. They said that to all outward appearances, you were modest and respectable."

She glared at him. "It was either be modest and respectable in public or risk my stepfather's temper. Believe me, that wasn't who I was inside."

His jaw tightened. "They also told me you were left penniless, with no man to protect you."

She nodded, bewildered. If he understood all of this, then what was he so intent on learning? And why was he so angry? Simply because she hadn't told him any of it?

"So you found out you had no means of support, but you had a father in London. You and Charity set out for London. That much is understandable."

He paused, his eyes playing over her face. Not certain what he wanted of her now that he knew so much, she held her tongue.

"What I don't understand," he said softly, "is why you chose to go on the stage. Why not find employment more suitable to your upbringing—a position as a governess, perhaps?"

"I told you before—Charity had a friend in the theater."

Abruptly he straightened. Crossing his arms over his chest, he smiled, though it didn't bring any warmth to his eyes. "That doesn't explain why you didn't use your real name once you arrived. Or why you didn't take more active steps to find your father. It took me a week to convince you to tell me you were looking for him. You could have shown that ring to any number of people who'd have brought you to your father. Why didn't you?"

She couldn't meet his eyes. "I wanted to be discreet."

"Rubbish. Try another tale, my lying swan. While you're at it, explain why a 'proper girl' would turn into a wanton in the city. And don't tell me any of that nonsense about its being the only way to protect yourself. Other actresses manage to live respectably and not be troubled by forward gallants."

"I could see no way to fend them off—"

"Stop it!" he thundered, leaning down to trap her in the chair again. "Stop lying to me! You came to this city and set yourself up as a wanton amongst the actresses with a purpose in mind. I want to know what that purpose is."

He was so desperate that it frightened her. "Why do you care?"

Torment gleamed in his eyes. "Because I'm afraid I know what your purpose is, and it smacks of a deeper treachery than I'd thought you capable of."

Suddenly she couldn't bear it anymore, his presuming to pass judgment on her. She shoved him back, then leapt to her feet, feeling as if he were smothering her, closing her into a tight box of condemnation without even seeing the real her. She was tired of pretending to be someone else, especially with him.

As she paced, unable to meet his eyes, the words spilled out of her like corruption from a lanced canker sore. "Is it treachery to want to punish the one who abandoned my mother and me to a daily torment? Is it treachery to want vengeance for being discarded without a thought? Is it?"

He remained ominously silent.

"You want to know my purpose? All right, then. I came to London to punish my father. I came to humiliate him before all the world and make him ashamed to lift his head in public." She whirled to face him, and added in a voice bitter and low, "I came to make him suffer for his crimes by being the bastard daughter of his nightmares. That's my darker purpose, my treachery."

Chapter Sixteen

"Trust not your daughters' minds
By what you see them act."
—William Shakespeare, *Othello*, Act 1, Sc. 1

Colin could only stare, stunned into silence. This wasn't what he'd expected. He'd been certain that her plan for vengeance centered around exposing Walcester as a traitor.

But he should have known that Annabelle always defied expectation. "You wanted to *humiliate* your real father?" he choked out, still taken off guard.

"Aye." She turned her back to him. "I thought to be the kind of daughter no man would want to own. Then I planned to reveal my identity publicly once I determined who he was."

"I don't understand."

"Of course you don't," she said bitterly. "Your father claimed you—a little late, perhaps, but he did. Mine didn't. As far as I can determine, he didn't care one whit that he'd fathered a child."

"Perhaps your mother never told him."

"That's not the point!" she hissed. "Because

my father couldn't keep his blessed 'sword' in its sheath, Mother was consigned to a life of hell. You say you understand about the murder." Her voice thickened with pain and anger. "But you weren't there. You don't know what it's like to see your mother, normally mild as a nun, take a knife and plunge it over . . . and over . . . and—"

She broke off on a sob, and with guilt eating at him, he gathered her up in his arms.

"There was so much blood," she whispered against his shoulder. "It . . . it splattered Mother . . . it splattered me. Mother was screaming like a madwoman. She just kept stabbing and stabbing—"

"Hush," he murmured, stroking her hair. It was killing him to watch her relive it. "Oh, please, dearling, hush."

"Don't you see?" She lifted her lost, haunted gaze to him. "She died because of me, because she wanted to protect *me.*"

"It wasn't your fault," he said fiercely, cupping her face in his hands. "It was your stepfather's. Never forget that. *He* was the one who began the torment; your mother merely ended it. And thank God for it, too, or he might have killed *you* one day."

"All the same," she said in a ragged voice, "I should have stopped her from killing him. I tried, I really did, but she had this sudden incredible strength . . ."

"Yes. That often happens in situations of this

kind." With his heart in his throat, Colin rubbed the tears from her eyes. "You couldn't have stopped her. When someone is in a fit of passion like that, they're nearly invincible." He'd seen it happen in fights, when a man was so enraged that he lost all control.

Still, he'd never had to watch it happen to someone he loved and respected. It must have destroyed her to witness it.

She was nodding now. "Invincible, yes. The squire was long dead before Mother stopped. One of the reasons the judge had no mercy for her was that she was so brutal. Of course, he didn't care why. He . . . he simply sentenced her to hang."

Of course he had. As Annabelle had once pointed out, a man was king of his castle in England. No matter how he ran roughshod over his family, they were supposed to take it. Her mother must have suffered a good deal at the hands of the squire to have broken that unspoken law.

"I was there at the execution," she whispered, tears flowing down her cheeks. "I watched her hang."

His blood chilled. "For the love of God, why?"

"I—I thought I'd cut her down and bring her to a surgeon who'd revive her." Her voice hardened. "But they wouldn't let me near the body. Charity took me away once she was h-hoisted . . . but"—her voice broke—"I—I heard she didn't die for some time. Oh, sweet Mary, if I couldn't stop her from killing him in the first place, I should have saved her from that at least!"

"Sh, sh," he murmured, holding her close and fervently wishing he could wipe it all from her memory. "It sounds as if you did everything you could, dearling, short of calling down a miracle from God."

"I d-did that, too," she choked out. "H-he didn't give m-me one."

That sent Colin over the edge. With a low moan, he lifted her and went to sit by the fire, cradling her in his arms, whispering soothing words, stroking her hair as she gave herself up to her tears, to the unbearable sadness that he'd seen in her time and again. He let her cry. He didn't try to hush her or kiss her. Instead, he comforted her, giving no demands and asking no questions.

It felt so good to hold her, to know that she trusted him with her pain, that he kept her against his chest long after her tears had subsided, her hand clutching the now-damp cloth of his vest. Shifting her in his arms, he reached for the flagon and poured her some wine. With a grateful look, she sipped it.

She stared up at him, a sudden wariness coming over her now that the worst of her grief was past. "You do understand why I had to punish my father. I had to make him suffer the way Mother suffered. He took her innocence and abandoned her. He had to pay for that."

Colin wrapped a lock of her hair about his finger, then lifted it to his lips to kiss. "I can see why you'd want revenge, but I still don't understand how you meant to get it."

Sniffling, she set the wine aside and laid her head on his chest. "I thought if I appeared to live scandalously, my father would be shamed before his peers. No man wants a daughter who's an actress on the stage."

"Most nobility consider treading the boards to be one step above whoring," he agreed.

She winced. "I—I had this dream, you see, of destroying his reputation by flaunting myself and eventually revealing my parentage."

"But you had to find him first."

"Yes. I took his surname . . . and . . . and . . ."

When she paused, he held his breath. Would she mention the poem? He was loath to ask about it when she'd finally begun to trust him. He wasn't supposed to know anything about it.

"I—I took a nickname," she finally whispered. "I didn't tell you this before, but my father left my mother a poem signed with the name 'The Silver Swan.' That's why I wore that brooch and why Charity and I coaxed the gallants into using it for me. All I knew was my father's surname and that nickname, so I used it on the stage, hoping to draw him out."

His heart leapt to hear her finally tell him everything. She trusted him at last. Still, how could she not have known the significance of the name she'd taken? "This poem," he prodded. "Why did it have such a strange signature?"

She shook her head. "I don't know. At first I couldn't think what to make of it. Then I assumed it was some sort of . . . I don't know . . . nickname he used with his friends." A sudden fear lit her face. "Until today."

"What do you mean?" he asked sharply.

Quickly she related the story about the man accosting her in the box at the theater and trying to find out why she went by "The Silver Swan." Colin's blood chilled. Walcester, damn his hide. How dared he go so far?

Colin shifted her on his lap. "What did the man look like?"

"I didn't see. He never left the shadows. But he had a gravelly voice and carried a cane."

Colin gritted his teeth.

"Was it my father?"

"I think so."

"I don't understand why he fears my using his . . . his nickname. Unless . . . I mean, I have to wonder if it had anything to do with the task he asked of my mother."

Colin stiffened. "What task?"

She swallowed. "Mother told me that my father gave her that poem to pass on to his friend in the village. She did, but after his friend read the poem, he thrust it back at her and told her to leave."

"For the love of God," Colin muttered under his breath.

"It sounds as if my father were involved in some intrigue. What could he have done that makes him so fearful now?"

Clutching her against his chest, Colin groaned. He had a pretty good idea of what it might be. "It doesn't matter what he did. You must promise to abandon this foolish quest of yours for revenge. Your father could be dangerous."

"I know," she whispered.

He tipped up her chin until she was staring into his eyes. "Listen to me, dearling. I'm not saying Walcester doesn't deserve to suffer for what he did to your mother. But if you endanger your life to punish him, then he has won. He has destroyed both you and your mother and proven he can do as he pleases without answering to anyone."

Her mouth trembled. "I know."

Not quite able to believe she was agreeing with him, he murmured, "This isn't about him or your mother or your stepfather. This is about you and your pain. It won't be assuaged by hurting him, I assure you." His throat felt raw. "The scars on your back won't heal because he's been punished. Nor will the scars on your soul. You must set about healing them by putting the past behind you and finding some new future."

A soft smile lit her face, giving him hope that she was seeing the sense of what he said.

Encouraged by that, he went on. "I have no right to ask, but will you promise to abandon this plan of yours before Walcester gets some wild idea about what you know of his past and decides to hurt you?"

She stared at him a long moment, then lifted her hand to stroke his cheek. "Yes. If you wish it."

His relief was so profound it stunned him. He hadn't expected her to agree. "Thank heaven. Walcester is a foe to be feared."

She eyed him uncertainly. "You don't truly think he'd try to kill me, do you? I mean, I know he doesn't know I'm his daughter, but he's not the kind of man who would murder someone, is he?"

Damn, all of his deceptions were coming back to haunt him. He should tell her the truth—that Walcester knew who she was but didn't care. That Colin had been lying to her all this time.

But how could he, when she'd just begun to trust him?

He tightened his arms around her and spoke as much of the truth as he dared. "I don't know, dearling. I discovered some things in Norwood about your father that give me pause."

"What?"

"It's all very confusing, but apparently he was at Norwood shortly after the Battle of Naseby. After he sent your mother to Norwood to deliver that message, three Royalists who'd escaped capture until then were caught and the papers of Charles I confiscated by the Roundheads. The man who arrested them said they were betrayed by a traitor in their midst."

Shock showed in her features. "You think my father was the traitor?"

He couldn't see any other explanation. "'Tis possible, though I don't know for certain. But I mean to find out." He cupped her face in his hands. "I tell you this only because I want you to know what a risky game you've been playing. I hope you mean it when you say you'll abandon your vengeance."

Her eyes grew solemn. "I do."

"I swear it would destroy me if something happened to you," he admitted hoarsely. "The very thought of it strikes terror to my soul."

She blinked, then covered his hands with hers and gazed up at him with a look of such guileless love that it made something twist in his chest. Before he could even think, he was pressing his mouth to hers, determined to make her forget about her father and the Silver Swan and the terrible things that had happened at Norwood. To make her care only about him.

He kissed her a long while, the blood rising in him, searing him, rousing his hunger for her. When he drew back, her eyes flamed with the same hunger. It fairly slayed him. "Hell and furies, it's been the longest two weeks of my life."

"Of mine, too," she admitted with a shy smile.

"I suppose I understand why you took my ring off and sought to hurt me while I was gone. You were right. I should have told you what I was doing. Still, I don't think I could bear again to see you mauled by a lecher like Rochester."

"Don't worry. As soon as I return to Aphra's, I'll put your ring back on and never take it off."

He smoothed his thumb over her lips. "This time you'll keep your promise to be mine and mine alone?"

"Aye, this time I will, my lord." Then she added archly, "But only if you promise the same."

He bit back a laugh. "Easily." Clasping her hands, he held them to his chest. "I swear, Annabelle, by all that's holy, to be yours and yours alone, to have no other woman in my bed, in my thoughts, in my heart."

"In your heart?" she echoed.

And in that moment, he knew. He wanted this vow to be forever. He would *never* want another woman in his life. He knew it as surely as he knew that the sun rose and set every day.

"Annabelle," he rasped, "I think our promises are not enough."

Her eyes went wide. "What do you mean?"

"I want a more lasting promise." He brushed a kiss to her lips, then added in a whisper, "I want to marry you."

Chapter Seventeen

"Excellent wretch! Perdition catch my soul
But I do love thee! and when I love thee not,
Chaos is come again."
—William Shakespeare, *Othello*, Act 3, Sc. 3

Annabelle gaped at him. Surely he hadn't said what she'd thought. "Marriage? But . . . but . . ."

"Does that mean you don't wish to marry me?" He lifted her hand to his lips, grazing the knuckles with a feathery caress.

"Please, don't toy with me like this. We aren't of the same station."

A fierce light entered his eyes. "You're the daughter of an earl and the granddaughter of a knight, are you not?"

"Yes, but—"

"And that's not what matters, anyway. What matters is that I love you, dearling." He looked a bit shocked that he'd said it, but then he nodded, as if to himself. "I mean it. I love you. I want you in my life, in my future, in my soul. Losing you would drive me quite mad." He ventured a smile. "So you see, to save my sanity, you *must* marry me."

How she wanted to believe him, but how could she? It was preposterous that he should stoop so low. "Colin, you must be sensible. I'm an actress with a scandalous reputation. Not to mention a bastard."

"So am I, remember? You and I are meant for each other. Who else could I find who would understand my sorrow and my peculiar sense of humor, who wouldn't secretly be embarrassed to be wed to me, who cares not a farthing for my money and position? Who else?"

"Surely you could find a wife who isn't—"

"Intelligent? Talented? Kind? Aye, I could. But I don't want to marry a stupid, boring, cruel woman." He caressed her cheek. "I want to marry *you.*"

She ducked her head, not wanting him to see the hope shining in her eyes. He couldn't do this. There were so many reasons it was unwise. Yet she couldn't stop thinking of her dream of growing old with him, of sharing his future.

"Is it that you don't love me?" he asked. "Because I believe I could *make* you love me in time."

"Dear heaven," she muttered, "if you actually try to make me love you, I shall burst into flame."

He tipped her head up, his eyes gleaming with satisfaction. "Then you *do* love me."

"It would be foolish of me to do so," she said, still afraid to let him in. "Because if you marry me, you'll be the laughingstock of London."

"I don't care."

"I do," she said softly. "It would kill me to hear people mocking you for having an actress wife."

"Then we won't live in London." He stared earnestly into her eyes. "We'll go to the colonies, where no one will know or care about your past. I've been considering it of late. I want some purpose beyond whiling my time away at court or serving the king. I only hesitated because I couldn't bear to go alone. But if you went with me—"

"You're serious," she said incredulously.

"Yes." His eyes glittered . . . with determination . . . with desire . . . yes, and perhaps even with love. "How shall I prove it? Shall I circulate a poem among the court that extols your virtues and announces my intentions? Shower you with jewels? Cry my love from the rooftops?"

Her eyes widened. They were the words a gallant would say, yet she could almost believe he meant them. "I've had enough of poems," she whispered, trying not to turn into a puddle of mush before him. "And you already know what I think of your jewels."

That brought a faint smile to his lips. "Then something else." He trailed his finger down into the neck of her shirt. "Kisses, caresses, sweet words. They're all yours, my love, if you want them."

"If you *mean* them," she said lightly, though her heart was in her throat.

He slid from beneath her to kneel before her. "Surely there is some way to prove that I do. What trial do you require of your swain to prove his devotion? Shall I beg?"

"Don't be absurd," she mumbled.

With eyes alight, he removed her embroidered slipper, then caressed her instep. "Shall I kiss your feet?" he asked, then pressed his lips against the top of her foot, sending shivers of delight up her leg.

Desire struck her with such force that she felt faint.

"Tell me what you want," he asked in a low, seductive voice.

Her pulse beat madly. What she wanted was *him*, naked and at her mercy.

As soon as the idea sprang into her mind, she knew that was *exactly* what she wanted. Men had always told her what to do, what they demanded, while she was expected to comply or be beaten for it. But for once a man was asking what *she* wanted. A man was telling her that she could choose her path.

And it was the man she loved. What could be better than that?

"Take off your boots," she said, a little shakily.

He blinked and stared at her a long moment. Then he smiled. He sat back to tug his heavy, mudsplattered jackboots off and toss them aside. As if guessing at her game, he lifted an eyebrow.

"Stand up," she commanded, more firmly this time.

He did so without hesitation. He must have ridden hard from Norwood, for his traveling clothes were rumpled and dirty. Yet she found him more dangerously attractive than ever, particularly when his eyes blazed with need.

Emboldened by that, she said, "Take off your vest."

"I'll do you one better than that," he quipped as he undid his sash, then unbuttoned his vest. "I'll take it all off."

"No," she said quickly. "I get to choose."

He cocked his head at her and then nodded. "Ah. I see."

She could tell that he *did* see. There was no condemnation in his face, no male posturing pride. He removed his black velvet vest and no more. But it was enough to show his aroused member standing boldly beneath his breeches.

She knelt in the chair, wondering how far he would let her go. "Now the shirt and cravat," she whispered, and he immediately complied, tossing both to join his vest on the floor.

Sweet Mary, but the sight of his bared chest nearly undid her. The blond hair sprinkled over it folded into a line in the center of his chest, which darkened the closer it moved to his groin.

Colin's eyes were gleaming, his smile dark with promise as he watched her. Not a hint of embarrassment crossed his face. If anything, he looked cockier than usual.

Well, she knew how to erode *that*. She stood and shrugged off her coat and vest, then removed her shirt and threw it aside.

His gaze went right to her bared breasts, and his arrogant smile faltered. He reached for her, but she said, "Not yet," and brushed his hands away. Then she moved behind him and hugged him close so her breasts flattened against him.

He sucked in a sharp breath, and she smiled. He was hers. She could do whatever she pleased with him. And the fact that he was allowing it made it sweet beyond reason. With a heady joy, she ran her hands over the muscles of his chest and teased the flat nipples. A groan escaped his lips.

Oh yes, having him at her mercy was wonderful. Pressing kisses over his iron-hard back, she trailed her hands down his chest until she reached the band of his breeches. She undid the button and his breeches slid to the floor.

Now he wore only his long drawers and his stockings held up with leather garters. But when she reached for the ties of his drawers, he caught her hand. "That's enough, my demanding temptress," he murmured, lifting her hand to his lips. "You'll drive me insane if you don't let me touch you, too."

"I thought you said I could ask any trial of you," she whispered. "Well, your trial is to let me touch you until I've had my fill."

He moaned. "Hell and furies, you've chosen a good one."

"I know." She fought to keep the laughter from her voice as she unfastened his drawers. She slid the kerseymere down his firm hips and muscled thighs, kneeling to kiss one bared buttock.

He swore, but she merely laughed as she unbuckled his garters, then removed his stockings and drawers. He kicked them aside. For a long moment, she savored the sight of him from behind—broad back and shoulders, lean but muscular hips, and well-formed legs. She ran her hands over the expanse of male muscles, watching fascinated as they flexed beneath her fingers. Then she circled back around to stand before him.

The arrogant smile was gone. In its place was a look of such ravenous hunger it fed the heat building in her belly. She swallowed, then lifted both hands tentatively to touch his chest.

That was all it took to break Colin's control. Before she could halt him—not that she would have—he'd clasped her so tightly in his arms she could hardly move, much less resist.

He started to kiss her, then stopped an inch short of her mouth. Never had she seen him look so forbidding and mysterious . . . and so very determined.

"Have I passed my trial?" he growled. "Have I let you touch me until you had your fill?"

She was tempted to say no, yet it felt so good to

be clutched against him. "I suppose it could be considered—"

He blotted out the words with a hard kiss. There was nothing slow or leisurely about the way he plundered her mouth and ground his hips against her. He was less than gentle when he lowered his head to tug greedily at her breasts with his mouth, laving them with his tongue until they felt tight and tender as ripe berries awaiting picking.

Dropping to one knee, he darted his tongue into her navel as he worked loose her breeches. He slid them over her hips with a grin and murmured, "I never thought I'd be undoing breeches for someone I wished to bed. It feels odd."

As he bared her to his gaze, he went very still. Then, with a low groan, he kissed the soft thatch of hair between her legs. "Doing this, however, feels perfectly right."

He tasted her there, then drew back to grab her half-full goblet and trickle the wine between her legs. She shivered at the cold sensation, but in seconds his warm tongue was roughly lapping her . . . first her thighs, then her damp curls, then deeper to tease and taunt the swollen petals. She gasped as he began to caress her with his mouth in earnest, his hands clasping her hips to hold her still as he buried his face in her most private place. Her breath quickened, and she clutched his head to her.

Within a matter of moments, his caresses

brought her to the point of unreason. A sudden sweet burst of pleasure made her arch up to stand on tiptoe, and she lost her balance. It didn't matter, for Colin caught her, cushioning her fall with his body so they ended up on the floor with her sprawled atop him.

He shifted her until she straddled him. Staring up at her, he brushed the hair back from her flushed cheeks. "You know, dearling, if we're to continue this very interesting test of my love, we should go to my room, where I keep my sheaths."

She groaned at the unwelcome intrusion into her sensual haze. Trust Colin to have remembered the sheaths.

Then a startling realization hit her. "I thought you planned to marry me."

"I do."

"Then it hardly matters if I . . . if I find myself with child, does it?"

A smile tipped up the edges of his mouth. "No, dearling, I don't believe it does." Then he pulled her head down to his and kissed her long and deep as he cupped her buttocks.

His hard flesh pressed up against her belly. It hadn't occurred to her until that moment that there might be other positions in lovemaking than the one they'd used the first time, but now strange, intriguing thoughts flitted through her mind. She stroked his staff experimentally, delighted when it leapt to her touch.

His smile grew forced. She fondled it as he watched, not stopping her. How very interesting. She raised her hips.

"Yes," he murmured. "Ride me, dearling. I would give much to see that."

"I'm . . . not sure I know how."

"Oh, yes, you do," he said dryly. "You're a natural wanton."

She frowned.

"'Tis a compliment. There are few inexperienced women who need so little teaching to make love as you do. And trust me, while most men want a respectable wife in the drawing room, they want a wanton wife in the bedchamber."

"Well, at least you'll have one of those," she said tartly.

"I'll have both," he corrected her, then urged her over his jutting member. "Though at present, I want the wanton." Next thing she knew, he was sliding up inside her, hot, hard, and heavy.

It was nothing like the first time. She felt no pain, and only a little pinching tightness, but it gave her a delicious sense of power to be on top of him. When she moved and he gasped, she decided she definitely liked this position.

"Annabelle, love," he whispered, "don't stop."

Ah, his pleasure was now dependent on *her* whim. She stared at his brow, shiny with sweat, at the clenched muscles of his face, and realized that he'd relinquished control on purpose, to please her.

So she began to move, to please *him*. Dear heaven, how she loved him. She had only one thought, one purpose—to give him the same pleasure he gave her.

Yet somewhere in the joining of their bodies, she discovered that their pleasures were as intertwined as strands of thread. When she ground against him, they both gasped. When he caressed her breast, they both grew aroused.

She leaned forward, bracing her hands against his chest as they rocked together with quickening strokes. But she didn't set the pace alone. Their bodies rode together, pounding, thundering, lifting and teasing. Their rhythm blended with the roar of the blood in their ears and their sweet wanton cries until he gave a mighty thrust and she arched back to receive it.

They reached the peak of bliss together.

It took several moments for her to regain awareness of their surroundings, to realize she was clutching his arms, leaving tiny half-moon marks on them with her fingernails.

His eyes were closed, his mouth parted, and sheer ecstasy shone in his face. He drew her down to his chest and cradled her against him. They lay there entwined for a while as he stroked her back and she relished the feel of his hard body beneath her.

"I love you, Colin," she murmured. The words felt so freeing that she had to repeat them. "I love you. Truly, I do."

"Good." He pressed a fierce kiss against her hair. "Because I swear, Annabelle, if you ever leave me, I'll die."

Chapter Eighteen

"Those have most power to hurt us that we love."
—Francis Beaumont and John Fletcher,
The Maid's Tragedy, Act 5

The woven rug hardly helped to soften the hard floor. Yet Colin didn't move or ask Annabelle to move from her contented sprawl atop him. The hardness served as a kind of penance, even if it barely assuaged his guilt.

He should have told Annabelle about his real reason for first pursuing her. After all, she'd told him everything. He was certain of that. In return, he'd kept back something she would want to know.

So why couldn't he bring himself to tell her?

Because he was afraid that she'd be so hurt, she'd lose her trust in him and suspect all his motives.

'Sdeath, he had to tell her sometime. He couldn't risk her finding out some other way. Yet wouldn't it be better to marry her first, to prove his intentions were honorable? Yes, of course. They'd marry as soon as possible, and then he'd tell her. She'd be angry for a while, but she'd not be able to doubt his love for her.

Hell and furies, how he did love her. He hadn't realized it until he'd said the words, but then it was as if scales had fallen from his eyes. How could he not love her? He'd never known a woman who was his match not only in wit and lust for life but in being a bastard reared as nobility, who'd suffered all the pains of rejection and only become stronger for it. She was as daring as a man, but with the softness and caring of a woman. He could think of no one else who could follow him to the colonies and face head-on the trials they were sure to encounter.

If she was willing to leave London's glittering society. She hadn't said for certain that she would. What if she truly enjoyed the wild life of town?

Then he remembered her bitterness when she'd spoken of the gallants at the theater. Perhaps she'd grown as disillusioned as he.

His arms tightened around her. He certainly hoped so. But in the end they must come to a decision about their future together. After all, there could be no one else for him. Annabelle had been right—there *were* other women he could have married, of higher station, greater fortune, and impeccable reputation. But he'd never been like his peers, searching for ways to enhance his position in London society. He was far more concerned with finding a woman he could live with, and at last he'd found her.

Later he'd think about what to do with Walcester, for he must do something, if only to make certain the earl never tried to hurt Annabelle. It had all happened so long ago. Perhaps it would be best if Colin simply kept his knowledge to himself, or better yet, used it as a lever to get Walcester to agree to some terms on Annabelle's behalf. Could Walcester truly be involved in some conspiracy to overthrow the king *now*? It seemed unlikely.

"Colin?" she whispered.

"Aye, my love?"

"Am I hurting you?"

He smiled. "Nay, but the floor is doing a fine job of stiffening my back."

Immediately, she slid off to kneel at his side. "You should have said something! Oh dear, I'm sorry I—"

"I'm teasing you," he said with a laugh. "You'll have to get used to my teasing if we're to be married the long years I intend." He sat up. "Although I do think it's time we moved our . . . er . . . discussion to a more comfortable room." His gaze darkened. "Like my bedchamber."

To his surprise, she blushed.

He gave a hearty laugh. "Hell and furies, no wonder you're such a fine actress. You're as unpredictable in life as you are in the roles you play."

She managed a trembling smile. "And you, Lord Hampden, are a smooth-tongued rogue."

"Aye. 'Tis what makes you love me."

At her wisp of a smile, he stood and offered her his hand. "It's down the hall, but we ought to put some clothing on before we go sneaking about the house. Don't you think?"

Laughing, she donned her clothes and slippers but he noticed she didn't bother with the stockings. Instead, she stood, her adorable calves bared and her hands on her hips, waiting for him to dress.

He pulled on his breeches but didn't worry about the rest. Then he took her hand. "Come, my love, let's see if we can get to my room without being spotted."

Like two mischievous children, they peeked out into the hall. Colin pointed out the door to his rooms. Then, seeing no one around, he slapped her rump and whispered, "Quickly now, dearling," and watched her run laughing ahead of him as he followed at a more sedate pace.

But as she reached the door to his rooms, Colin heard shouting in the foyer below. She paused with her hand on the door. He motioned for her to go in, but she stared at him wide-eyed, for she'd apparently recognized the voice of the man shouting.

So had he. It was Walcester.

"I know he has returned," the gravelly voice echoed up the stairs. "I have ways of knowing these things. He's here, and I will see him!"

"His lordship is not to be disturbed," the footman said.

"He'll see me, I tell you," Walcester growled,

and they could hear his steps coming up the stairs, punctuated by the clicks of his walking stick. "He'd damn well better."

Gritting his teeth, Colin motioned for Annabelle to enter his bedchamber. When she stood frozen, her eyes wide and fearful, Colin opened the door, intending to thrust her bodily through it. Then Walcester rounded the top of the stairs and spotted them.

For a moment, the three of them stared at each other, Walcester full of rage, Colin equally angry, and Annabelle stunned.

Walcester was the first to speak. "This certainly explains a great deal. Damn you, Hampden, how long have you been back in London, cavorting with her while you pretended to be helping me?"

With a sinking in his stomach, Colin heard Annabelle's sharp intake of breath. He glared at Walcester. "I distinctly heard my servant tell you I didn't wish to be disturbed."

Walcester's face was mottled with rage. "You deceitful bastard! You had no right to trot off to the country instead of doing as I asked. Two weeks you've been gone, but instead of coming imme-diately to my house upon your return from God knows where, you avoid me to bed this . . . this chit!"

"Get out, damn you!" Colin snapped.

But the earl was beyond reason. "Don't try to tell me you did it to find out her secrets for me. You're like all those other randy bucks who can't keep their cocks in their pants and their minds on their obligations!"

"What obligations?" Annabelle asked, her face ashen. "This horrible man can't be . . ." Then her tone sharpened. "Oh, but of course he is, which means he's my—"

"I'll explain it all later, love," Colin said, his throat tight. 'Sdeath, he was losing her. He had to get Walcester out of here.

"'Love'?" Walcester growled. "I see you've pulled the wool over her eyes well, haven't you?"

Annabelle stared at the earl, pain etched in every line of her face. "You're Walcester, aren't you?"

For the first time since he'd arrived, Walcester turned his gaze on Annabelle. "The *Earl* of Walcester," he snapped. "Show some respect to your betters."

She gave a bitter laugh. "I'll be sure to remember that, *Father.*"

Anger twisted his mouth as he looked her over. "You're a wanton, girl. No matter what your blood says, you're no daughter of mine."

Annabelle flinched as if struck, obviously not as pleased with the outcome of her vengeance as she'd expected. Then her hurt expression twisted into one of defiance. "What did you expect? When you forced a gentlewoman to share your bed and then set her loose among the wolves, you should have known you'd breed a wanton. I'm only taking after my dear old father."

"I was never a whore!" the earl said as he lunged for her.

Colin stepped in front of her. "If you ever call her such names again, I'll slit you from throat to toe."

"Well, she's certainly got you fooled, hasn't she?" Walcester glared past him at Annabelle. "Doesn't it bother you that she's played the wanton with every man in your acquaintance? Do you enjoy having a mistress bring you another man's leavings?"

"Let me tell you something about your daughter—"

"No!" Annabelle cried as she clutched his arm.

When he turned to look at her, his heart sank to see the wounded anger on her face. "I'm going to tell him the truth. I won't let him continue with these base opinions."

"Haven't you done enough already?" she hissed. "Spying on me? Lying to me about . . . about what you felt?"

"I did not lie to you!" he bit out, seared through by her words. When she just shot him a mutinous stare, he barked at the earl, "Walcester, give us a moment alone and I'll tell you everything you wish to know."

The earl clenched the top of his walking stick as if it were a club, but moved off to the other end of the hall.

Colin said under his breath, "I won't let him think you a whore. It serves no purpose."

"Oh? It doesn't prick his pride? Look at him. He's furious. And ashamed, as he should be."

At the desperate purpose written in her eyes, something twisted inside him. "You promised to give up this insane vengeance."

"As you knew I would when you . . . when you seduced me and spoke sweet words to me . . . and, devil take you, told me you loved me!"

"That was the truth!"

Tears glittered in her eyes. "Please, Colin, don't torment me anymore. You've fulfilled whatever cursed obligation you had to him . . . Just leave me be!"

Guilt swamped him at the look of betrayal on her face. He should have told her the truth when he'd had the chance. "Let me make it up to you, love. I know I deceived you about my association with Walcester, but I meant everything I said tonight."

"What are you two whispering about?" Walcester bellowed. "I want answers, damn you!"

Annabelle rounded Colin to face down the earl. "I'm happy to give you answers, *Father*. My mother was Phoebe Harlow Taylor, whom you bedded, then abandoned while she was with child."

"I didn't know she was—"

"She had no choice but to marry a squire, who dedicated his every waking hour to making her miserable." Annabelle planted her hands on her hips. "Thanks to you, Mother had a painful life and a more painful death. She was abused and tormented by the man who hated her for bearing *your* bastard."

When Walcester seemed at a loss for words, she went on relentlessly. "So the next time you see me on the stage or hear of my scandalous exploits, you remember what you did to my mother. Because from now on, everyone will know I'm the Earl of Walcester's daughter. Everyone!"

"Annabelle, don't do this," Colin growled, but she ignored him.

"And you know what else?" she hissed. "The Silver Swan will rue the day he abandoned my mother to the torments of a cruel man. Because I am going to be an unforgettable daughter. Most unforgettable."

Walcester paled. "What do you know about the Silver Swan, you damned impertinent wench! You'll tell me what you know or I'll shake it out of you!"

When Walcester reached out to grab her, Colin stepped forward, but she was already fleeing down the stairs.

"Come back, damn you!" The earl strode after her. "You come back here, girl, or I swear you'll regret it! When I get through with you—"

"Leave her be!" Colin ordered. Bad enough that the woman had stirred up a hornet's nest with her taunt about the Silver Swan, but now she thought to wander about the city alone in the dead of night? No matter how angry she was, he couldn't let her.

But before he could go after her, Walcester blocked his path. "What did she mean? How much does she know about the Silver Swan?"

"You've just wounded your daughter beyond repair," Colin growled, "and all you can think about is your damnable code name? Hell and furies, man, don't you have an ounce of feeling in those veins?"

For the first time since Walcester had arrived, Colin saw ambivalence flash over the stern face, but it was quickly masked. "When your past is as treacherous as mine—when all you've worked for is in jeopardy of being ruined because some girl has taken it into her head to destroy you—you can't coddle yourself. Feelings are dangerous. You should have learned that by now."

He had, in the king's service. And that was precisely why he planned to leave it. Because he wanted to feel again. He wanted to live without trying to guess the meaning behind every smile.

Which was why he must find Annabelle. He had to make her see that he regretted what he'd done, or he just might lose his soul.

"You owe me answers," the earl went on.

"And you will have them," Colin snapped. "In a moment."

He shoved past the earl and raced down and into the street. But she was gone. Damn it all. How could she be gone so quickly?

"Your lordship," his footman came up to say, "the lady took a hackney that was waiting for the earl."

"Did she say where she was going?"

"No, my lord. I'm sorry."

His blood froze in his veins. She was out there alone and hurting, and it was all his fault. As he headed back into the house to dress, he told the footman, "Fetch me a fresh horse. And call for my coach to carry the earl wherever he wishes."

Walcester, standing in the foyer, heard him and growled, "I'm not going anywhere until you answer my questions, damn you!"

Colin stared him down. "Fine, then stay here until my return. But if you want to know what she knows, what *I* have learned about the Silver Swan on my own, then you can damned well wait for your answers until I find her."

Chapter Nineteen

"Heaven has no rage like love to hatred turned,
  Nor hell a fury like a woman scorned."
—William Congreve, *The Mourning Bride*, Act 3, Sc. 8

Annabelle warmed herself at the fire she'd made in the hearth of the tiring-room. No one would look for her at the closed theater so late in the evening. Not even Colin.

Colin. Tears clogged her throat. How could she look at him again, knowing that he'd been in league with her father all along? Had he been lying to her every time he said he cared?

No, she couldn't believe that. And perhaps he'd even meant it when he said he loved her. But what did he know of love when he couldn't tell her the truth, when he could make an alliance with her enemy, then hide it?

Like a creeping poison, Colin's assurances to Walcester that he would tell the man everything after speaking to her seeped into her mind. Devil take him and his promises! A sob choked her. He knew what she'd been through and seen what a blackguard her father was, yet he still intended to fulfill some obligation he felt to the man?

The thought of Colin and her father together sent pain slicing through her. Had Colin given the earl daily reports about the drugged tea and her naivete and her pathetic tears when she'd asked him to stay in London? For heaven's sake, how closely had Colin reported to that wretched creature who'd sired her?

Dropping into a chair, she tried to blot out the memory of making love to Colin, but it was too recent, too precious to ignore. And she kept seeing Colin's anguished expression when her father made his appearance.

Her anger dug in its heels. She didn't care if Colin had felt remorse over not telling her of their association; it still stung that she'd bared her soul to him and he hadn't done the same.

Had he intended to keep it a secret from her forever, to marry her and never tell her that he'd been spying for her father?

Marry her. Her blood chilled. What if he hadn't meant it? What if that had been another ploy?

No, that made no sense. He'd already heard all her secrets and taken her to bed. He wouldn't have offered marriage unless he actually *wanted* to marry her.

Her hand balled into a fist in her lap. But how dared he offer marriage to her while carrying on such a deceit? And how dare her father use her and

Colin to further his own hidden aims? He deserved the vengeance she wished to visit upon him. What a spiteful, horrible man!

Except that her vengeance wasn't turning out as planned. He might find her reputation a torment, but it no doubt made him all the more pleased that he'd abandoned the woman who'd borne him such an outrageous daughter. She'd wanted to make him feel remorse, but he clearly didn't know the meaning of the word. So her dreams of retribution were just that—silly dreams. Lord Walcester wasn't the kind of man to beg forgiveness or dissolve into bitter, regretful tears. All he'd cared about was her knowledge of his nickname.

She sat up straight. Had Colin told the truth when he'd hinted that her father might be a traitor? Surely he wouldn't have said such a thing about his own friend unless it was true.

So her father had to have been a spy for the wrong side. And he'd dragged her poor mother into it, too!

She thought through the poem. If "the bard" referred to Shakespeare, then perhaps "Portia" and "Beatrice" referred to two of the three men Colin had said were arrested. Perhaps men her father had betrayed.

A chill struck her. No wonder the earl had cautioned her against using his alias.

Had Colin known all along? She didn't think so.

He seemed to have found out most of his information in Norwood.

The door to the tiring-room opened, startling her. But it was only Charity.

"I thought I might find you here. Y've got everyone worried, you have. His lordship is beside himself wanting to find you."

"Where's Colin now?" Annabelle asked. "He didn't come with you, did he?"

"Nay, since you weren't at our lodgings he went to Aphra's to see if you might have gone there. And he sent me to the theater."

Sir John stepped into the room behind Charity, and Annabelle groaned. So much for staying hidden. "What's *he* doing here?"

"I didn't think Charity should be roaming the streets in the middle of the night alone," he snapped. "Nor should you, for that matter."

Right now Annabelle had little patience for Sir John. "Doesn't your fiancée keep you too busy to be concerned about your mistress, sir?"

Sir John flushed but pulled Charity close. "Aye, my fiancée is keeping me quite busy."

Charity gave a shy smile. "John's asked me to marry him, he has. He's going to withdraw his offer for the viscount's daughter in the morning."

Annabelle arched an eyebrow. "Really?"

Sir John's face hardened. "Listen here, I won't let you or Mrs. Behn poison Charity any longer with your hardhearted views about men. I'll admit I neglected her feelings in the past, but that's all changed. Charity has helped me realize that our love is more important than any social position."

The sweet smile he cast Charity tore at Annabelle's already wounded heart.

"My father was a merchant," he continued, "and my mother a chambermaid when they fell in love and married. So you see, I have a rather humble lineage myself. I gained a knighthood only because of service to the king. For a time, I forgot that my parents had been happier in their love than any of the nobility I know with all their titles and wealth. I nearly threw away my only chance for happiness."

"I set you straight, didn't I, love?" Charity whispered.

Sir John nodded. "When it came right down to it, I couldn't stomach the thought of losing you."

To see them billing and cooing was nearly more than Annabelle could bear, but Charity deserved this second opportunity for love.

"At any rate," Sir John said, turning back to Annabelle with a softer expression on his face, "I hope you'll wish us happiness."

"I do." She meant it, despite her pain at seeing them together. She managed a smile. "I truly do."

"Now y've got to go after Lord Hampden," Charity said fervently. "'Tis time for you to find yer own happiness."

Annabelle's smile faded. "I'm afraid you'll have to let me handle Lord Hampden in my own way."

"But—" Charity began.

"Nay, love, she's right," Sir John put in. "You must let them work out their own problems."

Annabelle yearned to tell Charity of all that had happened, but Charity's loyalties were with Sir John now, and Sir John would report to Colin whatever she said. Dear heaven, she was surrounded by spies. No doubt Sir John had known all along what Colin was doing for Walcester.

Or had he?

"Sir John," Annabelle blurted out. "Do you know the Earl of Walcester?"

"Of course. He's a powerful man."

Annabelle bit back a harsh retort. "Is he also a friend of Lord Hampden's?"

Charity was regarding her suspiciously, but Annabelle ignored her.

Sir John shrugged. "You could say that. I don't know that the earl makes many real friends, but Hampden does feel indebted to the man for saving his life once during the war. Walcester was also the one who got Hampden his position in the king's service."

Her heart sank. No wonder Colin felt obligated to aid her father. Owing so much to the man, Colin would never help her bring the earl to justice. For all his secrets, Colin was an honorable man.

But her father didn't deserve such consideration.

"Why do you ask?" Sir John said.

"No reason." She cast Charity a warning glance, hoping the maid would keep quiet with Sir John.

Charity stiffened. "John, love, could you give me and Annabelle a moment alone?"

He nodded, then left the room.

"What the devil is going on?" Charity demanded.

"The earl is indeed my father. And Colin has been spying on me for him."

The color drained from Charity's face. "Are you sure?"

Annabelle nodded. "I don't think Colin intended for me to find out. He must have known how it would hurt me. But I know now and he's upset. The thing is, I've also learned something else about my father. And I can't keep silent about it. But Colin would want me to."

Planting her hands on her hips, Charity stared hard at Annabelle. "So what are you planning?"

With a sigh, Annabelle asked, "Would you do one favor for me?"

"Anything."

"Would you fetch my special box from our lodgings and bring it to me here? The key is in the binding of the book of poems on the bureau."

Charity regarded her quizzically. "Aye, but why?"

"Please don't ask. Do this for me, and I'll be forever in your debt."

Shrugging, Charity turned toward the door. "Whatever you wish."

"And, Charity? Don't tell Colin about it, and whatever you do, don't tell him where I am."

Charity's eyes narrowed on her. "What are you up to?"

"You'll know soon enough," Annabelle said. "Now go."

To her relief, Charity nodded and left.

The earl was a traitor and Colin could never do anything about it, not considering what he owed the man.

She, however, didn't owe her father a thing. But she still owed her mother. Clearly Lord Walcester had seduced Mother so he could use her for his own traitorous purposes, or else why had he fled? And why else was he so panicked over Annabelle's uncovering his actions?

Thanks to him and his machinations, Mother was dead. And though Annabelle had promised Colin to abandon her vengeance, that was before she'd learned that he couldn't get justice himself for Walcester's treachery because of the debt he owed the man.

So it was up to her to make sure the earl received justice. Colin had warned her that her father was dangerous, but surely the only way to protect herself from a dangerous man was to make sure he paid for his crimes. Colin might not approve, but she couldn't let him harbor a traitor, no matter what obligation he felt.

That decision made, Annabelle began to search for a costume. She had to look her best tonight.

For she was going to meet a king.

AT MIDNIGHT, ANNABELLE stood in the small room off the Privy Stairs of Whitehall Palace, waiting for William Chiffinch to return from sending her message in to the king. She stared about her, clutching her box against her chest and wondering what His Majesty would think when he saw her here so late, dressed in the finery she'd borrowed from the theater.

Not that it mattered. After she laid out her case, he'd be set straight, even if her note hadn't already quelled all interest he might have in her body.

A moment's guilt assailed her. What she was about to do was unforgivable. Even if her father ever could find it in his heart to accept her, he'd not do so after this. Despite reminding herself that her father was almost certainly a traitor and she was doing this for her country and her king, she knew that was only half true. She was doing this to punish him—for abandoning Mother, for not caring about what happened as a result. And for making Colin spy on her.

She choked down her tears. She wouldn't think about Colin, not now. Opening her box, she looked for her father's ring to remind herself of his treachery. Instead, she caught sight of Colin's ring.

Emotions flooded her—pain, resentment, longing . . . and yes, love. Despite everything, she loved him, so very much. And he'd undoubtedly be furious when he heard what she'd done.

Yet she had to do this. As long as Lord Walcester feared her knowledge of his past, he'd hound her. The earl was a hard man, and the only message he would understand was a hard one.

She tucked Colin's ring into her apron pocket. The earl might deserve punishment, but Colin did not, so the king mustn't learn the truth about their affair. She couldn't bear to think of Colin being arrested simply because he'd fulfilled some ancient obligation to the treacherous Earl of Walcester.

Chiffinch appeared in the doorway. "His Majesty says he will see you, madam, but he can only give you a few moments. He has guests."

Guests? Oh, of course. Rumor had it that the king rarely went to bed before dawn.

Annabelle followed Chiffinch up the Privy Stairs and into the king's chambers with growing trepidation. His Majesty was presiding over a small supper. She recognized an actress from the king's company and Barbara Palmer, the king's current mistress, who flashed her a glance of scathing contempt as she entered. The Duke of Buckingham, one of the king's advisers and Barbara Palmer's cousin, was there as well. Unfortunately, so was Lord Rochester.

The king met her with a sober expression. He was much taller than she'd expected, and handsome, with thick brown hair that fell past his shoulders, a sensuous mouth, and heavy-lidded eyes. No wonder the women all wanted him.

Still, he could not compare to Colin.

He watched impatiently as she fell into a deep curtsy.

Offering her his hand, he murmured, "Good evening, Mrs. Maynard. I do hope you've fully recovered from your illness."

She was so nervous she nearly forgot what he was talking about, but she caught herself in time. "Yes, Your Majesty. I'm feeling much better these days."

"That was a very interesting message you just sent me," he said tightly. "I hope it wasn't intended as a ruse to capture my attention."

"Nay, Your Majesty!" She glanced around the room, then swallowed. "But if it please you, I would prefer to discuss the matter in private."

The king regarded her oddly, then nodded and led her into an adjoining room. As he shut the door, he said, "You claim to have information regarding a traitor to the Crown. You do realize what a serious charge that is?"

She sucked in her breath. "Aye. But I assure you that my suspicions aren't based on hearsay or speculation." She drew herself up. "Nor do I speak merely as an actress. I speak as the illegitimate daughter of the Earl of Walcester."

Now she had his full attention. "What in the devil are you talking about?"

"I'm the earl's by-blow, conceived shortly after the Battle of Naseby in a town called Norwood."

The king's eyes narrowed. Obviously he knew about both Naseby and Norwood. Perhaps he even knew of her father's presence there. "You have proof of your parentage?"

"Aye." She took out the signet ring and handed it to the king. "He gave this to my mother. It bears his coat of arms, as you can see."

The king's eyes narrowed. He turned the ring over in his fingers with a frown.

Then she handed him the poem written by the Silver Swan. "He also gave this to her."

He scanned it quickly, then paled. "You'd best tell me everything."

She related an abbreviated version of how her mother and father had met and how her mother had come by the coded poem. Then she told him why her mother had married the squire. She told him her mother and stepfather were dead but didn't say how, ending with the fact that she'd come to London penniless to seek out her father, though she made no mention of her plans for vengeance.

When she finished, the king looked astonished. "This is most disturbing." He read the poem again. "Buckingham!" he shouted, making Annabelle jump.

The door into the other room opened and the duke entered, along with Lord Rochester. Annabelle's stomach sank. Had the king not believed her?

"You were well acquainted with what happened at Norwood after the Battle of Naseby, weren't you?" the king asked Buckingham. "Wasn't the Earl of Walcester questioned in connection with the incident?"

"Aye, Your Majesty. I was one of the men who questioned him."

"Didn't he claim to know nothing of the three Royalists who carried the papers until after they were arrested?"

Buckingham's eyes narrowed. "As I recall, that is true, sire." His shrewd gaze flitted to Annabelle, then back to the king.

"You know Mrs. Maynard, I suppose," the king said, waving his hand toward her.

The duke nodded with a knowing smile.

But Lord Rochester said slyly, "Aye, Your Majesty. We *all* know Mrs. Maynard."

"If you must listen in," the king snapped at Rochester, "keep your tongue in check. This business happened while you were still a pup, so I doubt you have anything to add."

Annabelle relaxed. After what had occurred earlier in the evening, Lord Rochester no doubt itched to strike back at her.

His Majesty returned his attention to Buckingham. "Mrs. Maynard claims to be Walcester's illegitimate daughter. I have reason to believe she tells the truth.

Lord Rochester's eyes widened and she could feel his gaze on her, probing, resentful.

The king handed Buckingham the poem. "Madame Maynard claims this was sent by Walcester to someone in Norwood shortly before the men were arrested. Do you remember the names the men were using?"

"Anthony Gibbs, Benedict Cooper, and Paxton Hart." Buckingham read the poem several times over as Annabelle waited, resisting the urge to twist the overskirt of her gown. She mustn't appear anxious, or they'd never believe her.

When he reached the bottom, he murmured, "Ah yes, the Silver Swan. I'd forgotten that was his code name." His gaze shot to her.

"So you think he probably did write it," the king said.

"It does look like his hand."

The king turned to Annabelle. "To whom was your mother supposed to give this?"

"All she told me was that my father, Captain Maynard, sent her into town with a description of the man." She related the rest of it for the duke's benefit.

A calculating expression crossed Buckingham's face, giving her pause, though the king didn't seem to notice.

"I'm curious, Mrs. Maynard," Buckingham said. "Why have you chosen to bring this to our attention?"

"I wish to see justice done. All I have seen of my father tells me that he is dangerous. I felt it my duty to expose his treachery to those who could end it, before he has the chance to do any more damage." She added truthfully, "And before he can hurt me for what I know."

"I see." Buckingham read the poem again. "It seems to me, Your Majesty, that this is a message in code, governed by the reference to the bard. It contains the three names of the men who were taken."

He showed the king the paper, gesturing to a line. "Here 'Portia' is meant to be read as Anthony, since they were both characters in *The Merchant of Venice*, and 'Beatrice' as Benedict, from *Much Ado About Nothing*. Down here, 'heart' is meant to be Paxton Hart. The 'martyr's plain' no doubt refers to St. Stephen's Street, where the men were staying. 'Tis clear that Walcester wanted to identify them for the benefit of the soldiers, who promptly went to arrest the men there."

This was the first time Annabelle had heard where the men were captured. That line leapt into her mind—*Far away from the martyr's plain*. If her father had wanted to betray his companions, why would he have sent a message bidding the soldiers to tread far from that street?

"What a nasty business," the king said. "Yet it

does seem as if you are right. What of the rest of the message?"

Buckingham folded the paper and tucked it into his pocket. "Mere words to throw the reader off the scent. You know how these communications work— a lot of frivolous material to cover up the meat."

Annabelle was no longer paying attention to Buckingham. She raced through the poem, trying to remember the key phrases. *Your heart you must keep close and mute.* If that referred to the *man* Hart, then why would her father admonish the soldiers to keep him silent, but not the others?

And what about *Lest ye be forced by crown-less hands / To sing the hangman's lullaby*? Were the crown-less hands Cromwell's men?

A cold chill swept over her. What if she'd been wrong about the poem? Might it be a warning?

That made no sense. Her father had no reason to hide the fact that he'd tried to warn the Royalists. Only if he'd *betrayed* them would he want to keep her silent.

Still . . .

"Your Majesty?" she said. "It seems to me that the last line of the poem might have meaning."

As Buckingham shot her a wary glance, the king said, "Oh?"

"The line about the crown-less hands—"

"Means nothing," Buckingham said smoothly. "Unless it refers to the Roundheads' desire to take the crown from the king."

"No, I meant—"

"I think you'd best leave this sort of thing to the men." Buckingham fixed her with a cold gaze. "You're quite talented on the stage, Mrs. Maynard, but sorting out coded messages is not within your purview."

For the first time, it dawned on her that there might be more to Buckingham's determination to keep her silent. She'd best tread carefully.

"Perhaps you're right, Your Grace," she said in a conciliatory tone, "but I do know more about the situation than any of you, since my mother was there."

"We should speak to the mother, you know," His Majesty interjected.

Annabelle stifled a sigh. "I told you, sire. My mother is dead."

"Ah yes, you did."

The door to the room opened, and Barbara Palmer thrust her head inside. Sparing a contemptuous glance for Annabelle, she forced a pout to her lips for the king. "I swear, why are you three taking so long? I thought we were going to play whist. Peg and I are near to tears with boredom waiting for you."

His Majesty flashed his mistress an ingratiating smile. "Just a moment more, darling. State business does sometimes intrude, you know."

"State business." Barbara's tone was snide. "Of course." She glared at Annabelle, but at Buckingham's dismissive nod, she shut the door.

"In any case," His Majesty told Annabelle, "Buckingham is correct. You must leave it to us to address the problem now, my dear. Buckingham is well versed in the ways of spies. I have complete faith in his ability to sort out the truth." Clearly, the king no longer wanted to be bothered.

Buckingham looked pleased with himself, which worried her. What if she *were* wrong? Now that she thought on it, the poem could be interpreted more than one way. "Your Majesty, I think perhaps I've been hasty—"

"So like a woman to be fickle," Lord Rochester drawled. "Have you suddenly figured out that Hampden won't take kindly to your exposing his friend as a traitor?"

Annabelle paled. "Lord Hampden has nothing to do with this," she said, trying to sound nonchalant. "I can't imagine why you'd think he would."

"Can't you? He *is* your lover, is he not? Or have the two of you had a falling-out?"

Buckingham seemed perturbed. "I don't see what Hampden has to do with this."

"Come, Buckingham," Lord Rochester said, his lip curling with disdain. "The girl prances about the stage under her father's own code name, and suddenly Hampden, Walcester's only ally in London, displays profound interest in her. A bit too pat, don't you think? It smacks to me of a conspiracy."

"Nay!" she cried. "What conspiracy?"

Lord Rochester shrugged. "Walcester's been

deliberately misleading his peers all these years about what happened at Norwood. And to what purpose? Does he have secret ties to the king's enemies? Are he and Hampden up to some treachery?"

"That's an outright lie, and you know it!" she cried. "You're merely angry because Lord Hampden shamed you at the Blue Bell tonight."

Lord Rochester glared at her.

"What's this?" the king asked.

"Lord Hampden put his sword through his lordship's breeches for his scandalous behavior toward me," Annabelle said with scorn. "Lord Rochester was behaving like a drunken lecher . . . as usual."

The king hid his laugh behind a discreet cough.

That only seemed to infuriate Lord Rochester. "The fact remains that Hampden and Walcester have been intriguing together. Hampden obviously knew about the whole thing and sought you out for that reason. For all we know, the two of them made you part of it until you came to your senses and decided to do your duty by your country."

"Your Majesty," Annabelle pleaded, "all of this about Lord Hampden is sheer nonsense! Lord Rochester is just being spiteful because—"

"Enough!" the king said wearily. "Listen to me, Mrs. Maynard. You have presented us with important evidence, and for that we are grateful. Now you shall have to trust me and my advisers to sort out the truth." He gave her a condescending smile. "These are weighty matters. I promise that we are more qualified to deal with them than you. You have done your part. Now you must let us do ours."

"But—"

"Are you questioning the integrity of His Majesty or his advisers?" Buckingham asked sternly. His eyes sparkled with something that looked suspiciously like triumph.

Why did he seem so pleased with all of this? "Nay." She fought the trembling in her belly. Dear heaven, she could say no more without giving the king insult. But how could she let Lord Rochester sway them with his insane lies?

"Then that is settled," the king said and turned for the door, obviously ready to return to his mistress. "Buckingham, we must discuss this at length in the morning. Something must be done about Walcester." He cast Lord Rochester a considering glance. "Hampden, too, if indeed he is involved."

Annabelle stood there, helpless to stop the madness. They'd taken it out of her hands. But, sweet Mary, what had she done?

"Rochester, will you accompany Mrs. Maynard downstairs?" His Majesty said as an afterthought.

Rochester practically licked his lips over the prospect. "Of course, sire."

"I can see myself out, Your Majesty," she said.

"*I'll* see you out," the Duke of Buckingham inexplicably put in.

"Very good," said His Majesty, opening the door

to the other room. "Come along, Rochester. We have friends to entertain."

Buckingham led her out the door leading to the Privy Stairs, but as soon as they were alone, he murmured, "I have a suggestion for you, Mrs. Maynard."

"Aye, Your Grace?" She was still reeling from the rapidity with which they'd gone from scarcely believing her story to condemning both her father and Colin.

"I wouldn't speak to anyone of what happened here tonight, if I were you."

She stopped short to fix him with a suspicious gaze. "Why?"

His lazy smile didn't mask the cruelty about his eyes. "I have more influence with the king than you could ever dream of. One word, and I can make it seem as if you, too, were part of this absurd conspiracy of Rochester's."

Only with great effort did she keep from letting him cow her. "Surely His Majesty isn't so lacking in discernment as to think that a frivolous actress like me would be interested in such boring affairs."

Buckingham's eyes rested on her bosom. "Perhaps. But then, as you saw just now, His Majesty would rather dally with his mistresses than concern himself with matters of state. He will listen to me when I suggest that he keep your name out of the entire affair—for propriety's sake, of course."

She sucked in a breath. "And what do you wish of me in return?"

"That you do not mention that poem to anyone, especially Lord Hampden."

Her control slipped a fraction. "His lordship had nothing to do with it!"

He smiled. "Yes, well, we shall see. But in truth, I have no doubt he's innocent, and I'm sure the king realizes it as well. Rochester can spout absurdities when he's angry, but that doesn't mean anyone will credit them."

The tension in her chest eased a little.

"Nonetheless, your lover *is* Walcester's friend. If justice is to be done and your father to be punished, we mustn't have Hampden stepping in to confuse the interpretation of the poem, if you know what I mean. Better that he not know about the poem at all."

Her pulse quickened as the truth hit her. Buckingham didn't care what the poem really said. He hated her father and was taking this chance to rid himself of an enemy.

Instead of delighting in that, she only felt guilt. It was one thing to betray her father if he was a traitor, and quite another to see him pay for a crime he hadn't committed.

She didn't know why he'd hidden the truth about Norwood all these years, but what if he'd had just cause? What if she'd just set into motion the condemnation of an innocent man? He deserved to suffer for abandoning Mother, but if she were honest, she had to admit that he hadn't been the one to torment her, and Mother hadn't been hanged for any crime that *he* had done.

So what kind of woman was she to send her own father to the gallows? Nay, she couldn't do it, for it would make her as low as he.

She certainly couldn't let them take Colin. And no matter what the duke said, if Lord Rochester had his way, Colin would be implicated.

"You do want to see your father arrested, don't you?" Buckingham said with an oily smirk. "To see justice done?"

Aye, justice. Not murder.

She had to find a way out of this. She had to save Colin and learn the truth about her father. But Buckingham would be no help to her, that was certain.

She forced a smile. "Justice. Of course."

Buckingham nodded his approval, then took her arm once more and continued down the stairs.

Yes, she would do whatever she must to see justice done for both Colin and her father. Because in the end, it was her soul that lay in the balance. And she had finally decided that she wanted to keep it.

Chapter Twenty

"He that would govern others, first should be
The master of himself."
—Philip Massinger, *The Bondman,* Act 1, Sc. 3

Hell and furies, where is Annabelle?

Colin pulled his horse up before his town house in the early-morning hours. He'd spent all night in search of her—at the Blue Bell, at her lodgings, at Aphra's lodgings, even at Sir John's house—but she seemed to have vanished. By the time Sir John and Charity admitted that they'd seen her at the theater, she'd left there, too, to go nobody knew where.

And he still had to deal with the damned earl. Assuming the man was still at his house, which was by no means certain.

But of course Colin couldn't be so lucky. The earl was waiting for him as soon as he entered, apparently having sat there in the foyer the whole time Colin was gone. And he looked it, too, although Colin felt little sympathy for him.

"Did you find her?" the man demanded as he clasped his cane and shoved to a stand.

"Why do you care?" Colin snapped.

The earl scowled. "I don't. But since you refuse to do as you promised and keep flitting off about the countryside—"

"I've been in Norwood for the past two weeks," Colin said baldly. He paused to let that sink in and was rewarded to see Walcester pale.

"Why?" the earl asked hoarsely.

"To find out what Annabelle and you were hiding."

Walcester glanced over at the servants, who were listening with great curiosity. "Perhaps we should have this discussion more privately."

"Indeed," Colin said, though at the moment he didn't care much about preserving the man's reputation. Especially if the earl was as guilty of treachery as he feared.

Colin led the man to his study. As soon as they entered, Walcester rounded on him. "What did you discover in Norwood?" he demanded, his gaze fearful.

"That everything Annabelle said last night is true and then some. Annabelle's bastardy often made her the target of her stepfather's punishments, so her mother went mad one day while her husband was beating Annabelle yet again over some minor infraction, and she plunged a butcher knife through his heart."

A strange mix of emotions crossed Walcester's face, but Colin could summon no pity for the man.

"That's why, after Annabelle witnessed her own mother's hanging, she came penniless to London, hoping to find you and have her vengeance."

At last Walcester showed some hint of feeling, fixing Colin with the kind of astonished grief people wear when they first realize a loved one has been taken from them. "Phoebe was hanged?" Walcester asked in a still voice.

"Aye. Apparently, her death was slow and painful."

Walcester muttered a ragged oath. "Poor Phoebe. I never loved her as deeply as she loved me, but she was a sweet slip of a thing, given to tender words and very timid."

"Except, I take it, when you bedded her." Colin's voice hardened. "Unless you raped her."

"Good God, no!" Walcester protested. "'Twas not a rape. We cared for one another. I wouldn't have left her behind if I hadn't been forced to."

"You mean when your Royalist companions were all taken prisoner and the king's papers confiscated?"

Walcester suddenly looked quite old and weary. He leaned heavily on his walking stick. "I suppose you should tell me what else you found out in Norwood."

Should he even give Walcester the chance to explain? The earl was a liar and a spy and probably not to be trusted.

Then again, though he suspected the man of

being a traitor, he had no proof, and he couldn't in good conscience pursue the matter without it. He should at least hear the earl's side, if only to help in sorting through the lies.

Colin walked over to the brandy decanter on his desk and poured two glasses. When he offered the other to the earl, the man waved it away.

With a shrug, Colin sipped some. "I spoke with the Harlows' housekeeper. She told me you'd spent three weeks in the Harlow home recovering from injuries, though she didn't know, of course, what you'd been doing with Phoebe Harlow."

"We were very circumspect."

"Yes," Colin said dryly, "until you left her alone with a babe in her belly."

"And she was married off to the squire. I know all that," Walcester bit out. "What else did the housekeeper say?"

"That you fled after the three Royalist spies were arrested. There was talk that they'd been betrayed by one of their own."

"Aye, they had been." Turning away, Walcester walked over to the fireplace.

Colin stared at him incredulously, hardly able to believe that Walcester would admit his treachery so freely. "You sent a message by Miss Harlow to someone in the town."

Walcester whirled to stare at him. "How did you know that?"

"Annabelle told me. Her mother gave her the

poem your message was hidden in and told her it was written by her father. Annabelle, of course, didn't realize what it was, but I found it among her things and realized its significance at once. I just didn't understand why you gave it to her mother. Until I went to Norwood."

The earl went rigid. "The poem. Where is it? Where does my . . . daughter keep it?"

"Why?"

"Don't you see? It proves everything."

"I figured as much."

Walcester couldn't mistake the accusation in Colin's voice. "No, you don't understand. It proves that I warned them about the traitor in their midst!"

That took Colin by surprise. "You mean, it wasn't *you*?"

"Good God, no!" the earl protested. "But there was one, and in the end he succeeded in getting them captured. Obviously Phoebe failed to deliver the message, and as a consequence the Royalists were arrested."

Colin regarded Walcester warily. He didn't think the man was lying, yet something wasn't right. "Annabelle insists that her mother did deliver the poem. Your friend read it and then told her to leave."

A desperate look entered Walcester's eyes. "The girl must be lying." At Colin's fierce frown, he said hastily, "Or mistaken. Perhaps Phoebe delivered the poem to the wrong person." He let out a chuff of exasperation. "Something had to have happened or the men would have been saved."

"I don't understand. I heard that you claimed not to even know the three men were in town. Why? If you did your duty back then, you'd have no reason to hide your involvement." And no reason to spy on Annabelle.

"But I *didn't* do my duty—that's the point!" Walcester snapped. "My duty was to save those men, to tell them they had a traitor in their midst." His expression turned grim. "My duty was to prevent them from being drawn and quartered and the king's papers from being confiscated. Perhaps if I had, the war would have ended differently and our late king might not have been executed."

His voice grew rough with guilt. "Instead I sent a woman to do my duty, and she failed." Walcester shook his head. "Do you know what my enemies would make of that? They would think me a coward or, worse yet, suspect me of bungling it on purpose, of being a traitor. All manner of things might go wrong, and my political career would be over."

"That's why you've kept it secret? Because you didn't go yourself?"

A faraway look crossed his face. "Aye. I shouldn't have sent a woman to do my work."

Silently Colin agreed. Poor, innocent Phoebe Harlow should never have been forced to aid Walcester in such a dangerous task. "Then why did you?"

"Because I *was* a coward. The soldiers were everywhere, and I knew if they caught me I'd die a spy's death, drawn and quartered like the rest."

Colin stared hard at him. "Why didn't you tell me this before?"

"So you could scorn me? Would you have helped me if you'd known? Nay. You would have been contemptuous, and you would have washed your hands of me." His voice lowered. "Or worse."

A sadness filled Colin as he realized what the earl meant. "You've been a spy too long, old man, if you think I would have betrayed you." This was what came of a long career looking over one's shoulder. A man started to suspect even his friends of treachery.

"Perhaps you wouldn't have, but you know damned well that others would if they learned of it."

Walcester had a point. If the earl were exposed as a coward responsible for setting in motion the events leading to Charles I's execution, it would indeed ruin his political career, if not open him to charges of treason.

"If you don't believe me," Walcester put in, "then look at the words of my poem. They prove my innocence."

Colin ran through the words in his mind. "I can see that the line about keeping quiet or being forced 'by crown-less hands / To sing the hangman's lullaby' is a warning about being caught by the Roundheads, but who were Portia and Beatrice?"

"Don't you know your Shakespeare, Hampden?

Portia saves Antonio's life in *The Merchant of Venice* and Beatrice fell in love with Benedict in *Much Ado About Nothing*. Three Royalists were fleeing the Battle of Naseby with the king's papers when one was wounded and they had to take shelter in Norwood, posing as wealthy merchants. Two of them took the names Anthony and Benedict. The message was for them."

"And the third?"

Walcester's expression grew fierce. "Paxton Hart. *He* was the traitor. He sent word to the soldiers at the Harlow house where the Roundhead captain was supposed to be dining. Only he wasn't there, and you know how soldiers are. They couldn't decide anything without first finding their captain. Besides, they thought they had plenty of time. But they didn't reckon on me, of course. Since I was staying there, I heard everything. That's when I sent the message."

"That they should keep Hart 'close and mute' and 'tread' far from 'the martyr's plain.'"

"The inn where they were staying was in St. Stephen's Street." Walcester sighed. "I didn't dare write the message out the way I wanted, in case it fell into enemy hands, but I knew 'Benedict' would understand. So I sent Phoebe to him with it, because I feared to go myself and risk capture."

"Instead you risked Phoebe's life, for the soldiers would have been no kinder to her if she'd been caught."

Walcester blanched. "I'd hoped the coded message would protect her, but you are right. I should have done my duty and gone myself. Everything might have been different, then. I always assumed she never delivered the message."

"Or perhaps the soldiers moved more quickly than you bargained for."

"Probably," Walcester said sadly.

Colin shook his head. What a tangled tale. Yet Walcester couldn't blame himself entirely. The traitor was as much to blame as any.

"What happened to Hart?" Colin asked.

"They killed him with the others. They weren't foolish enough to keep a man alive who'd betrayed his own companions." Walcester paused a moment. "You know, the worst of it wasn't that I trusted Phoebe to do my work, but that she wouldn't have been regarded as trustworthy by anyone else. Her father was a Roundhead. Yet it . . . it didn't worry me. She said she loved me, and I thought she didn't care about political matters—"

"I doubt that she did." Colin managed a reassuring smile. "A woman in love can be fiercely loyal." He thought of Annabelle. A woman in love could also be easily wounded. He'd tarried here too long.

First he had to ensure one thing. "Walcester, you do understand that Annabelle knew none of this." Until he'd told her.

"Yes, you've explained that. I suppose if she had,

she'd have found some way to punish me with the poem, since . . ." A look of chagrin crossed his face. "Since, as you say, she has some cause to hate me."

"'Some'?"

He blanched. "Perhaps more than some." Each word seemed wrenched from him. Then he scowled. "But for God's sake, man, you don't understand how it galls to see one's daughter playing the wanton on the stage! I have no children. Then I discover that I do have someone of my blood, and in the same day I learn she's become a wild trollop—"

"I can set your mind at ease about that. Annabelle's wantonness was a part she played and no more. The only man she ever bedded was me, and that only because I seduced her, as you seduced her mother."

Walcester's eyes widened in disbelief, then outrage.

Colin faced him squarely. "Aye. Annabelle is no wanton. I can testify to the truth of that. She merely wished to humiliate you, and it seems she succeeded."

"And intends to continue at it," Walcester said with wry bitterness.

Colin's insides knotted. "Now see here, Walcester. You're not to do anything about those threats Annabelle made. You'll leave that to me."

The earl forced a smile. "Don't worry. Any fool can see that you have more influence with her than

I." He surveyed Colin with grim satisfaction. "You care for my daughter, don't you?"

Colin met his gaze without a hint of remorse. "I love your daughter."

Walcester's mocking laugh grated. "For God's sake, why?"

"She was hardy enough to survive her childhood and daring enough to take on all of London society, which is more than you were willing to do. What's more, until you showed up today and tore her heart to ribbons, she was willing to bestow mercy upon a man who neither asked for it nor deserved it."

Walcester colored.

"Now," Colin went on, "if you'll excuse me, I intend to find your daughter and beg her—on my knees, if necessary—to forgive me for conspiring with you. Then I intend to marry her, if she'll still have me."

"Marry her?" Walcester said in astonishment. "You and Lord Falkham with your common women."

Colin arched an eyebrow. "She's no more common than you are, for your blood runs through her veins."

"True," the earl grumbled, surprising him. "I suppose I can hardly complain if you choose to make her respectable. I can't believe the girl would refuse. She'd be a fool not to marry you."

"Fear of being thought a fool doesn't always stop Annabelle from doing what she wishes."

"You have my permission to tell her I approve of the match."

A sarcastic retort sprung to Colin's lips, then died when he saw the wistfulness in the hoary earl's features.

Somehow Colin managed to keep the coldness out of his voice. "My association with you hasn't exactly endeared her to me, so telling her you've given me your blessing would probably prompt her to refuse my proposal at once. But if you wish, I'll pass some other message on to her from you."

Like a man who had lost his bearings, Walcester stared about him. In his world, men with titles never dreamed of marrying women of small wealth and bad reputation. But the war had changed a great many things for Colin—judging people by their rank and wealth was one of them.

"Aye, pass on a message to my daughter," Walcester said. "Tell her . . . that I'll claim her." He hesitated, then his voice grew firmer. "Aye, you tell her that. She'll be a bastard no more."

Colin wanted to retort that society would never let Annabelle forget she was a bastard if Walcester claimed her. She'd almost be better off as Annabelle Taylor, the squire's daughter whose mother murdered him, than as Annabelle Maynard, the earl's bastard. And Annabelle would benefit most from the words *I'm sorry*.

But Colin held his tongue. After all, Walcester at least *thought* he was making a great concession. And though Annabelle might not accept the earl's offer, it might soothe her pain to know he'd made it.

He stared at the earl, whose brow was knit with worry about his political future and whose hands clutched the walking stick, and Colin felt a stab of pity for the lonely old man. His dreams of power were his only sustenance.

Colin put his hand on the earl's shoulder. "I'll tell her," he murmured.

But first he must find her.

He returned to Aphra's and spent several hours there, hoping Annabelle would appear, but she didn't. After a while, he had to face the fact that she wasn't returning. By then, the long day and night had taken its toll on him. First his grueling ride, then his discussion with Annabelle and their time in the study . . .

A bitter smile crossed his face. He could hardly complain about *that*. For one sweet moment, he'd had her entirely within his grasp, before Walcester had arrived and shattered everything.

As he reached his town house and handed his horse off to the groom, he vowed that he'd find her if he had to comb all of England. Somehow he'd make her understand and forgive him for deceiving her.

His footman greeted him at the door to take his cloak. "The woman who accompanied you home last evening is in the drawing room awaiting you, my lord. I wasn't certain whether I should allow her to stay, but she simply would not go."

"You did the right thing," Colin said, relief coursing through him.

When he strode into the drawing room, his heart leapt at the sight of the slender form asleep in an armchair before the fire. "Annabelle."

Her head came up and she rubbed her eyes.

"Where have you been?" he cried, going to her side.

Her expression of sleepy confusion faded to one of wariness.

How long had she been here? And where the devil had she gotten such a lavish silk gown? It was all he could do to keep from gathering her up in his arms, but judging from her expression, he dared not.

She settled herself demurely in the chair, her gaze dropping from his. "I need to speak with you, if you'll spare me a moment."

"Spare you a *moment*?" he said incredulously, wounded by her formal tone. "I'll spare you a few years if that's what it takes. I have to explain—"

Her gaze shot to his, dark with worry. "There's no time for that. Let me say what I've come to say, and then I'll leave you alone."

Oh no you won't. But he didn't say it. He must handle this carefully if he were to get her back. "Very well. Speak your mind."

Now he noticed what she held clutched in her arms—the box he'd seen on her bureau. Ah, hell. That couldn't be good.

She rose to face him. "I've done a terrible thing."

The blood pounded in his ears. "And what is that, dearling?"

The endearment gained him a quick surprised glance before it changed to something that looked oddly like guilt. She looked heart-wrenchingly beautiful in the gorgeous gown, part of her hair swept up and tied with a ribbon while the mass of it cascaded down her back. It made his blood race to see her thus.

"You know that poem I told you about? The one my father gave Mother?"

His gaze flew to the box before he caught himself. He reminded himself that she didn't know he'd seen the poem, that he'd drugged her to get a glimpse of it. One more secret for him to make penance for. "Yes. I remember."

"After I left here, I—I was so angry with you and my father. I could tell that you were indebted to him, and it hurt to think you'd helped him."

"I helped him in the beginning," he put in. "He saved my life once, so I didn't feel I could refuse him when he asked me to find out what you were up to."

"Yes, I see," she said almost distractedly.

He plunged on, blindly afraid of that strange distraction. "But I took the trip to Norwood on my own, because I'd already fallen half in love with you and had to know what I was getting into. I swear to you, that's the truth."

She stared at him with a gut-twisting sadness. "It doesn't matter anymore. I've done something far worse, I'm afraid, than anything you could ever have done."

"What do you mean?" Dread built slowly in him when she kept glancing away, as if looking at him would kill her.

"I went a little mad after I saw the two of you together." She paused. "You'd already told me that you thought my father was a traitor."

At that statement, his eyes narrowed.

"I read the poem again," she continued, "but I could make no sense of it. It did seem to me, however, that I ought to do something. If my father truly was a traitor, he deserved to be punished." Her voice grew more distant with every word. "I knew you wouldn't stand against your friend, and I knew of no one else who had the power to see that justice was done." She drew in a sharp breath. "Except perhaps one man."

A cold chill struck him. "Who?" he asked.

"His Majesty," she said in a small voice.

He felt as if someone had just knocked the wind out of him. She'd gone to the king after all the pains they'd taken to keep her safe? Was that why she was dressed this way? His blood rose at the thought of the king speaking with Annabelle in the dead of night. Surely that wasn't the "terrible thing" she spoke of. Surely she wouldn't have let His Majesty lay a hand on her.

"You went to the king?" was all he could manage.

Her words came out in a rush. "He was with Buckingham and some others. I showed him the poem; I explained everything, but it all got turned around, and before I knew it Rochester was accusing you of treason and Buckingham was calling for my father's arrest and—"

She broke off with a sob. "Dear heaven, Colin, I didn't want to hurt you! You may not believe this anymore, but I do love you. That's why I had to warn you about what they intend."

He didn't know whether to feel relieved that the king hadn't touched her or horrified that she'd told the king stories about him and Walcester. Hell and furies, had she been that angry?

"Perhaps you should start at the beginning," he said through a throat thick with pain. "Tell me everything."

It took him several minutes to get the entire story out of her coherently, but when at last he understood what had happened, he realized she'd not tried to implicate him in treason. What she'd done was certainly serious and would no doubt have dire repercussions for Walcester, but Colin himself was not in any real danger. And it was his safety she seemed most concerned about.

On that, he could reassure her. "Don't worry about me, my love. If indeed His Majesty believes Rochester, he'll simply have me questioned and then dismiss the matter. Rochester isn't out for blood; he just wants to repay me for humiliating him. I can handle whatever he throws at me."

"Don't you see? It's bigger than that now," she whispered. "If they prove that my father was a traitor, then you'll be seen as one too!"

"Your father wasn't a traitor," he stated. "I can assure them of that. In fact, he was something of a hero if they can be made to realize it."

Fear crossed her face. "What do you mean?"

He didn't want to increase her guilt, but she would learn the truth eventually. Quickly he related all her father had told him. The longer he talked, the paler she grew.

"Dear heaven, what have I done?" she whispered.

"When they question Walcester, he'll explain everything, and when I add my testimony—"

"You don't understand!" she broke in. "Buckingham will do anything to destroy my father. The duke will never let them hear the truth."

She seemed so sure that it worried him. He forced a lightness into his tone. "Nonsense. Buckingham's a fair man. I'll admit I've been away from court for some time and I'm not as familiar with the political alliances among the nobles, but Buckingham was always Walcester's ally. Surely he'll champion your father."

She shook her head. "Buckingham accompanied me out of Whitehall. He warned me against showing you the poem. Of course, he didn't know that you already knew of it, and I certainly didn't tell him."

"What did you say?"

After she recounted the conversation in a few terse words, a terrible sadness stole over him. Damn Buckingham. The duke was powerful enough to ensure her father was punished. Certainly Walcester would never finish his years in England. Most likely he'd be exiled like Clarendon, his dreams of political power ended forever.

She stared into the fire. "So you see, my father will be destroyed no matter what you or I say. Buckingham may not care about ruining you, but he is certainly determined to ruin my father."

He couldn't resist saying, "That should make you happy."

Shame flooded her face. "Nay. Though I had some dream of making him regret what he did to my mother, I never wanted to see him exiled or imprisoned or . . ."

She trailed off, but he knew what she didn't dare to voice. She'd already seen one parent hanged. She didn't wish to see another suffer the same fate.

Her woeful expression roused every protective instinct within him. "Listen to me, dearling—"

"Don't call me that!" she burst out, half in tears. "I don't deserve it. I've ruined your life and betrayed my own father to a pack of hounds eager for his blood. Don't pretend you feel anything but contempt for me now!"

He strode up to clasp her face in his hands. "I feel a great many emotions at the moment, but contempt isn't one of them. Yes, I'm stunned by all you've told me, but I know you felt it was your duty."

Tears streamed down her cheeks.

He wiped them away with his thumbs, wishing he could wipe away her pain, too. "And I'm hurt that you didn't feel you could trust me with the problem, but I do understand. If I'd been more truthful with you, this would never have happened."

Her gaze shot to his, the yearning in them so palpable he felt his heart twist in response.

"But mostly I'm sick with fear that you won't believe me when I say I love you. Because I do, no matter what you've done, no matter what happens."

Chapter Twenty-One

"The quality of mercy is not strained,
It droppeth as the gentle rain from heaven
Upon the place beneath: it is twice blessed;
It blesseth him that gives and him that takes . . ."
—William Shakespeare, *The Merchant of Venice*, Act 4, Sc. 1

Annabelle could hardly believe Colin. "I've ruined your life. And the life of your friend, my father."

A sardonic look crossed his face. "Walcester can take care of himself, dearling." His eyes softened. "As for me, the only thing you've done is make it impossible for me to live without you. From the moment I first saw you onstage, I knew I had to have you for myself, regardless of what Walcester wanted." He let out a shuddering breath. "I haven't lost you, have I? Can you forgive me for spying on you, for not telling you about my friendship with your father?"

When she lowered her gaze in confusion, reminded yet again of how he'd deceived her, he added hastily, "It wasn't as bad as it looks. Even as

I arranged our first meeting, I didn't just have Walcester in mind. I did as he wished only because I found you so intriguing. But after I began to pursue you, I went to him once and that was just to discover what he was hiding."

Once. But what had he said? "Did you tell him about . . . what we did?"

It seemed to take him a second to figure out what she was talking about. Then he clutched her to him. "Hell and furies, of course not! What kind of man do you take me for? I told him about the ring, and I asked him if you were his daughter. That's when I found out you were from Norwood, for he remembered your mother."

"When was this?" she asked in a hoarse whisper.

He remained silent a moment, then sighed. "After we made love the first time, while you were asleep."

Sorting through her memories, she winced. "That physic you gave me was a sleeping draught, wasn't it?"

"Aye. While you slept, I searched your room and found the key to your box. I read the poem and then I went to Walcester. But I didn't tell him about it then, because I wasn't sure whom to believe or trust."

"That's when you decided to go to Norwood."

He nodded, a strange expression of despair on his face. Did he really care so much? Then another realization hit her. "That's why you were so cold to me that morning. Why you acted so strangely when you left me at Aphra's."

"Aye. I knew you were lying to me about the Silver Swan, and I feared you had some dire purpose in mind."

She tried to back away, but he held her tight. Though it still hurt to think of him distrusting her, she'd never completely trusted him either.

"I've told you everything now," he murmured, nuzzling her hair, "every way I've kept the truth from you. And I believe you've told me everything as well. So tell me: Am I to lose you because I couldn't trust?"

She shook her head.

"I love you," he murmured. "You've said you love me. Can't we go on from there and make a new beginning?"

"So many secrets, so many roles." She gazed at him with longing. "Can we really say we love each other when our love is built on lies?"

Determination shone in his eyes. "There were some truths between us from the very beginning, dearling. I never lied about wanting you. And though I didn't tell you about my association with Walcester, in every other way, I was myself with you—a shade too quick-tongued, perhaps, about everything, but truthful."

She believed him. She didn't know why, but she did.

He stroked a tendril of hair from her face. "Nor

were you as deceitful as you seem to think. You never lied about your pain. Even when you disguised it, I could sense and understand it, because I've suffered a similar pain. And you never lied about your innocence, which showed in your every word and smile."

More tears stained her cheeks as she was filled once more with the overwhelming shame of what she'd done. "There's little enough innocence in me now."

"Aye. You've learned that the world can be crueler even than your stepfather was. And perhaps for the first time, you've committed an act that's left you feeling genuine guilt. But it's also helped you learn what you really want for yourself. It's helped you find the core that is Annabelle, the woman beneath the roles."

"I don't know who Annabelle is anymore."

He smiled. "I do. Annabelle is too softhearted to see her father go to prison, despite what he did to her mother. Annabelle is the kind of woman who'll take on a king before she'll relinquish her dignity. She's strong enough to withstand a beating, though I hope to God she never has to again, and kind enough to feed oranges to street urchins. Yet there's a part of her that wants to shed her roles and simply live."

Dear heaven, how could she let a man like this slip away? She'd known many a gallant and none of them had ever seen into her soul the way Colin did. "You make me sound much better than my father."

Colin's eyes went hard. "Your father's a bastard, dearling, no matter what his lineage. When he calls you names, it's truly a case of the pot calling the kettle black."

The way he leapt to defend her touched her. "You don't seem fond of him."

"Believe me, loyalty and fondness are not the same thing," he said, arching one brow. "But I'm very fond of his daughter. So tell me: Is his daughter very fond of me?"

His earnest expression made her breath quicken. "I'm fond of the Colin who gave Aphra enough rent money to last her a lifetime—"

"Which she used for a wild supper," he said wryly.

"Aye. And I'm fond of the Colin who told me about sheaths and protected me from the king." Her voice dropped to a whisper. "I'm very fond of the Colin who said he loved me and promised to marry me and take me to the colonies."

His slow smile made her heart catch in her throat.

"Then you're fond of me, dearling," he said in a husky whisper, "for there was and is no other Colin."

The words brought her more happiness than she could bear. "Then I suppose I'm quite inordinately fond of you."

"Thank God, Annabelle." He nuzzled her neck. "Hell and furies, how I love you."

He began kissing her then, and she gave herself up to it with pure delight. For the moment, her fears were eclipsed by the fire in his touch, by the heat his impassioned avowals had roused within her.

Then her joy was shattered by a loud knock at the front door.

"The servants will get it," he murmured and tried to resume kissing her, but she drew back to listen as the footman opened the door.

Surely they couldn't have come for Colin already.

Then they both heard a loud voice announce, "I'm the captain of His Majesty's Guard. Is your master at home?"

She clutched at Colin's coat. "They've come for you. Oh, sweet Mary! You've got to escape! You can't let them take you!"

He seemed more irritated than afraid. "You mustn't worry," he said. "Everything will be all right. Just stay here, and I'll speak with them."

"Colin, no!" she cried, but he was already striding into the foyer, closing the door of the drawing room behind him.

The man was insane if he thought she'd hide in here while the soldiers took him off. She hurried into the foyer, her heart in her throat.

"Good day, my lord," the captain said with a bow.

"Good day, Captain," Colin responded. "Can I be of service to you?"

The captain looked decidedly uncomfortable. "His Majesty has given me orders to accompany you to the Tower. My men await us outside."

Sweet Mary, they really were going to arrest Colin. If she ever caught sight of that wretched Lord Rochester, she'd do more than bite off his fingers—she'd plant a knife in the spot Colin had deliberately missed.

"His Lordship has done nothing wrong," she couldn't keep from saying. "Why is he being taken to the Tower?"

"Annabelle," Colin said firmly, "go upstairs and stay there until we leave."

The captain took one look at her extravagant gown and apparently decided she was Colin's wife.

"My lady," he murmured, bowing again.

"What is my . . . what is his lordship charged with?" she asked.

Colin's face went stony. "Captain. May I have a moment alone with my lady?"

The captain nodded.

Colin pulled her back into the drawing room. "Listen, dearling. You mustn't involve yourself in this. It's a tricky business, and if I'm to survive it, I must comply with whatever is asked of me. Otherwise, they'll assume I truly am guilty and I'll be dead for sure."

"But you've done nothing!"

"Aye, and the king will realize that the moment I present my case. Don't worry." He flashed her a wry smile. "The king has a certain fondness for me. He'll throw me in the Tower for a few days to satisfy his honor. 'Tis his way of disciplining his nobles. Last year, Buckingham himself had a stint in the Tower, as did Rochester for eloping with an heiress."

She knew about that, but the strain in Colin's features belied his assurances. This was, after all, a far more serious offense. "Can't you simply tell them you knew nothing about my father and had nothing to do with his spying on me?"

He forced a smile. "I could. But as much as I dislike him for what he's done to you, I can't betray him. To do so would truly make me a man of no morals."

She fought back tears. "Don't you see? Thanks to me, he's lost for good. You mustn't let him take you down with him!"

"It will be all right," he repeated.

This was all her fault. She had to find a way to stop this insanity! "Perhaps if I go to the Privy Council and explain the poem—"

"You know they won't believe what you say— not now, after you've come forward with a different story. They'll simply say the same ridiculous things they said before—that you're a woman and too emotional to be trusted. 'Tis better for you to simply stay out of it and hope for the best."

But she couldn't stay out of it. She couldn't!

"Promise me you'll do nothing to jeopardize

your own safety." He gripped her shoulders. "I'll go mad in the Tower if I think you're risking your life or . . . or your dignity for me. Promise me you won't go to the king or Buckingham or Rochester!"

She sucked in her breath. He was right. None of them would help her anymore. But perhaps she could find another way.

"I promise," she whispered.

But she wouldn't promise not to try to save him. She'd find a way to stop the madness. Somehow.

He searched her face a moment. "Do you have my ring?"

She stared at him distracted, then bobbed her head and drew the band from her pocket. He slid it onto her finger, then lifted her hand for a sweet kiss.

"Wait for me, dearling," he murmured. "Someday we'll have the chance to be together without all this. I promise."

Then he released her and strode out to the captain. She watched him go, her blood pounding in her ears and her hand tingling where he'd kissed it. She wished she could believe him. But despair reared up in her as Colin left with the captain.

She flew to the window and looked out, her despair growing as she saw the guardsmen who moved to flank Colin, their expressions serious. She couldn't let this happen!

But how to stop them? Colin was right—it would do her little good to speak with the king again. He'd obviously made up his mind, as had Buckingham.

Why were men such fools? They were more concerned with political connections and power than with the truth. All they saw was what they wanted to see.

Her entire career had been a perfect example of that. Colin had seen through her roles, but no one else had. The other men had merely seen a scheming actress. Dear heaven, they'd believed her more easily when she was playing a role than now, when she was telling the truth.

That was when it hit her. Her blood began to race as a plan formed in her mind, one of outrageous, ridiculous proportions. Yet it might work.

She hurried out into the foyer, where the footman was still standing with his mouth open. When he saw her, he told her with a faintly disapproving air that his lordship had said to make her comfortable in the house until his lordship's return.

"I need a coach," she said in the most imperious voice she could muster. "I must be taken to a friend's house at once."

"But his lordship said—"

"I'll be returning, I assure you, but I have to speak with my friend. If you want to see your master free, then please do as I ask."

His eyes widened, but he followed her command. A short ride later, Annabelle climbed the stairs to Aphra's rooms and opened the door, relieved to find the woman poring over a book.

"Annabelle!" Aphra exclaimed. "Colin's been

looking for you everywhere! What has happened? He wouldn't tell me anything."

"He's been taken to the Tower." She told her friend everything, relieved when Aphra didn't condemn her for what she'd done.

"That explains one thing, in any case," Aphra remarked. "A messenger came from Buckingham this morning with a purse for you. He said to tell you that His Grace considers it a small payment in exchange for your cooperation."

Annabelle groaned. "Dear heaven, he truly hates my father."

"What are you going to do?" Aphra asked.

Annabelle clasped her friend's hands. The money from Buckingham could work into her plan quite nicely. "You want to be a playwright, do you not?"

"Yes, but I don't see—"

"I need you to write a scene. It's got to be the best thing you've ever written and very convincing."

"What on earth are you talking about?" Aphra asked.

"It has to be good enough to free my father and Colin, good enough to be performed before your most discriminating audience yet."

Aphra's eyes narrowed. "Who?"

"His Majesty."

Chapter Twenty-Two

"Plots, true or false, are necessary things,
To raise up commonwealths and ruin kings."
—John Dryden, *Absalom and Achitophel*

Soft violin music wafted from the musicians'
box to where Annabelle sat in one of the special boxes, the one next to the king's. It felt odd to
sit across from the stage instead of behind it. It felt
odder still to wear a mask, although she knew no
one else would remark on it, since plenty of women
did at the theater.

Yet except for the mask and her seat in the box,
tonight was no different from any other night at
the theater. Her hands were clammy with both
nervousness and the rush of excitement that came
before a performance. She still wore a costume,
even if it was just an expensive gown she'd purchased with Buckingham's money in a very ostentatious manner.

If everything went according to plan, however,
her audience would be far more limited . . . and far
more discerning than usual. Oh yes, this would be

the role of a lifetime. It had to be absolutely convincing, or His Majesty would never believe it.

Thank heaven Sir William Davenant had agreed to help her and Aphra by pushing up the production of George Etherege's new play, *She Would If She Could*. Etherege was popular with the wits and gallants, so she and Aphra had reasoned that a new play of his would draw most of fine society.

And it had. Everyone of any consequence was there. The seats had been filled by two o'clock, even though the performance wasn't scheduled until three-thirty. Still, she'd not been able to rest until the king and Buckingham arrived. Once she'd heard noises in the box next to her and had recognized the king's bored tone and Buckingham's lazy one, she'd relaxed.

Now, if only her plan worked. She hoped she could say Aphra's skilled lines with some degree of sincerity and that Aphra's first attempt at acting would turn out well. Charity would certainly do her part with ease.

The curtains opened, and the first part of her plan fell into place as the theater owner himself announced that Mrs. Maynard wouldn't be playing the part of Lady Cockwood as scheduled. Mrs. Shadwell would play the part instead, Sir William Davenant stated, to some isolated boos from the wits.

As soon as he left the stage, the whispering started in the pit. Annabelle could see one gallant after another beckoning to Charity, who moved about and muttered first in one ear, then in another. Fortunately, no one noticed her sitting alone above the pit. Not that they would have recognized her with her mask on.

Everything was in motion, yet Annabelle couldn't relax. So many things could go wrong. It was a good thing Sir William hadn't asked them too many questions. He would throttle all of them when he realized how they intended to disrupt the big night.

As she waited, she fidgeted in her seat, unable to dull the edge of fearful anticipation in her blood. Her anxiety was only slightly alleviated when she heard Sir Charles Sedley enter next door and repeat to His Majesty the rumors Charity had circulated below. When His Majesty laughed, she relaxed a fraction. Sir Charles hadn't been in on the plan, but he was perfect. His Majesty had taken the first nibble at the hook, thanks to Sir Charles's gossiping tongue.

Time passed far too slowly after that. She felt as if she were watching it all from underwater. But at last Henry Harris made his entrance onstage and spoke the lines she'd been waiting for. It was time.

Right on cue, Aphra swung open the door to Annabelle's box. "Annabelle Maynard! I should have known you'd be skulking about in here, hiding behind a mask! You ought to be ashamed of yourself!"

"Keep your voice down, Aphra, if you please!" Annabelle retorted in a stage whisper that would carry quite easily to the box next to her. "I don't want Sir William to know I'm here. He thinks I'm ill."

"So he does." Aphra dropped into the chair next to Annabelle and squeezed her hand before continuing in a scathing tone, "But we both know why you don't wish to tread the boards tonight."

The voices in the next box had grown quiet as well as those in two of the other boxes. Annabelle bit back a smile and made her tone haughty. "I don't know what you mean."

"I heard what Charity's telling everyone, all that rot about you not taking the stage because you're distraught over your newly found father's arrest. You ought to be ashamed for letting them believe such lies."

"I *am* distraught over my poor dear father's arrest," she said in the sarcastic tone she'd perfected when sparring with gallants. "Here I am, having just found him, and now he's being whisked away from me."

"Such fustian, and you know it! If you hadn't lied about that poem, he wouldn't have been arrested at all."

Annabelle gave a dramatic sigh. "I didn't lie. My father did give that poem to my mother to deliver to someone in Norwood."

"Aye, but to one of the Royalists, as you well know. You didn't bother to tell them, did you, that the poem was sent to that Benedict fellow, or that the line about Hart was meant to warn his friends that their companion was a traitor. Nor did you happen to mention that the reference to 'crownless hands' referred to the Roundheads. That poem clearly stated that if his companions didn't leave St. Stephens they'd be captured. Of course, you kept that all quite secret."

Now a gallant was looking up from the pit at them. He nudged his companion and they focused their eyes on the two women conversing above them. She and Aphra had pitched their voices to stand out slightly over the hum of audience noise that always accompanied the plays, so she knew that anyone who paid attention would hear them.

"I didn't see the need to tell His Majesty everything," Annabelle said smugly, but wondered if the men in the next box could truly be so dense as to not realize this was staged. Then again, they'd been pretty dense in other matters.

Besides, it didn't matter if they figured it out. She'd still have made the situation public in a way that the king dared not ignore.

"Aye, you told them exactly what you wanted them to know," Aphra hissed. "I take it you didn't tell them that you hold your father responsible for abandoning your mother."

"That was none of their affair," Annabelle said with a sniff.

Aphra gave a mocking laugh. "Nor did it suit

your plans. I hope you're happy now. An innocent man is in prison because of your lies. Thanks to you, your father is being treated as a traitor instead of the hero that he was."

"Why do you care about my father anyway?" Annabelle said in her stage whisper. "You know it was monstrous of him to abandon my mother and me. What does it matter to you if I wish to avenge that?"

"I don't care a whit for your father. But thanks to your insane desire to see vengeance, my friend Lord Hampden is in the Tower. That's what you should be ashamed of. After all, he *was* your lover."

"Was. Until he ran off somewhere to meet another woman, leaving me here without so much as a shilling to see me through his absence."

Aphra sighed loudly. "Yes, well, he is a wastrel, but I could have told you that. In any case, you landed well enough on your feet."

"What do you mean?"

"I know about that tidy sum Buckingham sent to you this morning in payment for your lies about your father."

They both heard the gasp in the next box, but Annabelle continued the conversation as if she'd not noticed at all.

"I suppose you'll want some of it now to help you pay off your debt," Annabelle said hotly.

"Well, I have been lodging you at my house. I

don't think you should begrudge me a little of Buckingham's money."

Now the people in the fourth box over were straining forward to hear the conversation, which had risen in loudness since they'd begun. Annabelle shot Aphra a questioning glance through the slits of her mask. How long should they continue this before they'd said enough? The first act was ending, and once the interlude came, they'd not be able to be heard by anyone, even His Majesty.

Annabelle gave an exaggerated sigh. "All right, then. I'll give you some of it. Trouble is, the gold's not going very far. This gown cost me nearly all of it, though it was worth it to be able to buy a decent gown for a change. I swear, Lord Hampden was terribly lax about such things."

"That's not provocation enough to have him put in the Tower, for God's sake," Aphra retorted slyly.

"I didn't have him put in the Tower. That was all Rochester's doing. He was angry, you know—"

A tap at the door to the box made her break off. Sweet Mary, it had taken them long enough.

Now the more difficult part of her performance would begin. "Enter," she said, making her voice sound more normal.

Lord Rochester opened the door, his face blanched in rage. "Mrs. Maynard? It is you under that mask, isn't it?"

Annabelle nodded her head regally. "I wish to be alone just now, Lord Rochester."

"I beg your pardon, madam," he said, his tone heavily sarcastic, "but His Majesty has sent me to request that you accompany me to his box."

She dropped her mouth open in feigned surprise. "Oh, dear heaven, is His Majesty here tonight?"

"Yes." His eyes shot daggers at her. He, at least, was not fooled by her little scene . . . but then, he wasn't the man she needed to fool.

Rising to her feet and flashing Aphra an exaggerated look of horror, she followed Lord Rochester into the passageway and then into the next box. His Majesty had apparently sent away everyone but Buckingham. They'd also pulled the curtains to cut off the noise of the theater, although every eye was probably on those closed curtains.

She only hoped enough people had overheard her and Aphra's conversation to ensure that the king couldn't take her statements lightly.

"Mrs. Maynard," the king remarked, his eyes cold on her as she curtsied. "If you would be so kind as to remove the mask—"

"Of course," she murmured and did as he asked.

It made it easier to see his face, which looked flushed even in the dim light of the sconces.

"'Tis very rude of us, we know," the king said, "but we couldn't help overhearing your conversation with Mrs. Behn."

I should hope not, given how hard we worked to make sure of it. She feigned a stricken expression. "Oh, dear heaven, I had no idea that—"

"We must say, your conversation has us disturbed, very disturbed indeed."

It was all she could do to keep from looking at Buckingham to see how he was taking this.

"I don't know what to say," she murmured.

"You've said enough already," the king snapped. "Egad, what kind of woman would deliberately set out to ruin a respectable man like your father?"

She drew on all her acting abilities to look devastated. "Oh, Your Majesty, 'tis not at all how it sounded. Aphra is peeved at me, so she has made up these insane accusations—"

"Enough of your lies. Lord Hampden as well has pointed out the alternate interpretations of the poem. We did not believe him, of course, because Walcester is his friend and we assumed he was misled, but now we see that he told the truth after all."

"But, Your Majesty—" she protested.

"Silence!"

The king turned to Buckingham, and only then did she dare venture a look at the duke. He kept his features carefully indifferent, but she could see the anger seething behind his eyes. He definitely understood what she'd just done. And now she'd made an enemy of him, though it couldn't have been helped.

"Buckingham," the king said in a stern voice that made her quake for the duke, "how do you suggest we handle this terrible situation?"

Buckingham regarded her a moment longer with glittering eyes. Then he turned to the king with an ingratiating smile. "I would humbly propose that Lord Walcester be released, Your Majesty. It appears that a gross error has been made."

The king nodded wearily, for the first time not looking quite so in command.

Had His Majesty really believed her little scene? Or had he simply been forced to accept her presentation of the matter because he knew if he didn't, his subjects, many of whom had also heard the exchange, would rise up in outrage to demand the earl's release? After all, it wouldn't do for him to appear to mistreat a hero at the word of a lowly actress. He had enough trouble dealing with his subjects' dislike of his many mistresses and their pensions.

It didn't matter why; her father was going to be released. But no mention had been made of Colin. And she could hardly ask about him when she'd been pretending indifference to his plight. Still, how could they keep him imprisoned now?

"Your Majesty, what are we to do with Mrs. Maynard?" Buckingham asked.

She caught her breath. She'd deliberately ignored the possibility that they might punish her for falsely maligning a noble, but deep down she'd known to expect it. That was the way these things were handled. Horrible memories filled her mind . . . her mother's cell, her mother's last ride to the gallows, her mother with the noose about her neck . . .

"What do you think?" His Majesty asked, turning a shrewd gaze on Buckingham.

Annabelle's heart pounded, but Buckingham's hatred for her might work to her advantage. Everyone now knew he'd given her money to keep silent, so they would assume, if he ordered some cruel punishment, that he was retaliating, and that wouldn't look good either.

Buckingham stared at her a moment, obviously itching to torment her. Then he said in a bored tone, "She's a woman, Your Majesty, and women are weak in matters like these. They think only of their petty emotions and strike in fury without giving the matter the more considered thought that a man would."

Annabelle tensed. It was so like a man to consider a woman's maneuvering to be motivated by petty emotion, while his own was motivated only by sound logic. Buckingham had schemed more than she had, and would get only a few words of disapproval from the king for it. While she was to be given . . . what?

"Why not order that she be dismissed from the duke's players?" Buckingham went on. "That way you'll prevent her from continuing her scheming among the nobility. I think that's a suitable punishment."

Aye, he would think so. An actress dismissed from her company generally had one of two choices—find a protector or sink into the darkness of the whorehouses. And since she'd offended every nobleman's sensibilities and betrayed her father,

Buckingham no doubt thought she'd have only the latter choice.

But she knew better. She'd always find a way to survive. The theater had taught her that.

The king appeared to consider Buckingham's suggestion. Then he nodded. "That sounds most appropriate." He leveled a stern gaze on her. "Mrs. Maynard, we hope that, away from the theater, you will reflect upon the error of your ways."

She'd best make a token protest. "But, Your Majesty, how will I live? I have nothing but my profession."

Charles II waved his hand dismissively. "You should have thought about that before you embarked on this terrible scheme. Now begone. We are fast tiring of your deceitful countenance."

After falling into a deep curtsy, she stormed dramatically from the king's box. As soon as she'd moved into the passageway, Aphra met her, but Rochester was standing there watching them, so she couldn't say a word to her friend.

With hurried steps, she left the second tier, conscious that the interlude had begun and people would soon be milling about. She had to get out before that. The story of what she'd done would be spreading through the theater, and she didn't feel like enduring the murmurs and contemptuous remarks.

How odd—now that she'd finally succeeded in making herself truly scandalous, she didn't care.

It was probably a fitting punishment for a woman who'd betrayed her own father. Well, at least she and her father were even on that score. He was once more the revered member of the nobility, and she was, as always, the despised bastard.

But it no longer bothered her. After tonight, she knew she could do anything she put her mind to. By heaven, if Colin weren't released in a few days, she'd manufacture some other scheme for his release.

Feeling a little better, she walked through the foyer, doing her best to maintain her role of affronted actress. Just as she passed Sir William's tiny office near the front doors, however, two hands reached out and dragged her forcibly inside, shutting the door behind her.

Thinking some forward gallant had waylaid her, she whirled, a hot retort on her lips that died when she saw who'd grabbed her.

"Colin!" she exclaimed. "But . . . but how? I thought . . ."

He frowned, but the twinkle in his eyes belied his attempt to look severe. "Now, now, dearling. I could hardly stay in the Tower with Buckingham buying you gowns and Aphra calling me a wastrel, could I? Besides, having left you without so much as a shilling, I had to at least correct that injustice."

She colored. "You heard . . ."

"Aye." He grinned, all pretense of anger gone. "Leave it to you to find a way to make the king eat his words, and before an audience, no less. I assume he did eat his words when he took you aside."

She nodded, unable to keep back her exuberant smile. "My father's been freed, although Buckingham's mad as a hornet about it."

"Not surprising. He's just found himself outwitted by a woman, and isn't quite certain if it was intentional or simply bad fortune on his part." His grin faded. "Annabelle, dearling, you are amazing."

Her breath caught in her throat at his searing look. With a low cry, she threw herself into his arms and he clasped her so close, she exulted. He was safe and free, and he wasn't angry at her!

"We have but a moment," he murmured in her ear. "As soon as the interlude is over and the next act begins, we have to leave before someone figures out that you're not at all peeved to see me. I've got a coach waiting to take you to an inn on the outskirts of London. I'll meet you there in my own coach and then we'll set out for my estate at Kent. But we mustn't be seen together until then. I wouldn't have all your machinations go for naught."

She pulled back. "I'm sorry I had to make you sound so pathetic, but I didn't want them to realize I was trying to save you. Speaking of which, how on earth did you get here?"

He opened the door a crack and peeked out to see if the interlude was over yet. "They released me this afternoon, so of course I went looking for you and finally ended up here. Charity saw me enter and told me I'd best hide in one of the boxes or I'd ruin everything. Of course, she didn't explain what I'd be ruining, or I'd have put a stop to it. You shouldn't have risked yourself like that, dearling."

"Yes, yes," she muttered impatiently, "but how did you get released?"

He smiled. "As I told you, His Majesty could hardly condemn me on such little evidence. He did make one suggestion, however, to squelch any talk that might arise."

"What?" she whispered.

Colin's eyes twinkled. "He suggested I leave England for a while, at least a few years. He pointed out that the colonies would be a likely place for my talents."

"You know His Majesty won't expect that of you now. You can stay if you like."

His expression grew sober. "I don't want to stay. Do *you* wish to stay, my love? Does the theater mean that much to you?"

She managed a shaky laugh. "You may have been given a suggestion, but I was given a command. The king has ordered that I be dismissed from the company."

"Whose idea was that?" he asked, glowering.

"Buckingham's. Who else?"

Colin regarded her with narrowed eyes. "Did Buckingham really give you money to keep silent or were you making that up?"

"Oh no. He really sent me a bag of gold." She

grinned. "And I really bought this gown with it, too."

"Wonderful." He chuckled. "That part had everyone in the theater silently cheering, I'm sure. Most of them hate Buckingham."

"True, but now they hate me more. I'll be considered the worst harlot imaginable, ruthless and scheming to have my hallowed father imprisoned. I suppose that's mostly true anyway, even if I thought I had good reason for it."

Colin clasped her chin and stared into her eyes. "You just did a very noble thing. I know it, and so do your friends. No one else matters."

She swallowed. "I didn't do it solely for my father. I thought I was doing it for you, too."

"I know." He pressed a kiss to her forehead. "That makes it no less noble. You gave up your vengeance for me. That means more to me than you can ever imagine."

"Yes, but now you've been made to look a fool for being my lover."

"All I care about is having the woman I love beside me when I set off for my new home." His jaw tightened. "Can I count on that?"

She stared up at him. He still wanted her. Despite all that had happened, he still wanted her. Sweet Mary, what had she done to deserve such a man?

At her hesitation, he said, "I know I've been a rogue in the past, but—"

"Hush," she murmured, putting a finger to his lips. "Surely you know I love you. But you must be mad to want a woman of such scandalous reputation as I."

"Where we're going, no one will care, dearling. Let me set you straight on this. I love you. If I wanted to live in England, I would, and I'd marry you all the same. I'd say to hell with all the naysayers, as I have ever since my father first brought me here. We'd simply be the most scandalous couple in London."

His voice deepened. "But I want to marry you and go to a place where you and I can begin again, where no one knows or cares that we're bastards, where there are no memories of hangings to torment you and no court manipulations to disturb me. I want to own my soul again. Will you go with me?"

How could she resist him when he offered her something she'd wanted all her life? A place where she could be herself, where the one person she cared about knew her tormented past and didn't care. A place where she could love and be loved.

A smile spread over her face. It was Annabelle, only Annabelle, who gave the answer.

"I'll follow you to the ends of the earth, Colin Jeffreys." Her love for him swelled with sweet delight within her. "Yes, my love, I'll go."

Chapter Twenty-Three

*"A brave world, Sir, full of religion, knavery, and
change: we shall shortly see better days."*
—Aphra Behn, *The Roundheads*, Act 1, Sc.1

Annabelle and Colin stood on the deck of one
of Sir John's ships, waiting to set sail. Sir John
and Charity had liked the idea of starting afresh in
the colonies, so they, too, had decided to make the
trip. They'd married only a week ago, not long after
Colin and Annabelle's quiet private wedding at his
estate. Sir John and Charity were already below,
settling into their quarters.

But Annabelle had wanted to watch the ship
leave, to say goodbye to England. No, her memories weren't all fond, but they were her memories,
after all. They had made her what she was, and she
wouldn't go without making some sort of peace
with them.

"Shall you miss the theater very much?" Colin
asked softly, pulling her against him.

She thought of the months she'd spent treading the boards. "I don't know. I did enjoy the time

I actually spent onstage, the experience of holding people in thrall." She sighed. "But once I left the stage, I was never allowed to be myself. I always had to fend off advances and think up sharp retorts for the wits."

"It can be a hard place, I suppose."

"For a woman, it can." She paused. "I think . . . I think perhaps the theater isn't ready for women yet. I don't think a woman with any character or depth of feeling will truly enjoy treading the boards until she's allowed the same freedom to work that the actors have."

"And the same respect?"

She nodded and clutched him tight. Colin was completely different from any man she'd ever known. He took it for granted that women should have some privileges. He seemed to guess her thoughts before she spoke them. It was a constant amazement to her.

Staring up into the sky, she thanked God for this man whom she loved with every breath in her body. Then she realized that she'd just said a prayer— her first since God had abandoned her mother to the gallows. She watched the seagulls dipping toward the ship and felt the comfort of Colin's close embrace. Yes, God had chosen not to save her mother. Yet he'd given her this other wonderful gift, this caring, loving man. A tear slipped from her eye. Perhaps it was time to put her anger toward God aside as well.

Her throat tightened as she laid her head on Colin's chest. Aye, God had been watching out for her all this time. He'd given her Colin. How could she hate him after that?

As peace stole over her, she stood in Colin's embrace, awaiting the ship's departure. Suddenly she felt him tense.

"What is it?" she asked.

"Your father."

Startled, she searched the docks, her heart beginning to pound when she caught sight of the balding figure walking toward the ship. "What does *he* want?"

Colin shook his head as they went to greet the earl. She'd heard he'd been freed, but she hadn't seen him since that terrible night at Colin's house. Colin hadn't either, although he'd told her in detail about their last encounter and her father's statement that he'd claim her if she wished. No doubt he'd changed his mind about that after she'd gone to the king.

Her father took Colin's proffered hand and came on board, standing there awkwardly, looking about. Colin stood between him and Annabelle, but her father saw her anyway and stiffened a little.

"I hear you're taking my daughter off to the colonies," he muttered to Colin, though his watery eyes stayed fixed on her face.

In the bright light of day he looked older. Strangely enough, she pitied him. Colin had told her that he had no family, no heirs, only his political aspirations to keep him company. Such a lonely life he must lead.

She met his inquisitive stare without flinching.

"I'm taking my *wife* to the colonies," Colin retorted. "And I'd thank you not to do anything to upset her."

"It's all right, Colin," Annabelle said. "I wish to speak with him a moment."

At her pleading expression, Colin nodded reluctantly and stepped aside. Her father surveyed her from head to toe, seeming pleased by her demure gown.

"Sir," she said, her throat tight. She couldn't call him "Father." "I would like to know something. Before she died, my mother said that you were the only man she'd ever loved. Did you perchance love her, too? At least a little?"

She had to know, perhaps because Mother had found so little love in her life. Or perhaps because knowing that he and Mother had conceived her in love would make everything else bearable.

His eyes misted over, and his broad hand gripped the top of his cane. "If I've ever truly loved anyone, it was your mother. She was a sweet, giving woman, and I truly hated leaving her behind."

Annabelle swallowed, unable to say anything.

"Annabelle," he continued, astonishing her by using her name for the first time, "if I'd known about you, I believe I would have gone back." He began to nod. "Aye, I do believe I would have."

Tears welled in her eyes—of grief, of pain for lost chances, and yes, even of happiness. "I'm sorry I went to the king about the poem," she whispered, and suddenly she knew this was what she'd been waiting for, the chance to find some sort of absolution.

He gave her a trembling smile. "I'm not. For many years, I've lived in fear of having it be known what a coward I was. When at last it was all made public, I knew only relief. Now I can have some peace. Besides, they've not been as harsh toward me as I thought they might be. They pity me for my treacherous daughter and gloss over my sins. You must have painted quite a picture in your little scene at the theater."

Then he gave a raucous laugh. "I hear you gave Buckingham fits. It was worth a few days in the Tower to hear how my sharp-tongued daughter made a fool of that duplicitous snake before His Majesty and everyone."

He looked as if he might say more, then fell silent.

An awkwardness descended upon them both. The other times they'd spoken, it had been with acid words. With all the bitterness evaporated between them, there seemed little to say. The silence was broken by the call of "All aboard!"

He glanced about him, then fixed her with a yearning gaze. "You'll tell me if I have grandchildren, won't you?"

She glanced at Colin, who smiled. Then she

nodded. When her father flashed her a grateful look, she added impulsively, "And you may visit them anytime, if you wish, although I admit it will be a long journey."

"I may surprise you and accept that invitation someday." He stepped forward and, before she realized what he was doing, leaned over and pressed a kiss to her forehead. "May God keep you well, daughter."

As he turned to go, she caught him by the arm and stretched up to kiss his dry cheek. "And you," she whispered through the tightness in her throat.

He nodded, his eyes misting again, then walked back to the edge of the ship, where he was helped off by a crewman.

Colin came to her side. "Are you all right?"

She nodded, swiping away a tear with the back of her hand. He drew her into his arms, and she laid her head against his chest, her love for him so intense she could feel it in every part of her.

"You know, it's odd," she whispered, "but all this time I thought that all I wanted was to hear him say he was sorry for what he'd done, that he regretted it. He didn't really say that even today, did he?"

Colin remained silent, somehow knowing she expected no answer.

"Yet I didn't care. Because he said enough. He finally said enough."

"Do you wish you were staying now, so you could get to know him better?"

She lifted her head to gaze at him. "Nay. The only person I want to know better is you."

A slow, secret smile crossed his face as the wind whipped his golden hair about him like a halo. Crewmen scurried around them, casting off and hoisting the sails. Then the ship slipped away from the dock, and Colin steadied her in his arms as the vessel rocked.

He looked out at the ocean, at the sun-drenched morning, then gazed back at her, that smile still fixed on his face. "Then I can think of no better place for that than a whole new world, can you?"

She drew his head down to hers. "I think a whole new world should just suffice, my love."

And as he took her lips in a kiss as dark and mysterious and alluring as the land for which they were bound, she sighed and gave herself up to a new role, the only one she'd ever truly wanted to play.

Herself.

Epilogue

"Still in the paths of honour persevere,
And not from past or present ills despair:
For blessings ever wait on virtuous deeds;
And though a late a sure reward succeeds."
—William Congreve, *The Mourning Bride*, Act 5, Sc. 3

Colin strode through the door of his Virginia plantation house only to have his four-year-old son Marlowe hurtle through the air to clasp him about the knees.

"Papa, come quick!" the towheaded child cried. "Mama's crying!"

Colin hoisted Marlowe up into his arms and looked at him fondly, having to squelch a laugh when he saw the solemn face that still held a trace of the greasepaint his mother had been letting him wear for playing. There was no way he could explain to Marlowe that his mother was simply a little teary-eyed these days with a new baby in the house.

So he ruffled his son's hair instead. "It's all right. Let's go see if we can't cheer Mama up." With Marlowe riding his hip, he continued on into the drawing room, where she was undoubtedly working on the pair of leggings that Marlowe had been begging her to make so he could dress up as an Indian.

But Annabelle wasn't sewing. She sat in her favorite chair, a piece of paper in her hand and their two-month-old daughter sleeping in the bassinet at her feet as she wept great silent tears.

His pulse raced as it did every time he saw her truly upset. He let Marlowe slide down his length to the ground. "What is it? What's happened, dearling?"

He'd forgotten that a ship had come in today bearing letters from England. What news could she have gotten that would make her look so distraught?

She swiped the tears from her eyes as she glanced up from the letter. "My father is coming to visit."

It took him a moment to realize what she was saying. "Walcester? He's actually coming here?"

She nodded. "On a ship that left with the one that came in today, but stopped in Jamaica. He should be here in only a week."

With Marlowe clinging to his breeches, Colin went to sit beside her on the settee. Marlowe climbed into his lap as Colin put his arm around Annabelle's shoulders. "Rather short notice, I'll admit, but I don't see the problem."

"You don't see the problem?"

"No, I don't. Don't you want him to come?"

She turned her tearstained face up to his. "Oh, I don't know. I do want him to see Marlowe and little Aphra, and that is why he says he's coming. But . . . but the house is out of sorts, and I haven't had the new curtains done yet, and everything is such a shambles!"

Colin couldn't prevent a hearty laugh. As she stared at him with wounded dignity, he surveyed the drawing room's practical but attractive furnishings. He thought of Annabelle climbing out of bed less than a week after childbirth and insisting that she couldn't lie abed forever. Then he looked down at his son, whose mother always had time to fashion a cape for him from an old sheet or kiss his bruises . . . or feed him a rare orange.

Love swelled up in his throat so thick he thought it might choke him. He bent to kiss her temple. "If this is a shambles, then I have to see what you would call a well-ordered house. There's not a thing wrong with our home, dearling."

Her lower lip trembled. "And . . . and I'm f-fat, Colin."

This time he managed to contain his laughter as he scanned her trim figure. Her breasts were a little plumper from breast-feeding, and her waist a trifle thick, but she was still the loveliest woman he'd ever laid eyes on. "I see. You've just had a child, and your waist is what . . . two inches larger than it used to be before you got pregnant? And that makes you fat?"

"I want him to like me," she whispered.

Suddenly he realized what really had her worried. She'd never before had to be with her father, and it was terrifying her.

"Marlowe," Colin said softly, "go tell Bessie that Papa said to give you a treat. All right?"

Marlowe nodded and, with one last worried look at his mother, trotted off into the kitchen.

As soon as the boy had left, Colin drew Annabelle's head down onto his shoulder. "My love, your father would have to be deaf, dumb, and blind not to like you, and even then he'd have a hard time of it."

"I know he still thinks of me as a wanton woman."

"That will be put to rest the moment he sees you here."

"And—and he'll never be able to forget the things I did, not just to him, but on the stage."

"You're right, and that's why he's coming."

With a startled expression, she drew back to look at him.

He rubbed a tear from her face. "He wants to see his daring, saucy daughter again, the one who braved London society to make one man take responsibility for his actions. I don't blame him. His saucy daughter is well worth getting to know."

Her eyes met his, still teary, but a smile was beginning to spread over her face. She lifted her hand to stroke his stubbly cheek, and he felt every muscle in his body go taut. Would she ever stop having this effect on him?

Then she threaded her fingers through his hair and gazed at him shyly. "Do you know you're the most wonderful man I have ever known?"

There was no mistaking the desire flaring in her eyes. It had been a long two months. "I have to be. How else could I keep up with my very intriguing, very delightful wife?"

She giggled as he curved his hand around her neck and drew her head closer. "Don't forget 'wanton,'" she whispered.

He stared into her face, now flushing prettily at her daring statement, and a cocky grin crossed his lips. "My intriguing, delightful, wanton wife."

Then he showed her that being wanton could have advantages for them both.

Author's Note

The Battle of Naseby is a real one, and the king's papers *were* confiscated after the Royalists lost, leading
to a major shift of sympathy toward the Parliamen-
tarian New Model Army and away from the king.
Some speculate that the letters uncovered as a result
led directly to the execution of Charles I (father of
the king in my novel).

Several secondary characters in this book are real
historical figures: Charles II, the Earl of Rochester,
the Duke of Buckingham, Sir Charles Sedley, and
Sir William Davenant (actual owner of the theater
where the duke's players performed). But the one
who most intrigued me was Aphra Behn. Female
writers owe her a great debt for being one of the first
Englishwomen to earn her living as a writer. A spy
and an adventuress, she swaggered about Restora-

tion London with the best of the rakes, and produced seventeen plays in seventeen years, as well as thirteen novels and several collections of poems.

Because of her broad-minded ideas about love and sexual freedom, her works weren't given the same attention as those written by the Restoration rakes. But she demonstrated forcefully that women have the talent and ability to write for the stage and for publication, thus paving the way for generations of women writers to come. We all thank you, Aphra!

Turn the page for a sneak peek
at the next book from *New York Times*
bestselling author Sabrina Jeffries!

If the Viscount Falls

Coming in spring 2015 from Pocket Books

J ane Vernon was impatient to be gone from Mrs. Patch's. She was dying to know what Dominick Manton had discovered. Was it possible he'd actually found her missing cousin? Could that be why he was taking so long? Perhaps Nancy had simply stopped for a few nights at Ringrose's Inn, and he was coming back to give them the triumphant news.

But when the Viscount Rathmoor arrived, nothing in his grim expression said that he'd found Nancy. Dom *had* discovered something, however. She could tell. And it was clearly something he didn't want to share with Mrs. Patch.

Jane impatiently waited through the goodbyes and repeated assurances that they would keep Mrs. Patch informed of what they learned, and by the time they were in the street, she was fit to be tied.

"All right," she said without preamble, "what took you so long? What did you find out at the inn?"

He walked with such long strides toward the Elephant and Castle that she had to hurry to keep up with him. "I learned that Nancy arrived there around noon on the day you left Rathmoor Park. And then she apparently vanished."

"What?" Jane seized his arm. "What do you mean, 'vanished'?"

He stared over at her. "No one saw her leave. Unfortunately, that doesn't tell us much, because not all of the ostlers from that day were working today." Frustration crept into his voice. "They said I'd have to return tonight to speak with everyone who would have been here then. But . . ."

When he hesitated, she shook his arm. "But *what*?"

"One of the ostlers said that when he asked if he could fetch a hackney coach for Nancy, she told him there was no need because she was meeting a friend."

Jane's heart began to pound. "Mrs. Patch?"

"I doubt that." Eyes hard and brittle as emeralds glittered at her. "She would have said 'aunt.' Besides, 'meeting' implies that Nancy expected someone to come there for her. And you heard Mrs. Patch say she never ventures from her house."

This got worse by the moment. "Perhaps Nancy has a female friend in York."

"One you've never heard of? Never met? How likely is that?"

Oh, the man was so infuriating! "I take it you're determined to believe that Nancy was meeting with a lover."

"As I said—it's the most likely explanation." When she frowned at him, he said smoothly, "Certainly the ostler's words don't fit *your* pet theory—that she was kidnapped."

Seething with worry and anger and frustration that he could be such a . . . a *man* about this, Jane dropped his arm and quickened her pace. "You are attributing a great deal to one remark by an ostler." She turned onto the street that led directly to the inn. "He might have misheard or misunderstood the fact that she really was heading to Mrs. Patch's."

Dom followed her. "Without telling the woman ahead of time? Didn't Mrs. Patch say that Nancy always sent a note before she came?"

"She also said that murderers run rampant in the streets of York, but I don't hear you quoting the woman on *that*."

"Yes, but, Jane—" he began in that condescending, arrogant tone of his that pricked her harder than any embroidery needle.

"So that's it," she bit out. "You've got your mind made up. Nancy ran off with a lover, and you're washing your hands of the whole thing."

"Can you give me a good reason why I shouldn't?"

Something in his voice made her glance at him.

He was regarding her as a naturalist regarded a beetle he intended to dissect.

That's when it dawned on her—Dom wanted to unearth her secrets. *Nancy's* secrets. And somewhere between Winborough and here he'd deduced that she was hiding some.

A shiver ran down Jane's spine, and she jerked her gaze from him, fighting to hide her consternation. "Merely the same reason I gave you before. Nancy could be in trouble. And it's your duty as her brother-in-law to keep her safe."

"From what?" he demanded. "From whom? Is there more to this than you're saying?"

Ooh, that he was so determined to unveil the truth about Nancy while hiding his former collusion with her scraped Jane raw. "I could ask the same of you," she said primly. "You're obviously holding something back. You have *some* reason for your determination to believe ill of Nancy. I wonder what that might be."

Two can play your game, Almighty Dom. Hah!

He was silent so long that she ventured a glance at him to find him looking rather discomfited. Good! It was about time.

"I am merely keeping an open mind about your cousin, which is more than I can say for you," Dom finally answered. "She isn't the woman you think she is."

"Because she wouldn't give in to your advances twelve years ago, you mean?" Jane would make him admit the truth about the night they parted if it was the last thing she did! "Perhaps that's why you're determined to blacken her character. You're angry that she resisted you and went off to marry your brother instead."

"That's a lie!" When several people on the street turned to look in his direction, Dom lowered his voice. "It wasn't like that."

She stifled a smile of satisfaction. At last she was getting a reaction from him that was something other than levelheaded logic. "Wasn't it? If you'd convinced Nancy to marry you, you might not have had to go off to be a Bow Street runner. You could have had an easier life, a better life, in high society than you could have had with me if you'd married me. Without being able to access my fortune, I could only have dragged you down."

"You don't really believe that I wanted to marry her for her money," he gritted out.

"It's either that or assume that you fell madly in love with her in the few weeks we weren't able to see each other." They were nearly to the inn now, so Jane added a plaintive note to her voice. "Or perhaps it was her you wanted all along. You knew my uncle would never accept a second son as a husband for his rich heiress of a daughter, so you courted me to get close to her. Nancy was always so beautiful, so—"

"Enough!"

Without warning, he dragged her into one of the

many alleyways that crisscrossed York. This one was deeply shadowed, the houses leaning into each other overhead, and as he pulled her around to face him, the brilliance of his eyes shone starkly in the dim light.

"I never cared one whit about Nancy."

She tamped down her triumph—he hadn't admitted the whole truth yet. "It certainly didn't look that way to me. It looked like you had already forgotten me, forgotten what we meant to each—"

"The devil I had." He shoved his face close to hers. "I never forgot you for one day, one hour, one moment. It was you, always you. Everything I did was for *you*, damn it. No one else."

The passionate profession threw her off course. Dom had never been the sort to say such sweet things. But the fervent look in his eyes roused memories of how he used to look at her. And his hands gripping her arms, his body angling in closer, were so painfully familiar . . .

"I don't . . . believe you," she lied, her blood running wild through her veins.

His gleaming gaze impaled her. "Then believe this." And suddenly his mouth was on hers.

He was kissing her. *Kissing* her, curse him! That was *not* what she'd set out to get from him.

But, oh, the joy of it. The *heat* of it. His mouth covered hers, seeking, coaxing. Without breaking the kiss, he pushed her back against the wall, and she grabbed for his shoulders, his surprisingly broad and muscular shoulders. As he sent her plummeting into unfamiliar territory, she held on for dear life.

Time rewound to when they were in her uncle's garden, sneaking a moment alone. But this time there was no hesitation, no fear of being caught.

Glorying in that, she slid her hands about his neck to bring him closer. He groaned, and his kiss turned intimate. He used both lips and tongue, delving inside her mouth in a tender exploration that stunned her. Enchanted her. Confused her.

Something both sweet and alien pooled in her belly, a kind of yearning she'd never felt with her fiancé. With *any* man but Dom.

As if he sensed it, he pulled back to look at her, his eyes searching hers, full of surprise. "My God, Jane," he said hoarsely, turning her name into a prayer.

Or a curse? She had no time to figure out which before he clasped her head to hold her still for another darkly ravishing kiss. Only this one was greedier, needier. His mouth consumed hers with all the boldness of Viking raiders of yore. His tongue drove repeatedly inside in a rhythm that made her feel all trembly and hot, and his thumbs caressed her throat, rousing the pulse there.

Thank heaven there was a wall to hold her up, or she was quite sure she would dissolve into a puddle at his feet. Because after all these years apart, he was riding roughshod over her life again. And she was letting him.

How could she not? His scent engulfed her, made her dizzy with the pleasure of it. He roused urges she'd never known she had, sparked fires in places she'd thought were frozen. Then his hands swept down her possessively as if to memorize her body . . . or mark it as belonging to him.

Belonging to *him*. Oh, Lord!

She shoved him away. How could she have fallen for his kisses after what he did? How could she have let him slip that far under her guard?

Never again, curse him! Never!

For a moment, he looked as stunned by what had flared between them as she. Then he reached for her, and she slipped from between him and the wall, panic rising in her chest.

"You do not have the right to kiss me anymore," she hissed. "I'm engaged, for heaven's sake!"

As soon as her words registered, his eyes went cold. "It certainly took you long enough to remember it."

She gaped at him. "You have the audacity to . . . to . . ." She stabbed his shoulder with one finger. "You have no business criticizing *me*! You threw me away years ago, and now you want to just . . . just take me up again, as if nothing ever happened between us?"

A shadow crossed his face. "I did not throw you away. *You* jilted *me*, remember?"

That was the last straw. "Right. I jilted you."

Turning on her heel, she stalked back for the road. "Just keep telling yourself that, since you're obviously determined to believe your own fiction."

"Fiction?" He hurried after her. "What are you talking about?"

"Oh, for pity's sake, why can't you just admit what you really did and be done with it?"

"What I really did?" Grabbing her by the arm, he forced her to stop just short of the street. He searched her face, and she could see when awareness dawned in his eyes. "Good God. You know the truth. You know what really happened in the library that night."

"That you manufactured that dalliance between you and Nancy to force me into jilting you?" She snatched her arm free of him. "Yes, I know."

Then she strode out of the alley, leaving him to stew in his own juices.

DOM STOOD DUMBFOUNDED as Jane disappeared into the street. Then he hurried to catch up to her, to get some answers.

She *knew*. How the devil did she know?

The answer to that was obvious. "So, Nancy told you, did she?" he snapped as he fell into step beside her.

Jane didn't reply, just kept marching toward the inn like a hussar bent on battle.

"When?" he demanded. "How long have you known?"

"For ten years, you . . . you conniving . . . lying—"

"*Ten* years? You knew all this time, and you didn't say anything?"

"Say anything!" She halted just short of the inn-yard entrance to glare at him. "How the blazes was I to do that? It's not as if I encountered you anywhere. You disappeared into the streets of London as surely as if you were a footpad or a pickpocket."

She planted her hands on her hips. "Oh, I read about your heroic exploits from time to time, but other than that, I neither heard nor saw anything of you until last year when you showed up at George's town house to get Tristan freed from gaol. It was only pure chance that I happened to be at dinner with Nancy that day. As you'll recall, you didn't stay long. Nor did you behave as if you would welcome any confidences."

Remembering the cool reception he'd given her, he glanced away, unable to bear the accusation in her eyes. "No, I suppose I didn't."

"Besides, it hardly mattered that I knew the truth. I assumed that if you ever changed your mind about making a life with me, you would seek me out. Since you never did, you were clearly determined to remain a bachelor."

His gaze shot back to her. "It was more complicated than that."

She snorted. "It always is with you. Which is

precisely why I'm happy I'm engaged to *someone else*."

That sent jealousy roaring through him, predictably enough. "Yet you let me kiss you."

A pretty blush stained her cheeks. "You . . . you took me by surprise, that's all. But it was a mistake. It won't happen again."

The hell it wouldn't. He intended to find out if the past was as firmly in the past as she claimed. But obviously he couldn't do it here in the street. He glanced up at the darkening sky. Or right now.

She followed the direction of his gaze. "Yes," she said in a dull voice. "Looks like we will have a rainy trip back." She headed into the inn yard. "Perhaps if we hurry, we can reach Winborough before it starts. Besides, we've got only three hours until sunset, and it's not safe to ride in an open phaeton after dark."

She was right, but he didn't mean to drop this discussion. He needed answers, and once they were on the road, he meant to get them.

He strode into the inn yard, his mind awhirl. He'd never been one for snap judgments, which was precisely what made him a good investigator. He liked to be sure he had all the facts before he sorted them by their implications and importance so he could come to some conclusions.

With Jane, though, getting all the facts was proving difficult. She was obviously too angry to tell him rationally what he needed to know. And he was too unsettled to make sense of what little she'd said.

Fortunately, calling for his phaeton, putting the top up, and getting them on the road gave him time to settle his thoughts. Certain things seeped into his memory. Such as how Jane had called him "Saint Dominick" three months ago, which at the time he'd thought odd for a woman who should have believed him a fortune hunter. Or how she'd spoken of being tired of "waiting" for her "life to begin."

Good God. She really *might* have been talking about him then. About waiting for *him* to come after her. All this time . . .

No, he couldn't believe that. She'd only been seventeen when they'd ended things, and women that age were still feeling their way in life. She couldn't possibly have been carrying a torch for him all these years.

Why not? You've been carrying one for her.

He stifled a curse. Nonsense. He'd cut her out of his heart.

God, he was such a liar.

They were now well out of the city. She sat quietly beside him, obviously uncomfortable after what had happened between them.

She couldn't be any more uncomfortable than he was. He could still taste her mouth, still feel the moment when she'd turned to putty in his arms. He was aware of every inch of her that touched him. Her hand lay in her lap, so close he could reach over and take it.

Or perhaps not. The last thing he needed was her shoving him off the phaeton, which she was liable to do right now if she took a mind to it. She was damned angry.

Though he wasn't entirely sure why. She was now engaged to a very rich, very well-connected earl, all because Dom had set her free. So why did she look as if she wanted to throttle him?

Nancy. The chit must have made everything sound worse than it was. "Tell me how much your cousin told you about our . . . supposed dalliance."

"Everything, as far as I know." Jane smoothed her skirts with a nonchalance he might have believed if he hadn't also noticed how her hands trembled. "That you coaxed her into making it look as if you were making advances to her. That she then convinced Samuel Barlow to help get me into the library without suspecting, so I could see your manufactured tableau."

Nancy *had* told her everything. "She promised she would never say a word."

"I gave her no choice." Jane's voice lowered to an aching murmur. "I'm not the fool you take me for, you know."

"I have *never* taken you for a fool."

"No? You didn't think I'd notice when you made no further attempts to court Nancy? Or any other rich ladies? There was no gossip about you, no tales of your fortune hunting. It wasn't long before I smelled a rat."

Blast it all. "So you went to Nancy and forced her to tell the truth."

Jane got very quiet. He glanced over to find her looking chagrined.

"Actually, I sort of . . . tricked her into it. I claimed that I had encountered you in Bond Street, and you'd revealed the truth then. I told her I just wanted to hear her side of things."

A groan escaped him. "In other words, you deceived her."

"Pretty much." Jane fiddled with her reticule. "It wasn't difficult. Nancy isn't, well . . ."

"The brightest star in the sky?"

Jane winced. "Exactly. She's fairly easy to manipulate. Indeed, that was all it took to have her blurting out everything. That you told her a bunch of nonsense about how I would be better off without you—"

"It wasn't nonsense," he interrupted. "You *were* better off without me."

"Was I? You don't know that."

"I do, actually." He clicked his tongue at the horses to have them step up the pace. "Do you know where I lived for my first three years as a Bow Street runner?"

"It doesn't matter. I wouldn't have cared."

He uttered a harsh laugh. "Yes, I'm sure you would have been delighted to share a garret above a tavern in Spitalfields with me. To eat only bread and cheese four days a week in order to save money.

To forgo coal in the dead of winter so we'd have enough money to pay the rent."

"That does sound dreadful." Her voice held an edge. "But that was three years of the twelve we were apart. What about later? After you started to have some success?"

"I didn't move out of the garret because of any great success. I moved out because I . . . was traveling too much to sustain lodgings in London. That's how I spent the rest of my time as a runner."

In Manchester and wherever else the Spenceans and their ilk were fomenting rebellion. But he couldn't talk about that, not to her. She would never understand those difficult years, what he'd done, what he'd been expected to do. How could she? She was a lady encased in a castle of privileged living. She didn't know anything about the struggle between the poor and the rich. He wouldn't want her to.

"That was your choice, though, wasn't it?" she said softly. "Not all Bow Street runners travel."

He tensed. "No, but neither do they make much of a living. I was paid far more for . . . er . . . traveling than for catching criminals in London. I was able to save up enough to start my business concern precisely because of all those years when I was willing to go anywhere for my position."

To take any risk. To spy on his fellow countrymen. It still left a bad taste in his mouth.

"And what about after you started Manton's

Investigations? That was four years ago, Dom. If you had wanted me, you could have approached me then."

"Of course," he said bitterly. "I could have marched up to your uncle's house and begged you to marry me. To forgo your fortune, leave your comfortable position, risk being cut off by all your friends and relations so you could marry a man whom I was sure you considered a fortune hunter."

"Yes. You could have."

"And you would have gladly accepted my suit. Even though you could have had your pick of the men. Even though you had an earl and a marquess sniffing at your skirts—"

"You knew about the marquess?"

He cursed his quick tongue. "The point is, you would have been a fool to choose me over one of them. And I was astute enough to realize it."

"No, the point is that you'll never know whether I would have accepted your suit. You didn't offer it. You never took the chance, and that is your loss."

The words stabbed a dagger through his chest. She spoke as if she'd given up on him. But of course she had, hadn't she? She'd accepted Blakeborough's marriage proposal. And given how hard she'd fought twelve years ago not to jilt Dom, she was certainly not going to jilt Blakeborough.

What if Dom *had* asked? What if he had blundered into her life again and wrenched her from everything she knew?

No, that couldn't have ended anything but badly.

It had begun to drizzle. Since the phaeton top extended only so far, he pulled out a blanket to put over their laps to keep some of the damp off. When he took the reins in one hand so he could reach over to tuck the blanket about her, she froze.

So did he, painfully aware of his hand lingering on her thigh. He had half a mind to stop the phaeton, drag her into his arms, and kiss her until she softened and remembered what they had been to each other.

But she did remember. She'd made that clear earlier. She just no longer cared.

He drew his hand back and the moment blew away on the breeze.

A stilted silence fell over them. Mile after mile of dreary gray seeped into his blood, weighing him down. He didn't know which was worse, being without her entirely all these years or being so close and not having her.

After a long while, she released a sigh. "Do you even regret what you did to end our engagement?"

"No," he said tersely. He could feel her gaze on him.

"After all this time," she said tartly, "you still think you and Nancy did the right thing?"

"Absolutely." It was the truth. Wasn't it?

Another uncomfortable silence stretched between them.

"Nancy regrets it," Jane said at last. "She says

she regretted it from the moment she agreed to go along with it."

He was tempted to point out that Nancy had certainly hidden her regret well behind her triumphant marriage to George. But pointing that out would merely put Jane on the defensive again regarding her cousin. Jane seemed determined to believe Nancy some sort of saint, and until he had more facts, he couldn't dispute her view. Which was precisely why he had to investigate further.

"So, *are* you going to get to the bottom of Nancy's disappearance?"

Good God, did the woman read minds? "I think I must. You made a valid point earlier. If Nancy *has* been duped by some fortune-hunting scoundrel, it would be unwise to let the matter lie."

"You mean, because he might hurt her," Jane said, her tone anxious.

"Because he could hurt Rathmoor Park and Nancy's future along with it. Her dower portion comes out of the estate's income. Any husband she takes on will want to look after her interests and won't care what strain that puts on Rathmoor Park." Or how much trouble it caused Dom.

Shock emanated from Jane's side of the phaeton. "You know, Dom, whether or not I was better off without you, it's clear that *you* were not better off without *me*."

"What's that supposed to mean?"

"You used to have a heart, to care about people." She uttered a ragged oath. "Or perhaps I just thought you did. Perhaps you were always this cold-blooded, and I merely missed it."

He bristled at the accusation. "And what is it that makes you think me cold-blooded? The fact that I questioned the need to rush off after Nancy?"

"The fact that you only seem to see the financial aspects of this. She's a woman alone. That should secure your concern."

"I lost my concern for Nancy the day she married George," he snapped.

"So that's what this is about. She married your enemy, and that made her your enemy as well."

He tightened his grip on the reins, not sure what to say. "I suppose you could see it that way."

"Well, she's still my cousin and my friend, so I hope you have enough . . . softness left in your heart toward *me* that you would search for her on my behalf if not on hers."

"Don't worry, I'm not so 'cold-blooded' as all that," he said irritably. "Tristan and I will return to York tonight to speak with the ostlers at Ringrose's Inn who weren't there today. Then we'll comb the town, see what more we can learn." Dom shot her a hard glance. "You'll only get in our way, so you should stay with Lady Zoe at Winborough."

"That's probably best," Jane shocked him by saying.

So she was agreeing with him now? Was that because she feared he would attempt to kiss her again? Or because she'd learned what she wanted to know from him and now only needed him to find Nancy?

Either possibility chafed him.

They traveled farther without speaking, but when he caught himself humming some doleful notes from Mozart's Requiem Mass, he winced. Damn it, there were things he wanted—he *needed*—to know from *her*. "Jane, have you been happy all these years?" *Was my sacrifice worth it?*

When she didn't speak, he looked over to find her regarding him with a stark gaze that chilled him. "You don't have the right to ask. You didn't attempt to find out or ensure that I was, so think whatever makes you sleep better at night."

And she called *him* cold-blooded?

She squared her shoulders. "But I do intend to be quite deliriously happy from now on. I intend to marry Edwin and have his children and live to a ripe old age surrounded by people I care about. I assume that sets your mind at ease."

It should have. But it damned well didn't. Because for the first time, he saw his life laid out before him, devoid of Jane in a different way from before. And it made him want to howl and gnash his teeth.